UPPER hand

a Cedar Tree novel

by

Freya Barker

UPPER HAND, a Cedar Tree Novel

Copyright © 2015 Margreet Asselbergs as Freya Barker

All rights reserved.

No part of this publication may be reproduced, distributed, or transmitted in any form or by any means, including photocopying, recording, or by other electronic or mechanical methods, without the prior written permission of the author or publisher, except in the case of brief quotations embodied in used critical reviews and certain other non-commercial uses as permitted by copyright law. For permission requests, write to the author, mentioning in the subject line: "Reproduction Request" at the address below:

freyabarker.writes@gmail.com

This book is a work of fiction and any resemblance to any person or persons, living or dead, any event, occurrence, or incident is purely coincidental. The characters and story lines are created and thought up from the author's imagination or are used fictitiously.

ISBN: 978-0-9938883-8-0

Cover Image: **Reggie Deanching of R+M Photography**

Cover Model: **Alfie Gabriel Gordillo**

Cover Design: **RE&D - Margreet Asselbergs**

TABLE OF CONTENT

DEDICATION

To my readers, who have so graciously embraced the characters in the Cedar Tree series. I strive to live up to your expectations and am awed by the incredible response I receive with the release of each new novel.

You all make writing even more rewarding!

xox

PROLOGUE

"Better wake up, you big ape. You've been tying up this bed long enough. I knew you'd be trouble the moment I laid eyes on you."

The last is said with a distinct tremor.

I'm so tempted to let the darkness surrounding me suck me under, but each time I feel myself slipping, this voice keeps pulling me back to the surface. I don't have to open my eyes to know who it is. That voice has stirred and grated on me equally over the past year. Deep and resonant most of the time, shrill some of the time, but there've been moments where it had some sweetness to it. It's those times that stirred my soul; gave me the promise of a world of softness underneath the bristles. A promise that had all but disappeared, until now.

Sure, her words are combative, but Beth's emotions are only too clear in her voice. She cares. She doesn't want to, that much is obvious, but she cares nonetheless. At least I think so. So far, I really haven't been on my game when it comes to her, and yet with every rejection and slight, she has managed to worm herself deeper under my skin. Damn.

The first time I laid eyes on her, she had soot all over her face and her dark hair had mostly pulled free of her ponytail. A strong, capable woman, I could see that from the way she stood straight. Despite her softer curves and the hint of fatigue around

9

her liquid brown eyes, I could see this was not a woman to cross. Not that I wanted to, quite the opposite in fact. Her defiant stance and pronounced hourglass figure shook me awake, body and mind. Immediately, I managed to piss her off.

"Well, aren't you a sight for sore eyes?" I remember wincing the moment those words flew from my mouth. From the look on her face, she wasn't that impressed either.

One of her eyebrows almost disappeared into her hairline, and her lush lips were pulled into an angry line. *Sonofabitch.* You'd think I'd learn after having already pissed off the owner of the place I was hired to do work on. The local diner in Cedar Tree was damaged in a recent fire, and I almost blew the job because of my runaway mouth.

It was hammered into me, growing up in the Deep South, to treat women like delicate flowers. Well, there wasn't anything 'delicate' about Beth, the woman standing across from me now, just as there'd been nothing flowery about Arlene, her boss and owner of the diner in question.

In fact, there wasn't a damn delicate flower to be found anywhere in or around Cedar Tree. I was making a name for myself pissing each and everyone of them off, at some point in time. The irony of it all was that my mom, although with the appearance of a true southern belle, had a spine of steel and a hand that was harder than my father's had ever been. Always dressed in frilly dresses, giving the illusion of fragility, she ruled the household and us boys with an iron fist. She'd always been our pillar of strength until cancer took her. My father gave up after that and didn't take long to follow her, and what remained of our family fell apart after that.

I tried to redeem myself. I tried hard with Beth, and although I'd struck up a friendship with Arlene and some of her friends, despite my shaky start, Beth never seemed to warm to me. She confused the hell out of me though. That foot, which has a tendency to stick itself in my mouth, got itchy whenever I was around her. There wasn't a time that our interactions didn't end up with Beth irritated or angry with me. Although recently, after I'd scheduled to meet a new client at the diner to discuss some work on her house, Beth had been more snippy than normal; almost as if she was jealous. After many months of trying to get in her good graces, I thought I'd found a crack in her armor. The next time I walked in the diner and saw her walking toward my booth, I figured it was time to push a little. So I got up and the minute she was within reach, I pulled her against me and was going to lay a kiss on her. I'd always been told that if you wanted something you had to be clear in your intentions. I figured nothing would get the message across better than a kiss. Right? Well, my lips had barely touched hers when she gave me an almighty shove to my chest and to my horror started crying. Not exactly the reaction I had hoped for.

"You—you caveman! Why would you do that?"

Before I could even form a response, she was running into the kitchen, tears running down her face. The kitchen where right at that moment half of Cedar Tree was assembled. Reckon that didn't only not go over too well, but it didn't go over too well in a very public way. I followed her, found her outside leaning against the dumpster, spouting some incoherent stuff about trying to kiss her when I was playing footsies with another. She could've spoken Greek and it probably would've made more sense to me. Seeming to make her only more upset, I left her and went back inside—eyes in the kitchen burning holes in my back.

I tried a few more times, until she told me to leave her alone, and she ended up hiding in the bathroom.

That's when I'd decided this was a battle that was perhaps not worth fighting or winning. As much as women are an enigma to me; Beth was a complete alien. A beautiful, loving—at least to her friends—and hardworking woman I'd spent a year trying to get to know, but the woman was an impenetrable fort. I'm all about fighting to get in, but at some point it'd be nice to be invited. I'm getting too old for this song and dance. Having loved and lost before, I can say I'd gladly do the loving part, but the losing is not something I'd volunteer for again. Especially not before we even get to the loving.

So with continued rejection bitter on my tongue, I started spending all of my energy on my contracts: the house renovations in Cortez and Naomi's place in town.

It's actually the last thing I remember, the old house behind the feed store. I think I was there, but the memory keeps going to black, like turning off the TV. A clear picture one minute and the next thing a blank screen. My head hurts, and momentarily forgetting about the woman in the room, my hand moves of its own accord toward my head. I haven't opened my eyes yet, but the gasp I hear is clearly from her lips.

"There you are. I gotta call a nurse."

Busted. For as much as I've started to embrace the dark, I know she'll just hound me until I open my eyes.

CHAPTER ONE

"He moved his arm," I reply excitedly to the nurse, who enters the room I've virtually lived in the last few weeks. "I thought there was something different about his breathing this morning, but that was all until he moved, just now."

"Mr. Mason?" She approaches the bed confidently, pulling a small flashlight from her pocket, as she carefully peels back one of his eyelids.

Before I got the news that he had been hurt badly and flown to Durango, I'd fought the feelings this man invoked in me tooth and nail. Successfully so, I thought, after having a few minor melt downs when my resistance was low but coming out swinging. He'd retreated to his corner, before stepping out of the ring completely in the last month. I ignored the pang of regret I felt every time he'd walk in the diner and would pointedly ignore me. So different from the entire time since we were first introduced.

Oh, he'd put his foot in time and time again. It just seemed to be his way to say the wrong thing at the wrong moment, but it was obvious the guy was a complete loss when it came to talking with women. One sentence from his mouth was even more insulting than the next. Yet, he remained incapable of reigning in the politically incorrect verbiage flowing from his lips without benefit of a hefty filter. Almost endearingly clueless, which is what made—makes—him so dangerous.

13

For all intents and purposes, Clint Mason was a decent man. A good man, who apparently never had the privilege of learning to communicate effectively with women. Real women that is. I'm sure some might be charmed by his redneck approach, but the apparent lack of respect for women was all in the eye of the beholder but not so much in his.

The simple fact that he'd found himself a place in the group of friends that made up part of the regulars at Arlene's—hell, even befriending Arlene after the major faux pas he made with her the first time they met—told me there was more under that southern veneer he was hiding behind.

A dangerous man for me; unlike the smooth-talking losers I'd hooked my wagon to, from time to time, until finally giving up men altogether. Clint in all his stumbling communications, as far from smooth with the ladies as possible, has proven himself a good, honest, and protective friend to everyone but me. My doing entirely, I've simply not given him the chance.

So, while I was telling myself to be relieved not to have to deal with his undesired attentions any longer, and erasing that one moment where his lips were close enough to taste from my mind, I was literally shocked into motion when learning he was en route to the hospital in critical condition. Tearing off my apron as I was running to the kitchen for my purse, Seb, cook, part owner and husband to Arlene, tried to stop me. Nothing would've at that point though, not even the sizable, tattooed, and very willful Seb. Shaking him off like a bug, I beelined it through the back door and to my junker of a car parked beside the dumpster. Praying for at least half a tank as I cranked the sputtering engine, I breathed in relief when the gauge showed only a quarter gone.

Can't remember exactly how I got here, ignoring messages and texts noisily coming in on my cell on the way, but I got here. Then I lied through my teeth so I could come in to see him. With the 'family only' rule in place for critical patients, I morphed myself into his fiancée. I almost snorted when I said it, from habit I guess, but the nurse at the desk swallowed it hook, line, and sinker. At least I think so, because I was lead to the Intensive Care Unit waiting room right away.

That's where I've been the past few weeks, holding vigil by this man's bed. Holding his cold hand, reveling at its size much like the man himself: big, bulky, and rough-looking. Cursing him for not waking up, for leaving us hanging.

It's not like I was only one trying, either. Every one of our friends have been here, talking, coaxing, and even pleading with him to wake up, but without results until now.

I watch the nurse flick the flashlight into his eyes and he squints, his hand uncoordinated as it tries to swat at the light. A relief washes over me so strong, my entire body seems to deflate. It isn't until the nurse talks to me that I realize the tears running down my face.

"You okay, Beth? Would you like me to call someone for you?"

Her gentle inquiry pulls me back in the moment, and I immediately dig my cell phone out of my purse.

"I will. Th— thank you," I mutter, dialing the one person who has been as anxiously awaiting Clint's return as I have, while the nurse continues her preliminary examination of his reflexes and tries to coax him to speak.

"He's waking up," is the only thing I need to say.

"On my way," the person on the other side answers before hanging up.

With the arrival of the doctor, I've been ushered out of the room, while Clint is subjected to a more thorough examination. He hadn't done much more than blink, so far. The nurse suggested I use the time to get something to eat, but I can't bring myself to move from my spot right outside his door. I should probably give Dylan a call. I've been staying with my son and his family for a few weeks now. Walking in, dead on my feet, after another day spent watching over Clint and doing little more than rolling into bed and sleeping. Only in the mornings would I allow myself an hour or two to enjoy my two-year-old grandbaby, Max, before my daughter-in-law, Tammy, would take him to daycare and I'd head back to the hospital for another day of vigil.

Frankly, I was glad to be out of the house, the tension between my son and his wife palpable. I've tried to talk to Dylan to find out what is wrong, but he isn't talking. Neither is Tammy, for that matter, and although she's never been my favorite person—a little too self-involved for my tastes—I hate seeing both of them struggle. They married so young, after dating only a few months and finding themselves pregnant. Dylan had just turned twenty-three and Tammy had still been in college. They struggled through his apprenticeship as a mechanic, where he made next to nothing, and more often than not, I'd had to help out when rent would come due at the beginning of the month. Once he was fully licensed though, his pay increased, Tammy got a part time job, and life had become a little easier for them, until now. I hate that as a mother and grandmother, I have no choice but to sit back and worry.

I am lost in my thoughts and don't hear anyone coming in until a hand falls on my shoulder.

"Hey. How is he?" The deep southern rumble is so like his brother's, I look up to find Jed's eyes full of concern.

"Not sure. The doc's checking him over right now."

"Has he said anything? Can he talk?"

They'd told us that even when he does wake up, he might not be the same man we remember. It's possible he'll have some lasting damage. My heart clenches at the thought of the big burly man, irritating as he might be, limited or changed in any way.

"He hasn't talked, has barely even opened his eyes. His arm just suddenly moved," I tell him, as he sinks down in the seat beside me.

"He won't be happy to see me, you know," Jed says wistfully. It's not the first time he's said something like that.

When Clint was first brought in, and I threw myself up as his 'next of kin,' I realized how little I knew about this man. Didn't know of any family or even a past. I'd never given myself an opportunity to know him better. All I knew was that the name of his company, Mason Brothers, would indicate there's more than one Mason. So I started digging and making some calls, finally locating Jed, Clint's brother, with whom he apparently lost touch years ago. Some kind of estrangement that Jed stayed very vague about, short of saying Clint bought him out and had taken over the company by himself. He hadn't hesitated though, when I explained who I was and why I called. Within half a day, Jed appeared at the hospital, and I never questioned who he was; the two so similar in build it was almost uncanny. My guess is Clint has probably five years or so on his brother age-wise, but other than that, the brothers favored the same genes quite obviously. Jed came in and immediately took over the running of Mason Brothers, no questions asked. He also never questioned my ruse with the hospital to be put on record as Clint's fiancée, something I immediately confessed to. From what I could see, Jed Mason was a decent, hardworking man, just like his brother. Puzzling.

"You don't know that," I suggest. "Surely, he'll be grateful that you dropped everything to be here, making sure his business is taken care of."

A snort is my only answer and rather than pry, I sink back in the quiet of the small waiting room.

"Beth?"

The nurse from earlier, I think her name is Kathy, sticks her head around the door when she spots Jed.

"Oh good, Mr. Mason, you're here too. Your brother seems to be waking up. Groggy still and not quite able to form words, but his eyes are open and his vitals are excellent. I'd normally say only one at a time, but I'm sure he would love to see some friendly faces. The doctor's done with him, so feel free to come in." She leaves with a smile.

I'm already on my feet when I notice Jed isn't moving.

"Not coming in?"

"Not sure he'll want to see me, Beth. I think maybe—"

"Nonsense. Come on, let's go." I grab his hand, and he lets himself be pulled across the hall into his brother's room.

Clint's eyes are closed when we walk in, but the moment the door clicks shut they shoot open and only widen when they fall on me.

"Beth…" Barely discernible he breathes out my name. A warm tingle spreads through me on hearing his faint voice.

"Clint," I say simply, getting lost in his dark eyes that swirl with emotion. Remembering we're not alone, I step aside to include Jed, but before I have a chance to say anything, Clint's eyes fall on the figure of his brother and turn instantly cold.

"Out."

"But, he's—"

"Get. Him. Out," Clint interrupts me, struggling to force each syllable from his mouth.

I'm shocked silent. Never have I seen him lose his temper over anything. Not even when I knew he was exasperated as could be with my persistent rejections.

"I should go," Jed says from behind me, "I never should've come. I just thought…" He lets his thought trail off without explanation before turning and leaving the room, shutting the door firmly behind him.

Turning back to the man in bed, I feel anger bubbling up inside. I don't know what happened between these two, but dammit, Jed doesn't deserve this.

"Well, welcome back to you, too," I bite off. "That's your brother you sent out of here. The same brother who dropped everything and came running the moment he heard you were in here. The same brother who has spent the past few weeks peddling back and forth between keeping your contracts on schedule and holding vigil at your bedside."

I can see my words are affecting him, because he flinches before turning his head away.

"How long?" His voice cracks from lack of use, and it almost physically hurts me to see him weak like this.

"Almost three weeks now," I whisper, ashamed for going off on a man who has just survived what easily could've been a deadly injury. Someone who has missed a chunk of his life he'll never get back, and we don't even know if there might be lasting effects.

"Jesus… What—tell me what happened?"

"You can't remember?"

I should've stayed in the dark. Cold as it has been, it's not nearly as brutal as waking up is. The harsh glare of that damn flashlight the nurse insists on aiming at my eyes, the pounding in my head, and the lingering smell of Beth in the room, long after the nurse escorts her out, is enough to make me want to crawl back under the surface of the dark pool I can still sense surrounding me. The doctor examining me asks numerous questions, which I only manage to answer in grunts and nods. Then he tells me I have a serious brain injury as the result of a violent attack and my mind goes blank. I'm obviously in a hospital and my head hurts like someone is taking a fucking pickaxe to it, but as to how I got here? I can't remember a damn thing.

When the door opens and Beth stands there, her name filters out on my breath. It hurts; talking. Feels unfamiliar as my mouth works around the words tumbling through my head, trying to line them up in order.

The moment I spot my brother behind Beth, my blood fires hot. The last person I want seeing me laid up in a bed, weaker and more vulnerable I can recall ever feeling, is that piece of shit.

"Out."

That single word bursts from me without thought or warning and stings the back of my throat, which is parchment dry. Beth tries to intervene but I won't hear it. He needs gone. Now.

After some whispering I can't hear for the raging of angry blood in my ears, he leaves the room and Beth proceeds to tear a strip off me. When she lets slip I've lost a few weeks somewhere, I have to fight down the nausea threatening to choke me. "I can't remember a damn thing," I admit. "All I know is that I was at Naomi's new place."

Naomi is Doc Waters, who's just purchased a house in Cedar Tree I've been contracted to renovate. I struggle to remember what I was doing, but I can't seem to.

Beth moves closer to the bed and sits down beside me, grabbing my hand to hold it between hers.

"Do you remember hiring on a new guy that day?" she asks cautiously.

I do, I actually remember picking him up in Cortez because he had no transportation. When most of my crews were finishing up jobs elsewhere, I'd needed an extra body, and this guy happened to call looking for temporary work. It had seemed serendipitous and I never checked his credentials. A sense of unease settled over me.

"Yeah? Why?"

The look Beth gives me should've been a warning, but what she says chills my blood right down.

"The man turned out to be Maxim Heffler. He must've knocked you out before he went after Fox."

My mind, still a bit sluggish, I struggle to put the names in place. When I realize the extra pair of hands I brought with me that day had been the murderer who'd been after Naomi and her son, Fox, for months, I feel sick.

"Fox?" I ask, dreading the answer.

"He's fine. A bit banged up but fine. And Joe is fine now, too."

"Joe?"

"Got shot in the scuffle, but Heffler got the brunt of that one—he's dead."

I have a hard time computing this news, and exhausted by the effort, I let myself slip into the darkness, Beth's hand still clasping mine.

"How is he?" Jed asks me the minute I walk into the waiting room.

"Passed out. He wanted to know what happened, can't remember a thing. He seemed in shock, and in hindsight, it probably would've been better to hold off, because one minute he was clinging to my hand and the next he was off."

"That nurse, who was here earlier, warned me we should expect him to slip in and out for a while. Don't beat yourself up, he'd want to know. I know my brother well enough for that," Jed offered gently.

"Still…" I protest, feeling guilty and second-guessing myself, tears welling in my eyes. I force them down and swallow hard. I'm not one to cry and most definitely not in public. *Right.* I give a little snort when I realize I've done it twice recently over Clint. So much for never spilling another tear over a man.

Despite my attempts at hiding them, Jed notices, stands up, and with a hand in the small of my back, starts ushers me out of the waiting room.

"We're going to grab something to eat. You're exhausted and I bet you haven't sat down to a proper meal in weeks. Am I right?"

"I guess. But what about Clint? What if he wakes up again?"

"We won't be further than five minutes away, and we'll let the nurses know so they can call the minute that happens. Okay?"

When I still hesitate, he stops to face me with his hands on my shoulders, holding me in place.

"You need to eat, Beth. You're no good to him if you start passing out."

Ha. Emotional blackmail. Works every time. Without a word I slip out of his hands and start walking to the nurse's station.

"So how'd you meet my brother?"

We were sitting in a booth at Digs, a restaurant across the street from the hospital, and I was working my way through a BLT sandwich. Jed had made short work of his burger and fries and was leaning back in his seat, sipping on his coffee.

"He was hired to work on the diner in Cedar Tree I work at." I shrug my shoulders, making it sound as casual as I can, despite the fact that my life had not been quite the same since.

"So how come he hasn't snagged you up, yet?"

The bite I just took from my sandwich threatens to go down the wrong tube, and I hack gracelessly to clear the crumbs from my airway. When I'd confessed to him early on that posing as Clint's fiancée had been just a ruse, I'd also assured we were just friends. He's never questioned further, until now, and it throws me off.

"What brought that on?" I answer his question with one of my own, once I've cleared my throat.

"It's obvious you care for him a great deal, Beth. You don't give up your work and your life, for weeks at a time, for 'just a friend'."

His smirk grates on me a little as I consider how to respond.

"Well, it's not been for lack of trying on his part. I'm just not one for romantic entanglements," I finally share, causing that damn smirk to get even more pronounced.

"Neither is he, so the fact he's tried with you says something."

"Oh come on; he's a charmer, he can't help himself," I sputter.

Huh.

I'd always thought Clint was one of those guys who would always prefer to have a willing woman by his side, always on the prowl. Had even suspected him of being a player, which was why I'd gotten pissed at him when he tried to tell me that woman, he'd had at the diner with him a while ago, meant nothing to him. I'd confronted him for trying to flirt with me when I'd just watched him charm her over lunch. I'd called him a player and when he'd then tried to kiss me, it incensed me. Hearing that he apparently isn't that kind of guy has me stumped. I'm usually a pretty good judge of character.

"Anyway," Jed continues, ignoring my silence, "I'm gonna stay and make sure the work is taken care of, but I think I'll steer clear of the hospital, from now on. Seems better for him."

I watch his shoulders slump and can't help but wonder what ever went wrong between these two brothers, but I wasn't going ask again. Instead I asked him a different one.

"How is it that you seem to have no trouble reading people the way you do—me in particular—when your brother is like a big blundering fool, who can't keep his feet out of his mouth?"

His chuckle soon turns serious when he fixes his eyes on me.

"Truth is, I'm the charmer in the family, all you get with Clint is straight up. Best remember that."

Not sure what to make of that, I open my mouth to ask for clarification, but Jed's already up and moving for the cash register to pay our bill. I guess he's done talking.

CHAPTER TWO

"Why don't you go home," I tell Beth, who seems to be here every time I open my eyes.

I've been in here for over a month now and am going nuts with the inactivity. Granted, I've only been aware for a little over a week, but it's been a fucking long and tedious week. The day after I woke up, they started me on physical therapy to try to get me up on my legs, which were annoyingly wobbly, but it didn't take long for me to regain a bit of strength and my balance. Now, I am ready to go home.

I'm sick of lying in bed, weak and miserable, with too much time on my hands. Feelings of guilt and helplessness are constantly in the forefront of my mind, and having Beth around to witness me at my weakest, just doesn't sit right with me.

As usual, she ignores me, only gracing me with a sharp glare from her eyes, inviting no further argument. God, that woman doesn't listen.

Finding out she'd been at my bedside right from the beginning, even pretending to be engaged to me to get in, had initially blown life into that little grain of hope still lodged in my chest. But when I discovered she'd been the one to find Jed and get him down to the hospital, and had been spending a lot of time with him, the hope quickly died down. Feels like deja vu, except this time I have my eyes wide open. I won't ever be caught off guard again, so that little bit of hope died a quick death. I made sure of it.

"I want to hear what the doctor has to say," Beth says, like she has a right to be here.

I'm about to find out if I'm cleared to go home.

Home has been Cedar Tree for the past year, where I finally used my half of the sale of my marital home after the divorce. Until then I'd rented, not wanting to put down roots anywhere. But with the friends I'd found there, and the general sense of community in the small town, I couldn't pass up on the fixer upper on the outskirts of town. A small three bedroom ranch-style house, all one level, in pretty poor repair but with a chunk of land that made it an attractive investment. Especially for someone with hands that could turn the place into a showpiece. At least that had been the plan until business started picking up at a steady pace, leaving my own house in a state of perpetual renovation. The living room and kitchen done, but bedrooms and bathroom still in their original, less than appealing state. I figure myself lucky now, that stairs are not going to be an issue going home. Although I'm regaining strength, I'm still moving around with the aid of a walker. Like a fucking geriatric, I shuffle behind the damn thing so as not to fall on my face. Balance is getting better, but each time I've tried to walk without it, I've ended up on the floor.

Just tried again to go for a piss, and Beth had walked in just in time to prevent me from going down. Receiving an earful—not the first one either—is what prompted my attempt to send her home. Should've known she wasn't just gonna go.

We don't have to wait long before my doctor pushes in to the room.

"You ready to get out of here?" he opens and at my eager nod, he finally cracks a smile. First one I've seen on him that I can recall. "Good. I've contacted the care facility in Cortez and they have a bed. They're expecting you this afternoon."

Okay, that's not gonna happen.

"What are you talking about?"

"You no longer need to be here. You still have a sizable blood clot between your skull and your brain, but it's shrinking as per the last MRI results. You'll need to continue on the anti-coagulants until it's dissipated. I strongly suggest a continued aspirin regimen once it does, to prevent further clotting, but your main issues are regaining strength and balance back. Something they're much better equipped at facilitating in Cortez than we are here in the hospital," he explains.

"Sick of lying in a bed all day long, Doc. I just need to go home."

"I get that, Mr. Mason, but since according to Ms. Franklin here, you're still living on your own and despite how well you think you're doing now, you'll be disappointed when you get home. You really need some round the clock care for a little while longer."

"I'll do it," Beth blurts out, startling herself by the looks of it. Frankly, I'm too stunned to object. Her eyes flick over mine insecurely before she straightens her shoulders and turns back to face the doctor. "I can be there."

"Beth…" I start, but she cuts me off.

"You want to go home? Then you're gonna have to suck it up, Big Guy. We have a new clinic opening up in town that Doc Waters is running, and she has a physical therapist working with her." Beth turns to address the man, who nods at Naomi's name.

"Good doctor. I've heard of her through the grapevine. Fine, let me put in a call to see if that arrangement is going to work," he concedes, looking at me sternly. "But you'll have to sit on this one, Ms. Franklin. I have a feeling he's going to give you a run for your money.

He's chuckling when he leaves the room and I almost miss Beth's whisper. "He already does…"

Not sure what I was thinking, blurting out that I'd look after Clint. Pretty impulsive and not quite processed through, but the thought of this strong bulk of man being laid up in a facility housing mostly the elderly is almost a travesty. I realize now it means I'll have to bunk in with him. From what I hear his place is all one level, and it makes much more sense than moving him into mine, where he'd be faced with stairs. Damn.

"What are you doing, Beth?" He wants to know.

Well, isn't that the million dollar question? Not willing to show my doubts about the arrangement, I shrug my shoulders and play it off lightly.

"Just spent more than a month at your bedside—a couple more weeks isn't a big deal if it gets you home."

The look on his face shows he's not quite buying my attempt at sounding casual, but he's not questioning me any further.

The tense quiet in the room gives me a chance to sort through the logistics in my head. Although I didn't bring a lot, I'm still going to have to pack up my stuff at my son's house. As much as I'm glad to be leaving the tension there behind, I'm going to really miss breakfasts with Max. Part of me wishes I was a little closer, so I could visit more frequently, but I'm also eager to get back to where I'm most at home—in Cedar Tree. I'll have to just try and keep better tabs on what's happening with Dylan. Perhaps if I'm not under his nose every day, he'll be more inclined to talk about what's bugging him.

"Beth, look…" Clint breaks through the silence. "I appreciate the offer, but I don't think it's gonna work."

"Really? So, what do you suggest then?" I'm sure he can hear the sharp edge to my voice. Dammit that man seriously can't see the forest for the trees.

"I could hire someone. I mean, it's not like it'll be for long—I just need to get my feet back under me."

"You'd rather have a stranger in your house and up in your business? Be my guest, Clint, if you've got that kind of money to burn. I'm gonna head over to my son's and grab my stuff, because either way, you're being released today."

I'm swallowing down the bitter taste of rejection as I get up and move to the door. Honestly, I'm not sure why it feels like I've been judged and found lacking. For the longest time he was up in my face with his clumsy ways. Now, he just seems eager to get rid of me. Well good for him, if that's what he wants.

At the door I look back at the man in the bed, his large frame having lost a lot of the bulk and his head shaved bald with the scars from his surgery still a bit angry looking. The same guy, yet so different from the good-natured big oaf I'd come to know. With a pang of regret I walk out the door, wondering if the changes would be permanent.

"Ms. Franklin!" Clint's doctor calls just as I'm passing the nurse's station on the way to the elevators. "Could I have a quick word?" He watches me as I approach him. "I just wanted to give you a head's up. Spoke with Dr. Waters just now, and she's agreed to monitor Mr. Mason's progress."

"Good, I knew she would."

"Also," he continues, "there are a few things you need to be prepared for taking care of someone recovering from an injury like Mr. Mason's. The physical effects are rather obvious, but you'll also need to consider the emotional impact and even personality changes these patients often go through. May not be easy to deal with someone who might be unpredictable and angry at times. In my experience, the bigger and stronger ones tend to fall hardest. It's not in their nature to be vulnerable. Keep an eye on him. Depression is not uncommon."

His tone is wistful, and the look he gives me is one of sympathy, while at the same time sizing me up. Checking to see if I'll be up to the task. Damn right I'll be up for it, if Clint hasn't already cut me off at the pass. Although I just walked out of his room, ready to throw in the towel; this information changes that attitude right around. Sure, I'll go to Dylan's house and pack my things, but I'm going to be right back here after that to bring Clint home. There isn't a person better equipped to take care of his ornery ass.

He can just suck it.

When I pull into the driveway, I'm surprised to find Dylan's truck parked out front. Strange. It's the middle of the day. I find him on the phone at the kitchen counter when I walk in. Seeing me he does a double take before turning his back to me.

"I'm gonna have to call you back—No, I can't right now— I'll get back to you." Snapping his phone shut, he turns to face me. "I thought you'd be at the hospital."

"And I thought you'd be at work. Guess we were both wrong. I'm here to grab my things, it looks like I'm heading back home today. Well, at least Cedar Tree. What about you? How come you're here in the middle of the workday?"

My question makes him uneasy, that much is clear.

"Forgot my lunch this morning, just came home to grab a bite," he says by way of explanation, turning his eyes away from mine. A sure tell sign he's lying; he never was good at that. Also, I distinctly remember him packing his small cooler with a stack of sandwiches this morning when I was in the kitchen, flipping pancakes with Max. Huh. The worry that had been niggling at the back of my mind makes its way to the forefront.

"Everything all right?" I can't help but ask.

"Yeah, just a bit of a hectic day is all."

He might've well said, 'back off,' in so many words; the message was clear. Although not normally my style not to push a little, I let it slide this time with so many other things on my mind. Something I'll come to regret.

By the time I get back to the hospital, having left a note for Max and Tammy saying my goodbyes and promising to come for a visit soon, I find Clint sitting, fully dressed in his own clothes, in a wheelchair in his room—waiting.

"Wow. I guess you've been given your official walking papers? Good, let me just get the car; I'll drive up to the door."

A guilty look flicks over his face but before he can open his mouth to respond, a familiar voice sounds behind me.

"Ready, my friend? The truck is parked out front. Oh, hey, Beth. I must've missed you coming in." I turn to find myself enveloped in Gus's arms.

Gus is a good friend and owner of GFI investigations. He came to Cedar Tree a few years ago for a case he was working on and ended up falling in love with my friend Emma and sticking around. He relocated his business from Grand Junction and settled in like he'd always been there. I'm a little surprised to find him here.

"What are you doing here?"

"Had a meeting in town and decided to pop in. Surprised to find our friend here sitting up and ready to head out, so I offered to take him. He didn't mention you were coming, though?" Gus throws Clint a sharp look, before smiling back at me. Clint's gaze is aimed at the floor. Ass.

"I guess I'm just that forgettable," I mutter, only half-joking. I'm pissed. Had I returned any later, I'd have found an empty room. "So what's it gonna be, cowboy? My ratty old Ford or Gus's shiny big Yukon?" I don't hesitate putting him on the spot. Seeing him flinch gives me minimal satisfaction, and I decide to shelve the 'discussion' I feel bubbling up for a time when I can tear a strip off him in private. "You know what? Why don't you go with Gus, it'll be more comfortable for you. I'll stop for some groceries in Cortez, since the contents of your fridge are probably well past their expiration, and I'll see you at home." Without another word I walk right back out of the room, ignoring the pained expression on his face. Fuck you, Clint Mason. Fuck you for making me feel like a fool.

"Not cool, man. Not cool at all."

33

I fucked up. Shouldn't be anything new, but I have a feeling I fucked up but good this time.

After Beth left my room earlier, I was already feeling like shit. I don't want to hurt that woman. Not for anything. The woman has been an absolute enigma to me. Though I freely admit that most women are mystifying to me, Beth has the unique ability to render me absolutely stupid. Frankly, I don't know what I want. Well, I do. My attraction to her hasn't changed. How could it? The woman is stacked just right and with the contrast of that sharp tongue and those deeply sensitive brown eyes, she's had me by the balls from the get go. Difference is, I'm feeling fucking weak and inadequate right now and don't want to run the risk of being yanked around by the gonads once again. Been there, done that, and have the bruises to show for it.

So when Gus walked in shortly after Beth left and offered to give me a ride, I thought…Fuck, I don't know what I was thinking. I'm an ass.

"I know. I'm an ass," I say out loud to Gus.

"You are. We have collectively not been able to pry that woman from your bedside since you got here. Everyone has chipped in to fill in for her absence, *and* yours, and you wake up with a giant burr up your ass, and treat her like that? She didn't say it, but I will on her behalf—fuck you, Clint."

Fucking hell.

If I already didn't feel like absolute crap, this would surely get me there. I look up into Gus's angry scowl and I 'suck it up,' like Beth would say.

"I'm sorry. You're right; she doesn't deserve that. I just don't…I mean…I'm struggling. She's my Achilles' heel, my soft spot, and I'm already about as weak as a goddamn newborn. I'm out of sorts," I finish weakly, although I never lower my eyes. At least that's something.

"I realize this can't be easy, but you can't go alienating the crap out of your friends. You already won't talk to your brother, from all accounts, even though he's busted his ass making sure all your projects are taken care off—we're the only family you have left, buddy."

Harsh, but very true. I reach out my hand as…well hell, as a peace-offering I guess. After a second, Gus grabs it firmly.

"You're gonna make it right with her." It's more of a statement than a question.

"Gonna try." Is all I can give him.

The drive to Cedar Tree from Durango feels much longer than I remember. I'm surprised at the obvious change in seasons already. Guess I missed most of the transition of fall. The big Yukon is comfortable enough, but who'd have thought that sitting up for an extended period of time could be so exhausting?

I'm relieved when we pull off the main road onto my drive, which goes back a ways to where my house sits. I haven't been here in over a month, and the place doesn't even look the same. What the fuck? When I look closer, I notice a few things that I sure as hell don't remember. For one thing, the old door on the double car garage had been hanging lopsided in its track since I'd bought the place, never having had a chance to replace it yet. But now, what looks to be a new graphite grey garage door is hanging in its place. Quite straight, I might add. The color matches the new damn front door, replacing the old dented one that had also been on my 'to do' list.

35

"What's going on?" I turn to Gus, whose earlier grim face now sports a smirk.

"Guess someone found your to-do list. You know how it goes."

He doesn't elaborate and frankly, I'm too tired and stunned to question him further. Been a long time since someone had done something like this out of the blue. On top of the little reality check Gus handed to me earlier, it seems Beth isn't the only one I owe a great debt of gratitude. Unfamiliar territory for me to be in this position.

When I optimistically open the car door and slide out, my legs can't seem to hold me up, but before I land on my ass in my own drive, Gus pulls my arm around his shoulders and hoists me up.

"Whoa, Big Guy. Slow down a spot, will ya? Gimme a chance to grab your wheels first."

Leaving me hanging on to the passenger side door, he makes quick work of grabbing the walker from the backseat and with a few experienced moves has it unfolded and positioned in front of me. I forgot this is par for the course for him, his wife Emma needs the use of a walker at all times, so he has plenty experience.

I dig through my pockets, hoping to find the keys I would've had on me when I ended up in the hospital, but come up empty.

"Don't know where my keys went."

"I've got a set," Gus responds before walking up the front path leaving me to look after him.

"You do?"

He turns around with a shrug of his shoulders and grin on his face. "Someone had to keep an eye on things here. Especially this last week since you woke up. Been a busy place."

With that he opens the door and walks in ahead of me.

Nothing's changed as far as I can see in the living room and kitchen, but there is a distinct smell of fresh paint, cut wood and something I can't quite put my finger on, coming from the hallway to the back of the house where the bedrooms and bathrooms are. When I walk through, it becomes obvious that someone's been doing a shitload more than just hanging a couple of doors. The two bedrooms on the left of the hallway have the doors open to reveal freshly polished wood floors with an obvious fresh layer of poly and light grey walls. No more dingy shag carpet or gaudy wallpaper with unidentified foliage on the walls. Well, fuck me sideways. A look on the opposite side of the narrow hall reveals the walk-in shower, I was hoping to build one day, in place of where the linen closet used to be. The old tub has been replaced with a huge over-sized modern claw-foot tub, and the raw stone tiles of the floor look just as I'd hoped they would against the glass subway tiles of the walls. Two bowl sinks, sitting on pedestal cabinets, are each topped with their own oval mirrors on the wall. This is fucking identical to what I envisioned. In fact, it looks like someone copied it straight from the notes and blueprints I had tucked in the center console of my truck. I walk through to the master bedroom at the end of the hall. When I open the door, my eyes flip up to the ceiling immediately. If I had any doubt before, the coffered ceiling that greets me is confirmation that whomever did this had my own plans in hand. Only one person I know is qualified for this kind of detail. Fucking Jed.

CHAPTER THREE

"Sixty-eight twenty-five, please."

The young girl manning the cash register snaps her gum, which reminds me I should pick up a supply. Chewing gum is my one addiction. I used to smoke, from time to time, but couldn't stand the smell of it on me. Gum chewing is a healthier habit to have. At least it gives my mouth something to do.

Grabbing a handful of packages, I pile them onto the belt for the girl to add to my bill.

"Seventy-two fifty," she says with barely contained impatience when I start digging for exact change.

I'd stopped at Safeway, just inside Cortez, to pick up groceries for Clint's place. Not having had the presence of mind to ask what he wanted—I'd frankly been too pissed off—I wandered the isles for a bit, trying to remember all the things he'd eaten before at the diner. Scary how my mind seems to have retained all those snippets of information from the past year and filed them away. By the end of my trek through the store, my cart was surprisingly full.

Loading the heavy bags into my old beater, I feel less and less sure about what I'm doing. With the anger at Clint dissipating a bit, I wonder if putting myself on the line, as I seem to be doing now, is actually going to help anyone. He's made it abundantly clear that whatever interest he might have had in me before he ended up in the hospital, really has passed. How ironic that at the same time he loses interest, I finally come to my senses when it comes to wanting …what? I'm not even sure what it is I'm looking for, but somewhere along the line I clued in that I was shooting myself in the foot. Sure, he isn't the smoothest operator, but he's a good man. From the first time I clapped eyes on him, he had me drooling. Exactly what got me riled in the first place; my physical reaction to his rugged good looks. Whenever that had happened before, I'd ended up with a broken heart, and I was done with that. Unfortunately, Clint bore the brunt of that. As a result, he gave up, which should've made me happy but instead, I'm hurting. Damn fool woman. So no, I don't exactly know what I'm doing, forcing myself on him like this, preparing to move in with him until he recovers. Buying his goddamn groceries. Not a damn clue, except that when I thought he might not wake up at all, or survive his injuries, I had the breath knocked out of me. The thought of not having him around was almost paralyzing. I knew then I owed it to myself to give this—Clint and me—a try. I hope to God I'm strong enough to survive if this all goes south.

Pulling up beside Gus's big Yukon in front of the garage, I wonder what Clint's reaction had been to all the improvements. I'd given Jed his keys, so he could pick up some things for his brother. He also needed the truck to keep Mason Brothers running. When Jed came in one day with the idea of finishing the work Clint had started on his house, I'd been sceptical, not sure if he'd want someone else working on his plans. But with his doctor continuing to hammer home to us that even if he woke up, there'd be no guarantee he wouldn't have permanent damage, I caved and told Jed to go for it. That had been two weeks ago, and Jed had managed to get some of the guys on their crews to put in a few extra overtime hours every day to get it done. Hell, the man had even driven into Grand Junction to pick up just the right bathroom fixtures one day. I hadn't seen any of it yet. Hadn't really seen the 'before' either, because the only time I'd ever been here was to drop off an order of food from the diner when he'd just moved in. I'd resolutely refused coming in when he invited me, and now I could hit myself over the stubborn head for that.

Before I have a chance to open the trunk to start unloading the bags, the front door opens and Gus comes out.

"Did you leave anything on the shelves?" he says, eyeing the number of bags in the car, before grabbing four of them at once and walking inside. Wiping my clammy hands on my jeans, I grab two of my own and follow him into the house. There's no sign of Clint. When Gus catches me looking, he tilts his head down the hallway to the bedrooms.

"He's lying down for a bit. Guess the drive home and the state of his house took the stuffing out of him."

"How was his reaction?" I ask, knowing that Jed would be on pins and needles.

"The house? He walked around in a daze and didn't say much, but he didn't get mad either, which I think is a good start. I do think he realizes his brother spearheaded it. Heard him mutter his name under his breath when he looked at the bathroom. Still can't figure out why someone like Clint, a genuinely good guy who never seems to lose his shit, would be estranged from his brother. Another good guy, from what I can tell. It just doesn't make sense," Gus contemplates.

"I have no answer for you. That's one thing Jed refuses to talk about and so far, Clint hasn't exactly been forthcoming either."

"Must've been a doozy. Let me just grab the last of the groceries from your car, and then I'll head out. I called Emma to let her know where I was, and she was ready to hop in her car to drive over here. Managed to hold her off, but I'm not sure how long she'll be able to resist if I don't get my ass out of here soon." Gus heads out the door, chuckling at his wife's need to take care of everyone. Even those who don't want taking care of. It's one of the things I love about Emma, she looks out for everyone, no exception. Luckily she has Gus, whose sole purpose is to look after his wife, and he does that quite well.

Ignoring the pang of envy, I start unpacking and putting away groceries. Gus comes in holding the last Safeway bags, along with my suitcase. Convenient that was in my car, it's all the stuff that I'd brought to Dylan's house.

"You want this somewhere particular?" Gus holds up my suitcase.

"One of the spare bedrooms, I guess. Is there even a bed?" I wonder, once again reminded that I might not have thought this through too well.

"One of them has a bed, I'll dump it in there."

Coming back into the kitchen, Gus suddenly pulls me into a hug, surprising the shit out of me.

"Call when you need anything, okay? Even a break from that cranky shit in there. I'm sure this can't be easy for a man like him, being laid up like this. I don't suspect it'll be easy on you either, so if you need out of the house, just give me or Emma a call."

Releasing me, he walks out, leaving me standing alone…in Clint's kitchen. Weird.

I must've fallen asleep, because when I open my eyes, dusk is coming in though the large picture window in my bedroom. I lie there for a bit, listening for sounds coming from the house, but it's quiet. Last I remember, I heard Gus and Beth talking in the kitchen before my body gave in to the heavy draw of sleep.

I have to steady myself on the walker, sitting beside my bed, when I try to get up. The constant dizziness is starting to piss me off. Even when I turn my head too abruptly, my world starts spinning. It takes a few minutes before my equilibrium settles and I can actually stand. I'd discarded my jeans and shirt when I went to lay down. Clad only in my boxers, I shuffle to the bathroom for a much needed piss, feeling about twice my forty-six years. Walking in I'm struck again how perfectly accurate to my vision this bathroom turned out. Knowing I likely had Jed to thank for it did not sit particularly well, though. But it didn't stop me from admiring his handiwork. He'd always been a talented son of a bitch when it came to details and this work was no exception. The glass subway tile walls in the shower were testament to that, with bull-nosed edging around the top of the wall and intermittent L-shaped tiles neatly curving the corners, there isn't a flaw to be found. And trust me, I try.

With only sponge baths and two piddly showers to my name since landing in the hospital, I'm eager to try out the spray of the dual shower-head; one spray and one adjustable high pressure. I strip out of my boxers and am about to step in to the stall when the door swings open on me. Beth stands in the opening, her mouth hanging open.

"Jesus! Sorry…so sorry," she mutters, slowly backing out, but not before she gives me a good once-over, which immediately results in a very distinct physical reaction. On my part—or maybe I should say *of* my part. My cock is happier than I am to see her. I'm tempted to make a smartass remark, but for once I check my mouth, knowing that what usually comes out in her presence goes down the wrong way. I simply stare back at her and wait until her eyes make their way back to mine. It takes a while. Long enough for my brain to lose its hold on my mouth.

"Gonna join me or just stand there and watch me?"

Beth's eyes shoot up. If looks could kill, I'd be a sorry puddle on the floor. Without a word she walks out, failing to shut the door, but when I go to close it behind her, it swings open again and there she is: a couple of towels in her hands and a stern look on her face.

"Don't need you to go slipping all over the floor, just cause you forgot to bring towels. Typical…" She trails off, never finishing the thought, but before she stalks out again, she turns at the last minute, a hint of amusement on her lips.

"You may wanna keep that thing covered." She waves in the general direction of my dick, which seems to enjoy all the attention and perks up even further. "It looks dangerous."

Just like that, she's gone again.

Oh, sugar, you have no idea.

When I make my way to the kitchen after my first, christening experience under the new shower, where I finally sank on the floor after jerking myself to a release of impressive proportions for the first time since forever, I find Beth fussing over some pots on the stove. I like it, and I don't like that I like it. I had worked hard on getting her from under my skin, where she didn't seem to wanna be, and now suddenly she's everywhere I look. It's hard not to appreciate the hourglass shape of her body and the lure of her Gypsy-like looks. Dark brown eyes like melted chocolate, wavy chestnut hair, which I realize I'd never seen flow free, and lips that would turn a priest into a sinner: full, wet and a deep red. Immediately my imagination took me under her clothes, wondering if her nipples would be the same deeply flushed color. Or her pussy lips....*Jesus.* With a firm shake of my head, I snap myself out of it, at the same time causing another dizzy spell that has me grabbing the edge of the counter for stability.

"You okay?" she asks, eyeing me with concern written on her face.

"Yeah," I can't help but chuckle at myself. "Just gotta remember not to make any sudden movements, it sends the world spinning."

"Sit your ass down then, I've got some jambalaya on the go. Figured you'd be sick by now of the bland hospital fare, and what better way to wake up your taste buds than some good Cajun spices? Nothing like jumping in the deep end, right?" she says, turning around and filling a bowl. It's now I register the fragrant smell of spice that's been teasing my nostrils. My stomach immediately roars to life. When she sets the bowl in front of me on the counter, I have the first spoonful shoveled in my mouth before she can even turn away.

"Slow down, Big Guy, before you give yourself a stomach ache."

I fill a bowl for myself and sit down beside him at the counter, eating at a much slower pace and trying to ignore the proximity of his thickly muscled thigh. The same thigh that only half an hour earlier had been on bold display, along with its twin and the heavy ball sack that hung in the shadow of what may well be the most impressive bit of man flesh I'd seen in memory. The man is a fucking Viking god, all dark russet body hair with just a sprinkling of grey mixed in. Thick solid muscle covering his legs and chest, without being overly cut. His newly shorn bald head has a surprisingly nice shape and the thick scruff on his jaw a stark contrast. *He can pillage and plunder me any day of the week.* I have to smother a snicker at the thought and quickly stuff another bite in my mouth. I must've made a noise anyway, because Clint turns his head to me and tilts it to one side.

"Something on your mind?"

"Nope," I lie, fighting off the telltale blush that I can feel crawling up my neck.

"Mmmmm," he half growls, not helping matters down south for me.

Heel, woman.

"So," I attempt to divert attention, "did you rest okay?" A grunt is my only answer, but I plough on. "Did you get a chance to talk to Kendra?"

Kendra is the physical therapist, who is going to work with Naomi Waters at the new clinic in town.

"Yeah, when I went to lay down. She's coming by tomorrow for an assessment. Says since we'll start gently. We can do it here until the clinic opens this coming weekend."

Right. I'd forgotten about that; the entire town was invited for the 'open house.' Emma had mentioned it when she came to visit the hospital last week.

"Almost slipped my mind, that. We should go."

He looks at me with some reservation.

"You want to go to the opening?"

"Well, yeah? And you're coming," I add sounding more courageous than I feel.

A small twitch of his lips shows he's probably on to me.

"I am?" he challenges before leaning in, his face only inches from mine. "You're kinda bossy. Could get interesting, since I like to be the one in control, but I might make an exception."

Holy fucking Batman. There went my panties. In a desperate attempt to ignore the bright red flush on my face, the hard peaks of my nipples, and the flood in my undies, I try to bluff my way out of the danger zone. Those words teased the deepest of my fantasies that had never seen the light of day.

"Hardly a challenge now, Big Guy. You're weaker than a newborn calf." I had to go and say something and just like that, the flirting tease disappears from his eyes and his mouth draws a grim line before he turns back to his bowl.

The rest of dinner takes place in utter and extremely uncomfortable silence. Clint eats two bowls; his stomach is apparently made of steel since he doesn't seem to be bothered by the heat I added to the jambalaya. My own, on the other hand, is throwing up signals of distress. Well, shit.

I'd realized earlier when I'd needed a pit stop—one now that I think of it, I still haven't taken—that neither of the bathrooms in the small house provided much privacy; one attached to the master bedroom and the other too close to the living area for comfort. Yet another thing I hadn't considered when forcing my care on Clint. Ugh.

"Coffee?" I ask, sliding off my stool and grabbing the empty bowls to put in the sink.

"Probably keep me up all night," he confesses, looking rather sheepishly.

"Bought decaf. I have the same problem but still like my coffee after a meal."

"In that case, all right. I'll have one."

"Why don't you go sit in the living room, I'll bring it to you."

He has to hold himself up by the counter again, when he slightly stumbles getting off the stool, but I don't intervene. This is a man who self-admittedly likes to be in control. It can't be easy, like Gus said, to be struck quite helpless.

Suddenly it dawns on me why he shut down after that tantalizing come on. It was right after I told him he wasn't a challenge cause he's weak. I'm an idiot. Just kicked the guy in the balls when he was already down. Nice move.

"Extra sheets in the linen closet." Clint points out as he heads for his bedroom.

We've just watched the first two episodes of "Sons of Anarchy;" a series everyone raves about but neither one of us has seen yet, when he announces he's 'wiped' and needs to hit the sack.

"I already grabbed some. Spare bed is made. No worries."

Still he lingers in the doorway a little awkwardly.

"Look, Beth, you don't need to do this. I mean, I really appreciate it and all, but I don't want you to be put out. I'll manage."

Trying hard not to feel it as rejection, I take a minute to filter my thoughts.

"I know I don't need to. That's not why I'm here. Actually, I'm not sure why I'm here, just like I wasn't sure what I was doing at the hospital. All I know is I have to do this for me. Let me?"

Opening myself up like that causes a sliver of anxiety to snake up my spine, but now that I've made the decision to show myself, I'm not going to back down. Not even the long steady glare I'm subjected to is going to change my mind. It may shake it a little, but not change it. After what feels like along time, but was likely no more than a few seconds, Clint nods once and disappears into the hallway.

I slump back down in the couch that we'd been sharing just moments before. Holy crap.

Ten minutes later, when I hear a soft but steady snore coming from the room at the end of the hall, I slip into the bathroom and finally find relief from the constant gurgling and popping of my belly all night. I better start watching what I eat if I'm going to survive staying here without embarrassing myself thoroughly.

CHAPTER FOUR

"Hello?"

It's still dark outside when I open my eyes after the shrill ring of my cell phone wakes me. In a scramble to find the damn thing on the floor beside the bed, I knock over the lamp that sits on the floor with a loud crash. Dammit. So much for trying not to wake Clint. A goddamn nightstand would've come in handy.

"Ma? Where the hell are you?"

"Dylan? What's wrong? It's five o'clock in the morning." I point out after a quick glance on my phone screen.

"I'm at your house. I need a favor."

"I'm sorry—you're where?"

"At your house, Ma. And you're not here." He's starting to sound irritated, which only pisses me off more.

"Nope, I'm not. What the heck, Dylan? What is it you need? What's going on?" I can hear the panicky edge in my voice but I can't stop it. He's freaking me out.

"Ma, I gotta get back in time for work or I'll lose my job. I have Max with me. Tammy left yesterday. Just took off, leaving Max behind, but clearing out every last penny from my last paycheck. Can you look after him for a couple of days until I get sorted?"

My head is spinning with all the information he's slinging at me.

"Wait—Tammy left? Just like that? Did she say anything?" I fire off questions as soon as they formed in my head, not giving Dylan much of a chance to respond.

"Jesus, Ma. I gotta get goin or I'll be late. Can I explain to you later? You coming home?"

"You're gonna have to give me ten minutes, I'll be there in ten, okay?" I'm already out of bed and stumbling toward the bathroom by the time I hang up, when my path is blocked by a very large bulk. Not seeing much more than a shadow, I let out a scream and swing my arm with the phone in my hand, connecting with a solid wall of muscle.

"Beth! Christ, woman, it's me. What the heck is going on?"

Clint. Of course, the crash of the lamp must've woken him up if my nasty ringtone hadn't already. He grabs me by the arms, as much for his own stability I suspect, as mine.

"Something's up with Dylan. He's apparently at my house dropping off Max. Something about Tammy up and leaving last night. He sounds panicky, says he can't afford to lose his job, which he will if he doesn't get back to Durango in time for work. I gotta go."

I try to push past him, but he holds me firm.

"Why not tell him to come here?" Clint asks.

"I was trying not to wake you. I thought I'd be back before you got up. Look, I've got to pee and then I gotta go."

This time he lets me go but not without a warning.

"Wait for me to get my pants on. You're not going off half-cocked in the middle of the night without me. You hear?"

It's only because I need to get to my house fast, that I don't want to start an argument now. Otherwise his bossy ass would get it both barrels. I slam the door shut, quickly relieve myself, and brush my teeth before nearly barreling into him again as he comes out of his bedroom, this time pushing the walker in front of him and wearing clothes.

"Get dressed," he barks and I snap out of my stupor and beeline it into my bedroom, pulling on yesterday's clothes that I'd left on the end of the bed. By the time I step into the hallway, he's already walking into the kitchen grabbing the house keys off the counter. I snag my jacket off the dining chair and pat my pocket to see if my keys are in there. With keys in hand, and my phone in my pocket, I join Clint by the open door where he's waiting. After a bit of a struggle getting the walker folded and in the trunk, we're off.

"So what exactly did he tell you?" Clint wants to know.

"Not much, just what I said, Tammy left taking what little money they had in the bank but leaving that precious baby behind. Who the fuck does that?" The sudden burst of anger at my daughter-in-law is welcome. It distracts from the niggle of fear that is unsettling my stomach.

"Anything leading up to this? Did you know something was wrong?"

"Something was causing stress, I know that much. But each time I'd try to talk to Dylan, or even Tammy about it, they said everything was fine. Dylan can't lose his job, Clint. He's just started making some decent wages after many years of struggling. I know they have debts to pay off."

I hate it. Hate no longer having control over my kid's wellbeing. It used to feel so burdensome when he was little and there was no one but me looking out for him, but now—hell, I'd welcome back that kind of control. I have none now. Nothing but the love in my heart to do what he needs me to do so he can 'sort things out.' Oh dammit. How is that going to work with Clint? I throw him a furtive glance to gage his mood. Not much better than it had been, but I can't really blame the man. How the hell am I going to solve this?

"Quit staring at me, woman, and drive. We'll figure it out."

Despite his surly mood, I reach over and grab one of his hands resting on his knees and give it a squeeze. Feels good having someone solid to worry with. He squeezes back before putting my hand on the wheel.

"Eyes on the road, hands on the wheel. Reckon I've spent plenty of time in the hospital already, not looking for another go," he grumbles, but I can here a hint of a smile in his words.

"Whatever," is my intelligent comeback.

Christ, she's gonna get us killed.

I've never been a good passenger, not since I got my driver's license at sixteen. It's been on my lips to tell her to let me drive, but in all honesty, I trust myself even less right now— and that is saying something considering the hair-raising ride she takes me on.

When we pull up to Beth's place, a strange pickup truck is in the driveway. A man is sitting on the porch steps with a car seat beside him and a toddler in his arms wrapped in a blanket. Never having met Beth's son, I assume this is him. Beth parks, flings open the car door, and gets out, going straight for the little guy. Sweet isn't usually a word I'd associate with Beth, but seeing her with her grandson in her arms, snuggling him with a big smile on her face, it's oddly the only word that comes to mind. Her son, however, is not looking too happy and seems agitated, glancing over to where I'm sitting in the car. When I see him gesturing aggressively toward his mom, I decide it's time for introductions. Not wanting to end up on my face in the driveway, I manage to get myself and my walker out of the car and make my way over to where their voices are starting to carry.

"What the fuck, Ma? You're shacking up now? What are you getting out of this? You know he's just using you, haven't you learned anything?"

"Dylan! You're waking the neighborhood, would you simmer down?" Beth tries to keep the little boy in her arms calm while facing off with her son.

"Who is using her?" I turn to Dylan with my eyebrow raised. "From what I can see, you're the one who calls her at the butt crack of dawn, expecting her to drop everything and come running. And then you have the gall to browbeat her and question her or me about motives?" I'm seething and clenching the handles on the walker tight enough to turn my knuckles white. It's that or lay that snot nosed, self-righteous punk out on his ass.

"Clint…" Beth puts a moderating hand on my arm, which only pisses me off more.

"You know you shouldn't let anyone talk to you like that. As if no one can see you for more than a means to an end. I don't care if he's your son, he has no right to berate you like that. Come on, let's take that baby home. Little thing's about to fall asleep on you." I point out, watching the little boy fighting to keep his eyes open on his grandma's shoulder.

"And you," I turn back to Dylan. "You should grow the hell up. Sounds like you've had a rough night, and I get that you're overwhelmed, but you have no fucking right to take it out on the woman who is saving your ass. And from what I can tell, it isn't the first time either. Am I right?" From the way the kid lowers his eyes and the slump of his shoulders, I can tell he's run out of steam. That boy's got troubles and I get a sneaky suspicion it's more than his wife leaving. Watching him wrap his arms around his mom and son, that suspicion is only fueled when I hear him talking in a low voice.

"Sorry, Ma. I'm sorry, it's just all a fucking mess. I'll sort it—I promise—just look after Max for me, will ya? I'll be in touch." With a kiss on his son's head and only a brief glance in my way, he walks straight to his truck, ignoring his mother's plea for further explanation, and looking like he's carrying the weight of the world on his shoulders. Yup, he's got trouble. I make up my mind to put a bug in Gus's ear, see what he can find out.

I turn to find Beth standing a little forlorn on her front step with a now sleeping baby in her arms, watching her son drive off, and the worry is etched on her face. She knows it, too.

"Let's get the baby home," I say again and her eyes snap to mine.

"But—"

"Let's get off the lawn, go back to my place, put the little one down and figure it out over coffee. Okay?"

She simply nods and looks around her at the car seat and bag that were left behind on her steps. She tries to balance Max on her shoulder while making a grab for the car seat.

"Here, give that to me," I reach for the seat and plop it on top of the walker. Beth follows behind with Max and the bag.

"I've got to install his car seat." Beth points out.

"That's just gonna wake him up. Give him to me." I slide in the back seat and hold out my arms. After a brief hesitation, Beth leans in to deposit Max in my arms and his little baby body curls up against me easily. For a moment when Beth backs up, our eyes meet and a wan smile slips on her lips.

"That baby looks good on you, Big Guy," she teases, and I growl in response, which only makes the smile brighter. Good.

With Max boxed in with pillows on a quilt on the floor in Beth's room, we settle in the kitchen with a pot of coffee on the go. Beth's face is once again lined with worry.

"He's in trouble," she says when she catches me watching her.

"I know."

"It kills me, you know? Having him shut down like that. He's not usually so closed off and bad-tempered." She lets out a long shuddering breath, before adding. "Not sure what to do."

I take a minute to consider my response.

"For starters, we'll give Katie a call a little later and find out if we can borrow a travel bed, or crib, or something from them, so Max has a safe place to sleep. We can set him up in the other spare room, for now." Katie is married to Caleb, both operatives for Gus's company GFI. They worked together for years before their relationship developed into something lasting and they had a little boy, Mattias.

"You want us to stay?" Beth seems surprised and frankly, so am I. I'd been quite convinced I was done with her, especially after finding out she'd been playing nice with my heel of a brother. I hadn't wanted her here, but now that she is, I can't envision letting her leave. Not now.

"Seems like a decent enough solution. I mean for both of us. The doc doesn't seem to think I can fend for myself just yet, not being able to drive and all, and you're gonna need help looking after the little tyke. Seems like a win-win situation to me." Even to my own ears it sounds like lame excuse, and the look on her face tells me she's not sold on it either, but something inside me pushes me to keep her here at all cost. I didn't like the way her son's eyes were flicking around, scanning the darkness earlier. Although my gut instincts have let me down in the not so recent past, I'm not about to ignore the nagging feeling that whatever trouble he is in, he might just have dropped it on his mother's doorstep, as well. Yeah, she and Max were much better off here, where I can keep an eye on them.

"Look," I reason, "you have a job to get back to sooner rather than later, and it'll be some time for me to recover completely. You can't take off work indefinitely, and surely I can come in handy looking after a two-year-old, every now and then."

She snorts loudly. "We'll talk again when his energetic little body is fully awake, and we'll see how you feel then."

How bad can it be?

"Max, no. Don't put the remote in the toilet, buddy."

Two-year-olds apparently haven't quite grasped the skills of listening. My remote plunks wetly into the bowl and Max stands with a proud smile, watching it sink down. I just manage to save it from flushing down when my hand quickly grabs Max's little one going for the lever on the tank.

I had no idea—seriously not a clue—that a two-year-old angelic looking little boy, with dark curls and thick eyelashes that would make a drag queen happy, could wage such destruction on my house in just minutes.

Apparently Max is not quite potty-trained, as is evident from my soaking wet quilt now tumbling in the washer. Beth had to run out to the store before Kendra would show, to get some diapers which his father had failed to pack. Left me in charge; chuckling that this was a perfect opportunity for me to showcase my skills. *Fuck me.* She hasn't been gone more than ten minutes and already I have coffee stains on my carpet, the bottom cabinets in my kitchen have been emptied of all contents, which are now strewn over the whole house, and my TV remote is dying a certain death in the toilet bowl. I'm exhausted.

Half an hour later, Max has apparently run out of steam when his little head starts bobbing on my shoulder. He has a newfound fascination with my hairless head and spent the last five minutes rubbing his little hands all over it, while camped out on the couch beside me with some old magazine, which is now laying in strips around us. Trying not to look around me at the disaster in my living room, I rest my head back on the couch, closing my own eyes for a moment. I only register Beth's presence when I feel the warm weight lifted off my shoulder and hear her soft chuckles.

"You could've warned me," I groan, making her laugh harder. Squinting my eyes open, I find her smiling face burying in Max's little neck, her eyes warmly on mine.

"What—and spoil all the fun?" she whispers cheekily before heading down the hallway to the bedrooms, Max securely in her arms.

Slowly letting my eyes roam over my surroundings, I flinch at the mess. Strips of paper, pans and Tupperware containers, the contents of a box of cereal, and other random items are littered about. *Jesus.* I groan as I get up and make my way to the kitchen for the garbage can, hauling it with me to pick up the debris from every elevated surface, not trusting myself to bend down all the way. Apparently the little monster had found his way into Beth's bag, judging from the utilitarian cotton panties tossed on the dining room table. They stand in stark contrast with the lacy black and grey Victoria's Secret bra that hangs over the back of one of the chairs. I know it's Victoria's Secret because I'm inspecting the label with interest when a shocked gasp comes from behind me. *Busted.*

"What? Ohmigod, that little terror," Beth blurts out as she rushes to yank the bra from my hands and her panties off the table.

"Enticing combo; functional and frilly," I tease her, deepening the blush on her cheeks.

"Whatever. Stop looking at my underwear. Oh Lord, I have to get a lock on my suitcase," she mutters, stuffing the offending underwear in her pockets, not quite successfully, before snatching the garbage can from my hands. She makes short work of the rest of the scattered paper, scooping the containers and pans off the floor. It's done before I can even blink.

A knock on the door reminds me that I need to replace the batteries in the doorbell. Beth heads to open the door to Kendra, whom I've met only briefly once before, while I was working on the clinic. Kendra's face registers surprise when she follows Beth into the living room.

"Eh... you guys? If I'm interrupting something I can come back another time, you know?"

Beth looks at her confused and I can feel my mouth twitching. When Kendra indicates the pretty lace bra dangling from Beth's pocket, she blanches and pulls the offending lingerie out.

"Oh for fuck's sake!" she sputters, "we weren't…I wasn't… Nothing was going on, it's that little trouble-maker." She turns into the hallway leaving Kendra a bit befuddled.

"Her grandson, Max, is here and nothing is safe from him," I say by way of explanation. Apparently that's good enough for Kendra because she changes tracks immediately.

"How are you doing?" She zooms in on me and for the next hour she proceeds to question, probe, and challenge me, leaving me feeling like I've been wrung out and hung up to dry. Other than to offer a meek apology and a cup of coffee to Kendra, Beth has kept a low profile. It isn't until Kendra gets ready to leave that she appears in the doorway.

"Done?" she asks no one in particular, and Kendra is quicker than I am.

"For today," she says, like I'm not in the room. "First order of business is to ditch that walker and work on his stability. I've got an adjustable cane in the car, which will be necessary outside of the house, but inside I want him to try and get around without. He just needs to remember not to make any sudden movements and to turn his head along with his eyes. It's often the sudden eye-movements that trigger a shock to the equilibrium. That, and sudden changes in position; laying down, standing up, bending over—those are all triggers. Learn to move with control. I'll be back tomorrow and bring my needles for the headaches."

"Needles?"

Both women look at me and chuckle, but it's Beth who speaks. "One of Kendra's specialties is acupuncture. Didn't you know?"

Fuck no, I didn't know. Even though I manage to tough it out for the occasional drawing of blood, needles scare the shit out of me. The idea of being used a human pincushion is not at all appealing, and yet I manage to smile and hold it together.

"I look forward to it," I grind out between my teeth, making them laugh even louder not buying my bluster for a second.

CHAPTER FIVE

"Gammy, dwink fow me?"

Max's melodic little voice, which makes everything he says sound like it should be followed be a huge question mark, never fails to put a smile on my face. The dramatic rise in pitch toward the ends of his sentences as endearing as the perpetual smile on his face. Even though he has had nothing but a sunny disposition for the past few days, his abounding energy has me worn to the bone. I don't think I'm alone; Clint has crashed each night, not long after Max goes down for the count.

Thank God for decent nights and long naps, but this morning I think we could all use a change of scenery.

I pull my coffee out of the reach of Max's little grabby hands—again—and look over to the table where Clint is tinkering with some new drawings. Something he's taken to doing when he's not working with Kendra, playing with Max, or sleeping.

"What are you working on?" I try to engage him in conversation that's been sorely lacking in the days since we've been back in Cedar Tree. His moodiness is still present, and I've got to admit, it's starting to feel a little awkward staying here with Max, looking after him. Although he's been surprisingly wonderful and attentive with Max, he never says much more than the occasional one or two word answers to anything I ask him. Maybe inquiring after something he obviously has an interest in will get him talking. I can try.

His hands still and his eyes lift from the paper to look at me.

"Doodling," he says, before turning his attention back to the paper before him.

Not letting the one-word answer discourage me I push on.

"I was thinking we could go for lunch at the diner? Be good to get out some."

Truth is, I miss the place. Miss my friends. I feel I've been stuck in limbo for all this time, and despite the fact that Max is quite the distraction, I miss conversation; chitchatting with the customers, joking with Arlene. My ears ring with the silence once Max is down and with a chest full of feelings I've got nowhere to go with, I need some distraction. It wouldn't hurt to get away from Clint a bit too, since even with his lacking conversational skills, I find myself wanting to jump him. I don't like being on this side of the fence. Christ, I'm a mess. It hasn't even been a week since I basically forced myself on him, and here I'm already trying to get away. It's not like he'll need me much longer, I'm sure. He just uses the cane now outside, and although a bit wobbly at times, nothing at all in the house. All I do now anyway is cooking, cleaning, and laundry. Kind of like a glorified housekeeper for a very, very grumpy man. A different man than the one who'd chat, charm, and make friends everywhere, despite his foot-in-mouth disease.

His head lifts again and he tilts it slightly.

"Diner?" he says with a hint of smile on his face.

Well, alleluia! There's life in there after all. I plaster a moderate smile on my face to hide the inner jumping up and down I'm doing.

"Yeah. We'll take Max, see if Katie and Mattias will meet us there because the boys were gonna have a 'play-date' anyway this afternoon, and we can head into Cortez to see Kendra right after lunch?"

With the clinic not scheduled to open until after the weekend, Kendra had suggested yesterday he come into the care facility where she is finishing out her week. She wants to 'push his limits' a bit and says she needs her equipment to do that. Thinking I could use the time to stock up on some stuff we're running low on, I think about calling Katie to take her up on her offer to take Max for the afternoon.

Katie was a security specialist for GFI before Mattias was born, but now she chooses to stay at home with him. Oh, she still works, but mostly tech support while one or more of the guys are working a case. Having already offered, I have no doubt she'll say yes.

"Miss it?" he asks, surprisingly attuned.

"I do," I admit honestly. Mainly 'cause I suck at lying. "But with Max here now too, working would be complicated."

Clint shrugs his shoulders as he leans back in his chair, his attention now fully focused on me.

"Maybe—maybe not. Why don't you give Katie a call, see if she'll meet us and we'll check out how the diner is managing without you."

I waste no time and in short order have Katie on board, Max's stuff packed up for the afternoon, and am ready by the front door. Clint chuckles as he walks up to me, cane in hand, ripped jeans hanging off his hips, and a flannel shirt over a white Henley perfecting the picture of rugged mountain man. Together with his sheer size, the old cowboy hat he's taken to wearing outside perched on his bald head, greying scruff complete with fucking dimple, he takes my breath away. The cane doesn't do anything to minimize his impressive appeal. I find myself staring slack-mouthed when Max, who's sitting on my arm, slaps his tiny hand on my cheek, snapping me out of it.

"Gammy go?"

"Little guy seems as excited as you are to get out of here," his voice rumbles. The sound of it travels right down between my legs causing me to clench them together. A squirming little body in my arms reminds me how inappropriate my ungrandmotherly thoughts are, and propels me out of the door without a word.

"Here, I can take the bag," Clint says from behind me, tugging lightly on the strap over my shoulder, and I can feel the light brush of his fingers over my shoulder right through the layers of my clothing. While he stops to hoist the diaper bag on his own shoulder and lock the door, I'm already opening the car door to strap Max in his seat. When I straighten up and attempt to step back to close the door, I bump into a large body.

"A gentleman would've offered to do that for you, but when you bend over with that fine ass on display, I suddenly don't feel so gentlemanly anymore."

His breath tickles my ear and my body freezes in the spot. Mortification and arousal do battle for supremacy while I struggle for a smart come back. All I manage is an illiterate grunt, before slipping around the trunk of the car, keeping my head down to hide the telltale blush. His low chuckle follows me all the way into the driver's seat, and that's where my indignant self comes alive.

"What's with you?" I blurt out the minute his fine ass hits the seat beside me. "For days, no, make that weeks since you've woken up, you've been mostly a grumpy ass. And now suddenly you're going all sexy and shit. The hot and cold routine is giving me hot flashes," I mumbled the last, but apparently he hears because the car fills with the best sound I've heard in months—Clint throwing his head back and laughing without restrictions. I can't help but look over and take in the strong column of his throat and the strong white teeth showing between his lips. Fuck, those lips.

"Sexy and shit?" I lift my eyes from his mouth and find him looking at me with one eyebrow raised in question.

"Seriously? That's what sticks from all I said?"

"Well, no. The hot flashes made an impression too." He winks. He bloody winks.

"Very funny, Big Guy." I resolutely turn forward and start the car, Clint chuckling softly beside me, and Max clapping his hands enthusiastically in his seat behind me.

"Gammy, GO!" he yells from his perch. "Fwunny, big gah?"

I know I've been a bear. Both in attitude and in the urge to crawl into a cave and hibernate.

It all comes home when Beth turns those expressive brown eyes on me and suggests we go out for lunch. The barely contained eagerness is right there for me to see, even if her words try to veil the fact she is jumping out of her skin to get out for a bit. For someone raised as a 'southern gentleman,' I haven't done the moniker much justice by being less than pleasant to the woman who has put her life on hold to provide family for two lost souls, Max and me. She deserves more.

I've got to admit, after the sudden and shocking breakdown of my marriage to Luanne, kids never really beeped on my radar. First time that changed was the birth of Mattias, Katie and Caleb's son. I'm not sure if it was the fact that I had a front seat to Katie's pregnancy while renovating their barn, or whether it was the first time she shoved that little scrunched up and squirming ball of humanity in my arms. I never felt the loss of something I'd never had as strongly as when his little hand tried to squeeze the life from my much larger index finger. And the smell—no one ever told me babies smelled so fucking good. Well, at least until they crapped their pants, but that's what parents were for.

Second time I lost my heart was just now. Sitting in the car on the way to the diner, a smile still lingering on my lips from the heat I seem to have put back in Beth's eyes, I'm stunned to hear Max's little singsong voice coming from the back seat.

"Fwunny, big gah?"

When I turn my head, his little eyes are focused on me and unless I'm imagining things, his perpetual smile stretches even wider. Little bugger *is* talking to me. *'Big gah'*...Big Guy. Beth calls me that regularly, the last time just seconds before. Damn if the little tyke didn't pick up on it.

"Yeah, Max, that was funny."

"Fwunny. Hahaha?"

Beth snorts in the seat beside me at the same time I chuckle at Max's attempt at mimicking the sound of my deep belly laugh. I turn to her with the smile still on my face.

"He knows my name." I point out.

"Your name?" Beth teases, "I thought your name was Clint. But I'm happy to call you 'big gah' if you like?"

"You've been calling me by the only name that counts, and don't you forget it. Big Guy is made for me and believe it—it fits me perfectly."

Beth rolls her eyes at my thick innuendo, but not before she drops a quick glance at my crotch. *That's right, baby; that's exactly what I'm talking about.*

"Oh my gawd! Look what the cat dragged in."

Arlene is waving her towel in the air when we walk into the door. "Katie called earlier and mentioned you were coming, but I told her I'd have to see it to believe it. I could barely remember what y'all looked like."

Coming around the counter, Arlene walks up to me first and wraps me in a tight hug. Pretty tall for a woman, and she's damn strong too.

"Got my head healing, woman, don't need crushed ribs to set me back some." I smile down at her.

"Oh, please—like you even feel that."

Nevertheless, she lets go immediately before turning to Beth to offer her the same treatment.

"I miss your cranky ass around here, girl! It's dull without you bitching at me all the time."

Beth snorts loudly but returns the hug one armed with a big smile on her face.

"Yeah, well, I'm not gonna admit I missed your testy self, but I have to say it's good to be back. Now if you could stop squashing my grandbaby?"

"Oh hush, you know you love me," Arlene quips, as she releases Beth and elbows her for good measure.

"Only on Sundays," is Beth's response.

A familiar chuckle sounds behind me. "Good to see our live entertainment's back," Joe smiles as he walks around me. "Good to see you out and about, man. Had us worried there for a spot."

I can't help it, I blow out a sigh of relief. Not sure what to expect since the man got shot by someone I brought onto the scene, it definitely wasn't concern about my wellbeing. No, I figured I'd have a lot of apologizing to do when faced with Joe or Naomi, which is why I've avoided contact. Joe is all smiles though and apparently harbors no hard feelings. Still I need to ask.

"How are you? All recovered? Look, I'm sor—" But I'm immediately cut off by Joe.

"Not even going there, my friend. Max Heffler spent a lifetime manipulating people; his lawyers, cops, the judges. Hell, even his own family thought he could walk on water. Not your apology to make. Don't wanna hear another word about that."

He gives me a stern look and claps his hand on my shoulder. Nothing to do but nod back.

"Staying for lunch?" I want to know.

"Now I am."

"Gimme that little scrumptious nugget." Arlene holds her arms out for Max, who throws himself in her arms. With Max's little arms around her neck, she shows us to a large booth by the window, pulling along a highchair for the toddler. "Let me go talk to Uncle Seb and see what he can scrounge up for you," she says while strapping him in, expertly evading his grabby little hands.

"Everybody, coffee?"

A round of yes from everyone, and she's off to the kitchen where her other half rules the roost.

"No other wait staff?" Beth looks around worriedly. "Feels funny sitting on my ass when the place is this busy. Maybe I should go and see—" She's already halfway out of her seat when my hand on her wrist halts her.

"Sit down, Beth. You're allowed to have lunch without worrying about work today."

Beth's not impressed. Her eyes squint and I can feel the heat coming off her. Whoa.

"Don't you start telling me what I can and can't do, Clint Mason. Been deciding that for myself for the last thirty years, give or take. And let me tell you—that ain't gonna change," she hisses out. Yowza, I seem to have pushed a button. As quickly as I grabbed it, I release her wrist and sit back. Seems I haven't lost my knack for pissing her off. Best defense? Shut your mouth. Which is exactly what I'm doing. Damn Joe is chuckling beside me.

"Still at it, you two?"

"Fuck off," I mumble between closed lips for the sake of the little one, but it doesn't stop Joe from rearing back and howling.

I'm thankful for the distraction when Katie walks in with Mattias in the stroller, and just like that the booth is bustling with activity as the two boys sitting side by side in matching highchairs do their best to *out-cute* the other with their babbling and antics.

After we've all finished our lunch and wipe the remainders from the two kids, who *wear* more of theirs than they've ingested, Joe gets up to leave, clamping a hand on my shoulder.

"Hope we'll see you this weekend for the opening of the clinic. Can't wait to hear what you think of the finished product. Jed did a good job executing your designs."

At the mention of my brother's name, habit has my hackles rise and my jaw clench. If Joe notices it, he chooses to ignore it and with a wave to Arlene behind the counter, heads out the door. I can feel Beth's eyes on me. She's about to say something when Arlene walks up to the table with the coffee pot looking glum.

"More coffee?"

"I'm good, thanks," I hold my hand over my cup, my buzzing insides not needing more caffeine.

Both Beth and Katie have refills and Beth's keen attention has slipped from me onto Arlene.

"What's up, buttercup?" she asks Arlene, who shifts uneasily on her feet.

"Ahh, just the daily frustrations of running this diner."

"Like what?"

"Hard keeping anyone long term. Just got a call from the girl we hired just two months ago, Vicki? She quit. Says she found something a little closer to home in Cortez. Not coming back. Drives me effing insane when they do that—leave me hanging right before the weekend."

I can see the struggle on Beth's face and before I can stop myself I blurt out, "Beth? Since you miss this place so much, why don't you jump back in?"

A brief smile lights her face before it turns solemn.

"I can't. I mean…there's you and then Max. It just wouldn't work."

Katie catches my eye and I know what she's going to say before she opens her mouth.

"Why not? Seriously? I think it's a great idea. I can easily take Max for the afternoons and Clint is only a short drive away, he can call if he needs you for whatever reason. Everything doesn't have to hang on you. We all have a stake in keeping the diner running smoothly. Frankly, I don't think I can take Arlene any crankier than she naturally is," she says with a wicked gleam in her eyes. Arlene's mouth falls open and Beth tries hard to stifle a snicker. I don't—I throw my head back and laugh. God it feels good to be back here. Hiding out in my house is boring as shit, but with these people? Never a dull moment. I make up my mind to work hard on joining the land of the living again. With an amused expression, Beth looks at me intently.

"You haven't done enough of that lately; it's good to hear you laugh."

"Well, never mind that it's all on my account," Arlene sputters, "Glad I'm the subject of your collective hilarity. Besides, I'll have you know, I'm never cranky."

This causes a new wave of snorts and chuckles to her consternation, but before she has a chance to take off with her knickers in a twist, Beth stops her.

"You're wound to tight, Arlene, I keep telling you. I'm taking Clint into Cortez to see Kendra this afternoon, but what time do you want me in tomorrow?"

"Twelve to five or six okay? I'll get Julie to come in later, she prefers dinner shifts anyway." She tilts her head and looks between Beth and me. "You sure you want to? This gonna work for ya?"

Receiving nods from both Katie and I, Beth turns to Arlene. "I'll be here."

Leaving the girls to hammer out details, I grab my cane and follow Arlene to the counter.

"Hold up, I wanna settle the bill."

"Nah. Lunch is on me today," she says, as she turns around to face me with tears pooling in her eyes. I'm shocked at the sight, trying to remember the last time I've seen Arlene visibly emotional.

"Hey," I try, "we were just kidding."

She waves her hands, grabbing a napkin to blow her nose. "It's not that, you thick-headed redneck. It just feels good to have things settle again. Missed Beth around. Fuck, it's not natural not having her here, she's been part of this diner for donkey's years. Way before I even came on the scene. And you...as big of a pain in my ass you can be, I was really scared for a bit there."

The single tear that escapes her furious blinking has me walking around the counter, setting my cane aside and pulling her in for a hug. Arlene being Arlene, she struggles a bit in my arms until I tell her to 'settle,' and then she wraps her arms around my waist.

"Have you made your move on Beth, yet?" she mumbles against my shirt.

72

"Say what?" I feign ignorance, but Arlene is too sharp and pushes back, fixing her eyes on me.

"Don't play coy. You're like fucking spring in Canada, hot one minute and the next you're freezing her out. She cares, she's just stubborn."

"I know," I say simply, thinking to myself that this lunch has been cathartic in more than one way. I'm ready. Ready to get back in the saddle. With a glance at Beth, who seems to be sneaking peeks at our interaction, I give Arlene a kiss on the head and thank her for lunch, before heading back to the table, my eyes not leaving Beth's the entire time.

"That was a good lunch," Beth says as she starts up the car.

We just helped Katie secure Max's seat in her car and hauled his bag over to her trunk. My mouth got the better of me when I accidentally called her '*little lady*,' something that seems to slip out naturally for me but earned me an elbow in the ribs from the '*lady*' in question. Beth secured Max in the backseat next to his buddy, and we watched them drive off with plans to pick him up when we get back to town.

"Great lunch," I say, really meaning it. I've been a fucking pussy, hiding away, but today's shown me that the friends I've made here are the real deal.

CHAPTER SIX

"So on Monday morning, I'll see you at the new clinic?"

I've just been put through my paces by Kendra, who seems happy with the progress I'm making. She follows me through the front door where I sit down on the bench, waiting for my ride.

"Yes. I hope I can get behind the wheel soon though. I'm not a very good passenger," I admit, making her chuckle.

"Didn't peg you for one, but I don't think you've got long to wait. Already I can tell your balance is improving. And what do you think of the acupuncture? Are you getting used to it?"

This time it's my turn to chuckle. I was plenty freaked out beforehand, but honestly could not feel the first needle go in. Not a thing. That's not to say it is entirely painless, since the needle she placed at the base of my neck today hit a spot that is still sore now, but she swore it would bring relief. I have to admit, my head feels clearer now than it has since I woke up.

"I'm still not a fan of needles and reckon I'll never be, but my head feels good. So if you must, you can poke me again on Monday."

"Good. In the meantime, I'll see you tomorrow at the open house, right? Naomi tells me you'll be there."

Damn. I know the chance is good I'll bump into Jed there, and that is not something I'm looking forward to, but I owe it to my friends to be there.

"Yeah, I'll be there."

"Awesome!" I smile at her youthful exuberance as she walks off to find her car, following her with my eyes. She's gotta be in her mid thirties, but she's as peppy as a twenty-year-old. Cute, but not for me.

The familiar squeal of a car door has me swing my head around to find Beth leaning on the roof of her junker, looking at me through slitted eyes, before turning to wave at Kendra as she pulls out of the parking lot. *Interesting.*

"Ready to come or do you need to enjoy the view a bit more?" she snaps, immediately lowering her eyes from mine and turning red. Dropped her guard for a minute, while I'm not a gambling man, I'd stake my bank account on the fact that is jealousy I'm hearing.

"Nothing like the beauty of a spring afternoon," I tease her, but she just slips in her seat when I approach the car. Once I'm settled in and buckled up, I turn in my seat to look at her.

"Except perhaps the fully seasoned abundance of a gorgeous twilight." Fuck if I know where that drivel comes from, but regardless, it flies out of my mouth.

Beth's gaze flicks to me before she drops her head to the steering wheel and starts laughing. Okay? Not sure that's the reaction I was hoping for but still, it's better than making her cry. Takes her a minute to compose herself before turning her eyes back on me

"That is the corniest shit I've ever heard, and Clint? If you're looking to charm a woman? Don't call her 'fully seasoned' or compare her to twilight. Neither are particularly flattering." Thank God she's still smiling a little. I need to seriously work on thinking before I speak.

CRXO

I can't believe I blurted that out like a jealous school girl. I'm fucking forty-six years old and made myself look like a damn fool when I caught him looking at Kendra, who's at least ten years younger. Of course Clint being Clint, he immediately takes the burn off by coming up with possibly the most cringe-worthy line in history. The man is a lost cause when he tries to 'handle' a woman. Someone really should muzzle him before I shove *my* foot in his mouth one of these days.

"Did you want to stop somewhere?" I ask, aiming for a much needed diversion from the embarrassing incident.

When I don't get an answer, I turn to look at him and find his eyes on me, a smile tugging at his lips. Damn him for being so handsome. "What?" I prompt and the smile is now out in full force.

"I don't need to go anywhere, but did you get all you need?" he asks breaking the tension that is simmering between us. For a minute there I was ready to climb over the centre console and kiss that mouth that's been tempting me for so long. A small blush creeps up my cheeks as I think of the extra large pack of batteries I picked up.

"Yeah. I'm done. Except a quick stop at my house to grab a few things," I respond a bit breathlessly, thoughts on how I plan to use those batteries to ease my recently revived libido swirling through my mind. The knowledge of him sleeping just down the hall every night has wreaked havoc with my determined mindset that sex is something reserved for a younger crowd. It's been a long time since I've had any kind of physical release that involved a whole other person. The last couple of years I hadn't even craved the vibrator gathering dust in my bedside drawer.

Damn Clint. Being in his proximity constantly has my creaky body respond in unexpected ways. If I don't relieve some of the built-up tension, I really am bound to jump him at some point. Better to take matters in my own hands, so to speak.

"I'd love to know what's on your mind—what's got your face all scrunched up like that." Clint's deep rumbling voice startles me, and when I stop at the traffic light, I sneak a glance. His eyes are tracing my face with an intensity that I can feel stroking over my skin like fingertips. Just like that he is playing my body again, without ever touching me.

With every ounce of my resolve, I pull my eyes from the intense contact to focus back on the road and opt to say nothing.

My phone starts ringing in my purse, which is tucked in beside Clint's large feet.

"Would you mind grabbing my phone? It might be Dylan finally calling back."

I've been trying to get a hold of him ever since he dropped Max off, without success. I'm hoping it's him. I've been worried about him, especially since getting a message the number was no longer available when calling his house yesterday. Thankful to find his cell phone hadn't seen the same fate yet, I've been blowing it up with voicemails and text messages. So far no response.

"It's Dylan," Clint says looking at the screen.

"Can you answer it? I'm gonna pull off."

There's an empty church parking lot coming up on my right and I pull into it as I hear Clint say, "Hello?".

"Think you'd better talk to your mom about that." Clint hands the phone to me with an angry look.

"Honey?"

"Ma. I have to leave town for a while. I've got this job offer that I can't refuse. Can Max stay with you?"

"How long, Dylan? I'm just about to start working again. What's going on with you? I'm worried." I rattle off when a deep sigh interrupts me on the other side.

"Ma, please… I'm fine, I gotta go. Take care of my baby for me? Love you."

And just like that he's gone and when I frantically try to call back, fear creeping up on me at the despondent tone of his voice, the call goes immediately to voicemail.

"Goddammit, Dylan," I mutter to myself, trying three more times to get through, when Clint covers the phone in my hand with his.

"Was going to do this on Wednesday already, and now I wish I had; we're gonna talk to Gus, girl. See if he can find anything out."

"Something's wrong, Clint. I can feel it." I struggle to keep the impotent tears at bay when I feel his hand stroking my cheek, and my breath stills in my throat. He's never touched me like this before. When I lift my eyes, I see compassion in his eyes, but also something else—something darker. It's making me squirm in my seat.

"I know. Fuck, I knew it when he dropped Max off Wednesday morning. We'll figure it out, sugar."

With a variety of emotions constricting my throat, I simply nod before slipping the car in drive again and pulling out of the parking lot.

"Big gah!"

We've barely stepped inside when Max comes barreling to the front door, passing right by me and latching himself onto Clint's leg, nearly knocking him off kilter. Blue, Katie's dog, walks up languidly behind and nudges me with his big head, making sure I'm not left out.

"You guys the welcoming committee?" I smile over my shoulder at my grandson, but he's still smiling up at Clint. Little traitor. It does melt my rusty heart a little when I watch Clint smiling back and ruffling Max's hair.

"Go say hi to your Gammy." Clint nudges Max, who's like a little trained Pavlov dog when Clint speaks and immediately swings around and treats me to a big smile and a leg-hug, pushing the big dog out of the way.

"Gammy, see?"

Max grabs my hand and pulls me to the kitchen, where Katie is working on her computer at the dining room table. Mattias is sitting on the floor, surrounded by those oversized Lego blocks. Duplos I think they call them.

"Hey guys," Katie says, "I wasn't expecting you back so soon. Thought maybe you'd take the opportunity to grab some dinner?" She's wiggling her eyebrows up and down with a fool grin on her face, looking back and forth between Clint and I.

"Stuff it, pipsqueak. You're about as subtle as an eighteen-wheeler on a bicycle path."

"Actually," Clint pipes up, "maybe we should ask Katie? See what she can come up with on Dylan."

Katie whips her head back to me. "Why? What's up with him?"

I spend the next couple of minutes going over the tension in their house, Tammy leaving suddenly, and Dylan showing up at my house at the crack of dawn to drop Max off. I remember almost word for word our phone conversation from earlier. Not difficult, since he never said much to begin with. Katie's fingers are already flying over the keyboard, while I'm telling her what little I know.

"Where does he work?" She wants to know and I give her the name of the garage. She then proceeds to question me on his home address, Tammy's family, where they're from. Do I know if they'd had any specific problems in the marriage before, and if I know about financial issues they might have. I don't have a hell of a lot to tell her. Clint sits at the kitchen table keeping an eye on the boys, while at the same time listening in with a keen ear.

By the time we have Max and his things loaded up, my head's still buzzing with the virtual interrogation, despite the fact that Katie's assured me she'll start digging around. I'm just getting in the car when I remember something.

"Wait!" I call out to Katie who's already walking back in the house with Mattias on her arm. "We never talked about baby-sitting Max."

"Not much to talk about," Clint points out, "I'll sort it out with Katie in the morning. I'm not totally helpless with him." He seems almost insulted.

"Never said you were, but—"

Katie pipes up, "No buts, you just do your thing and Clint and I have Max covered between us, okay?"

"Fine." I throw my hands up in surrender. "I really appreciate this, you know?"

"Just roll with it, Beth. Being on the receiving end of help isn't something you're accustomed to, but you'll get the hang of it."

Clever bitch. I throw a sharp look at Clint, who is chuckling at Katie's teasing words, before sliding behind the wheel.

"Later, little lady," he waves at her before closing his door.

With a quick simple dinner under our belts and Max down for the night, I walk into the kitchen to find Clint at the counter measuring out coffee grinds.

"Decaf," he clarifies.

I slide onto a stool and find myself staring at his broad back underneath the flannel shirt he's wearing. I have to shake my head to clear the increasing R rated thoughts he seems to generate on a more frequent basis lately. Forcing my eyes away, I stare out into the darkness outside the window instead.

"Penny for your thoughts."

When I look back, Clint's eyes are studying me intently. It's become awkward with him getting better every day and me still around. Not like he really still needs me here twenty-four seven. He gets around the house fine, and aside from needing groceries and being driven around for now, he seems able to look after himself just fine. I like being here with him—not going to deny that—but I'm afraid to get too comfortable in this man's house, in his presence.

"I should probably be moving home, you know. Not like you need me around all the time." I wince at how passive aggressive that sounds. Like I'm willing him to ask me to stay. He doesn't; instead he rubs a hand over the now permanent scruff on his jaw and regards me through slitted eyes.

"Yeah? Getting tired of me already?"

"Not saying that," I scramble. "Just that I'm sure you're craving your peace and quiet. I'm not exactly easy to miss and Max...well, a two-year-old Energizer bunny is not your usual speed either."

"Hmmm. You worried about me or about you?"

"I'm not sure what you mean?"

I shift a little uneasily on my stool as he suddenly pushes back from the counter and makes his way around it. With both hands he grabs my seat and turns me around so I'm facing him. And he's close—in my face close, especially when he puts his hands on either side of me on the counter, effectively boxing me in.

"You running again?" I can feel the breath from his lips on my own. Whatever control I was holding on my physical response to him just went out the window.

"Again? When was I running?" I pretend not to know what he's talking about, when in reality he has pegged me better than I'm comfortable admitting. I am running, and have been, knowing very early on the kind of power he'd be able to wield over me. I'm a coward.

"You've been doing that since I first clapped eyes on you and tried to let you know I liked what I saw. You're like a jumping bean; in constant motion before anyone has a chance to hold you down. And, sugar, I've been wanting to hold you down in a bad way."

Still boxed in and with nowhere to go, I can't avoid the slow descent of his mouth to mine. Not that I really tried.

The rich, potent taste of him is like a shock to my system. While his tongue is determinedly taking charge of my mouth, his hips insert themselves between my legs. My mind is urging to shut him down but the moment I move, his cautioning growl against my lips has me wantonly open my legs and lips wider instead. It's not like he is holding me down, and yet despite only our lips touching, and his prominent, very hard erection pressing between my legs, he has complete control. Slow deep sweeps of his tongue in my mouth, in rhythm with barely discernible hip rolls, have me whimpering in submission. All thought, but the taste and feel of him, disappears from my mind. Each time my hands involuntarily move to touch him, his deep growl vibrates through all my nerve ends in a delicious warning.

When his mouth finally pulls away from mine, I can't stop the little moan escaping me. His hands, which have been gripping the counter on either side of me, finally move to cup my face and tilt it up. The undeniable heat in the dark brown eyes looking down at me sends an involuntary shiver down my limbs.

"Can't have your hands on me, or mine on you; I'd lose all control," he mutters in a low voice.

"Would it be so bad to lose control?" I find myself whispering.

"Absolutely. Can't have what my hands or yours are touching distract from what my mouth is tasting."

Fucking hell.

What in blazes happened to the man, who just hours ago said all the wrong things, and yet has me melting at the words falling from his mouth now? Just as I'm about to point that out the shrill ring of a phone interrupts.

"Yours," Clint says, as he steps back from me and leaves a chill in his wake.

I get up on legs that are more wobbly than I expected, requiring me to grab onto the counter for stability. My phone is still in the pocket of my coat hanging on a kitchen chair.

"Hello?" I manage to catch it right before it goes to voicemail. "Hello?" I try again when the line stays silent. I pull the phone away from my ear and look at the screen. It says 'unknown number' so I try one last time. "Who's calling please?" Nothing. Not a sound except the loud click that signals a hang up.

"What was that?" Clint asks.

"Not sure. Never got an answer."

I'm still staring at the screen when the damn thing starts ringing again, and I almost drop it on the floor. Clint reaches out and grabs it from my hand before I have a chance to answer.

"Who the fuck is this?" he says, rather angrily, evident by the stark red of the surgery scar on his skull.

"Christ. Sorry, little lady, Beth just got a weird call is all. Thought whoever it was before was at it again. Yeah—sure, she's right here." With a sheepish grin he hands me the phone back. "It's Katie," he explains unnecessarily.

"Thanks, Einstein," I mumble, secretly pleased at the forceful display of protectiveness.

"Hey, Katie-girl, what's up?"

"You tell me first; what's this business about a weird phone call?" she demands to know.

"Nothing, probably just a wrong number, but did you find something?"

"Only that Dylan was evicted from his house last Tuesday for nonpayment."

"*Jesus.*"

"He apparently failed to pay rent for the third month in a row, and the landlord had no choice, since he wasn't returning his calls."

"How did I not know this? See this? I stayed there for a fucking month and I had no idea. Why didn't he say something? I could've helped."

I feel Clint walking up behind me and putting his hands on my shoulders in silent support.

"I don't know what to tell you, girl, but I'm guessing he may have felt he'd tapped you enough for money over the years? Wild guess…"

"Yes, possibly—probably, but I would never have allowed my grandson to go without a home, I wouldn't even have hesitated."

"Don't know what to tell you, honey. The landlord did mention that he was surprised to find the place abandoned already. The notice technically gave them a week to move out, but he said when he went to check yesterday, there was nobody there, and it looked like someone had packed in a hurry. Clothes and such mostly seemed to be gone and a bit of a mess was left in the bedroom, but other than that, he said it looked like they just up and left, leaving all furnishings behind, including the desktop computer. I told him you'd be in touch once you've decided what you want done with the stuff?"

I slump a bit and feel Clint's solid form against my back. "Not sure what to think. Should I pack it up? Put it in storage? I don't even know when he'll be back."

"I actually had a thought," Katie offers. "Gus has Malachi going to Durango to attend to some business tomorrow. I'd like to have Mal look over the place and at least pick up the computer? Who knows what he picks up on and besides, we may be able to get some information off that desktop. He can arrange to have the rest packed up and put in storage for you? At least it keeps it safe until you want it or Dylan comes back."

"I guess that's fine, I can't even think straight right now. I probably should give that landlord a call."

"Do it tomorrow morning, it's too late now. Just let him know Mal is coming and give him the GFI number so we can deal with details."

When I hang up with Katie, Clint turns me around and wraps me in his arms.

"I think I got the gist of it; he got kicked out of the house for not paying the rent and he left the contents behind. Something like that?" His voice rumbles in my ear.

I just nod my head against his chest as confirmation.

"We'll figure it out."

Again I'm momentarily stunned with the easy way 'we' slides off his lips and settles in my heart. How ironic, since just a short while ago I was ready to run in the opposite direction.

CHAPTER SEVEN

"Shhh, let Grammy sleep for a bit longer, little man."

I wake up to the high pitched voice of Max and Clint's quiet rumbling one. With startling clarity, last night's events filter my sluggish mind. Katie's call, the news she brought, and the scalding hot exchange between Clint and I it interrupted. After hanging up with her, the momentary heat was cooled and it wasn't long before Clint suggested we turn in for the night. He left me at the door to my bedroom, with only a peck on my lips, a longing in my chest, and between my legs. I can't remember much beyond that except crawling in bed and promptly passing out from what I'm sure was emotional fatigue. Only explanation since even now, after sleeping a long night, the needy ache of my body has me restless.

Reaching over the side of the bed, I grab the bag I quickly stuffed with unnecessary clothes we picked up at my house, to find my battery-operated buddy. A quick twist and the depleted batteries drop out and I slip my hand between the mattress where I've wedged their replacements. Fumbling under the sheets, one hand wanders to find the coarse hairs on my mound and my slit already wet and swollen. A little shiver has me draw in a quick breath of air as I part my lips with one hand, while the other slides the bulbous tip of my vibrator through, coating it slick and teasing my clit. A quick flick of my thumb and the low-grade buzz, muffled by the covers has me clench in anticipation. Instead of slipping it into my pussy, I slide it back and forth from my clit, where I allow it to linger, all the way to my perineum and teasing the rim of my puckered hole. Muscles already tensing, I know that it won't take much for me to reach climax. After building anticipation with a few passes between my lips and beyond, I slowly shove the sizable vibrator in my pussy, deep enough so I can feel the deep buzzing inside my channel and the twitching bunny ears hit my now over-sensitized clit. I regret not having more hands to pull and twist my nipples. My breasts ache to be sucked in between strong lips. My hand is working the vibrator in and out at an increasingly punishing pace. My breath hitches and all I hear is the rushing of blood in my ears. Almost. I pull my knees all the way up to my chest and slam the poor replacement for the real thing home hard. Squeezing my eyes shut to imagine Clint between my legs, pumping his big cock inside me, his heavy balls slapping against my ass; I come apart. My muscles squeezing and massaging the inanimate length still vibrating inside me. Out of breath and heart pumping, I fumble for the little switch that turns off the buzzing, which suddenly sounds loud in the small room. With a deep sigh I pull it out of me, leaving me sated and tender. *Good gawd.*

Fucking hell.

I'm standing with my forehead pressed to the door of Beth's bedroom, having just listened to her get herself off with some aid by the sounds of it. Goddammit, I'm so hard I could knock down the door with my cock. I wanted nothing more than to barge in there and watch, having been teased for over a year with just a vague concept of what Beth was hiding under her clothes. I'd planned on biding my time with her, making her needy for me in a controlled manner, but she just blew that plan right out of the water. Fuck, I want to go in there, but I just left Max in the borrowed highchair at the kitchen counter, coming to grab a wet wash cloth from the bathroom to wipe his sticky face. What I want to do with Beth will surely take more than a few quick minutes.

With a hand pressed against my painful hard-on, I walk into the bathroom, grabbing the washcloth I came here for and wetting it at the sink. When I turn around I almost bump into Beth, who's standing in the door opening, her mouth slack and soft, eyes heavy-lidded, and a deep flush on her cheeks. My growl is unintentional but rather instinctive and has her eyes widen in response. Trying not to stare at the puckered nipples pressing against the thin fabric of her nightshirt, I breathe in the scent of her. I'm sure my eyes betray me, but I stay in full control as I lean into her. Or so I tell myself.

"You always smell good, but the scent of your orgasm makes my mouth water," I whisper against the shell of her ear before slipping my body by her, making sure to brush against her breasts. A sharp hiss escapes her and is followed by a mumbled, 'Holy Christ on a broomstick,' making me smile. With the satisfaction of knowing the effect I have on her, I walk down the hall to the kitchen—taller than I have in a while.

Finding Max with apple jelly all over his face, as well as the counter, is a small price to pay.

When Beth finds us a little later, sitting on the floor with some of Max's toy cars, she smiles but it's tight. Should've kept my big trap shut, 'cause I can see her mentally retreating from the boundaries we've started shifting. She turns to the coffee pot in the kitchen. I hoist myself up off the floor, pausing momentarily until the dizziness dissipates, before following her there. I can see the moment she realizes I'm behind her, because her back straightens up and she freezes in place. Not letting it stop me, I step up right behind her, my front to her back.

"Didn't mean to make you uncomfortable, Bean, but that was fucking hot."

Like a shot she turns around and plants her palms on my chest trying to shove me back. I simply grab her hands and hold them between our bodies as I back her into the counter.

"Bean? What the hell is that? Some depraved sexual term I'm unfamiliar with?" Despite the fact that her eyes are burning fire into mine, she spits her words through tight lips; she still makes me laugh out loud. Don't think that earns me any points, though.

"As in jumping bean, woman. It fits you. Nothing sexually depraved about it."

She still looks dubious when I lean down and whisper close to her face, "Although I can't lie and say you don't stir up some depraved sexual fantasies, your interpretation of that name was all your refreshingly dirty mind."

Rolling her eyes in her head, she wiggles until I loosen my grip on her hands and back away. Only a little.

"You have multiple personalities or something, I've never met someone so confusing. One minute you're the ultimate charming southern gentleman, if you don't count the sexist default you fall into every now and then. The next you're a grumpy old coot who is most definitely not for social consumption, and now—now you're this horny, predatory sex fiend." She finally manages to slip away from me. This time I make no attempt to stop her.

"I'm gonna call Dylan's landlord to let him know Mal will be by, and then I have to get ready for work."

Clearly dismissed, I leave her sitting at the table keeping an eye on Max, who's happily playing on the floor and making her phone call, to go outside. I need a little cooling off 'cause things have gone from zero to high octane since last night.

It's pretty cold out this morning. Judging by the white residue left behind on the grass by an overnight frost, I have a feeling we'll be feeling the full effects of winter soon. The backyard is pretty big, but doesn't necessarily feel that way with quite the number of mature trees dotting the property. Since moving in, I haven't really done much with the space, other than throw some folding chairs on the patio made up of old pavers. Come spring I want to take some time and build a nice deck out here, but first the tree house. Don't know how I came up with the idea, but this big old catalpa tree halfway down the yard reminded me of a tree in my parents' yard growing up. It'd been an old one like this and I remember my father building Jed and I a tree house one summer. That's what I'd been drawing; my own tree house. Not gonna deny having the little man around didn't have something to do with it. I happen to think all kids should have a tree house growing up, especially boys. God, the shit Jed and I used to get into. Good thing my parents never found out half of it. But it'd also been the place where I'd kissed my first girl, Becky Fortnoy. Damn I couldn't have been more then twelve, if that. I chuckle at the memory of the chubby little girl from next door. She'd been Jed's age, was in his class actually, and he'd been hanging around her with his tongue hanging out for months. I figured being the older brother I'd test the waters for him. Damn, I was a shit back then. He'd been so pissed when he climbed up and found us in a sloppy lip lock, my hand holding on to her little budding breasts that fascinated me to no end. It was weeks before he even talked to me again. Yeah, now I could laugh about it, but then I hadn't thought it funny when my pops found out and tanned my hide but good. He made sure I was sorry for hitting on my brother's girl. Well, Pops, Jed got his own back in a big way.

Shaking my head to clear the not so good memories, I examine the tree for good anchor points for my design. Too bad it's getting cold, cause I wouldn't mind getting a start on it now. Max would love it.

I hear the sliding door open and Beth sticks her head out.

"Putting on another pot, you gonna have some more?"

"Yeah, I'll be right in."

I watch her close the door and move into the kitchen, where I can see her through the window over the sink. She hasn't said anything about Jed the last few days. I haven't asked either, I almost don't wanna know the answer. I wonder if this is Becky Fortnoy all over, with Jed biding his time while I make the move. No it fucking isn't; Beth'd been mine long before that shit showed up. I wonder if he's told her about what happened.

I spend some time rummaging through the old barn at the back of the property looking for usable lumber, but with the chill creeping into my bones, it's time to go in and see about that coffee.

"Did you get sorted with the landlord?" I ask, walking into the kitchen where Beth is just rinsing out our mugs from earlier.

"I did. He's gonna be out of town but says he'll leave a key for Mal with the next door neighbor. I also called Mal to let him know when and where."

"Good. I guess I better get hold of Katie and sort Max," I offer, reaching for the phone.

"Actually, I just talked to her, too. She says she'll pick him up after his nap, if that's okay? She's got a babysitter organized for the clinic's open house tonight and offered to keep Max there so we can pop in and just pick him up after."

"Sounds good to me."

I notice Beth chewing her bottom lip and reach out to pull it from between her teeth.

"What's on your mind?"

She snorts as her eyes flick to mine and she takes a deep breath before responding. "What isn't? Let's see, my son's in some kind of trouble and has disappeared off the grid. I'm about to start work in an hour and have my grandbaby to worry about while I'm gone. I'm living in your spare bedroom, and I can't figure out why I'm still here, but I don't know if I wanna go home. And you are confusing the hell out of me. Is that enough?" Her eyes are full of uncertainty as I weigh her words.

"Yes. It's plenty, but you can only eat an elephant one bite at a time." I lean back against the counter, put my arm around her shoulders and tuck her close. "Mal's hopefully gonna find out more today, after he's gone through Dylan's place. Max will be fine with me for a bit and will have a blast later with Blue and Mattias. And I like having you here. Max too. I'm glad you're here to help out. As for me confusing you—I thought I'd made it pretty obvious that I like you, Beth. Not sure where the confusion comes in, but let that be one thing you get straight."

"I just don't want to become dependent on you," she mutters against my shoulder.

"I reckon I should be the one worried about dependency here. Not you," I chuckle as she slaps my chest.

"What are we doing, Clint? This…thing we've got happening here—I don't have a very good track record. In all honesty, I'm scared of it."

I lift my arm and turn her around by the shoulders and pull her between my legs facing me.

"What we're doing here is acting on an attraction that's been brewing for a long time now." When she tries to turn her face away, I place a hand on her cheek and nudge her back. "A long time, Beth, and you know it. I admit that for a bit I thought I was never gonna get you to admit, let alone act on this *'thing'* we have, and I was trying to convince myself to let it go. To let you go. But now that I've had a sampling? Honey, there's no way we're not gonna explore the hell out of it."

With the tiniest of smiles teasing the corners of her mouth, Beth does a head plant in my chest, and I press my lips to the top of her head, smiling my own little smile.

"Gammy! See toy?"

Our little moment is interrupted by a wide smiling Max, who's been suspiciously quiet now that I come to think of it. In his hand he proudly holds what looks to be Beth's purple battery operated companion with a Lego man stuck on its bunny ears.

"Max!"

I want the earth to swallow me up. Right now.

Scrambling to distance myself from a howling Clint, I lunge at my vibrator clutched in Max's little hands. When I grab it from him, his big smile dissolves in a quivering lip. Realizing I've probably scared him shitless, I mindlessly drop the offensive toy and scoop the little guy up in my arms, just as the first crocodile tear starts tracking down his chubby cheeks.

"I'm sorry, baby. Gammy didn't mean to scare you," I coo in his hair, bouncing him in my arms to settle him. I'd almost forgotten the damn thing when a still snickering Clint comes up behind me.

"I've got your toy, Beth. Next time you need to '*play*,' you come to me; don't want you playing by yourself anymore." The low, almost dangerous rumble of his voice resonates all through my body before he disappears down the hall, my bunny in his large fist. But I don't have a chance to consider exactly what his words mean, when my cell phone rings. With Max still sniveling against my shoulder, I grab my phone off the table and check the screen. Dylan.

"Hey, honey?" I answer it, but am met with silence.

"Hello?" A man's voice sounds on the other side. Not Dylan's.

"Who is this?"

"I'm sorry, ma'am, I found this phone sitting on a bench along the river in Oxbow Park earlier this morning. I couldn't find anything identifying, so I called the last number dialed. Apparently that is you?" The voice sounds cultured with only the slightest hint of an accent.

"It's my son's. Where did you say you found it?"

"Oxbow Park? In Durango? Look, I have to go back to work, but how can I get in touch with your son?"

"Shit—sorry. I…" I'm scrambling to think what to do, when it comes to me. "I can have someone pick it up from you. Do you work in Durango?"

"I do, but I have meetings all afternoon. Perhaps I can get my secretary to courier it to you?"

"Sure, I'm in Cedar Tree. Beth Franklin, just send it to—" Clint scowls at me before glancing down at the phone he's just literally yanked from my hand.

"Who's this?" he barks in the phone. "Hello?"

With a grunt he disconnects and pins me with an angry glare.

"What the heck, Beth? Did you even know who that was?"

My initial surge of anger quickly subsides as I process his question. I didn't know. It could've been anyone.

"I…he…the call was from Dylan's phone. I thought it was him, I…I never thought…" I let my voice trail off before trying again. "He said he found his phone by the river in Oxbow Park. Wanted to return it. I was gonna give him my address." A sick feeling settles in my stomach as Max squirms in my arms. I put him down and he toddles over to his pile of toys on the floor, before I turn to face Clint and tell him exactly what was said.

"You know when someone finds a phone somewhere outside, the logical thing to do would be to drop it off at the nearest police station, right?" He points out and I have to agree. "I'm thinking we should let Katie or better yet, Mal, know about this. He's in Durango right now."

"I can't believe I was that dumb. Sorry." Damn, that word sounds rough coming from my mouth. I probably don't use it enough.

The anger long gone from Clint's face, he reaches out and grabs me by the nape of my neck, touching his forehead to mine.

"You're worried. He caught you off guard and who knows? He may well have been legit, but the fact he hung up the moment I got on the phone probably is a good indicator he didn't call with the best of intentions. And Beth? I'm sorry too—for getting pissed."

An excited Max interrupts the moment, by appearing from the far end of the hallway, one of my bras dangling from his hand and dragging half behind him on the floor to Clint's great hilarity. I manage to unclench his little fist from the strap, and while Clint picks my investigative little guy up, still chuckling, I go to return the damn thing to my suitcase. Just before I disappear into the bedroom, I hear Clint's voice say, "Think I'm gonna keep you here, little man. You know where to find all the good stuff."

CHAPTER EIGHT

"So damn good to have you back, woman."

Seb puts his arm around me and pulls me in for a side hug.

I hit the floor running so to speak, when I came into the diner just before noon. Saturdays are always busy for lunch and it looked like they got an early start today. The parking lot already filling quickly, I pull my car around the back, parking it next to the dumpster. With a quick wave hello, I throw on my apron, tuck my pencil behind my ear and pop a fresh strip of Wrigley's spearmint in my mouth. Ready for battle—and I've got to say, it feels good. The diner has been my second home— hell, at times it was my first home—for near thirty years. Hard to believe that what was supposed to be a part time job turned into a career.

Some career. I don't regret any of it though. Sure, I let myself get too distracted back when I should've been preparing for college, and before I even had a chance to get my head on straight, I fell in love with a boy who was destined for great things. Or so I thought. Joel and I met at Mesa Verde National Park where I worked during the summer of 1989 to save up enough for college. Joel Barnes was a tall, lanky university student from Chicago, who as an anthropology student was eager to work at Mesa Verde during the summer months. I think it was his eager need to learn as much as he could about the Anasazi and their way of life, that attracted me to him in the first place.

The friendship we struck up morphed into a hot heavy affair in no time, and when he had to go home for a family reunion that July, I cried at the thought of missing him, even just for the four days he'd be gone.

Turned out I'd had real reason to cry. I knew in my heart he'd been on that plane the moment the news hit that flight 232 from Denver to Chicago had crash-landed in Iowa. Funny how I felt his loss, even before it was confirmed he'd been one of the passengers who didn't make it out.

We'd only been together for six weeks and yet he left me with something to remember him by for the rest of my life.

Dylan.

I didn't find out I was pregnant until I was about to start college, and it changed my life on a dime. That was one of those occasions where the diner became my home because it literally was for years. Well, actually the apartment above it where the old owners let me live after my father kicked me out.

He was a hard military man with no tolerance for disobedience; not from his wife and certainly not from his daughter. I'd been so keen to head off to college in the big city, leaving my hometown in the dust. But when I found out I was going to have a baby, that dream evaporated with the need for support. *Ha.* Support—that's a good one. When I told my folks I was pregnant, my mother just clapped her hands over her mouth and said nothing when my dad slapped me so hard he split my lip. Then he packed up my clothes and tossed them on the front lawn. That'd been the last time I spoke to my parents. Oh, I'd see them around town, from time to time, but they never even acknowledged me. Not even when I was pushing Dylan in a stroller at Safeway and they came around the corner of the aisle. They never spared him or me a glance. That's when I knew it was me and my boy against the world.

When I was contacted by a lawyer years later, Dylan had been nine at the time, to tell me I was sole beneficiary of my father's will, I was shocked. I hadn't known that my father had died of a heart attack a month before, or that it happened not long after mom apparently succumbed to cancer. As much as Cortez is still a small town where nothing is secret long, the grapevine had failed on this one. I'd had no idea. The money I used for a down payment on the little house I bought to make sure Dylan had a home to grow up in. The pain and regret I tucked away safely, and I made sure never to make myself that vulnerable to anyone again.

I thought it worked. Until Clint.

"You seem miles away," Seb says.

I didn't hear him walk up behind me at the counter, where I'm refilling the condiment trays for the dinner crowd, when he slips his arm around my shoulders.

"I was. Years away, actually," I offer, turning my head to face him. "And I'm really glad to be back too. Missed you guys…and the diner."

"Why don't you head home? It's almost five anyway and Arlene and I can hold the fort until the help gets here. Been a busy afternoon, bet your feet hurt."

Yes, they fucking do. Funny how I suddenly feel my age, my body obviously quick to forget the demands of waitressing. Turning to find Arlene wiping down tables, I call out to her.

"Hey, your husband is sending me home. That okay with you?"

Her head lifts and she dismisses me with her hand. "Go, but have your ass back here tomorrow for noon. You can have Monday off."

I snort loudly.

"Diner's closed Mondays, Arlene. Don't make it sound like you're doing me a favor."

"Like I said, good day for you to be off. Now get gone, don't have time to drag my ass like someone I know. We'll pop in at the clinic later."

"You're a peach, I'll see you later," I smile when Arlene turns a glare on me. That woman loves me, almost as much as I love her, and she knows it. Grabbing my purse and coat, I drag my sorry ass to the parking lot in the back where the sound of a giggle has me turning my head. A stacked blonde is standing on the bottom step of the stairs going up to the apartment above the diner, her body hanging against Malachi's big frame. Katie's brother-in-law tilts his chin at me before turning his scowling face back to the Barbie around his neck. Seeing as he's busy, it would be awkward for me to interrupt with questions about Dylan's place, and I turn back to get into my car. I've barely turned the key when a tap on my window startles me. Mal gestures for me to roll down the window.

"Hey, Beth. Sorry about that," he says in his gravelly voice, looking back to the stairs where the blonde woman still lingers with thunder on her face. "Some unwelcome baggage from a job I did earlier this month that keeps on popping up."

I can't help but snort. "There's a way to avoid that, Mal. Keep it in your pants."

He chuckles softly at my words, shaking his head.

"Not as bad as you make me out to be, Bethie. If I was up to half of the shit you accuse me of, I'd be worn off to a stump."

Now I laugh out loud; a sound that apparently carries because I just catch the movement of Blondie stomping off around the side of the building.

"I've chased her away I think."

"Thank you. I didn't seem to be too successful." He smiles. "But I stopped you because I wanted to let you know that I got your son's computer—handed it off to Neil, who's back in town and at Gus and Emma's—and I got a couple of guys I know to help me pack up the rest. Most of it is in a storage unit near the airport, I've got the key and the paperwork upstairs. I can go grab it now or bring it with me tonight. I assume you're going to the open house?"

"I was planning to, yes. Just bring it with you. I don't know how to thank you for doing that, Mal," I tell him, putting my hand on his arm.

"You kidding? You've looked after me since I got here; feeding me and slipping into the apartment to clean when I'm on assignment. Don't tell me you thought I wouldn't notice. I notice everything, Beth," he says with that familiar arrogant tilt to his mouth. Gawd, whatever woman ends up taming him is one lucky bitch. "Oh, and before I forget, I'll pop by tomorrow to drop some shit off I brought back. Was gonna do it this afternoon but I got...held up."

"What do you have for me?"

"Didn't make sense to have little Max's room packed up and stuck in storage, when he could have it here. Figured he might miss his things."

Oh yeah, some girl's going to hit the jackpot with this one.

"Well, that was unexpected," Beth says, as she takes off her coat and hangs it in the closet by the front door.

We've just come home from the clinic's open house, where I had an awkward reunion with my brother. I'd figured he'd be there. Hell, hard as it is for me to admit, he must've worked his ass off getting the place done. Although exactly what his motivation is for being here in the first place, I don't know. I managed to be civil, at least with Beth around, but when she was chatting with Kendra, Jed approached me wanting to talk.

"I've got nothing to say."

"Maybe so, but I have enough for the both of us."

That threw me off a bit, because he's basically running my business, and I'm curious what the fuck he has to tell me, I tell him next week. That I'd be by at the office next week. Guess it was enough because he backed off then.

Then to everyone's surprise, Joe showed up in a tux and dropped to a knee before Naomi. Certainly caught her off guard, although she got him back when she tackled him to the floor knocking the ring right out of his hand. I chuckle at the memory. But his proposal doesn't really surprise me. Naomi's been the one for Joe for years, even when he still had his head up his ass. And Naomi? Let's just say Joe couldn't have found a better woman around anyway. Well, with maybe one exception. My eyes flick to Beth.

"The timing was, the sentiment wasn't."

"I guess," she mutters, as she passes me by in the direction of the kitchen. "Want some decaf?"

"Sure."

I watch her puttering around the kitchen, wondering whether I should call her on the strange mood she's been in since she got home. It's not even nine-thirty yet, by all accounts

103

early for a Saturday night. What better way to spend it than try and make some headway with this stubborn woman?

"You okay, Beth? You've been a bit off since you got home from the diner, is it that time of the month?"

With a clatter the spoon she was holding to scoop coffee grinds drops to the counter. I realize in that moment I probably just fucked up again.

"Say what?"

Damn that woman can look angry.

"I just meant that you seemed a bit off, like you weren't feeling well or something." I struggle to recover but once unleashed, there is no escaping the wrath of Beth.

"I'm off and so being a woman it *must* be my time of the month? Un-fucking-believable! You are such a Neanderthal, Clint. What do you call it when a guy is '*off*,' huh? Oh wait, that's right, men stronger than that, right? Not bothered by '*little*' things that would affect only us '*fragile*' women?" The sarcasm is dripping off, and before I have a chance to throw up a defense, she's back in action, the coffee spoon clutched in her hand, waving around like a weapon. "For your information, buster, I haven't had a period since the doctor removed my chicken coop twelve years ago!"

I swear I try to follow what she's saying, and I think I'm doing okay until she brings up a chicken coop. Confused I shake my head and repeat it back to her.

"Chicken coop?"

For a minute I think the dramatic eye roll is all I'll get for an answer, when in reality she's just gathering steam. Fucked up as it may be, it makes me harder than steel to see her all riled up. My cock is straining behind my zipper to the point of serious self-mutilation.

"Oh. Em. Gee. Yes, Clint. Chicken coop. The works. The baby factory. I had a hysterectomy, you baboon!"

Okay, sue me, but all I can think right now is the promise of sliding into her without the barrier of a condom between us. Fuck yeah.

"Tell me I don't have to explain to you what that is?"

Her hands on her rounded hips in challenge, she stirs the darker side of me. A challenge like that is not wasted on me and before she can blink I am on her. My arms pull her tight into my body, one hand sliding down to clasp that luscious ass and the other one tugging at the damn elastic band in her hair so I can weave my finger through.

Eyes wide and mouth opening in what I assume to be protest, I take away that option, forcing her to swallow her words when I slam my mouth down on hers. Hands that were braced against my chest in rejection, slowly curl to find purchase in my shirt as my mouth eats at hers in a dance for the upper hand.

I win.

Her whimper, along with the moulding of her body to mine, shows me that underneath that bristly fierce creature lives a woman who craves giving up control. Who despite the tight reigns she keeps on her life and everyone in it, secretly wants to let go. The knowledge that I'm able to bring that out in her makes my chest swell with emotion. *Fuck yeah.*

With Beth wedged between my body and the counter, I hold her head in place with my hand tangled in her hair, while the other hand goes exploring. Over her soft hips to the dip of her waist, skimming the slight swell of her stomach I can feel her suck in, to the weight of her breast overflowing my palm. I pull back slightly, leaving my lips barely touching hers and will

105

her eyes to open to mine. I need to see her reaction as I use thumb and forefinger to sharply pinch and tug on her nipple poking through the lace of her bra. The sharp hiss and instant darkening of her chocolate brown eyes tells me enough.

"Bed," I mumble against her mouth. "I need my mouth on you in the worst possible way, and I'll end up on my face if we don't get horizontal right fucking now."

I shouldn't be surprised to feel her stiffening up against me, but I'm not about to back off just because she feels insecure.

"I don't think—"

"Don't want you to think. Just want you to feel." Taking in a deep breath I give her a little. "Bean, *please*. Bed."

Taking a step back I take her hand and hurry as best I can down the hall. Don't want to chance those damn defenses going up, like I know they will the moment I take my hands off her. The woman runs rings around me everywhere, but in passion she yields.

We pass by her room and head straight for the master, where I sit on the side of the bed, pulling her body between my wide spread legs. I haven't had a chance to take her in with her gorgeous wavy hair down and take my time doing it now.

Uncomfortable under my intense scrutiny, as I let my eyes slide down the length of her body slowly, her hands start fiddling with the hem of her shirt by her sides.

"You know, I should—"

I can hear the uncertainty in her voice which pisses me off. For all her spark and fire, she shouldn't be anything but proud for all she is, instead of shrinking before my eyes.

"Eyes on mine," I interrupt her a bit curtly, waiting to have her attention. "Don't look away."

Without looking away, my fingers slowly start unbuttoning her top, starting at the bottom. Every time she makes to look away all it takes is a small sound or movement from me to have her attention back. I don't want her looking at what my hands are doing, I want her to feel what I see. Button after button slips free until the last one. My eyes still firmly fixed on hers, I carefully spread her shirt wide open and lean forward to run my tongue from the waistband of her jeans all the way up to the edge of her bra, dipping into her bellybutton on the way.

"Your taste is incredible, I don't think I'd ever need another meal if I could have my mouth on your body all day," I mumble with my lips on her stomach. She feels and smells amazing, and I want to see to confirm what I already know—that she is beautiful. Feeling a little bit like I'm charming a feral animal, my eyes let go of hers and drop down to where her gorgeous, soft tits are almost spilling from the cups and lower to the creamy white soft flesh of her belly. *Dayum.*

"Gorgeous…"

Her sharp intake of breath has me raise my eyes again. "You are, you know that? It doesn't really matter how hard you try to hide it with your ponytails and plain clothes—you can't camouflage this kind of beauty. Nor should you."

I grab her hips firmly in my hands to hold her in place.

"Now take off your bra," I say, my voice with a hard edge now.

Instinctively Beth's hands shoot up to cover her breasts and fire returns to her eyes making me smile.

"You don't get to tell me what to do," she challenges, but all I do is look at her without saying a word. A couple of minutes, not even, and I can see her determination wavering until finally she drops her hands away and reaches behind her to unhook her bra. Her breathing, high and shallow, is telling of anxious anticipation. The waiting for what is to come next and it's that sound I love. The sound of promises of things to come. The sound of the tender beginnings of trust. The sweet, sweet sound of letting go.

The moment the cups of the lace confection falls away from her heavy, slightly sagging breasts, my hungry mouth and hands are there; kneading and lifting, sucking and nipping, groaning into her flesh until I feel the sting of her hands scratching my head. *Yessss*. This is what I hoped to find. I bury my face in her soft tits, her heart racing under my ear and her fingers massaging my skull. Fucking bliss, and I haven't even been inside her body yet.

With my hands back on her hips, I move her back a little so I can maneuver her to sit on the bed beside me, her hands slide from my head and her mouth-watering tits sway with the movement. All it takes is a nudge to her shoulder to have her on her back on the mattress, and I lean in over her body, finding her mouth with mine in a possessive kiss. Not an easy task to get her jeans undone and down her hips with one hand, while the other holds her head in place by the hair, and I have to release her mouth to finish the job. Her creamy soft body is splayed out on the bed and momentarily has the breath stuck in my throat. Everything I fucking dreamed of is right here in full display. Cotton, waist high panties in stark contrast with the seductive Victoria's Secret bra I just had her take off, symbolizing everything that is Beth to me. Her tempting dark Gypsy beauty paired with the simple, undemanding but hard-working woman underneath. The combination as alluring as the lingerie she wears.

I don't notice the smile on my face until she starts rolling away.

"Where do you think you're going?" My voice comes out in a growl, pushing her shoulder back down in the mattress, and pinning her with my body.

"I don't particularly like being the butt of your inside joke, you asshat!" she spits, her fight only serving to make me harder, if that's even possible. Without hesitation I slip my hand under the elastic of her panties and without stopping to play with the surprisingly soft hair on her mound, my fingers dip firmly into her wetness.

Fuck me.

The slick heat I find between her swollen folds almost has me come in my jeans, but I manage to control myself and focus instead on her pleasure. The immediate response of her tight channel squeezing the two fingers I pump in and out of her, tells me she is close and I want to see her come undone. Pressing my thumb down on her clit as her hips come off the bed, I demand her attention.

"Eyes on me, Bean. I want you to let go for me."

"I don't...I...ohhhhh Jesus!"

Although she isn't quite screaming *my* name, the satisfaction I get from feeling her convulse on my fingers and watching her face go slack in release, is like no other. Letting her ride out her orgasm on my hand, I finally slide my fingers out and bring them up to my mouth, using my tongue to lick her taste off me, while she watches carefully with heavy-lidded eyes.

"That's gotta be the hottest thing I've seen."

The sound of her voice is lazy and the smile on her lips spells temptation, but before I have a chance to kiss the smirk off her face, the ringing of her phone pops our bubble.

CHAPTER NINE

"Don't get why you can't just have Mal drop it off here."

I've been moody since Katie called with apologies last night, but Max was puking up a storm. He'd apparently gotten into Blue's kibble, or so it looked from what he was upchucking. Beth ran out to pick him up and the poor kid did look miserable when he came home. She ended up sleeping with Max in her bed. As for me, if I hadn't just gotten effectively cockblocked by a two-year-old, I'd probably think it was funny. That kid is something else, constantly into stuff he shouldn't be into. A certain incident with some bunny ears comes to mind, and this time I do chuckle.

Doesn't last long though, when Beth announces she has to go to her place before work today. Mal is dropping off some things for Max he picked up when he was cleaning out Dylan's apartment.

"Because we'd only have to move it all to my place anyway when the doctor gives you the all clear on Tuesday. Might as well take it directly there."

I grumble because I don't like the idea of her going back to her place. Not at all. But she seems adamant. So damn independent, that woman. I'm sitting on the couch with the little man pressed to my side, watching cartoons. This is what I've been reduced to. When I look over my shoulder, Beth is leaning against the kitchen counter, her mouth twitching to hold back a smile.

"What's funny?" God I'm starting to fucking sound like a woman. Apparently it amuses Beth because she finally lets go of that smile she's been fighting and has a good chuckle.

"You. You're pouting. I never thought grown men could pout, but there you are; doing it." The twinkle in her eye lets me know she's half teasing, but still I slip off the couch, making sure Max's little body rests against the pillows instead of me and stalk over to where Beth is observing my every move. That's right, sugar, you watch.

"I don't pout." I stop right in front of her and box her in with my arms on the counter so she has to tilt her head back to look up at me. *Perfect angle*, goes through my mind as I cover her mouth with mine and insert my tongue in her mouth, claiming it as mine.

"Whoa," she exhales when I finally pull back. "What was that all about?"

"That was me making sure you understand that I. Don't. Pout."

Her snort tells me she's not half as impressed as I'd like her to be with my little dominant display, so I bend low and with my lips against the shell of her ear I make her a promise.

"You're playing with fire, Bean," I tell her in a low voice. "Keep it up and I'll have you over my lap in a heartbeat. Won't be laughing then."

"Why you…" Beth huffs annoyed, but I'm pleased to see annoyance is not all that plays in her liquid brown eyes; there is heat there too. She likes the idea of being put over my lap, and that leaves me with a boner the size of a tree-log at ten o'clock in the morning. Tempting, oh so tempting, to take this into the bedroom, or on the counter, I'm not that picky, but Max once again makes sure I keep it in my pants.

"Big gah?"

"Yes, little man, I'm coming." So to speak.

"He's still not feeling himself this morning," Beth points out. "Wonder if I should call Arlene and tell her I can't make it. I don't want to hand him off to Katie when he's sick."

"No need," I tell her, sitting back on the couch and settling a lethargic Max against me. "I've got him. You just go do your thing. Us men will be okay here."

"You sure?" she asks tentatively. I throw a smile over my shoulder that is intended to show her much more confidence than I'm feeling, 'cause what do I know about kids?

"Positive."

Falling for the bluff, Beth takes one last sip of coffee before setting her mug in the sink.

"Well, I best get ready then." Off she goes to her bedroom, leaving me with an unusually quiet Max cuddled up to me on the couch.

"Gammy?" Max sniffles into my shirt.

He'd fallen asleep half on my lap just an hour or so after Beth left to meet Mal at her house. With his little body warm and heavy on mine, it hadn't take me long to doze off either, after a virtually sleepless night. When his voice and the small hands patting my face wake me up, I find the TV still on, but the cartoons have morphed into the Sunday afternoon football game. Seeing as they're midway through the fourth quarter, I'm guessing it's mid-afternoon or thereabouts.

Looking at Max, I notice a bright red flush on his cheeks and his eyes are shiny. I lift him up and settle him completely on my lap before touching my lips to his forehead, something

I'd seen Katie do with Mattias to see if he's spiking a fever. I'm surprised at the heat coming off this little boy, and his subdued little sniffles that haven't stopped have me concerned. Before I can get to the phone to call Katie for advice, a rap sounds on the front door. With Max settled in my arms, his warm head resting on my shoulder, I open the door to find Gus on the step.

"Hey."

"Hey, yourself. Is that Beth's little boy?"

"Yeah, her grandkid, Max. Come in." I step aside to let Gus in. "Want something to drink?"

"Nah, I'm good. You sit down before you fall down with the tyke in your arms. I just came by hoping to catch you alone. I saw Beth at the diner earlier, dealing with the Sunday crowd, so I figured it was a safe bet. Didn't know you were babysitting, though." Gus takes a seat in the La-Z-boy beside the couch. "I thought Katie was looking after him?"

"He got sick last night, eating Blue's dog food," I try to explain, raising a chuckle from Gus. "But now I think it may have been something else that's had him sick all night; he's spiking a fever."

Gus leans forward and touches the backs of his fingers to Max's forehead, who doesn't even register it.

"Damn, he's burning up, man."

"I know, I was just about to call Katie for some advice."

Gus already has his phone out and is calling.

"Hey, Peach, are you busy? I stopped at Clint's and he's got Beth's grandbaby, sicker than a dog—what?—yeah, he's burning up—you sure?—Okay, see you in a few." He sits back and gestures with his phone. "Emma's on her way. She says she'll bring some stuff. Figured I'd call her instead of Katie.

Don't need my woman pissed for not giving her a chance to help. You know Emma, she's mother hen incarnate."

I chuckle at that because he's not wrong. His wife Emma takes nurturing to stratospheric levels, if not with food, with loving, which she does plenty of. Feeling a little better to know someone with some experience is on the way, since I know dick about kids, let alone sick kids, I settle Max a little better in my arms and turn to Gus.

"So what brought you here in the first place?"

His face instantly turns serious.

"This little guy's dad. Neil managed to get some data off the computer Mal dropped by yesterday."

I'm surprised, since Neil was there last night, at the clinic's open house and had some odd stare down going with Mal.

"Already? Does the kid sleep?"

Gus chuckles. "Hardly ever and if he does, it's not long. Besides, he's hardly a kid anymore—he'll be twenty-nine in a month or two."

"Pffff, anyone with the number 'twenty' in their age is a kid to me."

"Got a point," Gus concedes. "Anyway, from what he could see, Beth's boy has been into some heavy online gambling. Started with sports and over time ended up in online casinos."

"Really? From what I understand from Beth, he's making a reasonable income, but not nearly enough to be able to afford that."

"Neil says he appears to have won a bit in the sports betting, had some kind of football fantasy league he was part of that he won after the Superbowl this year, but then he turned to the casinos and hasn't been that lucky."

Worry for the possible implications starts sinking in.

"So what are you saying? Reckon he's gone to Vegas or something? Try his luck there?" I shake my head. "I don't get it. For all intents and purposes, he finally started getting his feet under him. Makes no sense."

Gus gives me a flat look.

"It does when you see the kind of spending his wife was into."

"No shit?"

"Woman had a hole in her hand the size of the Grand Canyon. A spending habit no average guy would be able to keep up with. And that's just what we can glean from the online Visa bills that were stored on the computer. Spa treatments every few weeks, purchase-accounts at Macy's online and at local boutiques. Not to mention the restaurant charges on there. The woman must've taken everyone in Durango out for lunch at least once. Living a bit above her standards to put it mildly. My guess is, he may have started gambling in hopes of staying on top of his financial situation, but I'm pretty sure addiction set in quickly."

"Dayum. That's gonna wreck Beth. That why you're talking to me, not her?"

Gus nods in response. "That—and the fact that I don't think he's headed for Vegas. I think he's in deep with some lenders. Four months ago he put a decent chunk of money down on the credit card, but he never stopped his online habits. Unfortunately, neither did his wife, so between the two of them they managed to blow fifteen-thousand dollars."

I whistle at that number, stirring Max in the process who'd fallen asleep in my arms.

"That ain't no chicken feed."

"Got that right. I'm pretty sure Beth doesn't have that kind of money lying around, and I'm equally sure she has no idea what her boy's been up to. I'd say he hit someone up for money he should've steered clear of."

Tilting my head back, I let the information sink in before reacting.

"Makes sense now. Why the wife took off kinda sudden, and why he dropped his son off at the crack of dawn and disappeared. One thing that bothers me some, though," I say, as I feel a tingle of unease settle in my stomach. "Yesterday morning Beth answered a call on her cell phone. The guy called from Dylan's phone, which he claimed to have found in some park. Tried to get her address from her, which the damn woman was about to give him if I'd not stopped her. Moment I got on the phone, he hung up. Don't think she gave him much more than her name and the town, but still."

"Actually, Mal told me about the phone thing. I didn't realize she'd already given out some details. Don't go jumping to conclusions, though," he says as he takes in the worry I'm sure is showing on my face. "My guess is you weren't your friendliest when you got the phone off her, and you may have just pissed off the guy enough to hang up on you. It's possible he really did just find the phone somewhere."

At my raised eyebrow he chuckles and raises his hands defensively. "I'm just saying, keep an eye on that woman and give me and the guys some time to get to the bottom of it."

Before I get a chance to say anything there's a knock at the door.

"That's probably Emma," Gus says standing up to get the door.

"Where is that baby?" I hear her behind me before she lets out a little squeal. "Gus!"

"Don't be walking by me without a proper hello, darlin'."

"I just saw you at lunch."

"Don't care."

After some smooching sounds I'd rather not have been witness to, later Emma comes into view, her one hand leaning on her cane and the other out with her fingers waggling.

"Gimmie that sick little baby."

"Sit yourself down first, then you can have him. He's been sluggish and feels like a little oven."

Once she's settled in the recliner her husband just vacated, I put Max on her lap. He barely reacts.

"Gus? Can you grab that bag I have hanging on my walker on the front step for me?"

In seconds Gus stands beside her handing her the bag.

"Got my hands full, honey. Can you dig out the little zippered pouch? It has an ear thermometer."

Smiling indulgently, Gus produces the thing and with some impressively swift movements, Emma has that thing shoved in Max's ear without him hardly noticing."

"A hundred and three. That's borderline, Clint. When's the last time he drank something?"

I struggle to remember if he has, when I see the half full bottle sitting on the kitchen counter. "Before Beth left, and that was at about ten this morning. Nothing since though."

"Okay, let's get some fluids into him. He's probably dehydrated, which could be why he's so lethargic. We'll see how he does, but you still better call Beth."

"Beth, phone!" Arlene yells, just as I'm finishing up with the last of my lunch tables.

Hard to believe three hours have gone by since I got here. From the moment I walked into an already packed diner and Arlene tossed my apron over the counter, I haven't even had time to go to the bathroom. Not that I'd notice the discomfort of a full bladder now; my feet are demanding all the attention. Christ, I'm getting old.

Handing the customers their bill and telling them they can settle up at the cash, I make my way over to the counter where Arlene is holding out the phone.

"You okay?" she asks as I limp up to take the call.

"Just feel fucking ancient today," I admit.

"Just today?"

"Kiss my ass, Arlene." I smile, glad to be back, despite the beating my body is getting.

"Gladly, but first talk to Clint. He's on the phone."

First thing through my mind is that something's wrong with Max, and I snatch the phone from Arlene's hand.

"Hello?"

"Beth, it's—"

"Is Max okay?" I blurt out, not letting him finish.

"Jesus, woman, give me a chance. He's spiking a fever. Emma's here and thinks he may be dehydrated."

"You called Emma before you called me?" I have a slightly hysterical pitch to my voice as I'm pulling off my apron one-handedly.

"What? No. Just bear with me, sugar. Gus was here. He's the one who called Emma 'cause Max was burning up. I just—"

"Burning up?" I can't help cutting him off again, but bits of information get stuck, and I can't hear a damn thing after. "How high?"

"Hundred and three." Clint's resorted to only answering questions now.

"On my way and call Naomi, see if she can see us at the clinic right away."

"Yes, but—" he tries.

"Be there in a few. Gotta go."

Slamming the phone down on the counter and dropping my apron next to it, I grab my purse that a worried-looking Arlene is holding out for me already. Smart woman, she doesn't hold me back with questions, but simply says, "Go".

It doesn't even take five minutes to get to Clint's house from the diner, but it's long enough for me to imagine the worst possible scenarios. By the time I get there, I'm almost in tears. I don't have time to question why someone who's never been prone to panic when Dylan was young, would find it so hard to breathe now?

When I run up to the door it's opened by Gus.

"Saw you coming," he says by way of greeting, but my focus is further in the room where Clint is standing behind the couch with the phone to his ear, and Emma is holding Max. I drop down on the couch beside her and she immediately hands Max over.

He's so hot. Like a little Coleman stove. His eyes are closed and his face is unnaturally pale, despite his obvious temperature.

Emma holds out a baby bottle of water and I take it, teasing it along the seam of his lips, but the only result is that he squeezes them together tighter.

"I know," Emma says. "I've been trying to get him to take it for the past ten minutes, but I haven't been able to get anything down. He's likely dehydrated."

"Right," I mumble, and then again, "right. I need to take him in."

Barely thinking straight for worry, I stand up and walk to the door with Max in my arms.

"Hold up, Beth. Where do you think you're going?" Clint's voice stops me in my tracks. I swing around, anger suddenly roaring up.

"A doctor, Clint. I should've known it wasn't a good idea to leave him behind with you."

I regret my words the moment they leave my mouth. The pained recoil I see on Clint's face only confirms I'm way out of line, but I'm sick with worry: for my grandson, for his father. Things are slipping out of my control and it leaves me shaky and mean.

"Naomi's waiting at the clinic," Clint's voice is flat as his eyes hold mine.

"I'll drive," Gus offers, and I'm not about to argue when he puts his hand in my back, leading me to his truck. He settles me in the backseat with Max, gets in and starts the truck. Just as we start backing out of the drive I see Clint and Emma making their way to my car. Clint is carrying a diaper bag.

"Emma's driving your car, so regardless what happens, you'll have some wheels. I'll bring Emma back here to pick up hers."

When I look at him in the rearview mirror, my confusion must be evident.

"Clint already sorted all of that before you walked in, Beth. He'd just finished packing a bag with a few things Naomi was suggesting. The different cars was his idea, too."

He doesn't have to say anything else. His point is made. I'm a total bitch, but the little shudder coming from Max has me shake it off and focus on the little guy.

Naomi steps off the porch when we pull up and starts opening the door on my side before Gus has even turned the engine off. With a quick smile at me, she reaches for Max.

"Let me take him."

I reluctantly hand him over and slip out of the car to follow behind her into the clinic, which is attached to her house.

"Burning up is right. Huh, baby?" she coos at Max, as she puts him down on the examining table in one of the treatment rooms. She undresses him expertly and carefully runs her hands over his body, pressing here and there. Then she listens to his heart and lungs and all the while, the little guy barely blinks his eyes.

"Not sure what caused the fever, but he's severely dehydrated." She points out as she slightly pinches the skin on his hands together and it takes a while to regain its shape. "I'm gonna see if I can get an IV in him and hopefully get him a little more responsive. You may want to sit down." She turns to me. "You look about ready to fall down."

I know it's Clint when I feel an arm come around my shoulders, guiding me to a row of chairs. Exhausted, scared, and running low on resistance I turn in his arms and plant my face in his chest.

"I'm so, so sorry," I mumble through the unfamiliar tears dripping from my eyes and clogging my nose. "I didn't mean—
"

His big hand covers the back of my head as he whispers close to my ear.

"It's okay. I think I get it." Which only serves to make me cry harder. Yup, I'm a bitch.

After ensuring Gus and Emma they didn't have to wait, and Naomi's promise Max would be fine once she gets his fluid levels up, they take off in Gus's truck with a vow to call them with updates. Clint isn't moving from my side, despite my attempts at sending him home with them.

"Forget it," he says again. "Not leaving without you and Max."

Four hours later, with a much cooler and more alert Max and with assurances he hadn't suffered anything major, Naomi lets us go with a sample pack of liquid antibiotics, just in case he has an infection that caused the spike. Although she thinks it's the loss of fluids from when he was tossing the dog food all through the night. Poor kid, that's a hard lesson learned.

Once home I head straight to Max's bedroom to drag his cot into mine, so I can put him down for the night. Been a long-ass day, the little one has some recharging to do and I want him close to me for the night. By the time I leave him asleep in his cot, I find Clint puttering about in the kitchen, cleaning some dishes and putting them away. A strong smell of melted cheese draws my eyes to the oven, which is on.

"What's that?"

"What? Oh, in the oven? Frittata." He shrugs his shoulders, turning back to the sink.

"I had no idea you could cook."

This time when he turns back around a slightly embarrassed smile lifts his mouth.

"I get by. I like it better when I'm cooked *for*, but I can handle basic stuff when I need to."

"Well, you can color me pleasantly surprised." I smile at him. Seeing the tightness in his responding one reminds me of the elephant in the room.

"I should—"

"I'd like to—"

"Let me go first," I ask. "I have no excuse for what I said. Well, I do, albeit a weak one, but I've learned that when you apologize the only way to do it is without reservation. So I first want to tell you I'm so sorry for saying that to you. You've been so great with Max—helping me look after him—I really don't know what I would've done without you, and you didn't deserve that."

Clint sees me hesitate and nods in encouragement.

"Truth is, I've been worried sick about Dylan and what he may have gotten himself into. I'm hurting for my grandson, whose mom was able to just up and leave him, and to top it all off, I'm a little bit out of my depth with you." My last words linger in the air as I look from under my eyebrows at the clench of his fists holding the kitchen towel.

"How so?"

For a minute I consider pretending I don't know what he's referring to, but the truth is I know exactly what he wants to know. With a deep breath in, I bite the bullet.

"I like my independence. Like having control of my life. But I can feel it slipping around you and I'm letting it. Letting you in with your—at times—overbearing personality, and take control. I find myself liking it, and I don't know how to feel about that."

Clint moves slowly closer as I'm talking, to where he can reach out and take my face in his hands.

"Maybe it's more a question of how you feel about me?" His voice reverberates through me while his eyes seem to search mine for the answer. "Besides, the only time I'm interested in taking over control is the bedroom," he adds with a tiny arrogant tilt of his mouth.

Oh boy, I'm in trouble.

CHAPTER TEN

Voicing her worry about her son convinces me to say nothing about the information Gus shared with me earlier, but that doesn't absolve me from feeling guilt for keeping information from her. Still—after a day like today, I don't want to add to the stress. I almost chuckle aloud when I realize every day seems to bring a new challenge, keeping me from opening up with her completely. Her admission that I affect her in such a way toys with my resolve though. Never been one to want to show the back of my tongue, but somehow Beth is different. Tough, resilient, and so damn stubborn, she's lodged herself under my skin so deep, I just know there's no way to get rid of her. Even if I'd want to.

"You're staring at me," she whispers, interrupting my musings. "Are you still mad?"

"Fuck no."

She tilts her head, as if waiting for me to say more. When I don't volunteer, she takes in a deep shaky breath and looks away.

"Okay. Good. I really am sorry."

"Stop saying sorry, Bean." The use of my nickname for her has her eyes flick up to mine. "It's all good."

"So when can we eat? I'm starving," she announces, and I gladly grab on to the distraction.

125

"Now. Sit down. I'll grab us some plates."

We spend the next ten minutes or so quietly eating—the silence not an unpleasant one. After putting the leftovers in the fridge and hand-washing the few dishes we dirtied, Beth makes us some decaf, and we sit down in the living room. Instead of sitting on the couch beside me she picks the chair. A moment later I understand why she wants a bit of distance.

"I'm thinking tomorrow I'll move Max and my stuff back home."

"Is that right?" I try to curb the urge to demand she stay here. There really is no good reason to; other than needing the all clear from the doc on Tuesday. I've just effectively proven, by managing to prepare a meal, that I can manage fine on my own. Slapping myself upside the head for that now. Only reason would be that I don't *want* them to leave. Trying to force Beth to stay would probably only cause her to run in the opposite direction harder.

"I just think the sooner we get back into our regular routines, the better it is." She makes her voice convincing, but her eyes betray her. If I'm not mistaken, she doesn't want to go as much as I don't want her to leave.

"If you think so."

"Why? You don't agree?"

I can hear the uncertainty in her voice and suddenly I don't want to play this guessing game anymore. I'm too fucking old not to be clear about what I do and don't want. I think Beth is too.

"Cards on the table."

She looks at me with what I swear is an odd mix of hope and fear in her eyes. "Okay?"

"I'm way past beating around the bush like this, Beth. I don't think I need to point out that I care for you—fuck, you're beautiful, capable, smart as a whip, and even though you like to show off that hard shell, I fucking know you have the softest underbelly."

A slightly embarrassed blush starts creeping up her face, but she doesn't look away from me.

"I reckon you noticed too that there was a brief period there where I wasn't sure it was worth the fight, but I was wrong. It most definitely is worth the battle. I agree there's a lot going on—" Before I have a chance to finish my thought, she sits up straight.

"Exactly," she jumps in. "That's why I think this is for the best. Hard to get a good read on what is possible with all that is happening around us. I'm thinking a bit of space wouldn't hurt."

"You didn't let me finish," I point out and with a little move of her hand she indicates for me to finish. "Not 'exactly' at all, in fact. What I was going to say was that the shit that happens in life, whatever it is, will always be there. If not this, then something else. Life isn't lived in a bubble, Bean, you should know that better than some. Every day there is more bullshit to face and let me ask you—doesn't it feel better not to have to face it alone?"

I didn't expect tears to pool in her eyes, but they're unmistakable, hanging onto the edge of her eyelids for dear life. The moment the first one rolls down her cheek, I reach out my hand. "Come here, sugar."

Hesitantly she gets up and when she touches my hand, I grab on and pull her down on my lap.

"I'm too heavy!"

"Shut it. I don't wanna hear that shit."

Settling a little against me—but barely—she starts talking.

"I just don't know what you want. Hell, I don't know if what I want is even possible."

"First off, anything is possible, but you've gotta open up to it. And as for what I want? I can't rightly tell you, but what I *can* tell you is that I don't want you to go. I'm not gonna keep you; it's your right to do whatever the hell you want, but I really just want you to stay here. I like you here. I like Max here. And it's gonna be lonely as hell with both of you gone, but I won't stop you if that's what you want."

Slowly her body relaxes as she confesses what's in her heart.

"I don't really want to leave, but I'm afraid if I don't that I'll come to count on you. It's a luxury I can't afford myself."

"Don't see why not. Can't figure what's wrong with counting on someone to have your back. Gotta confess though, it isn't something that comes easy for me either, given that the few times I did; it blew up in my face, but damn if I'm not willing to stick my neck out and count on you."

She's quiet for a minute and stares at her wringing hands in front of her. I lift her chin so she's forced to look at me.

"Not looking to change anything about you, Bean. I like you just the way you are. Gotta trust me on that."

She nestles her head against my shoulder and I press my lips against the side of her head.

"Will you tell me what happened with you and your brother?"

Fuck me. Of all the things to bring up. I knew it was coming after bumping into him at the open house, but damn I'm not ready for it. Beth has her eyes on me, trying to read me, and given that I just gave her a spiel about trust, and that my cock is hurtin' from her wiggling around on my lap and wants to see some action, I figure I'll rip off the BandAid.

"He fucked my wife."

"Your what? He what? Oh my God—that's…I have no words." Her hand grabs my arm that's resting on her legs. I know she's looking at me but I don't look back. Not interested in seeing anything but lust and maybe something else in those eyes, but certainly not pity. Fuck, I hate pity. "I never would've thought that of him."

A bitter chuckle bubbles up. No shit. I'd never expected that either.

"Luanne wasn't a happy woman. I tried to make her happy, but she just wasn't. To be honest, I'd had thoughts of leaving her, just never got around to it. She volunteered that information. Just came out one day and told me when we were arguing over something stupid. Can't even remember. My own brother?" I just shake my head, still not quite grasping how someone, who I'd been close to my whole life, would do something like that. "I confronted him and he didn't deny it. I went after him with my fists, but some of my crew heard the commotion and stepped in. When I got home that night, she was gone. House was basically empty. I insisted on selling the place once the divorce was finalized. Since I hadn't seen Jed again since that day, I had my lawyer approach him with an offer to buy him out of the business with the money from the sale of the house. I eventually moved Mason Brothers out of Georgia. Took me a while to build up again, but I always loved the raw beauty of Colorado, so I rebuilt here. That's the story."

"Where's Luanne now?" Beth asks quietly.

129

"Fuck if I know. I guess back in Georgia, although what the heck Jed is doing here, I still can't figure."

There hasn't been a sign of Luanne either. From what I gather Jed's here alone and staying at the motel just outside town. Not that I care much either way; I've hardly thought about her, but Jed's betrayal lives deep under my skin.

"Maybe you should talk to him?"

"Yeah, sometime this week. I have no choice, with him running my business," I grumble. "Enough about Jed, the conversation was much more interesting before we started on him."

Yowza.

Not quite the answer I expected. I've had some opportunity to spend time with Jed, but he never struck me as a cheater. Not surprised he wasn't willing to tell me what happened between him and Clint when I asked him.

Feeling the tension in his body, I try to get up off his lap but his sizable arm keeps me anchored.

"Clint, let me go."

"Not likely. You got me on the subject I hate most and still my cock won't stay still. Can't you feel it?"

Uhh, yes, I can feel it. Been trying to ignore his hard-on poking my ass, but damn, hard to ignore something that prominent. Still, I try to struggle against him, causing him to tighten his arm. With the other hand, he slides up from my belly, between my breasts, and comes to rest on my neck. I don't know why, but rather than threatening, it makes me feel soft all over. I don't do soft, but Clint seems to barrel right through that, like the bull in the proverbial china shop he is.

"You gonna keep struggling or you gonna let me take care of you?" His voice a deep rumble from his chest, and my body instantly responds. Nipples perking up, a soft warm wave in my lower body I know is wetting my panties right now; so turned on by voice and hold. He hasn't even touched any pertinent bits yet. It's not in my nature to stop fighting for myself, to give myself over, but damn if Clint's not making me with his voice in my ear and his hand on my neck.

I let my body sag back into his and immediately am rewarded with a deep approving growl. Yes, *this*.

In a reverse move, he lifts me off his lap and on my feet, grabbing a firm hold of my hand when he gets up himself. There's still a slight hesitation when he waits for his equilibrium to settle, before he starts moving toward the back of the house where the bedrooms are. At the mouth of the hallway I stop, effectively halting his forward movement.

"Max..." I'm suddenly aware of my grandson sleeping in my room, and the fact I put him there to keep an eye out through the night. One step and Clint is in my face, his hands now tilting my head.

"Gotta trust me, Beth. I'm too old to give you the attention you need on a couch, and I certainly am not going to with a toddler in the room. He's gonna be fine right where he is, we'll keep his door open so we can hear, but I'll be damned if I'm gonna delay getting your body under me to explore." His look is intense and his words have my knees wobbly. "You with me? I need a response, Bean."

"I think I can live with that." My voice sounds raspy and thin to my own ears.

With a little smile and a firm nod he turns around and continues pulling me into the bedroom. He leaves me in the middle of the room to walk back to the door, where he turns around to look me up and down thoroughly.

"When I get back, I want you naked and on that bed."

Automatically my head turns to take in the massive bed he's indicating. The bed where we were interrupted before I had a chance to live out the fantasies I've harbored every time I eye it from the doorway, imagination running rampant in my mind of what it would be like to finish what we started the other day. By the time I look back to the door, he's gone already, and I'm left unsure of what to do. I'm still standing in the middle of the room when he returns a few minutes later, a scowl on his face at finding me in the same spot he left me.

"You're not naked," he points out as he closes the door behind him.

The way his dark eyes scan my body have a shiver of dangerous anticipation running down my limbs and goose bumps rise on my skin. I open my mouth to say something smart, but the look in his eyes has my voice freeze in my throat. One of his eyebrows rises in question. I can't seem to stop my shaking hand from coming up to fumble with the top button of my shirt. The look of satisfaction that steals over his face as he sits down on the edge of the bed, much in the same spot he was before, is enough to have me lift my other hand to make quick work with the rest of the buttons. I should feel self-conscious, standing in the middle of the room, undressing myself in front of this imposing man, but strangely I don't. The lust in his eyes when he looks at me, and the way he unapologetically adjusts the hard ridge in his jeans have me feeling empowered instead. How it is possible that someone always so uncomfortably aware of her own body faults can become so bold under the intense scrutiny of this man? Every flick of his eyes and flare of his nostrils signals the effect I have on him. Before I know it, I stand in nothing more than my pretty white lace bra and my practical white cotton granny panties. What can I say? I'm all about the comfort and Clint doesn't seem to mind.

"Pretty, but not naked yet," he growls, his voice catching a bit.

"You're still wearing all your clothes," I point out and his eyes slide up from where they were teasing my breasts and bore into mine.

"Well aware, and that's the way it's gonna stay for now. Stop stalling."

For just a moment I hesitate, struggling to fight the slight edge of unease at the disadvantage I find myself at, but I remind myself of all the things he's just told me. The trust that is so important to him, and I find I don't want to resist. I want to give him that. My hands slide up behind my back. In one move I unclip my bra, and let it slide down my arms until it simply falls to the floor, exposing the breasts that long ago have given up their fight with gravity. The way his gaze locks in with my swaying boobs is an encouragement to slip my thumbs in the top of my panties and shove them down my hips. I belatedly realize that I haven't really had a chance to do any landscaping in recent days. Immediately my hands go to cover my pubic area, which is in definite need of some weeding.

"Nuh-huh," his grunt stops my movement and I drop my hands back to my side. *Au naturel* it is. "Come 'ere…"

With movements much more confident than I feel, I step closer and stop when my feet touch the toes of his boots. Still he doesn't make a move to touch me, leaning back with his hands in the mattress for support.

"Unzip me."

The short firm instructions should get my back up, but instead they send a tingle of anticipation straight between my shaky legs. His legs spread wide and I use them for leverage to drop myself down on my knees between them, but instead of focusing on his jeans, I grab hold of his boot first, registering surprise on his face. With a light tug, he raises his left foot a little, allowing me to pull the boot off and removing his sock. I repeat the same move on the other side before reaching for the tab on his zipper with one hand, while flicking the button with my other.

"Careful..." His voice is bidding, but the hitches in his breathing alert me to the fact he is as affected by this slow dance as I am.

As requested, I carefully slide the zipper down over the thick ridge pushing against it. The moment I pass over the bulk of it, the power of his erection pushes it down the rest of the way. Fucking commando. His engorged cock springs free right in the palm of my hand. Without thinking, I clasp my fist around it causing Clint to exhale on a hiss. Entranced by the deep red, almost angry color and the feel of its heat and power in my hand, I softly glide my hand up and down, mapping the heavy outline of the blood-filled veins marking it. A drop of pre-cum beads on the crown. Curious, I bend my head to lick at its taste, barely noticing the big hand releasing the elastic from my ponytail and twisting the hair at the nape of my neck. With his hand firmly in control, the taste of him on my tongue, and the musky scent of him in my nostrils, I feel a fresh flush of arousal pool between my legs. I flick my eyes up to see his mere slits between his eyelids as he watches my every move intently.

"Take me in your mouth, Bean. All the way."

The use of my nickname grounds me and with firm pressure on the back of my head he guides my opened mouth down on his straining cock.

I've never been a big fan of giving blow jobs, because it always seemed so disconnected. Guys close their eyes and draw inside themselves while you minister to them. Not so now. With his hand tightly wrapped in my hair to the point of pain and his eyes never once wavering from mine, I can't imagine a more intimate act than this. I keep one hand fisted around the base of his impressive dick, and with every move of my mouth down his length, my lips press against it. My tongue laps along the veins and under the rim of his crown, finding that soft spot to caress. A slight twitch of his eyelids the only indication how my lips and tongue effect him. But I see it—and I take note making sure to hit those spots again and again until his lips pull back from his teeth in an almost pained grimace. I let him slide softly from my mouth when he pulls my head back, but I can't resist hanging on to the plump head and sucking it hard before letting it plop from between my lips.

"Enough," his labored voice croaks. Lifting me to my feet he sets me back a step before ripping his shirt off and lifting his hips to slide his jeans down. "Climb on and fucking ride me," he says positioning himself back on the bed. I only take a minute to look at this gorgeous man laying himself out like a beautiful buffet for me to savor. Tattoos that wrap around his massive biceps and up his wide shoulders. The broad chest, sprinkled with dark russet hair and laced with silver trailing to a flat stomach and pointing the way to the deep red erection standing up straight and impressive—like a beacon calling me.

Planting one knee beside his hip on the mattress, I swing my other leg over his waist and his hands are immediately on my hips to steady and guide me. But instead of down where I expected him to want me, he pulls my hips toward his face.

My slight hesitation is noted and his face darkens.

"I'm fighting hard for control here, sugar. Don't fight me. I need my mouth on that pussy. Wanna taste you as you come on my face."

Oh my...

Without any further resistance on my part I let him maneuver me to where my knees are bracing his head on either side. Grabbing a pillow with one hand, he stuffs it under his head to raise it and pulls me down.

The first lick is not tentative—with his hands pulling my cheeks apart from behind he reaches to press the flat of his tongue firmly in the crevice between them, the rasp against my highly sensitized perineum a shock to the system. Without prompting, my hands come up to cup the weight of my breasts and my fingers twist at the nipples. Head thrown back at the sensation, I do as he asks—and start gyrating my hips on his tongue—riding his face for all I'm worth.

His deep groan in response vibrates through my flesh and the moment his teeth slip over the tight bundle of nerves and bite down, I burst apart in a blinding release. Before I can even catch a breath, I find myself on my back, Clint on his knees between my legs slipping an arm under my ass to lift me. With surprising ease he pushes me further up the bed, my ass now resting on his knees.

"Grab the headboard and hold on. This is going to get bumpy."

Without questioning him, I raise my arms and grab hold of the metal rods that make up the top of the bed. Clint grabs me behind the knees and pushes my legs up and wide and I can't help the sharp intake of breath at the extreme exposure I feel. His eyes flick to mine.

"You okay?" His voice is gruff with restraint, and I can't do much more than nod my head and whimper at the overwhelming feelings running through me. A slight shift of his hips has the broad head of his cock sliding along my entrance and poised there, he lifts me by the legs as he straightens up on his knees a little. With just my upper back and shoulder still touching the mattress, he surges home inside me, without warning. The scream leaves me before I can check it and immediately he stops all movement, staring down at me with concern lining his face. I'm not in pain—not really—more overwhelmed with the incredible sense of fullness stretching my suspended body wide open.

"Please…" The plea falls from my lips as unchecked as the clenching of my core around him; willing him to move.

"Please, what?" he forces out between his clenched teeth.

"Please…move. Fuck me."

The change in his face is immediate, from worry to a ferocity I've not seen before. Although his retreat is slow and measured, the punishing plunge seating him right back to the hilt is as fierce and uncontrolled as the expression on his face. My hands can barely hold on to the bars of the headboard as he unleashes a power that has his balls slapping loudly against my ass.

Nothing has ever even come close to this feeling of complete surrender to the mercy of this deceptively powerful giant of a man. When his movements become erratic and I can hear his labored breathing, I succumb to my second blinding orgasm as his roar of release echoes in my ears.

Freya Barker UPPER HAND

CHAPTER ELEVEN

The stillness that follows my collapse on Beth's body, after coming so hard it crossed my eyes, is only interrupted by the shallow panting from her lips. I haven't exactly found my breath yet, either. Still I roll off her, wincing slightly the moment I slip out of her. *Shit*.

"We're fine. I don't have the necessary equipment anymore, remember?" Beth mumbles through her still swollen lips, before I even have the presence of mind to formulate a question.

"Swear I'm safe, Bean."

"Figured as much since you were about turned inside out while you were in the hospital. And I can barely count the number of physicals and smears I've had since… Well, you get the drift."

I roll up on my side, my hand stroking the sweaty strands of hair off her face. Slowly her eyes open and focus on me.

"What'ya doin'?"

"Looking at you. You look so… wholesome."

I know I've said something wrong the moment her eyebrows screw together.

"Wholesome? Really? Damn, Clint. Just what a girl wants to hear after she's been fucked six ways to Sunday. Wholesome, huh?" I can tell she's working up a head of steam as she pushes

138

herself out of my reach and sits up. I can't help myself, my eyes immediately drop to the movement of those delicious tits.

"Up here." Her voice is sharp and if I'm not mistaken she's pissed. "Let me tell you what wholesome is; a sow nursing a new litter of piglets is wholesome. A plate of healthy vegetables is wholesome. Hell, even a pile of freshly churned earth is wholesome, but it's not something you use to describe the afterglow of the best sex I've possibly had in forever!"

Fuck. Wait, did she say it was the best sex ever?

"Best sex, huh?" I can't stop the conceited smirk I feel pulling at my lips. Fuel to the fire.

With a cry of frustration she throws her hands up and slips out of bed.

"That's what you pick up from that? I swear there's something wrong with you. A malfunction in your processing center or something. A short in your circuits. I'm going to bed." With that, she grabs her clothes off the floor and makes for the door, her butt jiggling with each angry step. I know it's bad, but I can't help imagining that pliable ass offered up to me as I slide in from behind. May not be the best time to bring that up though, I realize as she slips into the hallway. I jump out of bed to go after her and am immediately assaulted with a wave of dizziness. Too fast, dammit. I wait a second for it to pass, but by the time I step into the hallway she's already in her room with the door firmly closed. *Well, fuck.* There may not be a lock on that door, but she has Max in there and I'm not about to barge in there with my dick swinging. A quick step back into my room to pull on some sweats, and I'm back outside her door, hesitating. The muffled sound of sniffles can be heard, making the decision for me. Pushing open the door, I catch Beth just pulling some nightie over her head, and just like that, her amazing, soft, lush, beautiful body is gone. I know right away

139

what I should've said. She looks at me angrily but I can see the tears shimmering. I walk right up to her and open my mouth to try and make this right when she holds up her hand to stop me.

"Go to bed, Clint. I'm tired and you'll just wake Max up," she hisses.

I peek into the cot and see Max sleeping deeply, his thumb firmly lodged between his lips. He's out good; he won't wake up, but still I grab Beth's hand and try to pull her out of the room. Of course she resists, and I turn back on her, bringing my face close enough for our noses to touch.

"Don't want to wake up Max? Fine. Let's go, I gotta have my say and you're gonna let me."

When she threatens to pull away again, defiance written all over her body, I hold her still by the shoulders.

"You give me trouble and I'll have you over my shoulder so fast you won't know what hit you. And Bean? Don't doubt you'll be paying for that later." My voice comes out in a deep growl and she nervously licks her lips. I'm guessing my girl likes the forceful approach because her nipples underneath that butt ugly nightie have perked to attention. Good. I'm never going to walk away from a misunderstanding. Not with her— but her stubborn defiance pushes all my buttons and brings out my controlling side.

The dramatic eye roll is another challenge but at least she follows me out of the room, only to stop in the hallway when I try to go back to my bedroom.

"What now?"

"Not going in there again," she says resolutely and turns the other way, down the hall to the kitchen, this time leading me by the hand.

Well, fuck, this relationship may well be the death of me if she keeps on fighting me for the upper hand.

Flicking the light on she pulls out a stool and sits with her arms crossed under her tits and I instantly loose my train of thought.

"Well? You had something to say?"

Oh, that tone is grating on me, but I take a deep breath and try to think through my words.

"What I meant in there," I indicate toward my bedroom, "is that you looked amazing, your face was flushed and relaxed, your body beautiful and lush, and the word that came out was wholesome. You want to take that on as an insult, that's on you, but I certainly never voiced it as an insult of any kind. Quite the opposite."

She looks a little uncomfortable and suddenly I get the feeling there's a bit more going on.

"You jumped on the opportunity to get out, didn't you?" The quick flash of her eyes before settling them back on the floor is enough of answer, and I crowd her against the counter with my arms on either side of her.

"Why?"

"Dammit. Why won't you just let me throw a fit and walk away? That would be so much easier," she says softly, as if to herself. "That side of you—the way you are in the bedroom; I…" She shakes her head and goes quiet, but I've got the gist of it and am not about to let her bail.

"You liked it. You liked giving up control and you're not happy about that. Am I right?"

She just shrugs her shoulders, but that's not enough for me.

141

"I'll need some words, sugar. You liked the way I controlled you in there?"

"Yes! I did, and it's so not me. I like control—I need control. I promised myself I wasn't gonna blindly rely on anyone, and certainly not allow myself be bossed around, but I gave myself over to you on a platter. It's weak." She spits out the last as if it leaves a foul taste in her mouth.

"First of all, what happened between you and me has fuck all to do with bossing around or weakness, on either of our parts. It does have everything to do with trust. Me trusting you enough to show you a side of me not many have seen, and you trusting me enough to let me care for you. Nothing more, nothing less. Don't over analyze everything, Beth. Sometimes it just is what it is. It doesn't need to be boxed up and put on the right shelf."

"Okay."

"Okay?" I want to make sure I heard her barely whispered response correctly.

"Yeah, but give me some time, okay? This…all this, whatever it is, came up pretty fast. There's so much going on, I'm just a little overwhelmed." Some doubt still lingers in her eyes, and I'd like nothing better than to wipe all of it away, but I'm not going to fight her on this. I have a feeling the harder I push, the harder she'll push back.

"All this? It's called a relationship, Beth. I won't push, but let me just say I haven't been in one since my marriage. This is the first time I've cared enough to want it. With you. Don't push away because you think you're the only one a little scared of what it means. Cause you're not."

Her mouth has fallen slightly open at my confession, and I quickly press my lips to hers in a soft kiss before turning around and heading to my room. I know in my gut that she'll likely be gone tomorrow, back to the safety of her own place, but I won't stand in her way. Don't want her to regret any decisions she might feel forced to make later.

"Dwink?"

I crank one eye open to find Max standing up in the cot and eyeing me with a big smile on his face.

"Morning, sweetie," I croak, my voice rough from lack of sleep, and the few hours of muffled crying I did last night after Clint left me sitting in the kitchen.

I'm leaving today, and for some reason even though it's what I want, the thought makes me sad. It makes sense though, I tell myself, it's Monday and I don't have to be at work, plenty of time to pack up my shit. I want to get Max settled into his own bed, with his own stuff that Mal dropped off at my house on Saturday. It's not that I don't want Clint, 'cause I do. It's just that after being stuck in first gear with him for so long, I'm not trusting the sudden move into fifth—it seems a crash is inevitable, and I really don't want that to happen. I need to regain a little normalcy in my life. At least some part of what I can control. Finding my balance again after having let circumstances dictate my every move for the past couple of months. I'm lying here, convincing myself it's the best thing, for now, when part of me is wanting to stay so badly.

"Gammy?"

Right. Max is thirsty.

Sluggish from the less than full night of rest, I get up and lift him out of the cot, his little arms and legs wrapping around me. With Max clinging on, I walk us to the bathroom. After taking care of his night diaper and relieving myself, we wash up and head to the kitchen for his 'dwink.'

Clint is at the counter, watching our approach. I wish I'd spent some more time mentally preparing for what promises to be an uncomfortable day, judging from the tension hanging in the kitchen..

"Morning."

"Hey." I try for casual, but there's nothing casual about the intense look on his face.

"Did you sleep okay?" He reaches out to lift Max from my arms, who seems happy for the change of scenery, clapping his hands on Clint's scruffy jaw, making him smile before he turns his eyes on me, the question still there.

"Not much," I admit, choosing honesty. "I thought a lot about what you said last night. You're right; the thought of a relationship scares me. Hasn't worked so well for me in the past, but that doesn't mean I don't want it. With you. Which is why I'm going home today."

I don't know what I was expecting, but the smile Clint sports on his face certainly wasn't it. Registering my surprise he chuckles.

"Don't look so surprised, Beth. If I didn't believe you'll be back here, eventually, I'd fight you tooth and nail, but I need to make a point to you; I don't want or need to control you."

I can't hold back an incredulous huff.

"Just in the bedroom," I mumble.

"Just in the bedroom," he agrees on a smile, the shadow of his dimple only just visible underneath his scruff.

"Coffee?" I offer, holding up the pot in an effort to change the subject, and he lets me, nodding his reply.

Subject dropped, for now, but the atmosphere significantly lighter, Clint slips Max in the highchair and I set about making some toast for us.

Such a domestic scene. That is until we're interrupted by a knock on the door.

"I'll get it," Clint says looking me over head to toe. "You go get some clothes on."

No, not bossy or controlling at all. Although this time, I don't argue because I'm not comfortable greeting whomever is on the other side of that door in my nightie. When I go to grab Max, Clint beats me to it.

"I've got him, you go."

With a mock salute that has his mouth twitch, I head for my bedroom, while Clint makes his way to the door, Max sitting in the crook of his arm.

I make quick work of pulling on some jeans and throwing on a shirt and a quick brush of my teeth. I can hear the sound of male voices as I approach the kitchen, where Gus and Neil are sitting at the counter.

"Hey, guys."

"Morning, Beth. Sorry to barge in so early," Gus says apologetically.

"No problem," I wave him off before turning to Neil. "How long are you in town for this time?"

The youngest of Gus's team of investigators shrugs his shoulders. "However long the boss needs me here."

"Look," Gus draws attention back to him. "Neil picked up some intel last night. An APB went out on a car with the same description as Dylan's, after it was seen pulling away from a police raid on a warehouse just outside of Monticello. Cops were in pursuit for a bit, but lost him when they got clipped by a semi in an attempt to blow through an intersection. No one was seriously injured," he answers before I have a chance to ask.

"I don't understand? What's he doing in Monticello? Was he working there?" I know I'm rambling, but I'm trying to wrap my head around this information. Oh, Dylan, what have you gotten yourself into?

I feel Clint coming up behind me after putting Max down to play on the living room floor. His arm slips around my waist, providing a much needed anchor for my wobbly knees.

"The warehouse was a chop shop for luxury cars. A large well-run organization, with the stink of organized crime, which apparently has been on the FBI radar for a while. 'Collectors' drive the stolen cars from as far west as Las Vegas and Phoenix and south from New Mexico and Texas. The cars hit the warehouse and are stripped for the expensive parts. Once stripped they're virtually impossible to trace."

Dylan's words come back to me, *'I've got this job offer that I can't refuse,'* and sink like a stone to the pit of my stomach. Why didn't he come to me? I try to stop the sob that's pulled from my chest by slapping my hand over my mouth, but that only gets half the job done. I had a bad feeling right from the start but tried to ignore it.

"Sorry, darlin'." Gus's warm eyes almost do me in, and I swallow hard as I watch Gus and Clint share some unspoken message. "But there's something else you should know before the cops or feds come knocking on your door. Seems Dylan got into gambling some time back. We found some pretty compelling evidence that he may have sought the help of the wrong person to settle their debts."

This all comes as a shock to me. I would've sold my soul to help him out, if he'd only come to me. Even so, there is one detail in what Gus just tells me that nags at my brain.

"You said *their* debts?"

"Seems your daughter in law had expensive tastes," Clint rumbles from behind me.

In one twist, I turn around and slip free of the arms holding me.

"You knew?"

Anger bubbles up inside at the thought of something so significant being kept from me and flares even brighter at the guilty look on his face.

"You knew and kept this from me? You had no right!"

"Didn't seem necessary to worry you with it yesterday, Bean."

Oh no he doesn't. Ignoring the audience in the room I react.

"Don't use that name! Not now that you've shown me what a huge mistake I was about to make. Don't want to be controlling? Fuck you, Clint. It's all about control with you, deciding what the *little woman* can or cannot handle, and manipulating me with sex is so fucking typical. And the play you gave me this morning? I call bullshit. I'm going home."

With that I walk over where Max is looking at me wide-eyed, pick him up, and head for the bedroom. Max is surprisingly quiet and letting the anger feed my resolve, it takes me only minutes to grab our stuff together and stomp back out.

Making a point not to look at Clint, I give Gus a hard look, knowing he's the one who went to Clint instead of coming to me with that information. It puts him in the doghouse too, smack beside his buddy. Neil looks only slightly embarrassed, and at this point, I don't give a flying fuck. I grab a few of Max's toys off the floor and toss them in my bag, balancing Max on my hip. Without a word I'm out the front door, my grandson in one arm and an overflowing bag in the other. The cold hits me right away, making me realize I've forgotten our coats. However, before I have a chance to go grab them, Clint walks out with both mine and Max's in his hands, but when I try to take them from him he pulls them back.

"Beth..." There's a plea in his voice that I just don't want to hear right now. "Just let me put on Max's jacket, okay?"

I stand there holding Max while Clint works his little arms in the sleeves, trying with all my might not to burst into tears right now.

"I'll put him in his seat, you should get your coat on before you get sick, too."

I allow him to take Max from my arms, but in a childish act of defiance, I toss my jacket into the passenger seat and slip in behind the wheel—teeth almost chattering with the cold. I startle when Clint leans over the back of the front seat and holds something out to me.

"Here, I grabbed these. Max is gonna need 'em." I don't look at what he pushes in my hand. Not until he's safely backed out of the car and shuts the door. I don't really have to see to know he just pushed Max's medication in my hand. The sweet concern behind that hits me hard, and I quickly start the car and back up before I let those tears run unchecked down my face. *Damn.*

Tough. Standing here watching her drive away, but I'm letting her have this play. Fucked up as it may be, I think she needs to walk away with the upper hand this time, and I'm going to let her.

When I walk back in, Neil has an amused look on his face, but Gus's eyes are concerned.

"We messed that up," he says solemnly. "I've already put a call in to Mal, who's gonna keep an eye out until you can straighten this shit out. Don't need to tell you that the type of people that son of hers has gotten involved with won't stop at anything to get their money. The raid on that chop shop is only going to add urgency. Tell me again what he said when he dropped the little guy off and on the phone?"

For the next half hour we go over what little I know from firsthand observation and what Beth has told me. When Neil assures me he can keep track of her calls through an app he installed on the cell phone of every person in our group, I'm pissed. Gus jumps in to admit it was on his instructions Neil did it and would only be used in emergencies. So much has happened in the past few years to our friends that he wanted a chance to protect them should anything happen. Now that's something I can understand. Hell, I did the same with Beth, trying to protect her, although it didn't quite pan out the way I anticipated.

"Fine," I give in. "But I'm not going to lie to her again, not even by omission. So that phone app thingy? It's gonna come up and unless you want a mutiny on your hands, I suggest you inform whoever has that…thing on their cells."

"Understood," Gus replies without much enthusiasm. "But just for safety's sake, why don't you give Neil yours, so he can hook you up too. Yours is the only one we haven't had access to."

"Are you for real? You want to bug my phone?"

Gus just shrugs his shoulders unapologetically. "With you in the hospital there hasn't been an opportunity."

My instinct is to say hell no, but then my mind starts working. I'm planning to stick as close to Beth as she'll let me, and the thought of having that one extra bit of security in place may not be such a bad thing. I trust Gus.

With some lingering reluctance I fish my phone from my back pocket and hand it over to Neil. It takes him less than two minutes before handing it back to me.

"All done," is all he says, smiling his cocky smile. "It'll only be accessed in an emergency, but it may be helpful to know it has an emergency feature. Press the pound key three times and hit send and an alarm will go off on my computer or my phone," Neil continues. "Something we probably should inform everyone else about as well, if the cat's gonna claw its way out of the bag."

Not long after, the guys get up to leave, but Gus lingers by the front door, clapping me on my shoulder.

"Shouldn't let too much time pass before you go after her. These women here are made of strong and stubborn stuff. My guess is she'll hole up with her friends in no time, and they're even more impressive as a group."

Damn.

CHAPTER TWELVE

"He what?"

"I'm telling you it scared the shit out of me. Pulled right out in front of me, just as I was pulling into my street. Intentional too, I'm sure of it. The guy just sat there, pointed at me and then to his own eyes and took off again."

The sudden stop had jarred Max from the light doze he was drifting into and made him cry. Out of nowhere, this sleek black car pulled out of a drive and right into the road. If I hadn't had my wits about me, I'd have broadsided him. By the time I dislodged my stomach from my throat, the guy was already staring at me, sending shivers down my back.

"You need to call Gus, right now," Arlene urges. "If what you told me about Dylan, that he may have gotten involved with the wrong people, is true, then you've gotta take this seriously."

"Not calling him. I'm home now, Max is in his own bed, finally. I'm sure I'm just being overly dramatic."

"Fine, then I'm coming over."

Before I have a chance to dissuade her, she hangs up.

Sure enough, not fifteen minutes later, she's knocking at my door. Damn woman. She's not alone either; close behind her is Emma. The cavalry has arrived.

I wave them in and as seems to be the custom, they make their way into the kitchen where they both sit down at the table.

"What was the make of the car?" Emma wants to know. Being married to Gus, some of him must've rubbed off on her, because she looked to be all business. I stifle a snicker, because Emma looks far from a hard-nosed investigator with her riot of curls and sweet round face.

"It was a dark color; black or maybe deep blue, it was hard to tell. I don't know make but I know it was a four-door and looked expensive. Oh, and the back windows were blacked out. You know? That dark tinted glass?" I just realize that even in my shock, I was able to pick up a few details. Walking over to the table with mugs and the coffeepot, I see Emma open her mouth for the next question when her phone rings.

"Hey, honey." Her face goes from serious to soft at the sound of her man's voice. I can hear his rumble on this side of the table. Asshat.

"So. Wanna tell me why you're suddenly here and not at Clint's place?" Arlene pins me with a look as Emma's soft voice continues in the background.

"Not particularly, no."

"Spill."

Knowing she won't let up—it's simply not in her genetic make-up—I let out a deep sigh. "Fine. I found out that Clint kept some pretty important information from me. All in the name of not 'upsetting' me. Bastard. Don't know why he thinks he can just bulldoze right over me with his charm, feed me lines about not wanting to control me, when at the first opportunity he takes charge. Your Gus is no better." I point at Emma, who just hung up the phone and looks surprised.

"Why? What did he do?"

"Oh, he went to Clint with information about Dylan. Not to me, mind you, his mother, but to Clint. As if my constitution is to weak to take the news. Fucking men." I'm rolling now and open my mouth for the next volley when Arlene's hand on my arm stops me.

"You're pissed, I get that, but for God's sake woman, what information about Dylan?"

Just like that, my little self-righteous balloon deflates. Worked well as a distraction for the bigger issue, for a bit, but I can't ignore the real danger Dylan's gotten himself into.

"He's in big trouble," I start and in as much detail as I have, I tell them about the APB on his car, about the raid, and about the bit of news that these idiots had tried to keep from me, his gambling problems.

"I never liked that Tammy bitch," Arlene commiserates.

"You've only seen her twice. At a distance," I point out, an inadvertent smile on my lips at Arlene's fervent defense of anyone she considers her family.

"Doesn't matter, I could tell even from that distance she's got shifty eyes and dresses like she's a fucking runway model. Never liked her," she reiterates.

"So let me get this straight, Gus didn't talk to you about this but went straight to Clint? The man who all but two-three weeks ago was no more than a drooling vegetable in a hospital bed? Ohhh, I'm gonna have to have a word with that overbearing caveman." From the look on her face, he's in for it. "Now I get why he was calling to find out how my day was going, whether I wanted to go for lunch in Cortez. Bastard was trying to get me out of the way. Good thing I mentioned I was already hanging out with Arlene. I never said where we were, otherwise I'm positive he'd show up on your doorstep, too."

"Tell me about Clint."

I look at Arlene whose question surprises me. Far from the touchy feely type—much like me—this is something I'd have expected Emma or Naomi to ask, heck even Katie, before hearing it from Arlene's lips. All she does is raise her eyebrow impatiently.

"Not much to tell other than that he's a typical male chauvinist pig."

"Well, I can't argue with that," Arlene chuckles, having had her own run ins with Clint in the past.

"I actually don't think he's that bad," Emma pipes up. "He says things by rote, but I don't think he really believes them. More like an ingrained pattern, you know?"

"Ingrained or inbred?" Arlene jokes before focusing back on me. "But that's not what I was asking. Something's changed, I can almost smell it on you."

"God, I hope not," I answer, unable to keep the smug sound out of my voice. I did after all get my mind blown by the cretin last night.

"Oh Jesus, don't make that face, that's just creepy. You had sex with him, didn't you?"

Now it's my turn to raise an eyebrow but with a different message in mind.

Emma leans over the table conspiratorially. "And?"

"Bossy, big, and unbelievable."

Emma sighs as she leans back in her chair. "I wonder if these guys go to a special academy for that. They all seem to have those things in common."

"Bossy?" Arlene again whose uncanny intuition must've picked up on the vibe underlying that statement.

154

"You could say…" I let my voice trail off in an effort to steer clear of that particular topic, but Arlene looks at me through squinted eyelids.

"He better not be mistreating you."

I let that go, because frankly, I'm not quite ready to explore all the reasons why I enjoy giving up control in the bedroom—of all places.

Max's little voice provides the perfect diversion. By the time I have him cleaned up and settled into his own highchair—the one Mal had brought over—at the counter with a drink, nosy Arlene has forgotten all about Clint's bedroom prowess. She's so engaged in Max's limited babbling, she never even notices the knowing smirk Emma sends me. It's always the silent ones who see more than you're willing to show.

Realizing my kitchen cupboards and fridge are still empty, Emma suggests a move to her place for some lunch. Glad for the distraction from a growing sense of unease in my own house, I grab some things for Max before following them in my car across town. Max muttering happily to himself in the backseat puts a smile on my face, but I still have the presence of mind to check my surroundings carefully. I'm not ready for another encounter with the fancy car. There's been enough excitement for today.

I have no excuse other than that the house seems mockingly empty after Gus and Neil take their leave. I almost hang up when the phone turns over on the other side, but I figure I'd kill two birds with one stone.

155

"Mason Brothers, Jed speaking."

His voice has a dual impact on me; the instant anger, which seems to have become second nature when dealing with my brother, and regret for the loss of what was once a great relationship.

"You wanted a chance to talk."

"Clint? Yes, I do. Where are you?"

"Home."

"Is Beth with you?"

Immediately the leftover hairs on the back of my neck stand up. I don't like the sound of her name from his mouth, dammit. Automatically my defenses kick in.

"Beth is no concern to you," I bite off, struggling to keep my temper in check. From the other side all I hear is a deep sigh before he starts talking.

"I was only checking because I don't know how much you've told her about our history. I know I haven't said anything. Wasn't my place." He's being reasonable and I hate it.

"She's not here, if that's what you want to know."

"It is and I'll be there in twenty. I'm at the reno in Cortez."

With that he hangs up and I slowly put my phone down, trying to ignore the pounding in my chest. Other than that brief glimpse of him at the hospital and our very short but tense interaction in a clinic full of people, I haven't been in the same room alone with him since I beat the crap out of him years ago. Should be interesting.

It's more like twenty-five minutes when I hear the familiar sound of my own truck pulling up. The irony of that does not escape me. Truth is, we have the business to discuss, what to expect in the short term, and then there is the cesspool of our past that needs to be waded through. Despite the fact that I don't trust the man around Beth, I don't for a minute doubt that he's doing well by the business. The one we had built up together so successfully—and the same one I forced him out of, when he betrayed me by taking up with my wife. I was always more devastated by his betrayal then by hers. Had it been anyone else, I'd probably have walked away, wiping my hands clean of the marriage and glad to do so. But for your flesh and blood to…

The heavy tread of footsteps on the front porch, followed by a distinct rap on the door that apparently hasn't changed over the years—long, short, short, long—interrupts my thoughts before I can get myself all worked up again.

Opening the door Jed stands there, looking at me from under the brim of his ball cap. I try not to notice the pain and uncertainty in his expression. I'm sure it's close to matching my own. Standing back, I invite him in with a wave of my hand. Time hasn't been kind on him. At three years younger, we used to look a lot alike. Some had thought we were twins. But now he surprises me with his gaunt appearance, making him seem much older than his forty-three years. What used to be smile lines are now deep grooves that only emphasize the hollow look on his face. I can't help but wonder if I simply don't see the test of time as much on my own. Aside from the pesky silver strands that make my facial hair look grey. Jed's hair is almost completely gone that route. He looks old and tired, it gives me an empty feeling in my chest.

He comes to a stop by the couch and looks for silent permission to sit. Again I limit myself to a wave of my hand before I can bring myself to speak.

"Drink?" I manage.

157

"Just water if you have it."

Armed with two bottles from the fridge, I find him standing by the mantle that holds a few old family photos, his hat discarded on the coffee table. I brought them out after I bought this house, not sure why. Maybe as a reminder of good times or to make it feel more like a home, who knows?

"Remember that waterhole Dad used to take us fishing? I almost drowned there once, if it hadn't been for you." His voice is soft but I hear every word clearly.

"I remember," my voice croaks. "You were so gung-ho to hang that rope swing, you spent days trying to get me to take you. Then you went and hit your head on a rock we hadn't seen under the water on your first jump in. Damn, Pops was mad at us. Couldn't sit for a week after he was done tanning my hide." The bittersweet memory pulls my mouth into a reluctant smile.

Jed chuckles, the sound so familiar and yet it grates on me.

"So talk." I force both of us away from happier times.

Sitting down, Jed downs almost half his bottle before setting it carefully on the coffee table.

"Not sure where to start," he huffs out a bitter sounding laugh. "All the time growing up, I looked up to you. Always bigger, stronger, better and I aspired to it, but never quite was able to catch up. Mom and Pop didn't help with their 'wall of fame' of all your awards and diplomas, I think I had a second grade drawing make it to the fridge door once, that was about it. Don't really know why it was still under my skin after growing up. I honestly thought I'd grown out of it, but when Luanne showed up at my door in tears, claiming you weren't treating her right, I jumped at the opportunity to be better at something, for once." He pauses, running his hand through his messy mop, waiting for my reaction.

158

Well, other than the deadly grip I have on my water, I'm not saying a damn thing. Not sure what would come out of my mouth anyway.

"I need you to understand none of this is an excuse for what I did, but I've done a fuck-load of soul searching these past few years. Thinking about life, about things that are important, and things that I regret; and there are a lot of those. I've found ways to deal with most of those, but this? This is eating away at me. Was even then, although I would've denied it at the time."

"Why?" I'm finally able to speak.

"Because I always felt inferior to you, not by something you did, I realize that now, but it was there all the same. I'd always been a little in love with her, probably 'cause she represented another thing I couldn't have. She gave me an opportunity to gain the upper hand, for once. And she was only using me to get to you. Pretty fucked up." Again he stops to finish off the bottle, risking a glance in my direction, but I stay still.

"After everything went to shit, we tried to make something of it, but her heart wasn't in it—never was. If I hadn't been so high off scoring a fantasy, I would've realized, much sooner, that the fantasy was much better than reality turned out to be."

Restless, he gets up and walks back over to the mantle where he picks up the photo of him and I, side by side with a big catfish between us, one that Pops took.

"I'm so damn sorry. I honestly don't know what I was thinking. Got my own back though…"

He lets his voice trail off baiting me to ask, so I oblige.

"How's that?"

He chuckles to himself, shaking his head. "What do you think? Not even a year after we…after you divorced her, she

159

wanted to get married again. I had a good job and had the payout for Mason Brothers still in the bank, I figured I was pretty settled and this was probably a natural next move. A weekend in Vegas did the trick. Even then I remember thinking what a really fucking bad idea that probably was. I think it was not three months after that I found her in bed with my boss. I got a lawyer right away and filed for divorce, which I got, but not until after she cleaned me out."

I'm surprised at the pang of sympathy I feel for him. I should be laughing at the cheater being cheated, but all I can bring myself to feel is a deep sadness. I had never mourned the loss of Luanne, but always felt the loss of my brother deeply. Jed had already lost me, granted by his own actions, but then lost the woman he loved, his money, and I assume his job, since I can't imagine him going back to work after that.

"I'm sorry that happened to you," I say more sincerely than I'd anticipated feeling.

"Don't be," is his quiet response. "It was exactly what needed to happen for me to see what a self-indulgent little prick I'd been all of my life. I'll admit, I did go off the deep end a bit at the time, but that's done."

I can sense he's holding something back and I want to pry.

"How long ago was this?"

"Three years."

"Then why not come to me sooner? Why wait until I'm fucking hovering between life and death before you decide to show your face?" Some of my anger is slipping through, and now it's my turn to get up and walk around a bit to regain control.

"I was in jail until about six months ago."

"Say what?" The shock at his admission has me up in his face.

"Took a page from your book and beat the crap out of my boss when I found them. He didn't file charges though, until Luanne had her hands on the money, and then tried for attempted murder. That didn't fly far, not with the time lapse, so assault it was. Luanne testified against me and I was given two years. I'd just been out a few months when Beth tracked me down."

"I didn't know." I'm stunned, actually. As much as the beating I gave Jed had shocked me, never having been a particularly violent person, Jed in the role of aggressor seemed even more out of place.

"Had a lot of time to think in there, Clint. Not much else to do other than to try and steer clear of the other inmates. Or at least some of them." His eyes cloud over and it's on my lips to ask, but I don't. Instead I make a tentative suggestion, seeing that he obviously hasn't quite shed all the baggage he dragged out of jail with him.

"Have you ever talked to Seb?"

Don't really know why I suddenly feel the need to play matchmaker, but I know Seb had been in jail for assault. I figure he'd know better than anyone what it's like to be in there, and my brother might open up to him.

He looks at me suspiciously. "The cook at the diner? Why would you want to know that?"

"Because Seb did time for assault. I'm not quite sure how long he was in for, but if anyone would understand it would be him."

A little flare of interest shows on his face before he shuts it down.

"We'll see." Is all he will give me. So be it. I just nod and a slightly uncomfortable silence stretches between us. It gives me time to think. I hate to admit that hearing his side helps. It doesn't change anything but it does help. And for the first time I feel the old betrayal a little less. Suddenly I want to know about the crews, how the guys are doing, and the projects he's got going. He spends the next half hour getting me up to speed, and it feels good to talk shop with him. Been a damn long time.

"Well, I better get back to that crazy woman in Cortez," he says getting up from the couch. I know he's talking about Sarah Creemore, the woman Beth had seemed jealous of at the diner. I have to admit, she was a bit of an octopus, I never knew where her hands would turn up next. Had to be firm with that one to shut her down. She'd been bitchy ever since.

"Still going at her place? I never thought that job would take this long."

Jed snorts.

"It wouldn't have if she hadn't added new shit every week. She keeps asking about you too, and the kicker of it is; she does it while copping a feel from me." The look of abject horror on his face makes laugh out loud. Slowly his face changes to something warmer—friendlier. "Good to hear that again." He smiles and I shrug my shoulders a bit embarrassed.

"I'd forgotten what a funny fuck you could be."

"Give me a call after you see the doc tomorrow, I'd like to know what he says."

Before he is all the way out the door I call after him.

"Wait! Any way you could give me a ride to Beth's place? I'm kinda stuck. Doc hasn't cleared me for driving yet and you've got my wheels."

"Right, I should get my truck geared up. It's parked at the motel. Won't take much, just a proper lock box and a few tools, once you're back on the job," he says getting in the driver's seat and leaving me to fend for myself. He knows I'd get pissed with fussing.

"Does that mean you're sticking around?" I'm not one for pussyfooting and strangely the thought of him staying in town feels good.

"You saying I'd have a job?" he returns, making me chuckle.

"After seeing what you've done with the plans for my house, I'd say chances are good."

"Then I'll think about it."

"You do that." My smile gets bigger with each retort. We used to do this all the time when we were younger, bickering for the sake of bickering. Kind of like what life with Beth is like. Suddenly I'm in a hurry to see her. Two raps on the dashboard gets Jed's attention and with a hand motion I indicate for him to go.

"About your house, I'm sorry—"

"If you're thinking of apologizing to me, reckon you can stop that shit right now," I interrupt him, knowing I can't just let it go at that. "Thank you for that by the way. Don't know how you managed, but it's damn near perfect. 'Preciate it."

Jed's quiet for a while, until we're almost at Beth's place.

"*Near* perfect you say?"

I find myself still laughing as he pulls up her drive.

CHAPTER THIRTEEN

"What are you doing here?"

Takes me by surprise when I spot Clint relaxing in the swing on my front porch when I pull in the driveway. Everything about him looks casual, except the heat burning in his eyes. I just don't know whether it is anger or something else, I'm sure as hell still angry. Climbing out of the car, I almost forget I have Max in his seat in the back. *Jesus.* If it wasn't for his excited, "Big gah!" when he spots Clint through the window, I'd have easily left him alone in the car.

With Max insisting on being set down so he can run for Clint, I'm left without my shield. It makes me edgy so I go in for the attack. Clint ignores my question and continues to listen to Max's excited babble. His eyes never leave mine though.

Leaving Max in his care, I return to the car to grab the groceries I'd stopped to get on my way home from Emma's. The girls had picked up their interrogation over lunch again, until I finally caved and told them as much as I was comfortable with on how far Clint and my relationship had progressed. Gus and Neil's arrival saved me from spilling every last detail. I was surprised Gus came right up to me and pulled me into a hug, not only apologizing, but also letting me know Clint was a mess after I left. I'd already started coming to the conclusion that once again, Clint had meant no real harm by keeping the information from me, and truth be told, we did get kind of busy last night. It wasn't long after that I left.

By the time I have my bags out of the trunk and on my porch, Max has made himself comfortable on Clint's lap. The two of them look a bit cold and I feel guilty for making them wait. I step aside the moment I have the door open and gesture at him to come in.

"Thanks," he rumbles in his low voice as he passes me. His proximity is enough to have my resolve to go back to my own place wavering. I close my eyes and inhale deeply as he brushes by me. He smells so damn good; all man with a hint of wood shavings. I realize I'm still standing by the door with my eyes closed. When I look inside, Clint's on the other side of the hallway, a knowing little smirk on his face and his arms folded over his chest. I notice for the first time that he doesn't have his cane with him.

"Hey, where's the stick?"

"I'm done with it."

"Just like that? You don't think you should wait to see what the doc says tomorrow?" God I'm starting to sound like one of those nagging women.

"Don't need the doc to tell me my stability is improving. I can feel it."

A cry from the kitchen stops me from being snarky, and I walk in there to find Max with the garbage can spilled over. It isn't pretty, that garbage has been sitting in the can for a long-ass time. Last time I can recall emptying it was before Clint was attacked, and the lid hadn't come off the short period I was here this morning. Otherwise, I would've hauled the whole damn thing off the back porch. Poor Max has an unidentifiable mess covering him and it smells like dead animals.

"Damn, that reeks," Clint offers as he walks in behind me.

"No shit, Sherlock," I snap muttering my favorite list of profanities under my breath, while trying to dig my grandson from under the mess.

"Enough," Clint suddenly barks, stopping Max's crying instantly and startling me into silence. I grab Max and stand up.

"Beth, take Max and give him a bath. I'll clean up here." His voice is stern and that has my hackles up right away.

"I don't think you—" The rest of the words are caught in my throat when he steps in front of me, holds me in place with one hand and with the other reaches around and smacks my ass, making me jump.

"There will be more of that if you keep being so damn stubborn."

I open my mouth in protest, but his growl is enough to make me turn on my heels and take Max straight up to the bathroom.

Half an hour later, Max is in his own bed for a nap. When I walk into the kitchen, Clint just comes walking in from the sliding doors with what looks to be a clean garbage can dripping in his hand. The chill in the kitchen tells me he's had the door open for a while. Can't smell the stink as much anymore, thank God. The floor is clean and only a few of my groceries are sitting on the counter.

"I didn't know where you wanted those, I put the rest away."

Suddenly, the man who just thirty minutes ago was spanking my ass for speaking up, looks mighty sheepish with the offensive garbage can dangling between his fingers.

"I'll take care of it."

I have the stuff packed away in no time, while Clint has taken one of my new tea towels to dry the bin. I have to bite my lip so I don't bitch at him for not grabbing one of the old ones. Got to practice being nicer to the guy, so I turn my back to him and make us a fresh pot of coffee, chewing my lip the whole time. Besides, I figure we've got a 'talk' coming, and I'd feel much better with an extra shot of caffeine under my belt. The plop of the wet and now dirty new tea towel on the counter beside me has my head snap up. I swallow hard before grabbing it and without looking at Clint, make my way into the mudroom where my laundry is. He's testing my patience. When I walk back in he's on the phone, apologizing to someone for not being able to make their appointment on time. I didn't hear it ring, so I assume he's the one making the call, and my irritation turns into a full-out mini blow-out.

"Don't cancel your date on my account," I snap as soon as he ends his call. "Wouldn't want to have anyone miss out on your sparkling personality. Didn't take you long? Who've you got on speed dial?" I say all this while banging around coffee cups and milk. Trust me, I know I'm being a bitch. I also know that I shouldn't indulge that little bit of insecurity that always nags its way to the forefront when I feel threatened in any way. And I'm feeling it in a *big* way. Judging by the impact his 'omission' already had on me, it's a safe bet this man has the ability to break me, and that terrifies me.

"You about done?" he asks, with anger deepening the lines on his face. Already coming down from my little diatribe and afraid to do more damage, I give a little shrug. "Good. 'Cause now it's my time, and you're gonna shut it and listen."

I'm manhandled by the shoulders and pushed down on a kitchen chair.

"Hey," I voice a protest, but the furious glint in his eyes has me shut my mouth quickly.

"Shut. It."

Okay then. He stays leaning over me, one hand on the back of my chair and the other on the table, effectively boxing me in.

"Don't know why you're so damn stubborn," he starts, and I immediately open my mouth in protest. The don't-mess-with-me glare he sends me has me snap it shut again. "Good choice." He feels the need to point out. "You've been looking for excuses to pull away. I may not sound that savvy some of the time, but woman, I ain't stupid. Every chance you get, you try to put a wedge in what we've got going here."

"I should've been told about Dylan's troubles," I insist. Clint drops his head and sighs.

"Yeah, you should've. That's on me for trying to protect you. Not gonna keep shit from you again, even if it is with the best of intentions."

Okay, now I'm a little embarrassed about my crazy woman act. He obviously thought he was doing the right thing. *Ugh.* "Sorry too," I mumble, very uncomfortable with this apology stuff.

"Wait—did you just apologize?" I can hear the damn amusement in his voice, and I lift my head, shooting fire with my eyes. Well, at least trying to. It only seems to amuse him more, and he leans down and brushes a kiss to my lips while chuckling. So unfair. "I was just trying to do what I thought was best at the time, Bean. Trying to prevent you from getting hurt."

"I know…"

"And just in case you were wondering, that was Kendra on the phone. Wanted to reschedule to tomorrow after I see the doc."

"Oh." I do my best to avoid looking him in the eye, but he lifts a hand to the side of my neck and with his thumb lifts up my chin. I still see amusement on his face, but there is something warm there too. Something I might like to roll around in. I lean forward a bit and skim my lips over his. This results in his hand snagging in my ponytail and yanking my head back, angling me just right for his mouth to plunder mine with lots of lip and tongue. By the time he pulls back, the only thing securing me is his hand in my hair. I'm panting like a racehorse and am so focused on Clint, the shrill ring of my phone has me almost jumping out of my skin. He steps back, tags my phone on the counter, and hands it to me.

"Hello?"

"Why the hell didn't you tell me about the car incident?" Gus almost yells in my ear and from the look on Clint's face, he can hear every word.

"I forgot," I say honestly and watch as Clint's eyes darken.

"Jesus, Beth. I'd have never let you drive home on your own. Tell me exactly what happened."

So I do. I tell Gus everything I remember, and listen to him swear a few times, while talking to Neil in the background about some security or something. All the while I'm watching Clint's jaw clench harder. If he's not careful he's going to chip a tooth. He's pissed.

"Stay there, don't move. Neil's coming by to check out security at your house."

"I'm okay. Clint's here now." I volunteer.

"Clint? Let me talk to him." I hand the phone over.

"Yea," he says, walking away from the table and over to the back door with his back to me. I can't hear Gus anymore, but I can hear every word Clint's saying, and it's enough to get my hackles back up.

169

"She's coming home with me. You want to ramp up security at my place, send Neil over there. She's not staying here by herself." It's like he can feel my eyes burning holes in his back because he turns around to face me.

"Yes, we'll be there as soon as Max wakes up from his nap. An hour—sounds good."

As soon as he disconnects and tosses my phone on the counter, he's back in my space.

"When Max wakes up, we're packing what we need and you're coming back home with me."

"I'm fine here," I insist, which only makes his face go scarier.

"Yeah? You're so far up your own arse you can't even see the light, woman. How do you 'forget' to mention this to anyone?" He's almost yelling at me now, and let me tell you, the man is pretty damn intimidating when angry.

"I told Emma and Arlene. Then we got to talking about... Well, whatever, but anyway, I didn't think about it after that." Clint puts his hands on his hips and tilts his head to the ceiling. "*Jesus,*" I can hear him mutter.

"I'll be fine here," I try again, only to have him haul me out of my seat and against his chest.

"Gonna be the death of me, Beth. I swear to God. Think about Max then. I *know* you wouldn't want anything to happen to that boy. From what Gus tells me the group that ran that chop shop is a highly organized syndicate with lots of money. You know what that spells, Beth? That spells some seriously bad news. Your incident earlier today is a fucking warning. With Dylan in the wind, they're gonna try and flood him out through you. Or Max." He shakes me lightly with his hands on my shoulders.

I'm an idiot. I've been so preoccupied not getting sucked into the Clint vortex that I'm not thinking straight. This is fucking dangerous. So I tell him. "This is dangerous shit."

Clint drops his forehead to mine and wraps his arms around me tight. "No shit, babe. Seriously dangerous shit."

I snuggle right into his arms and hold onto him tightly. "I'm sorry," I mumble into his flannel shirt.

"S'Okay. I figured it wasn't gonna be a smooth ride."

Not sure I want to know what he means by that, so I wisely keep my mouth shut. For once.

"Hey, little man."

I reach out to grab Max, who just woke up, from his cot. All sleepy and warm, he cuddles right into my neck, and I feel his little fingers playing through my scruff. Beth is in her bedroom finishing her packing. I'd come into Max's room to start grabbing some of his stuff when he woke up.

Swaying from side to side with that little body curled up against my chest, I don't hear Beth coming in until I feel her hand on my shoulder. When I turn to look, I find her smiling sweetly, her eyes a bit shiny.

"You all done?"

She shrugs. "As good as. Just have to grab his stuff together." Rubbing a quick hand over Max's tousled hair, she turns to the dresser and starts pulling out his clothes.

"Neil's gonna be here soon," I point out. We'd talked a little and I'd suggested bringing all of the baby's own furniture home too. Surprisingly, Beth didn't object too much and after putting in a quick call to Neil, to ask him to swing by here first with his pickup, we'd started packing up stuff.

When Beth's got the entire contents of the little guy's dresser stuffed in a duffel bag, including his bedding, she takes him downstairs for a 'dwink,' while I take apart the furniture. As I carry the pieces of his bed down the stairs, Neil is at the bottom looking up.

"Sure that's a good idea in your condition, old man?" The smirk on his face tells me he's pulling my leg. Still.

"Shut it, boy."

That turns the smirk into a full-on smile. Little bastard. Okay, maybe not so little, since even though he's a few inches shorter than my six-foot-five, he's about equally wide. He seems to have grown every time I see him.

"Do you live at the gym?" I hand over the bed at the bottom of the stairs and Neil throws me a cocky smile.

"Nothing better to do."

"You could be chasing skirts," I point out. After all the guy is probably sneaking up on thirty and not half-bad looking, but his smile slides right off his face.

"Gettin' tired of that. Let me throw this in the truck and we'll tackle the rest together. Beth says there's a dresser?"

Not waiting for an answer, he's gone, leaving me to wonder why a good-looking kid in his prime would be tired of chasing skirt. Something's off.

Another two trips upstairs for the drawers and finally the dresser—a heavy sucker—and Neil drives off.

"You got everything?" I yell to Beth who is banging around upstairs, slamming drawers and doors. Max is on the floor playing with some Cheerios that probably aren't sanitary anymore. My mom used to say a little dirt would toughen the stomach. I figure it won't hurt him.

"Max!" From the squeal behind me, it's clear Beth doesn't necessarily share my mother's southern wisdom. She picks him up and sets him on her hip.

"Let's get your coat on, buddy." Two pairs of hands make relatively quick work of getting the two-year-old in his winter jacket and after slipping on our own and locking up, we're off.

"Mr. Mason? The doctor will see you now."

The skinny woman with the fire engine red hair behind the desk at the doctor's office is beaming ear to ear, like she's giving me the keys to the city or something. I struggled to look away from the clown-like do on top of her head the entire time we've been here, but with minimal success. It's like watching a fucking accident happen, you just can't turn away. Grabbing Beth's hand I pull her with me as we follow down the hall, where we're ushered into a small room with an examination table and one chair.

"The doctor will be right with you." Red throws her big smile around again with lots of teeth, reminding me a bit of a predator. The instant the door closes behind her, Beth yanks her hand from mine and sits down on the chair pretending to examine the poster on 'Early Signs of a Stroke' in great detail. Is she pissed?

"You pissed?"

Her head whips around and if I wasn't a big, strong man, I'd shrivel up at the deadly daggers she's shooting me. "Pissed? No Clint, I'm not pissed. Doesn't matter to me that you and that matchstick out there are making googly eyes at each other."

There's no way to hold back the laugh that bursts free, even though I know it'll likely get her more riled, so I throw back my head and let it go. But instead of anger when I look at Beth again, I see she's got tears in her eyes. Damn.

"Weird looking creature, isn't she? I was thinking clown, but matchstick works." Surprise spreads over her face and I bend down so our noses touch. "I get your experiences with men may not have been great, but sugar, the only reason I was looking was because I couldn't tear my eyes away from that hideous hair. Who the fuck does that?"

Her little smirk tells me the crisis has been averted. It better be, after I'd virtually begged her to come to my bed last night, only to be told she'd feel better sleeping with Max. Didn't sleep much, I can tell you that. For some reason the brakes she put on are still in effect, driving me up the wall, but I'd give her that one night. Tonight is another story.

A short knock on the door and then the doctor steps in the small room, clearly not made to hold more than two adult bodies.

"I'm just gonna wait outside, maybe give Katie a call to see how Max is," Beth announces. Before I can get a word in, she slips out. By the time the doc is done with me, I have an appointment for a follow-up MRI, instructions to continue building up strength with PT, but I don't mind because he also gives me the go ahead to drive and slowly start working again. Half days at first he insists, but I'll take it.

Walking into the waiting room, I see Beth's missing and turn to the freaky woman behind the desk, who seems to have turned up the smile a notch. *Brrrr*.

"The woman I came in with, did she leave?"

Now I get the fluttering eyelashes and an eager nodding of her head. I swear it looks like she's trying to dislodge something stuck in her eye. I barely manage a 'thanks' before I escape outside, after having to wait for her to give me a date for the MRI appointment.

I don't see her at first when my eyes scan in the direction of her rust bucket of a car. When I walk around the van parked beside it, I spot her, sitting on the pavement with her back propped up against the rear wheel, her hands covering her face. What the fuck?

"Beth?"

When she pulls away her hands and shows me her face, a hot fury gets my blood boiling. The bottom half of her face is covered in blood.

CHAPTER FOURTEEN

"Could you tell Mr. Mason I'll be waiting in the car when he comes out?"

I've spent the last ten minutes being glared at by the red-haired bimbo behind the desk, and I've had enough. I don't even wait for her response when I make my way outside, where cold fresh air instantly clears the claustrophobic feeling I got in that office. I pull out my phone as I'm walking to the car, following through on my plan to check on Max. Before I have a chance to hit the call button, I'm being yanked by my hair in between a van and my car. My phone goes flying as my hands automatically reach behind me to grab at whoever's pulling my hair. An arm slips around my neck and I am pulled against a hard body. Panicking I struggle furiously, trying to kick with my legs and scratching at the exposed wrist on the arm that is cutting off my air supply. I try screaming but nothing comes out.

"Keep your fucking mouth shut, bitch," a raspy voice whispers in my ear, engulfing me in a cloud of garlic and poor oral health. My mouth snaps shut instinctively. I'm suddenly twisted around and pushed back into my car, the offensive arm now pressing against my throat from the front. The owner of the arm is the driver of the car that cut me off yesterday in Cedar Tree. Cold fear settles in the pit of my stomach as I realize that since we're now in Durango, he was dead serious when he indicated he was 'watching me.'

"Where's your son?" he hisses, blasting me with another wave of his disgusting breath and I cringe involuntarily. "Where is that bastard?"

"I don't know," I manage to croak out, my hands clutched in his shirt to try and ward him off. When he sticks his face even closer to mine, I've had enough. In a defensive move, I pull my knee up as hard as I can but the bastard side steps so it glances off his thigh innocently. Now I've got him pissed off good. Removing his arm from my throat, he now grabs my jacket collar and slams me hard into the back door of my car, knocking the air from my lungs.

"Where? You bitch."

Still gasping for air, I just shake my head 'no,' something that obviously doesn't make him happy. Again he pulls me from the car by my collar and slams me back.

"I'm thinking I'll like spending some time getting the information from you." He starts pulling me away from the car. I really don't want to get slammed again, so I try to twist free by ducking down and under his arm. The sudden move has his hands slip off my collar, but before I can even run two steps, I feel him grabbing my arm and swinging me around, while his other hand comes flying through the air, straight at my face. I try to avoid it, unsuccessfully. I hear the crunch of my nose before the pain of the impact hits me. Holding me up with one hand, the other comes swinging again, but the sound of an approaching car stops him. He looks at the car innocently passing by furtively, before getting back in my face.

"Find your punk-assed son. You tell him, he needs to pay his debts or you and that brat of his will pay the price."

This time when the fist comes, I don't see it until it's too late, my eyes streaming tears. The impact I feel, but then everything goes black.

Next thing I know, I'm sitting with my back against the back tire, feel a warm trickle down my chin, and taste blood in my mouth. I hear footsteps. I try to make myself small and cover my face with my hands to try and fend off another attack when I hear Clint's voice.

"Beth?"

"Your nose is broken but not displaced. You're lucky. The swelling will go down with a few days, but you'll probably have twin shiners. Hits on the nose tend to give you not one, but two black eyes."

The young emergency room doctor hands me a prescription for some painkillers and leaves me alone in the room. Alone except for Clint, who is still seething and on the phone with, I assume, Gus.

"No. We won't need a ride. Cops are waiting to talk to us, but Beth doesn't want to talk to them—I don't know, why don't you try to talk some sense into her."

The phone is shoved in my hand. Clint turns his back and with agitated moves rubs his hand over his shaved head. I turn my attention to the person on the other side.

"Hey."

"Girl," Gus's voice soothes over the line and I feel tears stinging my eyes. Aside from being furious and barking orders at whoever was near, Clint had not shown even the slightest gentleness, and I've been sucking back the tears and the shakes all afternoon. "How are you holding up?"

"I'm okay," I sniffle, not even convincing myself.

"You've gotta talk to the cops, Beth. I get why you think it will hurt Dylan if you do, but the truth is in the end he's got more to fear from the goons after him than he has from the cops. Regardless of what he's done. Trust me on this. We'll keep you safe, but you've gotta tell them everything they want to know."

I let the silence stretch uncomfortably, using the time to contemplate my options. Not that I had many. I come to the conclusion that Gus is right, whatever consequences Dylan has waiting for him from the law, he's better off in their hands.

"Okay," I concede softly, causing Clint to swivel around and stare at me incredulously. I'd ignored his pleas for me to do the same, so I'm not really surprised to see the anger he was harboring shift to me. The moment I hang up the phone, he's on me.

"I'd like to fucking know what he said that convinced you so easily, since I've only been trying for the last few hours to get you to do what he managed in two seconds."

"Clint…" I try, but he won't have it.

"Don't fucking '*Clint*' me. I finally get some good news from the doctor, manage to escape the clutches of that scary bitch in the office, only to come outside to find my girl bleeding on the ground in the parking lot. Fuck, Beth…" His voice goes from dark and threatening to husky and soft in the span of that one sentence.

Instinct propels me off the bed, plastering myself against his back, which he turned to me again, slipping my arms around his waist and hanging on.

"Scared me, Bean. Can't remember being so scared ever before." His whisper is wavering with emotion and I just hang on tighter.

179

"I know, sweetie. I know," I whisper back. Because I do—I do know exactly how that feels. I know how it feels like your heart is about to be ripped from your chest when you see the person you love bloodied and hurt. When all you can think about is what *you* could've done to make a difference, when there really isn't a fucking thing. His hands come up and pry mine from around his waist before turning and sliding his back down the wall, until his ass is sitting on the ground. I don't need to think, I drop down immediately on his lap and wrap my arms around him again.

"I'm okay. I'll be okay. I'll talk to the cops, I'll stay at your house, I'll cooperate. I promise."

His face is buried against my chest.

"Excuse me, Ms. Franklin? About that statement—" The fierce look on my face when I turn my head to find the young officer, who was in earlier, sticking his head around the door, must've cut him off.

"I'll be there in a few minutes," I promise him. His eyes flick between me and Clint's head, still with his ear pressed against my chest. With a single nod, he backs out.

"You called me 'sweetie,'" Clint's muffled voice vibrates against my breast. I pull back a little, put my hands on his cheeks and tilt his face.

"I did," I say, trying to ignore the tear tracks staining his cheeks. He's scared and hurtin' for me, and I'm fucked. I so love this man. "If you're good, I might just call you that again."

The tease elicits a chuckle from him, and I lower my head until my lips find his. "Fuck, Beth, I—" My mouth silences him and by the time we pull back my heart is pounding a mile a minute.

"Me too, Clint."

An hour later the police drop us off at a car rental place, since they've towed my car from the clinic's parking lot. Apparently it is potential evidence at this point, at least as long as it takes them to check for any forensic evidence that might shed light on who this guy is.

Given the green light, Clint insists on driving. I try to pull down the mirror from the sun visor, but he keeps slapping my hands away. "Don't. Not until we get home."

Fuck, it must look bad.

"Oh. My. God!"

Right. So this is exactly what I didn't want Beth to be faced with, coming home from the hospital. I'd prefer it if she didn't see what that bastard did to her beautiful face, at all. But it appears the girls' posse has landed on my doorstep with entirely different ideas. And Arlene being who she is, there are no filters.

Beth's hands go immediately to her face as we get out of the car, trying to shield it from Emma, Naomi, and of course the verbal Arlene.

"I'm gonna kill that fucker. Emma, where the fuck is your husband? He needs to track that sonofabitch down so I can have my way with him." Arlene's voice spouts anger, but her eyes are full of tears.

"Arlene..." I start, before she turns on me.

"Don't you 'Arlene' me. Where were you when this was happening?"

Fucking direct hit that I feel in my gut.

Dropping her hands, Beth marches right up to her, getting in her face. "Don't you dare say another word to him. Leave Clint alone, he didn't even know I'd gone outside, Arlene. I know you love me and you worry, but don't you dare take it out on him!"

Arlene's mouth opens, but not a sound comes out. Then the tears suddenly flow and I raise my eyes to the clouds. Here I am, lone man surrounded by four sniffling women, and I almost wish I was in a coma again. Two arms come around me in a hug. "Sorry," Arlene's voice is soft—softer than I've ever heard it before.

"All good, sugar." I don't have to bend too low with Arlene, who's the tallest of all the women, to mumble in her ear. "Don't know about you, but this chill gives a whole new meaning to blue balls. Let's get inside."

With Beth flanked by Emma and Naomi, and Arlene still tucked under my arm, I unlock and lead the group in.

Emma takes charge of the kitchen, where in no time she has coffee on the go and something called, 'Madeleines,' in the oven. Some kind of mini cakes she's using my old muffin pan to make, by dropping spoonfuls to cover just the bottom. Smells fucking great though.

Naomi is looking Beth over, making sure nothing was missed in the ER. Being a former ER physician herself, having only recently set up shop locally with her own clinic, I guess she needs to make sure. Arlene is talking on her cell, giving an update to Seb, the cook and her partner in the diner, as well as her significant other. I'm sitting on a kitchen stool feeling the effects of the last hours when something occurs to me.

"Max. Jesus!" I grab for the phone and am about to dial Katie, when Emma puts her hand on my arm.

"He's fine. I checked with Katie while we were waiting for you. That's why she isn't here. She would've been but she suggested it might be better to keep him with her until things settled down a bit."

I shift so my back is to the room before addressing Emma. "The guy didn't only threaten Beth, he threatened Max, too," I tell her quietly. Her eyes widen slightly at that before squinting in angry slits.

"Cowardly bastard," she hisses. "Caleb's home. Katie told me he came in and already knew what'd happened. Does Gus know?"

"Talked to him when we were in the hospital, can't say I remember much of what I said."

"Gimme a sec," Emma says, pulling her phone from her purse on the counter.

"Hey, honey. — Yes, they just got home.— She's… gonna be fine." Her eyes flick over to the couch where Naomi is still hovering over Beth. "Just wanted to make sure you knew the guy apparently threaten that little cutie, as well. —You did?— Oh, okay. You wanna talk to him? —Love you, too." She holds out the phone to me. "Gus."

"I couldn't remember if I told you that or not," I jump right in.

"You mentioned something and I've been in touch with my contact at the Durango Police Department, who filled me in. Caleb and Katie will cover Max, and I've got Mal and Neil taking turns covering Beth. We just finalized two cases so the docket is clear. We'll get it sorted, Clint."

"I don't care what the cost. I've got money, and what I don't have I can make."

"Beth's family. Not gonna need your money." Gus clips.

"Beth's my woman. She got hurt when she was with *me*. I fucking know little or nothing about security, but I'll be damned if I let others take care of what's my responsibility." I get loud. I hear Gus, but he's got to understand this is for me to carry. One fucking way or another.

"Gotcha," is all he says before hanging up, but I hear the respect in that single word. He heard me. Looking at all the eyes turned my way, so has everyone else. So I do what I do best— hammer some nails. I head outside to my shed, grabbing my quilted work shirt from the hook by the door. For the next hour, I work on framing the walls for my design. I'm hellbent on having it up before the first snowstorm.

"You okay?" Beth's voice sounds from the doorway to my workshop, where she lets her eyes scan the interior. Not much to see, just some stacks of lumber, new and old tools, a floor full of wood shavings, and a few wagon wheels I aim to use at some point. Not sure for what yet. She takes it all in with a little smile on her battered face.

"Where is everyone?" I ignore her question because I don't want to let her know how *not* okay I am.

"I sent them away. Told them I wanted to rest, but I really just wanted to find you. Mal's here, though. He's sitting in his truck out front, refusing to come in. Says he can keep a better eye out from his truck." She shrugs her shoulders looking a bit lost.

"Come here," I tell her, putting down my tools, wiping my hands on a rag, and holding them out to her. Without questioning me, she moves right into my arms, a deep shuddering breath leaving her lips. Resting my cheek on top of her head I ask, "What can I do for you, my beautiful Bean?" I don't miss the sharp intake of breath or the little snort that follows and hold her a little tighter.

"Only you would call me that," she says, a smile in her voice.

"I'd better be the only one calling you that to your face," I grumble, to which Beth chuckles.

"Tell me what you're working on?" She moves from my arms and starts shuffling the drawings on my workbench.

"What is this?"

"I'll show you." I grab her hand and pull her out the door to the old catalpa tree in the yard.

"What am I looking at?" she asks when I turn her to face it, slipping my arms around her waist from behind and resting my chin on her head.

"Tree house." I feel the hitch in her breath before she turns in my arms and plants her face in my chest. "Boy needs a tree house." When she doesn't say anything, I go on to explain. "I've got time. Now that the doc's cleared me for half days at work, I can tinker around with it in the afternoons."

Lifting her face back, she looks at me with wet eyes but a smile on her face. "You're too much, you know that?"

"Far from it, but I sure hope I can be just enough."

Without another word, Beth leads me by the hand into the house and straight to the bedroom. With a little shove, she has me sitting on the side of the bed, inserting herself between my legs. Bending over, she kisses my head, before working her hands into my shirt and pushes it off my shoulders.

"Babe...maybe—"

"Hush," she stops me. "My choice. I need you."

Not about to argue with that, I allow her to divest me of my work shirt and the white T-shirt underneath, but when she drops down on her knees in front of me and goes for my belt, I grab her wrists.

"Not gonna happen. Not today." I let her know in no uncertain terms. I stand, pulling her up with me and start stripping her of the T-shirt she changed into after we got home. The other having been covered in her blood. Her heavy breasts hang beautifully in the lace cups of what undoubtedly is another one of her Victoria Secret bras, but since they're even more beautiful freed, I quickly undo her bra and strip it off her. There is so much vulnerability in the way she holds herself, I try to show her with my hands and my mouth how much I worship her body. I lave attention on her face, albeit very carefully, from her neck and shoulders to the soft swells with their dark pink nipples taut in my mouth. Finally nipping and licking my way down her slightly rounded belly that forms a perfect cushion when I'm laying between her legs.

Beth's eyes go wide when I slip down to my knees in front of her and slowly pull her pants and undies down to her ankles. Tapping one and then the other, I let her step out before I toss them aside, slipping my hands around to dig my hands into that fine ass, while I bury my face in her front.

"You smell so fucking good," I manage as my lips and tongue find their way to her pussy, already wet with her arousal.

Fuck me. I could die a happy man right this moment. Demanding as I like to be in the bedroom normally, this soft loving worship is what I need today. "Lay down for me, baby."

She settles on the edge of the bed before laying back, letting her legs hang open over the side, allowing me a clear view of her wet swollen pussy. "Beautiful," I murmur, sliding my fingers through her wetness. Listening to her breathing to tell me how to touch her.

"I could feast on you," I tell her before settling my mouth over her core.

CHAPTER FIFTEEN

I don't know how long I've been asleep, but I am starving.

Dusk is settling in outside the window and the house is quiet. Pulling on a discarded T-shirt from a pile of clothes on the side of the bed, I go in search of Clint, who apparently left the bed at some point, after bringing me to orgasm not once but twice. First with his incredibly talented mouth, and the second time when he fucked me sweetly before tucking me to his side. I must've dozed off in my postcoital daze, because I can't remember a damn thing after that.

The living room and kitchen are cast in shadows and there's no sign of him anywhere. Where the hell is he? A quick peek out the front door shows me the rental car is still there, and I know Jed still has Clint's truck.

A quick trip back to the bedroom to put on some proper clothes, and I'm out the door, toward the shed, figuring he's probably in there. Odd. It's dark in his workshop too. A little niggle of fear is starting to twist in my gut, and the hair on my neck is standing up. Now fully aware of the last of the light fading fast, I hurry back to the house, sneaking peeks over my shoulder. Whether it's just paranoia or someone is really watching me, fear chases me into the house, and I rush to slam the door shut. I need the phone. Rushing into the kitchen, I snatch the portable off the counter and immediately dial Gus's number, the first person I think of.

"Yeah?"

"Gus, it's Beth. I fell asleep and when I woke up Clint was gone. I mean I can't find him anywhere and the car's still here."

"Sit tight. I'm gonna call Mal. I'll call right back."

Before I even have a chance to respond he hangs up. I'm not liking this—not liking this at all. Suddenly, I need to know Max is all right, but I'm afraid to use the phone in case Gus calls back. So the next few minutes I simply stand there, panic sneaking through my body. I jump when the phone rings in my hand, almost dropping it.

"Gus?"

"I'm coming over now. Don't answer the door to anyone."

Suddenly feeling like eyes are on me, I slide down on the tile kitchen floor, my back wedged against the cupboards. I force myself to take deep breaths to try and slow down the loud pounding of my heart, when I pick up on a slight scraping noise. I still completely, not breathing until I hear it again. It's coming from the back door, sounds like someone's trying to get in. I frantically look around for a place to hide, but the only thing close enough is the laundry room, and that's on the other side of the fridge. On hands and knees, trying to stay in the shadow of the cabinets, I slowly move in that direction until a loud shout from outside freezes me in my tracks. What sounds like a scuffle ensues, complete with slaps of skin against skin and banging against the sliding door. It's so loud, I almost miss the knock at the front door, but when I hear Gus yelling my name, I get up. With a quick glance behind me that only shows a struggling mass of limbs, I run to the front door, which slams open when I'm just a few feet away.

"Fucking hell, woman. What—" Looking over my shoulder, Gus spots the fight outside my door and runs right past me to the back. He flips the lock on the slider and yanks it open, causing the wrestling mass to tumble into the dining

189

room. I recognize Mal but have no clue who the other person is, it's hard to see with the balaclava on his head that only leaves his eyes and mouth clear. I was half expecting the guy from the parking lot, but he was tall and this one is clearly smaller than Mal but fighting fiercely. The click of the safety coming off a gun stands out sharply and stops all movement, even before Gus speaks.

"Been a while, but I figure I still remember how to pull a trigger."

Mal uses the distraction to grab the other man's arm and twists it behind his back, snapping handcuffs on his wrist, before grabbing the other arm and securing that one too. Then he rips off the ski mask revealing a young man with blond hair and vaguely familiar features. He frisks the guy, coming up with a small gun, concealed in the pocket of his parka.

"Who the fuck are you?" Mal grinds out between his teeth, grabbing the kid by his collar and tossing the gun on the table. Gus tucks away his own gun, now that they have the guy handcuffed and under control.

"Lookin' for my sister," was his quick answer, eyes flicking back and forth between Gus and Mal, before turning to me. Suddenly I placed him.

"You're Tammy's brother. You're Brian." I'd seen him once or twice since the wedding, but always in passing. He looked like Tammy, though. Same narrow nose and wide set blue eyes. Even the color of his hair was the same. I remember thinking they could've been twins the first time I met him. Gus looks at him through narrowed eyes.

"What the hell are you doing here, breaking in?"

Brian's eyes turn back to Gus and he shrugs his shoulders. "Figured I'd talk to her," he says, tilting his head in my direction. "Maybe she'd heard something."

"With a gun? Normally people would use a phone or knock on the door. Not try to break in." Mal points out.

"How did you find her? Beth doesn't live here." Gus wants to know, and frankly, so do I.

Again a shrug of his shoulders and it appears Brian's had his fill of talking, slamming his mouth shut as his gaze lands on the floor.

"Where's Clint?" I ask, my mind swirling with confusion as I take in this bizarre stand off in Clint's house. Brian's head snaps up looking at me blankly.

"I don't even know who that is," he says belligerently, just as there's a sound behind me.

"The fuck?" Clint is standing in the doorway, looking at his front door, which is hanging from one hinge. Then he swings his head up and takes in the scene before him. Without thinking, I take a few running steps and throw myself in his arms. "What the hell, Beth?"

I swear, I've been gone for less than twenty minutes to find my front door busted in, and some random guy in handcuffs in my house, Gus and Mal hovering over him. Then Beth, who greets me like I've fucking returned from the dead.

Beth was still sleeping deeply when I woke up from a satisfied nap. She didn't even wake up when I went to clean up in the bathroom, so I figured I'd quickly call Jed and get our trucks sorted. I left a note for Beth on the nightstand and called Mal, who said he had eyes on the house. From where I had no fucking clue, 'cause I couldn't see his truck or him, but if he says he's there, then he's there. Jed picked me up in my truck and after switching out some tools over to his truck in the motel parking lot, I drove mine home again. Twenty fucking minutes tops.

"Anyone wanna tell me what the fuck is going on?" I bark, as I fold my arms around a sniffling Beth.

"I can," Mal volunteers. Thank fuck. "Just after you left, I see this guy sneaking around the side of the house to the back. I follow and catch him trying to unlatch the lock on the backslider. Beth apparently woke up to find you gone and called Gus, who in turn couldn't get a hold of me since I had the phone on vibrate and wasn't gonna alert this punk here by answering. He came through the front door… in a hurry."

"I left you a note," I tell Beth, whose fingers are clutched so tight in my back, I'm positive I'll have marks. Her head snaps up at my words.

"There's no note," she says, shaking her head.

"There is, sugar. On the nightstand." Without a word she releases her death grip and takes off down the hall to the master, coming back only minutes later with the familiar scrap of paper clutched in her hand and an embarrassed look on her face.

"It must've blown off when I threw back the covers."

"Come 'ere. You were worried about me?" I try to tease the embarrassment from her eyes, wrapping her back in my arms.

"Just worried something had happened before I could get proper return on my investment," she deadpans.

"Smartass. You know you'll pay for that." I smile into her hair.

"Right. Hold that thought. Gotta call the sheriff in on this, maybe he can get a straight story out of this guy, because breaking into a house just to talk to someone is not processing well. Besides, I'd still like to know how he knew where you were." Gus grabs the third guy's arm and starts marching him to the door. "I'm gonna secure him in the truck. Mal, you call and fill in Carmel, would you?"

The next ten minutes, until the brand spanking new sheriff gets here, is spent getting me up to speed as to who the kid is, what he claimed to be doing here, and on how come former Deputy Drew Carmel was suddenly sheriff. You miss a lot when you're out for a month. Apparently Drew was installed in office by the board, shortly after Joe permanently resigned to work with Gus at GFI Investigations. By the time there's a knock on the door we've haphazardly closed for now, to keep out the cold, I think I'm pretty much caught up. Not that I'm any less confused, which seems to be the general feeling.

Beth's still plastered to my side, which by the way I'm not complaining about in the least, when Mal lets Drew and a new deputy in through the wrecked front door. Almost immediately, the deputy leaves with Gus to switch the guy from his backseat to the patrol car and take him in to Cortez. Drew turns to Mal first for his recollection of events before turning to Beth.

"And how come Gus showed up, kicking the door down?" Beth, who's been very unnaturally quiet and subdued, goes stiff under my arm. "Beth?" Drew prompts when she's not exactly jumping to answer.

"That would be my fault."

Drew turns to me, a surprised look on his face. "I thought you weren't even here until after all this happened?"

193

"Technically, but I left Beth sleeping. She woke up not knowing where I was and called Gus, which was exactly the right thing to do." It's true, it had been the correct thing to do under the circumstances, and in hindsight, maybe lucky that he happened to walk in when Mal was struggling with the guy, cause from what I can figure, the dude did have a gun on him.

"Tell me your side, Beth, from the moment you woke up."

"I looked for Clint. He wasn't in the house and I couldn't find him in his workshop either. I was freaked out and called Gus."

"His workshop?"

"Out back, in that big shed. I figured for sure I'd find him there, but it was dark."

"And you didn't hear or see anything out there?" Drew pushes.

"I was uncomfortable. I remember the hairs on the back of my neck standing up, but no; I didn't see anything," Beth confirms, getting a little pissy at the prying questions. .

"Look, Beth, I'm just getting the logistics because it would seem you may well have been very damn lucky you didn't bump into him."

Apparently Beth hadn't yet considered that judging from the sharp intake of breath. "But he's Tammy's brother," she protests weakly.

"May well be, babe, but his story stinks," I point out. "You know it and I know it. He claims to only want to talk to you, but won't tell anyone how he found you, or why he's breaking into my house to do it. I'm not even gonna get started on that gun Mal took off him."

"Fine. I'm not a complete idiot, you know." Beth's cute when she pouts. Doesn't do it often, but it's a little bit of vulnerability that makes her somehow more approachable.

I tighten my arm around her shoulder and turn her body into mine, ignoring her resistance. Bending down, I whisper in her ear, "Watch that smart mouth. I have plans for it." Just like that her body settles against mine. I love how she responds. My cock loves it too.

Drew, his deputy, and Mal are off to Cortez with the hapless Brian, leaving Gus behind. He is talking on his cell just outside the front door. The moment he's done, I'm going to get his help rehanging the door he kicked down. Seems only fair. Beth was on the phone earlier, talking to Katie to check on Max. Katie and Caleb decided to keep him with them for security reasons. Beth was not on board with that at first, but when Gus reminded her that both Katie and Caleb are trained operatives, she had to admit Max would be better off with them for the time being. At least until this mess is sorted. What he didn't say was that Max was as much a potential target. I think she clued in fast though, because now she is puttering around in the kitchen, determined to 'feed' us. Guess she needs the activity. I had another one in mind, but it appears that's going to have to wait.

"Neil's on his way with some equipment to tighten up security here." Gus walks in, snapping his phone shut and grinning. "And don't be surprised when Emma shows up with food to feed an army."

"I'm cooking!" Beth yells from the kitchen, having obviously overheard some of that.

195

"Girl, you know my Emma; there's no way she would come over and *not* bring food. I'm guessing that before long there'll be more people showing up. After this morning's attack on you and now this, I'm thinking the Cedar Tree phone lines are humming. Everyone's gonna want to check in."

Both Gus and I have moved into the kitchen where Beth has half the contents of the fridge spread out on the counter.

"Bean. Don't you think that's a bit excessive?" I try, but am shut down with a fierce glare from chocolate brown eyes. Gus snickers beside me.

"Word of advice; don't come between a woman and her need to feed."

"Right," I confirm, my eyes still on Beth's where I see a hint of fear lingering. Wrapping my hand around the nape of her neck, I draw her to me, planting a soft kiss on her lips. "Right," I say again. "I'm gonna fix that door. Gus, give me a hand?"

Thirty minutes later, Emma is in my kitchen bickering with Beth. Gus and I have a new catch plate ready to go on the new doorpost—the old one having been splintered when Gus put his boot through it—and the door is ready to be rehung. Only thing left to do is put a new lock on it. It's around nine o'clock, getting pretty damn cold out, and I'm fucking starving, wanting to get this shit done. The crunch of tires on my drive alerts me. Gus, I see, is already alert with his hand on the butt of his gun, temporarily stuck in the back of his waistband so he'd have free movement of his arms. Guess he was comfortable enough to go without his shoulder holster but not going without the gun. Grinding to a stop is Arlene's truck. Figures.

"Where is she?"

"Easy, Arlene," Gus cautions when she comes marching up the steps, her face angry. But then Arlene has a tendency to get pretty pissed when something happens to her friends.

"Don't tell me 'easy', Gus Flemming. I just found out Seb was called twice today—twice—about shit going on with my girl, and he's in fucking deep water already for keeping it from me! Don't know why you wouldn't call me yourself. Not only this morning, but now. Good thing Emma gave me a head's up, or who knows when I would've been told?"

This is when I decide to intervene on Seb's behalf, because it'd been me calling both times and I purposely did it on his cell. "Arlene, simmer down. I asked him to."

"You what?"

"You guys were on the doorstep when we came home from the hospital, we didn't even have time to get in the house before you laid into me. Didn't want that whole circus twice in one day, so I asked Seb to sit on it for a couple of hours." I try, but as expected Arlene's not having it.

"Then you've just lost any brownie points you may have won over the last year, buster!" Oh, she's pissed. Right in my face, finger poking in my chest, and Gus, helpful as he can be, just leans back against the porch railing with his arms crossed over his chest, chuckling. Son of a bitch.

Then Arlene makes me mad. "That's my friend in there, we've been buds since we were kids, and you think you're gonna dictate when I can and can't see her? Got another thing coming, Clint." She spits out my name and is ready to march past me in the house, but this time I've got something to say.

"Wrong. I'm her man, and I will damn well do what I need to do to make sure she gets what she needs. This isn't about you, Arlene. This is about Beth and what is good for her." I raise my hand when Arlene opens her mouth to interrupt, 'cause I'm not done. "My woman, my responsibility, and when she's not at full strength, then my call too." I must've gotten loud, because I see Emma slip outside and lean against Gus, who immediately tucks her close, and I feel Beth's hand slide up my back. When I turn my head, she's looking up at me with a rare softness in her eyes. Usually they shoot sparks of one or another variety, but now they're soft, like melted chocolate. With one hand on the small of my back, the other now resting on my stomach, leaning in to my side, she turns to face Arlene who hisses when she sees Beth's face.

"Your face…it's worse now."

"Honey, I'm fine. Shaken up but fine. I had no idea Clint called—calling frankly never entered my mind—but I'm glad he called Seb." Arlene flinches at this and Beth is quick to finish her thought. "The scene in the parking lot, the hospital, and now this, I needed some time to process without a horde, however well intended, stomping down the door.

"But…"

"Hush. I know you want to rush to the rescue, and you guys are very good at that." I notice Emma's eyes widen a little when she finds herself included. "I appreciate it, but Clint's here. I look after him, and it would seem he looks after me, too. So let up, okay?" Arlene still looks like she wants to protest, but Emma's face has gone soft as her eyes travel between Beth and me.

"Right," she says. "Arlene come inside, give Seb a call to see if he can come over. We'll all have a bite, since between Beth and I we have enough food for an army. We'll let the boys finish up the door and Beth can tell us everything, all right?"

Gus bends down and kisses her temple before letting her go, and with her arm around Arlene's waist, she guides her inside. Ignoring Gus, I turn Beth so her front is pressed against mine, my arms around her.

"You good?" I ask, looking down in her upturned face, gently tucking a stray strand of hair behind her ear.

"Fine."

The significance of her little speech for Arlene slowly settles in to my chest, and I want her to know it didn't escape me.

I hold her a little tighter. Bending down, I touch my lips to hers and simply whisper, "Means the world."

Her own arms grow tighter and she whispers back, "Ditto."

CHAPTER SIXTEEN

"Hey, beautiful."

"Hey…What time is it?"

I've got to admit, having a man call you beautiful when you've been beaten black and blue, hair a tangled mess, and sleep crusting your eyelids together is a very new and very welcome experience. I try not to smile too big because I haven't brushed my teeth. Don't want to kill the illusion. Taking a quick peek at the clock on the nightstand tells me it's just after seven in the morning.

Shifting up in bed, I suddenly feel every muscle and bone in my body. Feels like I got plowed over by a damn Mack truck. I must've winced because Clint immediately puts down the coffee he's holding on the nightstand, fishes the bottle with my pills out of his pocket, and shakes two in the palm of his hand.

"Here," he says, holding his hand out to me. "Better knock it down fast. Second day after a beating is always worse."

I take the pills from him, pop them in my mouth, and wash them down with the coffee he picks up again and hands me.

"How would you know?" I ask after wrestling down the tablets. I've never been good at swallowing them. Clint chuckles, either at the question or the fact that my face goes funny when the taste of those damn pills gets stuck in the back of my throat. Complete with gagging sounds I throw back the rest of the coffee, near burning my mouth in the process.

"Well?"

"Grew up with a brother, Bean. We used to practice on each other. A lot."

I'm surprised he's smiling as he's apparently reliving good memories. Although, how beating the snot out of each other can be cause for smiles, I'll never understand. Regardless, a smile in relation to Jed is progress, it's got to be. "So have you been in touch? With your brother?" I ask, as I settle back into the pillows.

Clint moves to the other side of the bed and climbs in beside me, fully dressed in signature faded jeans, Henley, and flannel shirt. He gingerly tucks his arm around me and pulls me close. Because Clint is more comfortable than a few pillows against the headboard, I turn into him and put my cheek to his chest.

"Monday, actually. Was gonna tell you about it, but shit just kept happening. Mostly he talked and I listened. Not saying we're good, but we're better." His hand is lazily stroking through the ends of my hair, which is getting way too long and I snuggle in deeper. He really has a nice chest.

"Sorry your heart got broken, Big Guy. She was a bitch," I mutter into his shirt. It takes me a minute to realize the movement underneath my cheek is Clint's suppressed laughter and I promptly push up. "This is not funny."

His smiling brown eyes sparkle with amusement as he looks down on me.

"I love that pet name, and I love that you feel protective of my heart, but babe *she* didn't break my heart—my brother did. Looking back, I reckon she never really had my heart. Now how about you get your luscious ass out of bed. I'm cooking breakfast before heading out."

"You're heading out? Where?" I want to know. Flipping back the covers, I slip out of bed, tucking my shirt, or rather Clint's shirt that I've taken to sleeping in, down to cover my ass. When I turn, he's standing on the other side of the bed, a big grin on his face as he looks me up and down. "Well?" I have to prompt before his eyes slide up slowly over my breasts, that unrestricted hang closer to my belly button than I'm really comfortable with, and finally come to rest looking into mine. Damn grin is still there.

"Two things. I have to stop by the clinic and see Kendra. Realized this morning I totally missed that appointment yesterday, with all things going on. Since I missed Monday's too, I figure I at least owe her a coffee and an apology. Then I'm planning to meet Jed at the office, so he can get me up to date on the progress of current projects and work out a schedule with me." He purposefully walks around the bed and right up to me, wrapping those big arms around me. Standing with my face once again pressed against his chest, my arms snaked around his middle, half-naked in my bare feet, I feel dwarfed by his size. I like it.

"Maybe I should go check on Max. I mean, we can't just leave him at Katie's."

"Talked to Caleb this morning. He's doing some work from home and between him, Katie, and Mattias, Max will be taken care of. But Gus said he'd come to pick you up to head into Cortez, apparently the sheriff has some more questions."

I know that should concern me, but my mind was stuck on all the planning that'd gone on while I was still sleeping. "You talked to Gus, too? Busy morning already and it's not even eight."

He shrugs his shoulders. "Ready to get this day going, get our shit sorted, and start working on moving past it to where we can see our future clear."

When I tilt my head back, his eyes are warm on mine, holding a promise that I'm not sure I'm ready to contemplate, but it sure as hell feels nice. I lift up on my feet and touch my lips to his. "Let's get shit sorted then."

"So what you're saying is that Tammy's brother is the one who got Dylan hooked up with this Sam character? A member for a gang of car thieves?" I shake my head, still confused at the information that was suddenly burying me. Clint's hand tightens on mine. He'd decided last minute to switch his plans around a bit, when Gus came to the door with a very serious look on his face. Figured he should be with me for whatever news I was about to get thrown at me, and boy, was I glad he did. He hasn't let go of my hand since we sat down in the sheriff's office facing Drew.

"The gang supplies stolen cars to a crime syndicate running luxury car parts nationally and internationally. The chop shop they took down last week was only one of a chain of them. Turns out, Sam took it upon himself to use money that wasn't his to lend to Dylan, and when he wasn't able to come up with it in time, the syndicate discovered Sam's indiscretion and put the pressure on. Big time. Brian says he warned his sister, and she called him after a blow out with Dylan, who had no idea until then how big his problems were. She left and I guess that's when he decided to drop his boy off with you." Drew takes a sip of his coffee, which by the way, tastes like fucking tar. I had a sip of mine and put it as far away from me as possible when the astringent burn hit my tongue. I'm still trying to force my brain to process the information I'm getting, but without the aid of good caffeine it's proving to be difficult.

Gus decides to take over for Drew. "I thought initially maybe he was working for them. Those mechanics usually get great pay and it would've made sense he'd go for the bigger check in order to pay them off. Now it doesn't make that much sense anymore, because those guys aren't known for their charitable demeanor. Seems more likely he was doing something else there, but whatever it was, Dylan's now not only on the law enforcement radar, but on the syndicate's as well. In a big way." Gus puts a hand on my knee before continuing. "They want their money, Sam wants the money and even Brian is feeling the heat for his involvement from them. They're squeezing every angle and, darlin', I'm thinking since Dylan was spotted at the Monticello raid, it's no longer just the money. They just want him. Brian mentioned that word coming down is that anyone who hands over Dylan will be absolved."

"*Jesus*," comes out of Clint's mouth. I am too petrified to even move, let alone speak. Sure I've lived through some hairy stuff, along with everyone else. Everyone of my friends has been through some horrible trials in the past few years, but my response to those events was always one of action. Now? I can't even think, I'm so busy drowning.

"Beth?" Gus's voice penetrates and when I look up, I realize he's moved from the chair beside me to sit on the desk in front of me. Hadn't even noticed him moving. "I need you to listen carefully. We're not gonna let anything happen to you or Max, and I'm pulling in all manpower for this. Joe's on his way back from a job in Albuquerque to help. I've got Neil working on Clint's place, installing more security, outside cameras, and panic buttons in the kitchen, bathroom, and bedroom. Mal and Neil are going to continue to cover you, and Max is gonna stay with Katie and Caleb."

I try to protest that but Gus won't let me interrupt.

"Gotta be this way, Beth, I'm sorry. At least until we flush out all the players, and right now, as far as we can figure that's Sam and his band of car thieves and the syndicate. The first I expect is manageable, but the second is going to be tough. Their reach is far. Drew, Joe, and I will be working on clearing this shit up. In the meantime you don't do anything without coverage. Each time you step outside, for whatever reason, you should not be alone."

Swallowing hard, I try to stop my body from the trembling that's slowly started up in my limbs. Clint just clenches my hand harder, so hard in fact, it starting to feel numb.

"I want her put in a safe house somewhere. Some place where she'll be completely safe," Clint's voice sounds hoarse and I realize it's fear doing that. Fear for me. Despite the cold fist of fear around my heart, a warm tingle starts in the pit of my stomach.

"No."

All eyes turn back to me, surprised.

"I'm not going to do that," I tell Clint, placing my hand against his jaw. "If I do, they'll just move on to you or to any of my friends. Pressuring or threatening you for information. I won't do it, Clint. Not going to pass the hot potato. I couldn't live with myself if anything happened to you, or any of you because I was cowering in a corner."

"Beth, I'm telling you—"

"I said no. I know you want to keep me safe, and believe me when I tell you how incredibly good that feels, but I feel the same way about you. I'm sticking this out."

He drops his head, leaning against my forehead and whispers, "Killing me, my love."

My heart stops beating for a moment, before jumping into high gear, pounding so hard against my chest, I'm sure everyone can hear. Before I can properly process the fact that Clint just called me 'his love,' Drew decides to break up our little interlude.

"Right. Beth's correct in assuming they'll just move on to the next victim down the list. I'm going to try and convince the Durango PD to actively look for Tammy, who's apparently really disappeared off the grid, according to her brother, but don't hold your breath. Given that she took clothes and her car, they'll assume she chooses to stay away. They won't likely do anything unless there's evidence of foul play. I will also stay in close contact with Gus and keep him updated. Either of you need me, here are all my numbers." He hands both Clint and I his card.

"Do I need a license to carry a gun?" I blurt out, not entirely sure what possesses me but knowing I need to have a little bit of control back. Although, I've always loathed guns, I'm willing to put that aside for now. Maybe I'll feel less vulnerable.

A gun? She wants to carry a gun?

"You're allowed to have a gun, but to carry it concealed, you need a license. I can probably hook you up with one, but do you really think that's wise? Can you even shoot?" Drew asks Beth.

"I can learn."

"*Fuck me*," I let slip out loud, earning a scathing look from Beth. "Bean, I have a license to carry. I don't usually, but I'm going to now. No need for you to have one. I'm still not planning to leave your side. Besides, I know how to shoot."

From the look on her face, I didn't exactly help myself.

"Missing the point, Clint. I *need* to have some control—something I can do for myself. I know you're all big controlling apes at heart, but this '*little lady*' wants to be able to stand up for herself." The intended sarcasm does not go unnoticed and I tag her behind the neck and put my face close to hers.

"That's twice. Your ass is gonna be red," I tell her, hopefully low enough so only she hears, but from the muted chuckle coming from Gus, he got an earful too. Beth blushes a pretty red. Immediately my thoughts travel to putting that same pretty red color to her ass with my hand. I'm so distracted by the image, I realize too late she's out of her chair and walking toward the door with Drew in tow. Gus is still chuckling.

"Hands full with that one, maybe even more so than Emma was for me. But trust me when I say, when these women lay their sweetness on you, it's worth every fucking frustrating step it takes to get them there."

"I know it," I tell him, before following Drew out the door to where Beth is already filling out the necessary paperwork at the front counter. *Hell.*

By the time we get in the car, Beth is the proud owner of a fast-tracked permit to carry a concealed weapon, and she's happy with it in a way that has me concerned. I turn to Gus who slips into the driver's seat. "Do you have time for a drive to the gun store and shooting range in Mancos?" I ask him. He just grins as he turns over the engine and rolls into the road, going east.

207

"Was already planning to," he says, still grinning as Beth starts clapping her hands in the back seat.

"This is so cool!"

"Babe—this is serious," I growl at her and in return she sticks out her tongue to me. Now Gus is laughing out loud. "You guys are both nuts," I grumble, not at all happy with this turn of events but knowing there's not a damn thing I can do to stop her. Best I can do is try and make sure she's got a basic grasp. Fuck me sideways.

After picking out a small caliber gun for Beth, one that would fit in her purse, we spent about two hours teaching her how to take it apart and put it back together, load it, and hopefully only pull it out when absolutely necessary. Target practice was pretty hilarious with her popping her gum while she was concentrating on her aim and jumping up and down each time she hit even part of the body's outline. Although I almost had a heart attack the first time she did 'cause she was waving the damn gun around while doing it. A little more secure that she at least had a general idea of how to use it, Gus drove us home and left to do some 'work.'

Beth had just checked in with Arlene to let her know she'd be back tomorrow and I'd given Jed a call, telling him he'd have to do without me a few days more.

I'm not about to leave her alone if I can help it. Not that she'd be alone, Neil is at the house still working on the outside cameras and once done, Mal is apparently going to take his place keeping an eye out.

"You hungry?" Beth's voice comes from the kitchen, where she's been putzing around for the past ten minutes.

"I could eat," I tell her, walking up behind her and lifting her pony tail off her neck so I can put my lips there. "Whatcha making?"

"Grilled cheese, okay?"

"Sounds good to me," I pull out a stool and sit, watching her move around the kitchen. "How are you doing?" I ask softly when I spot the worry lines around her mouth. Sure she'd acted all excited while we were at the gun range, but I figured reality would slip back around her with a vengeance at some point.

"I'm fine."

"Beth…" I growl at her in warning, knowing full well by now that '*fine*' when from the mouth of a woman rarely means just that. Don't want her holing up inside her 'can-take-care-of-myself' cocoon again. "Talk to me."

"I'm freaked out is what I am. Happy now? I'm terrified for Dylan, still shaky over what happened yesterday, and I don't even wanna think about the possibility of something happening to Max. I have no control over anything right now and it freaks me the hell out!" She drops the knife in her hand on the counter, and I barely manage to snag her around the waist as she makes to run past me. She struggles for only a minute before she turns around and plants her face in my shirt, crying.

"No, Bean. I'm not happy at all. Not happy about any of it. Not about your son, or about this situation—and certainly not happy about the fact that you are still trying to carry the load on your own." On that, she stiffens in my arms, making to pull away, but I'm not letting her. I slide a hand alongside her neck and use my thumb to tilt her face up. "Listen to me. I need you to hear me clearly. There is nothing wrong with leaning a little when you need to." I feel the tight little shake of her head and can see her stubborn streak rejecting what I'm saying, so I cup her face in my hands and lean in close. "It has nothing to do with being capable or not, or being strong or not. It has to do with being smart enough to recognize you're not alone anymore and strong enough to know when to lean on that one person who will not let you fall." This time she hears me. Her eyes soften and new tears well up, but I want to make sure she gets it. "Babe—I'm that person. I won't let you fall. Not ever."

CHAPTER SEVENTEEN

"More coffee?"

I've been here for half an hour and am still getting strange looks. Shouldn't surprise me since my twin black eyes are slowly turning shades of purple and yellowish green. I tried to cover them with makeup but it looked even more ridiculous with than without, so I decided to go au naturel. Not so sure anymore if that was the right decision, though. Every eye in the damn diner is following me around, and I feel like a fucking monkey in a zoo.

Mal is sitting in the corner booth, nursing a coffee while keeping an eye out. My protection for the day, since I insisted Clint check on his business while I work. He wasn't very receptive at first, but when I pointed out I'd have a diner full of eyes on me, he finally gave in. I didn't know I'd be so close to the truth. Hate being the centre of attention.

"Sure." Mrs. Evans, who lives just down the street from Arlene and Seb, smiles at me when she says it, but doesn't bother hiding the concern on her face. "You alright, dear? I mean, it's not my business to pry, but I see a woman with a black eye, let alone two of them, and I can't help but think of the big fists that made them so." She shakes her head, but before I have a chance to say anything she goes on, "I was rooting for him, hoping he'd get his girl. Can't believe I had him pegged so wrong, honey. I'm so sorry."

In shock, I realize she thinks Clint did this. Oh hell no. If that is what people think, I need to straighten that out right now. Without hesitation, I stand up straight and look around at all of the faces turned my way. Almost the entire fucking diner is gawking, and even more so when they watch me slam down the coffee pot in front of Mrs. Evans and march over to the counter, where I pull out a stool and climb on top.

"I'd like everyone's attention?" I call out, before realizing every eye is already on me. Of course. I'm standing, teetering on a fucking stool in the middle of the diner. I *have* everyone's attention. "Right. So I have two black eyes and a busted up nose and I've seen y'all looking. Sweet Mrs. Evans just made it clear to me how small of a town this is, so instead of you folks speculating about what might've happened and making up all kinds of stories on your own, I'll fill you all in at once. I was attacked in Durango in the parking lot of a clinic by someone I don't know. Clint came out and chased him off. I'm fine, Clint is fine. Police report's been filed. End of story." Trying not to look at the semi-shocked faces of the diners, I start climbing down the stool when two firm hands grab my hips. I turn my head to find Seb with a grin on his face holding on to me. "Thanks," I mumble when I get down, suddenly pretty damn mortified.

"Atta girl, Beth. Beat me to it," Arlene pipes up from behind the counter where she's been shooting daggers from her eyes. Not at me, but at the gawkers. "Was about ready to start throwing condiment bottles." She indicates the row of bottles in front of her she's been refilling. Seb slings his arm around my shoulders and leans forward into Arlene's face.

"Better not, Spot. Insurance is high enough as it is. We don't need lawsuits and assault charges to raise it to astronomical proportions." Seb, generally laid back and good-natured, knows exactly how to handle the easily inflammable

Arlene. Good thing too since they've been together a couple of years now…and both are still breathing.

"Whatever." Arlene shakes her short blonde locks. "Love this small town, don't get me wrong, but everyone is always so damn nosy!"

Now it's my turn to chuckle. Because in front of me is probably the nosiest of them all, and I grudgingly have to admit I'm probably in second place.

God, I need a coffee. *That reminds me.* Giving Seb's waist a quick squeeze and winking out of one of my now purple eyes, I quickly make my way over to Mrs. Evans' table, where I so unceremoniously plunked down the coffee pot earlier, catching a chin lift and the tiniest of smiles from Mal, who's observing from the corner. Poor Mrs. Evans looks positively mortified when I approach. Reaching out her hand she clasps my arm.

"I'm so sorry." Poor thing had her bottom lip quivering and I'm quick to react, slipping in the booth beside her and giving her a good hug.

"Nothing to be sorry about, Mrs. Evans. You're looking out for me, and I really appreciate that, but I had to clear the air so people wouldn't start looking funny at Clint. He's the last person who deserves that."

"Well, I'm sorry I thought he had anything to do with it, too." She purses her lips. "Should've stuck with my first impression of him. A good man, who I knew would be perfect for you."

"Yeah? Well, he's nice enough, I'll give you that. And he takes good care of me." My thoughts automatically return to the day before when he'd vowed to have my back. He about melted me with those words, but I made him swear not to make me cry again the rest of the day, and he hadn't. We'd gone to the clinic to get him his work out with Kendra and give me a chance to catch up with Naomi. We had a quiet dinner at home and tried to invite Mal inside, who was keeping watch from his truck, but he couldn't be moved from his vantage point. Then we curled up on the couch, watched another few episodes of "Sons of Anarchy" and made our way to bed. Got a little heated there, what with the vision of Jax's nice tight ass still burned on my brain and the solid and hard-all-over body of Clint under my hands. It started wild and uninhibited and ended sweet and intense. There'd been one point where I was sure he was going to say something, but his mouth closed again. I swear he let me read all he'd wanted to say in his eyes.

A light cough draws me out of my head to find Mrs. Evans regarding me with amusement. "That good, huh?"

Shaking my head and laughing, I give her a kiss on the cheek, grab the now cold pot of coffee and get back to work.

"Beth—phone!"

Arlene's hollering from the kitchen doorway, causing every eye in the diner to go first to her before turning to me. Despite my earlier public explanation for my slightly battered appearance, it doesn't diminish the eyes from following me across the diner. By this time though, a lot of the earlier crowd has disappeared and been replaced with new diners, these come in before the dinner rush and for a second I contemplate a repeat of my earlier performance but I nix that plan quickly.

"Hello?" I answer when Arlene hands me the phone and walks into the diner to keep an eye out. I rest my shoulder against the door post when a small movement from the corner catches my eye. Mal is tilting his head questioningly. He's been sitting in that corner my entire shift and must be bored out of his brain right now. I shrug my shoulders at him.

"Hello—who's this?" I try again, but this time I can hear noises in the background. A rustling sound. Then I hear breathing, almost like panting…

"Beth…" The breathless, raspy voice is familiar.

I instantly snap up from the wall and my eyes fly to Mal as I answer, "Clint? What's the matter?"

"Beth… don't…" Then I hear a scuffle, a loud 'NO' and a big thud.

"Clint?" I'm yelling now, my hands barely able to hang on the phone. "Cl—"

"A choice, Beth," a clipped voice suddenly comes over the line. "Your son or your man. You have twenty-four hours to deliver your son, or I start sending your man back—in pieces."

Mal presses in beside me and pulls the receiver back from my ear so he can listen in.

"But I don't know where he is… Dylan…and even if I did, I can't…I couldn't!" I'm hyperventilating and Mal puts his arm around my shoulder, giving me a reassuring squeeze.

"Better find him then. I will call your cell phone in six hours from now. You don't answer? Your man pays the price." Then I hear a click. Gone.

"Where was Clint gonna be at, Beth?" Mal asks urgently keeping his hand on my shoulder and squeezing it when I don't respond right away.

"His office—meeting Jed to talk about the business. That's all I know." I lean forward with my head against the doorpost, vaguely registering Mal on his cell phone, when Seb moves in and maneuvers me into the kitchen, away from prying eyes. His arms come around me and his hand pushes my head in his neck.

"Bethie…" he mumbles. From behind me I can feel another body crowding me and just as I'm about to sink through my knees, I'm being held upright in a Seb and Arlene sandwich.

"That woman is a vulture, I'm telling you."

Jed's just finished telling me how Sarah Creemore, the client in Cortez whose house reno was almost done, had not left an opportunity by the wayside to get her hands on him. A slight shiver of disgust rolled down my back at some of the ways in which she'd tried to get his attention. Last one apparently a suggestion for a threesome between brothers. Yuck. Not that there's anything wrong with a threesome, necessarily. I might've tried that on once or twice, in my much, much younger years, when I was in college. But being in one that involved my brother? Not ever. I can't help the smile that steals over my face at the thought of Jed having to ward off an apparently very singularly focused woman.

"You laughing at me?" he asks, the side of his mouth lifting slightly. I just shrug, smile still on my face, which should be enough of an answer.

"Asshole," he mutters, shaking his head. "And by the way, you gonna keep wearing this thing? You look like some kind of cowpoke." He's playing with the brim of my cowboy hat, which I'd plopped on the desk when I sat down.

I run my hand over the fine stubble on my head, feeling the ridge of scar tissue left behind by surgery. "I've gotten used to it. Keeps the cold off my head."

"Guess you're keeping the bald head and the scruff then?" He rubs his own rather unshaven chin while still toying with my hat.

"Beth seems to like it," I point out, earning me a full on smile. Something I have to admit changes Jed's face right back to where I recognize him again. It makes him look his age, rather than about ten years older.

"She's a good woman. Rarely ever left your bedside, constantly in the hospital staff's faces to make sure you were getting all you needed. Hell, she even took to exercising your muscles while you were out. She'd read somewhere it could prevent muscle tissue from deteriorating and demanded to know why no one was doing it for you. When the nurse told her they simply didn't have the staff or the funding for that, she took it upon herself to do it. Pretty damn good woman, if you ask me."

I didn't know that. Granted, I'd lost a month and that was still at times fucking with my head. Despite the fact that I'd gotten up to speed on most things, no one told me about that. The thought of Beth caring for me so obviously, when I wasn't aware, hits me deep. I wasted my time with her. A fucking year I let her keep me at bay. As far as I can tell from what I know now, she's cared all along. Not going to waste any more though, the first chance I get, I'm gonna quit beating around the bush and tell her exactly how I feel. Been hinting at it, but never quite said the words to her.

"She is," I agree, "and the first chance I get I'm gonna let her know."

"Maybe it's the hat," Jed jokes. "Can't be your ugly mug, 'cause we both know I'm the better-looking one." With a flourish he plants the cowboy hat on his head. Tugging on it until the brim throws a shadow over his eyes.

"Wanna leave my hat alone?"

"Think I'm gonna borrow it and go out on the town tonight. I hear the diner's the place to go for picking up hot chicks. I'll wear the hat, see if it can make me lucky." He leans back in his chair, crosses his arms over his chest, and plants his feet on *my* desk, smiling widely.

I shake my head, just thinking about how easily we've reverted back to a familiar comfort level, not far from where we were before Luanne entered the picture, when the outer door of the office slams open. I watch Jed's eye's bug out, and I hear a gravelly voice behind me. "Mason?"

"That's me, what's all this?" Jed says, dropping his feet from the desk and sitting up straight. I start moving my chair around but before I have a chance to turn all the way, my world goes black.

"Sit down, Beth." Arlene is pushing me down in the chair in her office, off the kitchen, "before you fall down. Now talk to me."

Easier said than done, I'm not usually prone to panic but I'm fucking panicking now. Seb walks over with a tumbler of something and shoves it in my hand. "Drink," he orders, and without thinking, I toss back whatever's in the glass, only to feel it burning down my throat.

"Holy shit," I gasp, "what'd you give me?"

"Brandy. Got a bottle I use for cooking. Figured it would work well to knock the edge off the shock."

I shake my head to clear it and have to admit, the stuff had its merits, if only as a kick in the ass. "It's working," I tell him and to Arlene I say, "They've got Clint. Want me to trade Dylan in for Clint. I don't even know where he is." The panic is working its way back into my body, I can hear it in my own voice. I close my eyes and focus hard on keeping myself in check. When I open them again, Mal is standing in front of me, a concerned look on his face. That can't be good. Right?

"Gus and Joe are on their way to Clint's office now, babe. No one's answering phones, not at the office, not Clint's cell phone, or Jed's for that matter. As soon as they get a lay of the land they'll call. In the meantime, Neil is trying to see if he has any luck with the tracer on Clint's phone."

All I can do is nod, remembering something about some software Neil had installed on just about everyone's phone, allowing him to trace their whereabouts. My heart is feeling a spark of hope. In the meantime, I'm trying to block images of Jed laying dead in the office or Clint being maimed by these guys.

Half an hour later we're still waiting. Mal with me in Arlene's office, Seb in his kitchen while Arlene and Julie, who was called in for her shift early, are manning the tables.

"Should we call?" I ask Mal for the fifteenth time, and for the fifteenth time he patiently shakes his head and tells me they'll call. I've tried calling Clint's cell phone at least as many times, when finally Mal puts his hand on mine and takes my phone away.

"Beth," he leans in, his dark, almost black eyes looking intently in mine, "they'll call. I promise, honey. The second they know anything they'll call."

"O—okay," I stammer. Finally the tears get the better of me and start rolling down my face.

Hooking his hand behind my neck, Mal pulls me up from the chair, sits down, and pulls me down on his lap, wrapping his arm around me while the other presses my face in his neck.

"Fucking finally," he mumbles, "thought you were never gonna crack."

How long I've been sitting in on Mal's lap, face buried in his neck, I don't know. All I know is his shoulder is soaked with my tears, and I can't help but notice how good he smells. Outdoorsy with a hint of some spice. Nice. My little bout of hysteria over, I finally manage to get my crying under control and start to push back against Mal's hand, which is still cupping the back of my head.

"Mal, I'm too heavy. Let me up."

The hand at the back of my head is lifted away, but the one crossing my lap to the opposite hip is still holding me firmly in place. With his free hand he tilts my chin and focuses those dark eyes on me again. Obsidian, that's what they are. The perfect description. "You good?" he rumbles.

"I'm good. Well…better anyway." I try to get up, but he's still holding me down with his arm.

"Mal…"

"I'll let you go, but don't let me hear you talking about being too heavy again. That shit pisses me off. That padding you've got on you? Makes you soft, pliable—the way a woman should feel. I'm thinking Clint's a lucky man. Figure if I find me a woman like you one day—all soft and rounded in the right places, but hiding a core of steel—I'd count myself the luckiest guy alive."

Knew it before, but now I know for sure; some woman is going to count her blessings one of these days with Mal. He'd treat her like a goddess, I've no doubt.

"Thanks," I whisper, but just as I wrap my arms around his neck to give him a hug, a voice booms from the doorway.

"What the fuck?"

CHAPTER EIGHTEEN

"Buddy, you okay?"

The voice, vaguely recognizable, and the hand on my shoulder, giving me a gentle shake, wake me up to find Joe leaning over me. Disoriented, I look around to find I'm wedged in the tiny bathroom off my office, my torso twisted in the space between the wall and the bowl, and my legs spread and bent at the knees. Joe is standing between them and reaching out a hand.

"Can you move?"

I clasp the hand he offers and let him slowly pull me up to sitting. Aside from the wave of dizziness that should probably concern me, if I didn't have other things to worry about, I think I'm okay. It's then I notice that Gus is right behind Joe, just outside the doorway, looking at me intently while talking on his phone.

"Remember what happened?" Joe wants to know, and I tell him what I can, realizing as I'm talking that I haven't seen my brother yet, but I don't get a chance to. Gus slips in behind Joe, his cell now tucked away, and mumbles something to Joe I can't quite pick up.

"Sorry what?"

Gus's eyes shoot to me. "I said the ambulance is on its way."

"Is my brother okay?"

"Let's get you out of here first," he says, and between Gus and Joe, they pull me up and out of the tiny stall. I'm swaying a bit on my legs, trying to get my balance back.

"Whoa, my friend. Take a minute."

I should, but I'm more concerned about why they haven't answered my question, so I repeat it. "Where's my brother? Is he alright?" This time I can read the answer in their faces, and still I stumble past them to see for myself. *Fuck!* When I swing around, I pin Gus with a stare. "Who?"

"Not sure. I have my suspicions and Neil is trying to track a few things down, but for now he's in the wind. We'll find him though. Better fucking believe it." Gus's words are delivered with conviction, which makes me feel a bit better. Then he tells me about the phone call Beth received, and how they managed to find me, and there is only one thing on my mind.

"Take me to Beth."

"Buddy, we've gotta wait for the ambulance to check you out."

"Now. I have to see her now." I get right up in Gus's face. Not budging, he gives me a thorough stare down before I can see resolve slide over his face.

"Anything wrong, and I mean *anything,* we head straight for the hospital. You get me?" His voice is clipped and I have no desire to fight him on that. At least not once I've seen her with my own eyes. To Joe he says, "Change of plans, redirect the ambulance to the diner."

Within seconds they have me hustled into Gus's big Yukon, but not before I snatch up the cowboy hat that lies abandoned on the floor next to the desk. *Jesus.*

Normally, it takes about ten minutes to get to the diner, Gus does it in a little over five and pulls around to the back parking lot. Seb's eyes go wide when he sees me walking in the kitchen, flanked by the other two. He grins and with a lift of his chin indicates Arlene's office, where the door is cracked a bit. I push the door open further, only to have the breath knocked out of me at what greets me. Before I can even begin to process, "What the fuck?" bursts out of me.

"Clint..." falls from Beth's lips as she turns to face me, her face still wet with tears, sitting on the single chair the office contains, on Mal's lap. Leaping up she slams into me, fresh tears instantly getting my shirt wet. My arms close around her but my eyes never leave Mal, who calmly stands up out of the chair and steps toward us. Apparently not at all concerned that I just found my woman, on his lap, with her face buried in his neck.

"Good to see you standing, Clint. Beth was scared." With that, he claps me on my shoulder and slips past us out of the room, closing the door behind him. Point made.

With a bit of shuffling, I manage to plant my ass in the chair Mal just left and pull Beth on my lap.

"Beth, baby—look at me." I try to get her to lift her face from my chest but she burrows even deeper. "I'm fine. Just got knocked out, that's all. I'll be right as rain. Beth, please look at me."

Slowly her head comes up and her eyes, swollen from crying, turn into slits. "They hit you over the head?" she hisses, before repeating, "They hit you over the *head*?" in a significantly louder voice, before her hands come up and start smoothing over my face and around my head. "Oh my God, Clint; you're bleeding!" When she pulls her hand back, sure enough, it comes away with a trace blood clinging to her fingers. "We've gotta get you to a hospital."

"A scratch probably." I try to calm her, but she tries to push off my lap anyway. Grabbing her wrists to try and hold her still, I stick my nose in her hair and breathe in deeply.

I love this woman. Not that it's that big of a revelation. I've grown into it over a long period of time, but in this moment I feel it so strongly, I just say it, with my nose still in her hair and her body still struggling to get up.

"Love you, Bean," I mumble, torn to know my brother is missing but needing to not let one more moment pass before I make sure she knows it. Her body stills, and I lift my face from her hair to find her staring at me slack mouthed and her eyes big.

"Wha—what?"

"I love you."

Her eyes go soft. As soft as I've ever seen them and once again she does a face plant in my chest. "Baby…" she breathes, the heat of her breath coming through my shirt and touching my skin.

A short knock on the door is followed by Gus sticking his face around it. "EMT's are here," he announces, before backing away to allow two paramedics in.

Forty minutes later, after declared relatively healthy except for a small cut on my head, and alert, but left with a list of warning signs to look out for, the ambulance is gone. Beth is sitting on the desk, still reeling from the news that Jed is missing. I'm still sitting down, with Gus leaning against the doorway, briefing us on the course of events. He very pointedly includes Beth, making sure she's included in the discussion and making good on our joint fuck up the first time.

"For now, I suggest we move to your house," he says, looking at me. "You've got state of the art security now, motion lights outside, and then the cameras. Neil has screens set up to monitor and when that call comes through, in a few hours. He's gonna be ready to triangulate the signal to see if he can pinpoint a location on them."

Right.

Beth grabs hold of one of my hands that are clenched into white knuckled fists on my knees. Folding my fingers back, she slides hers in between and leans down to me. "Jed will be okay," she whispers, "It can't be any other way."

Now that I've seen Beth, know she's all right and coping, I want nothing more than to get out there and hunt those fuckers down, but I wouldn't know where to start.

By the time we've been force-fed Seb's admittedly fantastic goulash by Arlene, who wouldn't let us go on an empty stomach, it's nearing seven fifteen, and it's full on dark outside. Beth and I are in the truck with Gus, and Mal is driving Beth's car home. My truck is still sitting in the parking lot at my office, where Gus said to leave it for now, right beside Jed's truck. I've been hanging on to my cool this entire time, but it's wearing fucking thin. This inactivity when God knows what is going on with my brother is getting to me.

"You know we're not sitting still; Joe is out beating down every resource he has to find even the slightest of leads. Neil and Katie are working the computers at her place, and Caleb is getting in touch with every contact we have within the law enforcements agencies." Gus looks sideways at me. "I can feel the frustration and anger come off you in thick waves, eager to *do* something, thinking we're not *doing* anything. Truth is—we are. Every last resource is being pulled as we speak. Even Emma couldn't sit idle, and rather than have her come to the diner, I've asked her to look after the boys, so Katie has her hands free. Apparently, Naomi is joining her there as soon as the clinic closes at eight." He gives my knee a squeeze before turning his attention back to the road in front of him.

My head is spinning. Evidently, I've been so far up my own ass I didn't notice all this activity around me. Suddenly I find myself choked up when it hits me. They've got my back. I never even had to ask. A year ago I rolled into town, put my foot in it with just about everyone I encountered, and somehow, I got swallowed up in this community. This great group of people, who when the chips are down, all square up behind me. I shake my head and swallow hard, but it doesn't quite clear the stinging in my eyes or the fear burrowing in my stomach.

The moment Gus shuts the engine off outside Clint's house, he tells us to sit tight while he checks the house. Armed with Clint's keys and after a brief discussion with Mal, getting out of my car beside us, he disappears inside, leaving Mal standing in the driveway scanning the surroundings. I lean over and put my hand on Clint's shoulder.

"You okay, honey?"

For a moment he doesn't move, but then he turns in his seat, lifts my hand from his shoulder and turns it against his cheek, leaning into it with his eyes closed.

"Grateful for you, baby. And scared shitless that just now I've reconnected with my brother after so many fucking wasted years, I stand the risk of losing him." Slowly his eyes open and

I can see the emotions swirling around in them. "But it helps having you right here."

"Always, honey." I lean forward and touch my lips to his. A knock on the window shows Mal, who's motioning for us to come inside. The moment we're out of the car, Clint grabs my hand and laces his fingers with mine as I follow him into the house. Mal, apparently, isn't coming in, he just closes the door behind us and stays outside.

"Why's Mal not coming inside?" I want to know.

"Best to keep one set of eyes outside. Mal's eyes are the best ones around, at nighttime especially. I swear he's part big cat." Gus smiles reassuringly, but I'm still twitchy as all get out. Never did have any patience but this; this waiting around while Jed was out there, is testing my limits. I about jump out of my skin when a phone rings, but it's not mine. Gus grabs his from his pocket, looks at the screen and swears. Loudly. That does not make me feel good. I haven't moved from behind the couch and when Clint bends in asking me if I want a drink, I just shake my head. He heads into the kitchen and I just stand here, listening to Gus's conversation.

"Damien. Why do I get the feeling the feds are up to their fucking necks in this situation?"

Feds?

"The fuck you say!" Gus's voice thunders and has Clint come out of the kitchen, looking from Gus to me and back again. I'm frozen in the spot. I've seen Gus pissed maybe a handful of times since I've known him, since he's a good-natured guy. Angry once or twice in a stressful situation but never like this. Not ever. His eyes are mere slits and his face a deep red when he spits out his next words. "Got a woman here who's supposed to let those fuckers know in a few hours time, if she's made any progress locating her son. They're holding a man they think is *her* man ransom. Except it's not. They've got the wrong fucking guy! And you say you've had eyes on it the whole time? Then why the fuck did you not intervene?"

I can feel Clint stepping up behind me, wrapping his arms around my stomach. I'm glad for the support because my knees feel kinda wobbly. Gus seems to listen intently to what this Damien guy has to say, running his hand through his hair repeatedly. "Not going to do it, Damien. Not gonna beat a retreat because *your* case might get compromised. We're talking fucking lives here. Of people I happen to care about. You know you should've given me a head's up about this a long time ago. This shit? This is on you. Had you done what you should've, I could've been prepared. Now we're behind the eightball. Cause you fucked up." With that he snaps his phone shut and hauls his arm over his head to toss it, when Clint pipes up behind me stopping him mid-move.

"Gus. Reckon you might *need* that phone tonight," he says calmly.

Gus slowly lowers his arm and looks at the phone in his hand before slipping it into his back pocket, tilting his head our way. "Could do with a stiff drink, but given the circumstances, maybe a pot of coffee is the better option."

"I'll see to it," I mutter and grateful for something to do, I slip from Clint's arms and start a pot. By the time I've got a tray set out with mugs, sugar, and some milk, the coffee is ready. I carry the whole thing inside, where the boys are already having a quiet conversation that stills the minute I set the tray down. "It's clear you're trying to keep shit from me, but before you do, let me remind you of what happened last time you tried." I look at each of them before giving my full attention to the coffee. Once seated with my own mug, after having supplied the guys with theirs, I'm the one to break the silence.

229

"So what I gather from your side of that less than friendly conversation just now, is that your contact at the FBI knows more than they initially led you to believe?" I look at Gus and he looks right back at me, not saying anything.

After a minute of stare down, he shakes his head and mutters, "Stubborn as shit," before the corners of his mouth tilt up a touch. Lifting his eyes he turns them first to Clint, who's been quiet through our little stand off, shrugging and then turns them on me again.

"You cottoned on to the basic gist of it. Scoop is, they're no strangers to what's going on. And when I say that, I mean they've been working for a year and a half putting together a case against one Stan Jablonski. I've heard his name before, was a big name on the Denver scene but apparently has moved to the desert now and rules his syndicate from Vegas. Hanging with the big rollers now. Not a nice man, Stan. He's wanted for a laundry list of federal and state offenses, both in Colorado and Nevada. Feds tried to get something to go on for years, finally got a break last year when a guy was pulled over with a stolen luxury vehicle in Ouray and got into it with the cop. Facing not only theft but now assaulting a police officer, he talked. Feds came in when he mentioned the name Jablonski. Unfortunately he was found dead the next morning in his holding cell, but he'd already given the feds a thread, now all they had to do was unravel it, which is what they've been doing." He pauses and looks first at Clint, then back at me. I brace myself because something tells me what is coming isn't going to be good, judging by the silent communication he just held with Clint. "The FBI's had eyes on you from the moment Max was dropped on your doorstep," Gus says with a grave face.

"What? Why?"

"They were trailing Dylan. They know about his debt to Sam, who by the way is Sam Blazek, not just part of a ring of car thieves but one of Jabslonski's goons—something Tammy's brother either failed to mention or doesn't know—and coerced Dylan into becoming an informant."

It only takes me a minute to realize that that is not necessarily good news, especially when I combine that bit of information with what's been happening. "This Jablonski character knows, doesn't he?" I put to Gus, who only nods to confirm.

"Dylan was supposed to gather information for Damien's team, was confronted by Sam while going through some files, and the wire he was wearing was discovered in the resulting scuffle. The feds and local law enforcement were listening to the whole thing go down and stormed the place. In the scuffle they lost sight of both Dylan and Sam.

"That's the Sam who you mentioned before? Brian's friend?" When Gus nods, I sit back and feel Clint slip his arm around me and tuck me close.

"One and the same."

I'm still trying to process this information. "They sent my boy into a situation like that without any protection?" Now the blood started boiling good. "That Damien comes around, you're gonna have to stand in line, Gus. I'll be first getting my licks in."

Clint's hand squeezes my shoulder. "I'll help," his deep voice rumbles before he turns to Gus. "What I don't get, is why your buddy suddenly feels like sharing?"

"He's aware of what's gone down today and feels it's in everyone's best interest to share intel. Meaning he wants to know what I know and then tried to get me to shut down our investigation. He can try—it's not gonna happen."

I don't have to look at Gus to see how he feels about that, his voice is dripping with sarcasm.

I run through the events of the past weeks and reassess everything that's happened. "So they were out there watching when I got beat on?" My mind is spinning, but before I can verbalize what I'm thinking, Clint suddenly straightens up beside me when he clues in.

"Those fucking assholes! They're using Beth as bait, waiting around for either Dylan or one of those goons to show their faces, aren't they?"

Clint's outburst serves as an intro to a discussion on the moral code of the FBI, where he voices his displeasure *his woman* was hurt and his brother was taken, all right under the noses of the feds. Then Gus puts in his two-cents worth, pretty much agreeing to whatever Clint says. That leaves me inside with a still seething Clint, while Gus goes out to talk to Mal, to 'bring him up to speed.'

"You hungry?" I try to change tracks. That, and I also feel the sudden need to do something constructive, however basic it may be. When I don't get an answer, I turn and find him looking at me with a half-smile on his face. "What?"

"I could find other ways to keep you busy," he suggests, reaching out to play with a strand of hair that's slipped out of my ponytail, and I feel the slow heat invading my body.

"Bet you could," I say, leaning in to him, "but what with the two very hot, big security guys right in and out of our house, that might not be the best idea." I close the distance and lightly touch my lips to his. His arms surround me. He twists me so I'm sitting on his lap, my legs on one side of him and my back against the armrest. One hand slides up my back and twists my hair in his fist.

"Very hot?" he growls and I suppress a snicker. I figured he'd pick up on that. With his face an inch from mine he mutters, "Not the only thing I noticed you saying, Bean. I like the way you call this *our* house. Like it a lot." Then his mouth descends on mine, effectively cutting off the denial my lips are about to form, and his tongue sweeps in deep, eradicating the capacity for coherent thought.

I'm able to think after, though. When we're interrupted by one of said, very hot investigators, Gus, followed in by an also very hot Neil, who must've shown up while Gus was outside. After Neil rigs up my phone, with some doohickey that looks like an adapter, but is supposed to open a call to his laptop so he can listen in. I'm in my head all during his explanation. He'll record and track said call at the same time. Even after I've made some sandwiches, another pot of coffee, and watched all of them devour it. Now I'm cleaning up in the kitchen, and with my hands in soapy water. I think hard about how somewhere along the way I'd made the switch in my head from 'Clint's house' to 'our house', when the phone rings.

CHAPTER NINETEEN

"Got him."

These last minutes may well have been the longest of my life. I've been instructed to keep the guy on the phone as long as possible, to give Neil a chance to trace the signal, which apparently requires a certain length of time. Don't ask me what I all said, 'cause from the moment I answer the phone and he asks if I've found Dylan, it all becomes a blur. I know the guys had instructed me to try and avoid giving a direct answer right away. I manage to do that by asking about "Clint," who in actuality is standing right beside me, and distracting the guy with questions. He finally interrupts me with a curt, "I'll check again in six hours. Better have something real to tell me," before hanging up.

"Where?" Gus is instantly behind Neil, leaning in to get a look at the screen of his laptop, while pulling his phone out.

"South on the 160, looks to be around the Ute casino. I'm pulling up the satellite image of the general location now."

Fifteen minutes later, Clint's living room is full of activity. Gus and Neil are joined by Joe and Mal around the coffee table, now covered with detailed maps of the area. Clint has joined the cluster and I find myself on the outside looking in. The overwhelming need to *do* something propels me back in the kitchen for another pot of coffee. It's already close to eleven at night and from the sound of it, they're not planning to wait around for daylight, so coffee and something to eat would probably be good.

"Three possible locations," I hear Joe say when I join the group, armed with a fresh pot and a plate of sandwiches. "Mal, Neil, and I each check out one, look for activity. Gus, you can monitor from a central point. Whoever finds something, calls in and we come up with a plan of attack on the spot."

"I'm coming."

Every other eye in the room turns to Clint, but it's Gus who says something. "I get you, but—"

"Me, too," I throw in, straightening my back and lifting my chin at the almost tangible testosterone free-floating through the room.

"Hell no. Not gonna happen," Clint growls, his mouth drawing tight. The faces of the other guys are just as firmly set.

"Listen, I know you guys are all about protecting, but you don't know what you're stepping into and will likely need all hands on deck. I'd be safer with you than staying behind." I stand my ground, picking Gus to focus on, since he's the one calling the shots on this.

I know I've won when he lowers his eyes and shakes his head mumbling, "fucking stubborn women," before turning his eyes back on me and taking a deep breath. "Both of you stay in the truck, no matter what happens." He swings his pointed finger between Clint and I, but Clint doesn't even notice, he's too busy glaring at me. Whatever.

Not down with this plan at all, but Beth's got a point. Fuck.

While the guys hash out details, I move over to Beth, who's leaning against the dining room table and take a firm hold on her shoulders. Bending in with my face inches from hers, I make sure I have her full attention. "This is over, you and me are gonna have some words." I can feel a shiver going through her body and heat flares in her eyes, whether from anger or arousal I can't tell, and my cock doesn't care—it's rock hard. Damned if I don't know whether to lay her over my lap or fuck her on the dining room table. Maybe both. "Careful," I caution her in a low voice, "not a good time to play with fire, woman."

"Beth, give Katie a ring and fill her in?" Gus's voice interrupts, and I reluctantly lift my eyes from hers. Beth's light up and I realize she's getting off on this. Fuck me. She's enjoying it altogether too much. With a slight eyebrow rise to me, she grabs the phone and proceeds to explain in surprisingly concise and detailed terms what is going down to Katie.

"Gus—Katie wants to know if you need Caleb there."

"No. Max is his priority," Gus lifts his head to answer Beth, before ducking down over the maps again. Now I feel like a fifth damn wheel, but before I get a chance to wallow, Gus turns to me. "You armed?"

"I am."

"Good. Make sure Beth has hers locked and loaded, too. We're gonna roll out in fifteen; you and Beth in with me, everyone else in their own vehicle. We'll be setting up across the casino in the trees in front of the trailer park. Neil's gonna take the building to the east of the casino where Morning Star Lane makes a sharp turn. Joe take the one just south of the Ute travel centre by the Mobil station and Mal, you take the building by the north exit onto Morning Star. Neil, you've got all the phone tags activated?" When Neil confirms with a curt "*yup.*" Gus claps, stands up and says, "Let's roll guys. Make sure you're dressed warm, it's colder than a witch's tit out there."

Half an hour later, with Beth in the back of the Yukon, Gus and I in front, and each of the other guys in their own vehicles, the convoy of cars is on the road approaching the north cut off for Morning Star Lane. Joe and Neil continue on to the south exit to Westminster Road from where Joe turns south for the Mobil station, and Neil can get into the casino grounds on the north side. It's pretty dark on the road, but with what little light there is from the road and the few buildings around, you can see a bit of the surrounding landscape. Pretty desolate out here. Mostly desert and mountains with little vegetation other than sagebrush and like Gus said, freezing cold.

Mal is the first to turn off into a cluster of buildings just north of the casino, where he is to leave his car and continue on foot. Gus turns into a short dirt drive just past where Mal left off, leading to a copse of trees, sheltering the small trailer park. He maneuvers the truck so we have a good view of the road going both north and south. Not a lot of talking in the car, except for the guys reporting their progress over the phone.

Five minutes pass, then ten, and fifteen. Neil and Joe have checked in three times, but we haven't heard from Mal since he said he found a way inside.

"Something's up. I'm gonna check it out. When the other guys check in on the radio, give them the heads' up, and if they're clear, tell them to leave their cars in the casino parking lot and walk over here," Gus instructs as he grabs a portable radio and slips out, taking care not to slam the door. Beth doesn't waste any time and climbs over the back seat, plopping beside me in the driver's seat.

"What are you doing?"

"Always wanted to drive this thing," she says, immediately touching buttons and adjusting mirrors like a little kid. "It's huge!"

"Beth," I use my low voice in hopes of conveying a message but all I get back is a big smile ear to ear. Yeah, she's enjoying this far too much. "You're not gonna drive it, so stop messing with the dials. Gus is gonna flip." When she doesn't listen, I grab her hand and hold it. "Babe, enough. What if he needs to make a quick getaway or whatever? Don't mess with a man's settings."

"Don't mess with a man's settings?" she snorts before snapping the gum in her mouth loudly. I'm sure she's about to tell me how ridiculous that is, when I spot a car coming from the south and pulling in the drive. Luckily we're off to the side and partially hidden, but not ready to take chances, I push down Beth in the driver's seat and duck myself. Just as I see the headlights of the car slipping past us, Beth pushes my hand away from her head and pops up to check out the car, before ducking down again.

"What the hell, Beth? Stay the fuck down," I bite off, but she turns to look at me with a combination of fear and excitement in her eyes.

"That was him," she hisses, "the guy from the parking lot. It was him. They've gotta be back here somewhere. Let's go."

"Like hell. We'll call Gus on the radio, let him know. You're gonna stay here."

"But Jed...what if they move him before they get here?"

God, Jed. Only takes me a minute to make up my mind. Cupping Beth's face in my hands, I press a hard kiss to her lips before answering. "No, Beth. We don't even know for sure Jed's here. You get in touch with the guys and tell them what's up. Stay in the car and keep your head down. I'll go have a look." Before she has a chance to stop me, I'm out of the car and pull out my gun while following the now dimming headlights of the car.

Fucking Clint.

Grabbing the radio from the console, I press the button on the side. "Gus? Hello? You there?" Nothing but a crackling sound returns to me, so I try again. "Gus? Joe? Anybody out there?"

"What's going on," Gus's distorted voice comes through and in as few words as possible, I explain the situation. "Keep your head down and for fuck's sake, stay in the car. I'm heading back, can't find Mal. Neil, Joe, you copy this?"

"Copy. Nothing moving on my end," Joe radios back.

"Copy. Same here. Dead end." That's from Neil.

Reassured they're on their way, I slip open the door and slide out of the seat, ignoring the sound of Gus's voice, still talking. Closing the driver's side door with a soft click, I settle the gun, which had been in my purse on the backseat of the Yukon, in my right hand and head in the direction I saw Clint disappear. They think I'm going to leave my man to fend for himself, they've got another thing coming. My son caused this mess. I'm grateful to have had the presence of mind to slip on running shoes instead of my winter boots. Moving around on them is a lot quieter. I stick to the tree line alongside the path, in case anyone comes back down this way, but the further I get from the truck, the thinner the tree cover becomes. To my dismay, I discover that the wooded area really is only on the side of the road, because I can clearly see the group of trailers now. Other than the occasional tree, there isn't much cover at all. Damn.

Coming to a point where the path forks in opposite directions, in what appears to be a loop around the property. Outside of the loop all you can see is desert and some brush, but nothing much to hide behind. I'll do much better to stick to the inside and find cover between the trailers. Doesn't seem to be anyone around, the trailers appear to be empty, which makes sense given that these look to be vacation trailers. No one in their right mind would want to spend a freezing cold night in a trailer. Unless you're looking not to be found. After first looking to see if anyone is out there, I crouch as low as I can while running and beeline it to a spot between the first two trailers. When I get there, I drop down on hands and knees beside the trailer hitch of the one on the left, on a little patch of grass, catching my breath. I listen for any noises and peek around the side to see if I can spot the dark colored sedan parked somewhere. Nothing here. Looking ahead at the next two back to back trailers, I spot some movement about five trailers down the row. The sound of a screen door and some scuffling of feet, but before I can head toward it a large hand clamps over my mouth.

Fucking Beth.

Should've known she wasn't about to sit there and follow instructions like a normal person. No, not her. I get she maybe feels some responsibility, but Jesus, just yesterday she had her first go at a shooting range and before that hardly ever had a gun fit in her hand. On top of that, she's been worked over by this guy once already, she looking for a repeat?

"We get out of here, you and I need a meeting of the minds. Or rather, my hand has something to say to your ass. There are times you can throw your independence and attitude around, but babe, this is not one of them," I whisper in her ear, my hand still covering her mouth, not giving her a chance to talk back. "Serious pain in my ass you're turning out to be. Are you gonna listen to me?" Not sure whether to trust her when she nods her head, I slowly remove my hand, ready to clap it back over her mouth if she gets loud. Can't have that, not with the guy holed up in the white and grey Dutchmen trailer a couple of spots down. But she doesn't make a sound, only turns around to face me and her eyes are fierce. She grabs my shoulders and pulls herself up on level with my ear. Automatically my hands slide around her waist, but I'm pretty positive she's not preparing to whisper sweet nothings in my ear.

"I swear, if I just wet myself for real when you freaked me the hell out, I'm going to plan a horrible, horrible revenge," she hisses at me. Before she has a chance to build up more steam, I slam my mouth down on hers, tongue licking at the seam of her lips to gain entrance. She finally relents, after what I'm sure will be permanently scarring on my shoulders with her nails, and her rigidly angry body goes soft in my arms. Satisfied I've kissed the piss and vinegar right out of her, I release her lips, but leave my nose touching hers when I get down to business.

"About three or four plots up, Dutchmen trailer on the left. Stay behind me and tuck that gun away. Don't wanna get shot in the back." Without wasting any more time and not giving her a chance to respond, I move in front, tucking Beth behind my back.

By the time we pass the next trailer, we can hear muted voices. Two males, maybe three, arguing. Beth slips her hand in the back of my jeans, but doesn't say anything. The closer we get, the clearer the voices become, and I'm not liking what I hear. When one voice asks, "Where is the baby, '*Frajer*'?" in a thick accent, I assume it's Polish. At least it sounds European to my ears. I can clearly hear the response.

"Wasting your time. I don't know where he is and if I did, I wouldn't tell you." That's Jed's voice. No mistake. Beth hears it too, her hands holding on to my biceps now, squeezing. Then everything happens fast.

"*Bzdura!*" is yelled loudly and I immediately hear the sound of a struggle. Skin hitting skin. Without thinking, I pull myself from Beth's grasp and bridge the distance to the Dutchmen trailer in just a few large strides, yank the door open, and barrel inside, hoping the element of surprise is on my side. The large frame of a man is bent over and punching something, or someone. With one hand to the back of his shirt, I pull him off, revealing my brother, sitting in a kitchen chair, hands and feet duct-taped to it, and his face barely recognizable. *Bastards*. I swing my hand toting the gun around to aim at the guy I pulled off him, but the element of surprise has shifted. This time it's me who is blindsided. A sharp kick underneath my gun hand flings the gun up and out of reach. Too shocked at the condition of my brother, I'd delayed in making sure the guy was covered, and now I'd lost my one advantage. Fuck me. The big idiot comes at me with a huge grin on his face, ready to lay into me when he stops and looks over my shoulder.

"Don't even think about it." Mal's voice is barely a whisper as he steps around from behind me, a gun pointed at the idiot's gut. "Clint, grab the cuffs from the back of my belt," he tells me. I do as he says, doing my best to stay out of the way of Mal's gun, I cuff the guy's wrists behind his back. The idiot is still smiling, this time at Mal who calmly observes him.

"*Idiota*. He's dead already, he just doesn't know it yet," he says, and I follow his eyes to my brother, where I just now see the large knife sticking from his gut.

"Jesus, Jed!"

When Clint takes off toward the trailer, I'm frozen in place just watching him go. Stunned that he'd take off like that. I hear the physical altercation too, but the moment he yanks open the door, the sound stops. The sound of a scuffle propels me into action, but I don't get further then one step. Blocking my way is the guy from the parking lot a few days ago. The same guy who cut me off in the car. Only difference, this time he's not wearing his sunglasses and his eyes look black, as black as the barrel of the gun he's aiming at me.

"Well, well, well. How fortunate you show up here," he says in a thick Slavic accent, something that hadn't registered before, but this time I'm not distracted by his hands on me. Not yet anyway and if up to me, never. I put my hands behind me to find the knob on the hitch of the trailer I'm standing behind, leaning back a little.

"How much?" I ask, knowing I'll probably never get that money together unless I sell my house. But sell it I will, if it puts an end to this. The man just chuckles.

"There is no amount big enough to eradicate your son's troubles I'm afraid. He has crossed a dangerous man."

While he's talking, my right hand lifts away from the hitch and finds its way to the small of my back and under my coat, where the butt of my gun sticks out from my waistband. I had tucked it there when Clint told me to put it away. The guy doesn't even seem to notice, so full of himself and thinking too little of me. I bring my left hand forward and fiddle with the zipper of my coat, trying to get him distracted enough so I can pull my gun on him. The distraction comes a moment later, when I hear Clint calling out his brother's name and a chill settles over me. The second the guy turns his head, I have the safety off and pointed right at him. When he turns back, I see his eyes widen slightly, but before I even have a chance to pull the trigger, a red dot appears on his forehead and in the next instant he is on the ground, missing a good chunk of his head. *Oh my God, oh my God.* This is nothing like the shooting range. People don't get hit at the shooting range, and it's generally noisy. Yet I never heard this. I heard *nothing*. Just one minute he's standing and then he's not. Bile starts rising and I'm on hands and knees, puking out the goulash Seb made. I'm still dry-heaving when I remember Clint's voice. I don't think, and I try not to look at the dead man I jump over but continue to run toward the trailer, with only Clint on my mind. It's Gus who catches up with me at the door. He takes one look at me and grabs me by the shoulders.

"Beth. *Jesus.* Where are you hit?" His hands start to move over my head, unzipping my coat and running his hands over my torso. "What the…" That's when his eyes move beyond me to the shapeless form on the grass. "Honey…" With careful movements he slides his hand over mine and gingerly pries my fingers off the gun I'm apparently still holding. The crunch of gravel announces the arrival of both Joe and Neil, who stop in

244

their tracks, staring at me then looking beyond me at the man in the grass. Both immediately turn around and start scanning the surroundings, the three of them forming a barrier between me and the outside.

"Ambulance is on the way. So is the sheriff and tribal police," Neil speaks first, his back still turned to me.

Gus hands my gun off to Joe, who bites off a curse. I'm confused and I just want to get to Clint, so I start moving, but Gus holds me back.

"What the hell, Gus, let me go. Clint needs me."

I struggle to get free but his arms just wrap around me tighter. "Honey, he sees you like this, he's gonna lose it."

I stop fighting long enough to turn and look at him. "Like what?"

"We need to clean you up, you're covered."

With my heart racing I reach a hand up to wipe at my face. When I see the blood on my hand, I twist out of Gus's arms and start heaving again.

In the distance I hear the sirens approaching.

CHAPTER TWENTY

"Beth?"

Clint's voice comes through the curtain pulled around my bed. Don't really know why they want me to stay after the nurse cleaned me up and gave me a pair of clean scrubs to wear. I mean, it's not like I'm injured or anything, so I'm sitting on the edge, waiting for them to give me my walking papers.

As soon as the ambulance had arrived, the EMTs came straight for me. After I'd assured them I hadn't been hurt, that it wasn't my blood, they went inside the trailer. Mal had come out with a guy in handcuffs, who looked a little the worse for wear, but I still hadn't seen Clint. From what I could tell, things weren't good in there, but Mal quickly told me Clint was unharmed. Unfortunately, it turned out Jed was hurt and badly. Neil went and got the Yukon and Gus hustled me in the back, while Joe dealt with law enforcement, claiming I needed to go to the emergency to get checked out. Which is how I never got to see Clint. Until now.

His face looks haggard as he pulls aside the curtain and steps through, not pausing until he's wedged in between my legs, and cups my face in his hands.

"Baby, you okay?" he asks in a tired, soft voice.

"Fine, just fine. I tried to come to you, but they wouldn't let me. How's Jed?"

"In surgery. God, he was bad, Beth. So bad I thought he was gone a few times," his voice croaks. I wrap my arms and legs around him, trying to hold on as best I can while he dips his head down to rest his cheek on the top of mine. We're wrapped around each other like that for a few peaceful minutes, when I hear the curtain drawn back once again. Clint releases his grip on me but keeps his back to whomever's come in. I notice why when I release him and sit back. His cheeks are wet with tears and without taking my eyes of him, I address whoever stepped in, "Please, could you give us a minute?"

"I'll wait." I recognize Drew's voice coming from behind Clint and listen to the curtain closing behind him again.

From the table beside the bed I grab the box of tissues, and with a handful I carefully wipe the tears away. Clint lets me, his eyes never leaving mine, without saying a word.

"You good?" I whisper, my hand resting against his cheek and I feel him nod before his head dips and his mouth covers mine. A hard but meaningful kiss, and with his lips still touching mine he says, "Love you," before straightening up and calling for Drew to come in.

That part is less pleasant. Especially since this was the first Clint apparently hears about what happened outside. I'm still not even sure what happened. First thing Drew tells us that they were able to identify the dead man as Sam Blazek. I'm not surprised at that, but what I am surprised at is what he tells us next.

"Blazek was shot with a M1A tactical rifle or something very similar from a fair distance."

Clint sits down beside me on the bed, clutching my hand in his so hard, my fingers are about to lose function, but I'm not about to let go.

"We've yet to sit down with the other man, although we've identified him as Bogdan Lozinski, muscle for Blazek apparently. We're waiting for the FBI to come in on the interview. At some point, I'm sure they'll want to talk to you two as well, but for now you just have to deal with me. I need you to tell me exactly what happened."

For the next half hour, Clint and I alternate giving our respective accounts of that night's events. It isn't until we get to the end, when I've already cried over Clint's version of what happened inside that trailer, that I recount my experience outside. Clint abruptly gets up, moves to the end of the bed and bends his head, his knuckles white as he clenches the foot of the bed, releasing a litany of profanities under his breath. When I try to reach out for him, he shakes his head sharply. "Don't," he bites off and I retreat, hurt.

Drew observes the interaction and smiles at me gently. He's always been a good kid, even when still working as a deputy for Joe, he'd come into the diner and have such an even-keeled pleasant demeanor. He hasn't lost that gentle touch now, having worn the sheriff's badge for only a couple of months. I hope he never does.

"I'll take this back to the office, write up a preliminary report and when things settle down a bit over the next few days, we'll have you come in to sign a statement. In the meantime, I'll do my best to hold off Special Agent Gomez from barging in on you. How does that sound?"

"Thanks, Drew." I smile, despite still feeling the anger radiating from Clint, although he manages to growl, "'Preciate it."

With a small two-finger wave for me and a chin tilt for Clint, he disappears through the curtain, only to be replaced by the nurse who was in earlier.

"Okay then, let me do a quick check of your vitals, and then you're good to go."

Unnaturally complacent, I push up the sleeve of my 'borrowed' scrubs so she can get the pressure cuff on there.

"Why the vitals again? I'm fine, don't have any injuries, why hang on to me?"

The nurse tilts her head and smiles at me. "When your friend brought you in, you were showing signs of shock. Shallow breathing, pasty complexion, clammy skin, and your heart rate was all over the charts, in addition to a blood pressure which was coming up too low. You were showing mild signs of confusion, and although you appeared well able to communicate, there was a slight slur. All indicative of shock."

"But I wasn't even hurt."

"No need, sometimes highly traumatic events can induce shock even if there is no physical injury, although the symptomatology might be slightly different. We make sure with people over forty that they're not experiencing the early warning signs of heart attack. And you don't," she adds quickly, as she checks the readings, measures my heart rate, and jots it all down in a chart at the end of the bed. "All reads a lot better now and you're free to head out. Will you be with her?" she asks Clint, who is still standing by the foot of the bed.

"Won't let her out of my sight." Again with the growling. I twist my head to give him a glare, but it seems to bounce off him.

"Good. Well then, if anything happens, if you feel unwell, you start getting clammy again or get dizzy or confused, come back here right away, okay?"

"We'll be in the waiting room anyway, waiting for an update for a family member in surgery," I assure her.

"Stab wound to the abdomen?" she asks, obviously well informed, which admittedly is not hard to do. Cortez Southwest Memorial is not a big hospital. I nod at her and she goes on to say, "Why don't you have a seat in the waiting room, and I'll go see if I can find out anything on his condition, alright?" With that she leaves the cubicle, and I turn to Clint who is staring at me.

"Shoulda made you go back to the car," he says between clenched teeth. "Better yet, should never have left you there in the first place. I'd lost you today? I'd have been done for."

I get up off the bed and ignore the hand he lifts off the bed to ward me off. Without hesitation, I walk into his space until my front is plastered against his and my arms slip around his back, pulling him as tight as I can. Slowly the rejection seeps out of his body and he curls around me. One arm rounding my shoulders and the other hand sliding in my hair, pushing my head into his chest. Totally surrounded by Clint he whispers, "I swear, I wouldn't survive."

Blinking back tears I clench my hands into fists, holding onto the back of his shirt. "Honey…"

It takes everything not to punch my fist through a wall when I find out from the sheriff what happened outside, while I was struggling with that son of a bitch in the trailer. I'll be forever grateful for Mal showing up when he did. I might not have noticed the full extent of Jed's injuries otherwise, he could've bled out right under my nose. I'd never have forgiven myself. But the thought of Beth coming to harm when I was supposed to protect her, that would've ended me.

Still emotional and torn up over Jed, this news hits me hard. Hearing that she'd been forced to draw her brand new gun on a man, and then have his blood and brain matter blown all over her is upsetting enough. Strong though—fuck, is she strong. Even when I'm not sure she should be coming near me when I'm this close to losing it, she's sure enough for me. No hesitation when she ignores my attempt to keep her at a distance and plasters herself against me.

"I could use a hot drink," Beth says, shivering under the thin scrubs, "but first lets find the waiting room."

The waiting room is just down the hall, so I grab a thin hospital blanket off the bed, wrap it around Beth, and with my arm around her shoulders, take her there. Last thing I expect is the packed room that greets us. Emma, Arlene, and Seb are sitting on one side, Joe, Gus, and Neil on the other, and Naomi seems to be deep in conversation with a nurse I haven't seen around yet. The only one who seems to be missing is Mal.

It's Seb who gets up first, claps me on the shoulder, and wraps Beth up in a big hug before he's forced to give her up to the women, who flank her immediately and try to get her to sit down with them. Not Beth, she reassures them she's all right and comes straight back to me, leans in, and slips her arm around my waist.

That's how we stay for the next few hours, fueled by an endless supply of coffee and snacks from the hospital cafeteria, with the occasional pocket of soft conversation breaking the silence. It feels like a safe balloon, one where I feel the gnawing worries in my gut for my brother almost suspended, but when the door at the end of the hall opens, the balloon pops. I see the surgeon taking off his mask as he walks toward the waiting area, and my gut twists viciously. Beth curls into me deeper as both of us watch him approach.

"Mason family?" he asks and is surprised when a room full of people responds with '*yes.*' Beth's hand at my waist squeezes tightly, and I try and steel myself for what's coming.

"Mr. Mason was in very serious condition when he was brought in, having sustained a severe abdominal injury from a large blade knife. The knife almost completely severed a section of his large intestine, damaged his stomach and nicked his spleen. He also lost a tremendous amount of blood. We've had to remove the section of intestine that was damaged, repaired his stomach and removed the spleen. We also cleaned out his abdominal cavity of blood, stomach and bowel contents, but need to monitor him closely for infection. He's been continuously transfused but we are running short on stock." The doctor takes a look around the room and nods. "Luckily he is A positive. Anyone with A or O type blood can donate. I will have the nurse set up a station in one of the treatment rooms. We get him through to midday tomorrow," he looks briefly at his watch, "make that today, and we'll have a better idea of how we're doing. For now, he's through surgery, the active bleeding has been stopped, and he's been started on intravenous antibiotics preventatively. The next twelve to twenty-four hours will be a wait and see scenario." He nods around the room before saying, "I'll send Tracy in for those who'd like to donate blood." With that he's almost out the door before I catch him

"Can I see him?"

"And you are?"

"I'm his brother, please—I need to see him."

He hesitates for a moment, before giving in. "Five minutes and only you. Also, you'll have to be gloved and gowned, I'm not about to take any risks. His system can't take much more."

I follow him through the swinging doors, where I am outfitted, and a nurse shows me into a large room with three beds along one wall. Only one is occupied but it is hard to see by whom, because he is mostly obscured by a large number of machines, tubes, and hoses. I can hear the hissing of air being forced and the soft beep of one of the monitors surrounding him. I recognize what is visible of his hair and face. He looks old. Much older than his years. If I didn't hear the hiss of air going in and out of his lungs and see and hear the beep of his heartbeat on the monitor, I'd think him dead. There is no room to sit in the ICU, and I have to grab onto the foot end of the bed to keep myself upright. I stand to lose so much if I lose him. Years wasted on a woman who wasn't worth it from the start. Pain constricts my chest when I consider my only living relative, the brother I'd always considered my best friend before things went sour, might not make the night.

I move to the side of the bed and gently take his hand in mine. "I love you, Jed. Not gonna let a little nick get the best of you, are ya?" Careful not to disturb anything, I lean in and kiss his forehead, then his hand, before turning and walking from the room. Hardly notice the tears wetting my face.

When I walk through the swinging doors, Beth is waiting at the other side, her back leaning against the wall. She looks up, takes one look at me, and is in my arms holding me tight to her. My head bent down, face buried in the crook of her neck I let her hold me up. "Looks dead already," I whisper in her hair.

"He's not. He'll fight, if not for him, he'll do it for you." She sounds strong and convinced, and I hold on to that.

"Taking Emma home." Gus appears behind Beth and reaches over to put his hand on my shoulder. "She's worn out and still insisted on giving blood. Arlene and Seb are in there now. Neil's already done and has left to do some work. Naomi and Joe are hanging here to take you home when you're ready."

I let go of Beth with one arm and stick a hand out to Gus to thank him. Ignoring my hand, he curls his hand around my neck and pulls me in for a half hug. "Be in touch," he says, as he lets me go, turns, and walks down the hall. In the waiting room, Joe has Naomi cuddled up against him and both stand up when we walk in. Naomi walks over, giving me a hug while Joe slings his arm around Beth. "Joe's B positive, he can't donate, but he's gonna drive you home," Naomi says.

I shake my head, not wanting to leave, but Naomi isn't done. "Jed is well taken care of, Clint, but Beth is gonna crash any minute now. She was first in that room donating blood and won't sit down or rest until you do. I'll sleep here, so I'm close by. I swear I will let you know of any change." My eyes slide to Beth, who is leaning heavily into Joe. Not much different than the way I was hanging to her just minutes before. *Fuck.* Time to man up and look after my girl.

"Let's go," I tell her, "we need to get some rest."

She doesn't even object when I pull her from Joe's side and tuck her firmly against mine.

"Be obliged you could see us home, Joe."

"Happy to," is all he says before kissing Naomi hard, and making her promise to check in with him.

Naomi kisses both Beth and I on the cheek. "Promise to look after him."

"Thanks, Doc," I mumble, following Joe out the door, Beth tucked safely under my arm.

He's close, I can hear the wheezing of his breath behind me, and work my legs even harder. I can't see where I'm going because the night is dark, and I stumble over something, falling forward on my knees. I try to push myself up, but my hands keep slipping on the slick surface. "Beth," *I hear behind me. Franticly, I manage to scramble up partway, only to slip down again. When a sliver of moon peeks through the thick cloud deck, it illuminates a grossly distorted face lying only inches away. A vaguely familiar face, half of it gone, leaving a grisly bloody pulp in its place and I scream...*

"Beth! Jesus..."

Strong arms surround me. Slowly the softly mumbled words and familiar scent surrounding me starts penetrating and I stop struggling.

"Beth, baby. I'm here, it's okay."

My heart still pounding painfully in my chest, I become aware of where I am. In Clint's bedroom, in *his* house, with *his* body pinning me to the bed. The events of the past hours rush over me just as I'm trying to shake off the remnants of the nightmare. I prefer the nightmare. The tears I've somehow avoided all day and night, force their way up and out on a large sob.

"Let it out, Bean. Waited for this. For you to let it go," Clint mumbles in my hair, before rolling back and taking me with him. I'm draped over his chest, with his one hand tangled in my hair, pressing my face in his shoulder, and the other banding me around my back, and I let go.

After what seems like hours, when finally the tears start drying up, I lift my head to find him looking back. "I'm sorry," I mumble, slightly embarrassed.

The hand tangled in my hair tightens its grip, urging my head back down.

"No reason to be sorry. You had my back, I've got yours." His voice rumbles under my ear pressed against his chest. With his other hand he strokes from between my shoulder blades all the way down my ass, as far as he can reach, before sliding it back up. The shirt I'm wearing is bunched up almost around my neck and the slow firm strokes of his callused hand are causing my skin to heat and tingle. The hard ridge against my belly tells me Clint is as affected by our full body clench as I am, and I wiggle slightly against him.

"Bean," he growls, pulling my head up by the hair and sliding the other hand down my panties to clasp my ass, his fingers deep. My whimper is silenced when he locks his mouth on mine with a fierce intensity that pulls hard on my core. A rush of wetness slips between my legs, as the fingers of his hand slide deeper into the crevice of my ass.

"Jesus, you're soaked," he observes and suddenly rolls me over, his mouth and tongue never leaving mine and his fingers still playing in the arousal coating my pussy. "Wet for you," I mumble against his mouth. He likes that, judging by the groan I catch in my mouth before his forceful tongue stops me from talking.

My hands slide over his wide back and down to his ass where they find purchase. But they've barely copped a good feel before he leaves my mouth and pulls back, pushing my shirt up and off me before sliding his hand down, fingers snagging my granny panties and tugging them off.

Naked and exposed I lie underneath him, his eyes tracking every dip and valley of my body, and I feel not even a hint self-conscious. Not worried about my sagging tits, my swollen stomach, my neglected pubic hair, or my pitted thighs, because the heat in his eyes tells me he likes what he's looking at.

"*Beautiful,*" he says so softly, I can barely hear. "And all mine."

It's true. I'm his. A man who can make me tingle with a light touch of his working hands and flush with passion with only the stroke of his eyes over my skin can have me. Body, heart, and soul. That's when the words finally find their way to my mouth. Words the impact of which I've felt, and fought, for a long time already.

"I love you, honey." My voice is firm and full of conviction; Clint's eyes snap up from their lazy perusal and zoom in on mine. A fraction of a second he holds me right there, and shows me his heart in the shine of his eyes before pushing down his boxers. Dropping his weight between my legs, he traps my wrists in his hands by the side of my head, and guides himself inside me by feel alone. His focus never wavers. Beautiful.

"Tell me," he bites off between clenched teeth. I know what he wants to hear.

"I love you," I whisper this time, and when I go to close my eyes he stops me.

"Open," he orders, and totally against my nature, I comply.

With eyes locked on each other, our hands immobilized, and only our bodies moving with each other for maximum contact, time ceases to exist. When we finally race toward our climax, we do so together, watching the other come undone with the force of it.

"Love you, Bean," is the last thing I hear before sleep takes me, his cock inside me, and his weight on top of me a safe haven.

CHAPTER TWENTY-ONE

"Coffee?"

Gus walks into the waiting room with a tray of coffees. We've been here since six o'clock this morning, waiting for some news, but other than that Jed was stable through the night, there wasn't much more the nurse at the desk was able to tell us. I was told I could see him shortly, but that was about forty-five minutes ago.

"You're about early," Beth smiles at Gus, who sets the tray down on the coffee table in front of us, leaving us to doctor our own with the stack of sugars and creamers he pulls from his pocket.

"Don't need much sleep and I got an early morning phone call from Damien. Been up since." He takes a big gulp from his coffee before turning back to us. "Last night I left Mal to try and get a trace on the sniper who fired the shot. He was intercepted by a field agent, one attached to the FBI investigation into Stan Jablonski, who made it clear they were less than impressed with our 'interference,' as they called it. Turned into a bit of a stand off, ending up with Mal at the sheriff's office being grilled by none other than Damien Gomez, who appears less than pleased I haven't told my men to stand down."

Gus continues to explain how Damien wasn't too pleased when he pointed out that had he done as asked, a man would be dead now. Pointed out the feds might be willing to sacrifice for the greater good, but that's not how he or his men work, which made Damien even less pleased. From the sound of it the conversation was strained. Gus looks ragged, which only reminds me how lucky I am to have these people at my back.

"Thank you," I tell him quietly when he takes a break to toss his cup in the trash. He ignores me and forges on.

"Talked to Drew after, who was able to let me in on some of what he's learned. The guy you took down, Bogdan whatever the hell his name is, apparently was a tough nut to crack, but they managed to get a bit of information from him. Jablonski put the pressure on Sam to find Dylan, but put Bogdan with him to keep an eye out. He's Jablonski's man. Claims it took them a while to discover they had nabbed the wrong guy, since Jed apparently insisted he was you."

That gives me pause, thinking it would've been easy for Jed to let on they had the wrong guy, but instead he protected me by pretending to *be* me.

"Jablonski was furious, told them to get rid of him, but feeling things slipping out of control, Sam wasn't ready to give up and figured he could find out Max's whereabouts from Jed first." Gus notices Beth flinching at this and turns to her. "Not gonna let them at him, Bethie. Not a chance in hell. As we speak, Caleb and Katie are sneaking the boys to a safe place. Safer than Cedar Tree. Jablonski is anything but a fool even if his guys are. Even without Jed giving up Max's location, it won't take him long to narrow down where to look."

This time it's Beth who utters a tremulous, "*Thank you.*"

Gus grabs her hand as he shakes his head. "Family, darlin'. Yours and therefore mine. It goes without saying." Sitting back in his chair, he runs a hand through his hair. "We're closing in. Bit by bit. Bodgan claims it's Sam who stabbed Jed before taking off. No way of knowing—not that it makes a lot of difference who was actually wielding the knife. The guy's going down for kidnapping and attempted murder. And that's if he's lucky. Jablonski's reach is far, as far as the inside of a prison cell. We've seen evidence of that. FBI is trying to squeeze every last bit of information out of him before anything like that can happen."

"But who shot the other guy? Sam? I still don't get it," Beth voices what I'm thinking. I'm still not getting a clear picture.

"Mal says whoever did is highly professional. Trained and likely ex-military. No evidence left behind, other than a scuff mark on the bark of the tree Mal thinks he was holed up in. He never got a chance to explore further before he was hauled in by the FBI. Could've been one of Jablonski's men ordered to take him out before he fucked up even more, or it could've been the feds themselves who had eyes, but let too much slip for the sake of their case. Could be they had no choice when Blazek pulled on Beth. We may never find out."

At that we all fall silent, each consumed by our own thoughts, until the nurse from earlier pokes her head in.

"Mr. Mason? Would you come with me?"

I look at Gus, silently asking him to stick with Beth. A chin lift confirms he will, not that I had a doubt; he's had someone look out for us for a while now. Even last night he had Joe stay with us after he brought us home. Couldn't get him inside though, he stayed out in his truck. Keeping warm under the quilt and thermos of hot coffee Beth insisted on giving him.

I pull Beth to me and quickly kiss her mouth. "Back shortly."

"Right, honey," she says softly. Swear to God, I could be a hundred years old and never tire of Beth's brand of sweet.

This time when I walk into the room, I'm prepared for what I'll find. At least I think so, until I close in on Jed's bed, see his eyes open and looking at me.

"Hey," he croaks, his voice low and gritty.

"Jesus, Jed. She didn't warn me you're awake. That's good, man. So good. How are you feeling?" I ramble a bit, still shocked at finding him alert. I pull up a stool that is shoved against a wall and sit down, watching him shrug his shoulders.

"Not sure how I feel. Just know my gut's not doing great and my face is a mess. Other than that I'm just ducky."

I can't hold back a smile of relief before he talks again. "Not about to let a little nick get the best of me," he says, and I know even though he was out of it last night, he heard me.

"Fuck, bud, you scared me." I put my arms on the bed and rest my chin on my hands. He barks out a laugh before he can catch himself and wraps his arms around his stomach immediately, pain etched on his face.

"Fuck you for making me laugh, Clint," he bites out. "Consider the scare payback, for when you were laying in a hospital bed for a month, not waking up. You're getting off easy, having only a night of it."

Shit. He's right, and with that realization comes another one. One that I intend to set straight right away. "Never properly thanked you for that. Coming out here and dropping everything to keep the business afloat. I didn't act that way when I first saw you, but I am grateful." I hesitate, fighting myself to keep from automatically putting those shutters up again. The ones that have kept me from my own flesh and blood for way too many years. "Not just for that, though. Took guts for you to come. Don't know if I'd have had the balls, had the roles been reversed. I—"

Jed's grabs onto my wrist and his eyes are burning into mine. "Heard you last night. The feeling's mutual. Now let it go."

"Right. One thing; didn't go unnoticed, you never told them they had the wrong brother. I get you were protecting Beth and me, but word to the wise—pull a stunt like that again, and *I'll* beat your ass." I grin and the low chuckle from the bed sounds fucking amazing, even if he has to hold on to his gut.

"Time's up." The nurse who came to get me sticks her head in the door. "Gave you a little leeway already, but there are some tests waiting and the patient needs to rest. Dr. Jacob wants to keep him in the ICU until tonight. Barring any infections or other complications, he should be on the regular ward for visiting hours."

"I miss Max."

I'm bored out of my mind. Hard to imagine after the night we've had but there it is. I can't step outside the door without someone watching me, and there isn't a book that can hold my attention. To top it off, Gus strongly suggested I not go into work until this 'thing' is resolved. Not sure what or when that will be. The only thing Gus had to say was 'soon.' So I've baked trays and trays of cookies, just for something to do. The last twenty minutes, I've resorted to watching Clint in the backyard, building a platform of sorts in the big catalpa tree in the yard. Probably the most entertaining pastime of all, but even that started getting tedious. So with a fresh piece of gum, and dressed in a thick sweater, carrying a mug of coffee, I head outside.

"I do too, Bean. But you know it's safer this way." Clint turns and accepts the coffee, taking a deep drink.

"Aren't you cold?" All he's wearing is his hat and a flannel shirt, his jacket discarded on a pile of lumber by the shed.

"Nah. Physical labor warms you up. Keeps your mind off things too." He smiles at me with amusement in his eyes.

"Tried that. Have six dozen cookies to show for it. Not sure continuing on that track is advisable, given my already expanding waistline." This makes him chuckle. He hooks me by the neck, pulling me to him. It's not a hardship, standing in the crisp outdoors, my face planted in a hard broad chest, and breathing in the scent of fresh air, wood shavings, and Clint. His big hand slides up my back and under my hair to curl around my neck.

"I like your waistline," he mumbles in my hair.

"May not like it so much after I add six dozen cookies to it," I retort, snuggling in deeper when I feel the responding laughter vibrate in his chest.

"Sugar, your waistline could be twice the size and it wouldn't matter; the waistline comes with you, then I'm a happy man."

I tilt my head back to find his eyes smiling on me. "You're a charmer, Clint Mason."

"Hmmm," he hums, his eyes on my mouth. "Reckon I could think of a few ways to keep you entertained and warm."

Yeah. My body already tingling at the promise of his suggestive words, I stand up on tiptoes and touch my mouth to his lightly. Not enough it would appear, because the hand at my neck wraps in my hair, pulling my hair tight and his mouth angles over mine. I barely have time to tuck my gum in my cheek before his tongue forcefully demands entrance. *Yessss!* Pulling free his shirt in the back, I give a full body shiver at the feel of his skin under my hands while his mouth dominates mine. From zero to a hundred, my body is primed and ready as I whimper in his mouth.

"Jesus, woman. That mouth of yours should come with a warning," he softly growls as he pulls away and releases his hold on me, only to clasp my hand and pull me to the back door. "Not about to entertain an audience when I do what I mean to do to you, Bean."

Oh, I'm game.

I'm not so convinced a little later, when stripped of gum, clothes, and completely naked by Clint's deft hands, blindfolded with a tea towel, I'm trussed up like a holiday turkey with my hands tied over my head in his bed. I'm not sure, but Clint seems intent on playing. The sounds of drawers opening and closing is slightly unnerving, and the knowledge he hasn't removed any of his clothes makes me feel even more exposed. Especially when he lets the sleeve of his flannel slide over my skin, barely touching but there, causing goose bumps to appear. My hands clench into fists with every stroke for need of touching him.

"Honey…" I try.

"Quiet, Bean."

A brush of stubble on the inside of my knee sends shivers through my body and the repeat, a moment later, on the underside of my breast has my nipples pucker almost painfully.

"Please…" I breathe, only to feel his lips move against mine when he mumbles, "hush."

Callused fingertips, rough from manual labor, dance over my face, down between my breasts, over the swell of my belly, lifting away just before reaching the wetness gathering between my legs. I whimper at the loss. All I hear is my own heart pounding, and the harsh intakes of breath every time I feel his touch, suspended in anticipation for the next. A rustling sound has me tilt my head in its direction. I know he is taking off his clothes. I wait for the feel of his skin over mine, having memorized the sensation. I gasp at the unexpected scrape of something hard against my skin. I can't tell what it is, all I know is the light abrasion, that comes in sharp little scratches and long languid strokes, has every nerve in my body fully sensitized. I'm buzzing and open my mouth to plead for something, anything to end this sweet torture that has me lose any sense of time and place. But a light growl has me shut my mouth, tight. It's then I hear the heavy breaths, and it occurs to me; he's getting off on this as much as I am and an unexpected sense of power settles warm in my gut. I relax my arms, which have been straining against the binds, and let my legs fall open wide—giving myself over completely.

"There she is," he whispers only a breath away from my mouth, before nipping at my lips, his tongue tracing the contours. Teasing. At the same time his tongue slides inside and takes possession, his fingers plunge inside my pussy causing my back to arch off the bed. I can't help grinding down my hips on his hand at the sudden invasion.

"I own this pussy." His voice is deep and low against my mouth. I don't have it in me to argue about ownership, I'm too busy *feeling*. The slide of his fingers inside me, once, twice, has me so close to the edge, I feel their loss when he slips them from me.

"Appetizer," his voice rumbles in my ear, as I feel the touch of his fingers, coated in my arousal, painting my lips before his mouth plunders mine again. The spicy combination of our tastes is heady and the kiss leaves me breathless. Amazing what his mouth can do to my body, just by kissing mine. Other than our lips, there is no other contact, and it's like every cell in my body is reaching for him. When his mouth pulls away, I'm suspended once again. After the smooth wet slide of his fingers inside me and his tongue in my mouth, the abrupt scrape against the inside of my thighs is a shock to the system. No sooner has my skin adjusted to the harsh touch, it is replaced by the hot wet rasp of his tongue. Again my body shivers at the contrast, but when his mouth closes over my clit and sucks it hard inside his mouth, I'm up and over, shattering apart like particles in the wind. His mouth never leaves and with soft strong strokes of his tongue he brings me down gently.

"Could taste you all day long," he says right before a vaguely familiar hum hits my ears. Still lapping around my clit, I feel something slide inside me, the light vibration bringing my body to life again. That's where my BOB went.

She's fucking phenomenal.

I can feel the moment she gives herself to me. The muscles that strain under my hands go slack, her knees open wide in invitation, and her face now without tension, leaving her open and trusting. No fucking better high than that. Her skin even softer and her taste even sweeter now that all resistance has disappeared. The beautiful flush of her skin, wetness between her legs, and the hitch in her breaths the only measure of my effect on her. So responsive. Even the backscratcher Jed once gave to me on a lark, that for some reason I'd never gotten rid of over the years and had found a permanent spot in my shaving kit, came in mighty handy.

Fucking love playing with her. Bringing her to the edge before retreating, only to build her up again with a light touch. The moment I slide her own vibrator, the one I confiscated a while back from Max, between her swollen lips while biting down on her still sensitive clit, her body arcs off the bed and a guttural moan wrenches from her body. Before she has a chance to ride out her second orgasm, I'm between her legs, my hands pushing her knees up and open, sinking my aching cock into her. It doesn't take much and I'm right there. My mouth taking hers in a hungry kiss, I buck hard a few more times when my balls pull tight, and I shoot my cum deep inside her, as she swallows her own name from my lips.

"Yes, he's been moved to room 104. Mr. Flemming requested a private room."

The nurse at the desk smiles at my confusion.

"Mr. Flemming?" I repeat, turning around to find Gus right behind me.

"Be easier to keep an eye on him that way," he explains. "Things are heating up with the feds closing in on our man, and I'd rather not leave things up to chance."

Makes sense, even though I can't help but consider the lack of income coming from Mason Brothers, with neither Jed or I working right now. I should go in tomorrow to see what I can set up for next week and get in touch with the crews to check progress on the current jobs. So I tell Gus, who follows Beth and I to room 104. "Gotta go into the office tomorrow. See about the business."

"Tell me when. One of the guys will come with."

I stop outside Jed's door and turn to Gus. "How long are you gonna keep up covering the three of us—four, counting Max? You've got Caleb and Katie with Max, that leaves you and three more guys to cover three of us. Doesn't leave much time for anything else."

"Like I said, Damian swears he is close and has enough to hang Jablonski the moment he can get his hands on him. He keeps me in the loop, and I'm responsible for your security. I'm also still looking for Dylan. One way or another, this will be over soon."

"Can't wait," Beth voices what I'm thinking. "I need my boys back."

I'm worried we haven't heard anything from Dylan all this time, and I've seen the deep concern in Beth's eyes, too. We haven't talked about it much for which I'm glad, because I'd hate for her to have the suspicions I do about his fate.

"I'll wait out here," Gus says as I push open the door and let Beth go in first. Lingering a moment in the hallway I turn to Gus.

"Dylan?" I ask and he cottons on right away.

"Gone to ground in a way we can't seem to dig up. Could mean one of three things: Jablonski has him, which doesn't make sense cause he wouldn't be after Beth. Same goes for option two; he's dead, also doesn't make sense because of Jablonski and besides that his body would've likely turned up. And three; he has help—help from someone powerful enough to bury any trace of him. I'm voting three." His hand reaches around me for the doorknob. "Visit your brother, my friend. Let me do the worrying." With that he gives me a light shove into the room.

CHAPTER TWENTY-TWO

I hear the sliding door open and twist my head to see Beth walking toward me with my phone in her hand.

I'm making good headway with the tree house. The platform is mostly finished and I'm putting together the walls. They'll have to go up separately and I'll need someone to help me with that. The floor of the thing will be at about my eye level, which means most people would be able to stand underneath. I just didn't want it too high. Even if kids were to fall off, I'd rather have it be six feet than twelve. Max is going to love it.

I'm just trying to finish up the frame on one side before I clean up and head back into Cortez with Beth. Jed's doing much better and seems to have avoided any abdominal infection, which is a great relief. The past few days have really gone a long way to eradicating any lingering grudges. Life is too damn short to hang on to them; both Jed and I have been close enough to losing ours to make that really hit home.

Beth reaches me and puts her hand on my stomach, holding the phone up in the other.

"Left your phone in the kitchen. It's some woman for you." I reach out my hand but she presses the phone to her chest before whispering, "Says she 'needs' you, all breathy and sweet. Yuck," she says rolling her eyes.

I fight a grin as I take the phone from her hand. She's a nut.

"Mason."

"Oh hi, Clint." Sarah fucking Creemore. Should've figured. The woman was hard enough to shake off the first time. I lucked out when Jed ended up drawing her attention.

"What can I do for you, Ms. Creemore?"

"Please call me Sarah, Clint. No need to be so formal, after all, we did have lunch together."

The woman really rubs me the wrong way, so I keep my eyes on Beth when I respond. "Ms. Creemore, we had a business meeting after which my brother took on the work on your house. Now what is the reason for your call?"

"That's just it, you see? I can't seem to get a hold of Jed, and I have a big problem."

My turn to roll my eyes. From what Jed's told me, the bitch is making up shit to keep him busy. I'm sure this is just another ploy for attention. Beth is listening closely, her sweater wrapped tight around her to ward off the cold chill, but her mouth is tilted up at the sides. She enjoying this, the little minx.

"Jed's temporarily unavailable. What did you need him for?" I'm being short and borderline rude, but the woman seems unable to take a hint. She just keeps at it with what is probably supposed to be seductive with her sugar-sweet voice and silly giggles, but it only aggravates me more.

"I have a flood."

I wait patiently for more information, but when none is forthcoming, I raise my eyes to the sky and pray for patience.

"You have a flood."

"Yes, there must be a leak in the master bath somewhere because water is coming from the bottom of the vanity."

I lift my hat and scratch in frustration at the light stubble that's growing in on my head. Last I knew, Jed and his crew had finished the new master bath a week or so ago. *Dammit.*

"I have to be in Cortez later. I'll swing by in an hour or so. Check it out."

"Oh yay! That's such a relief," she titters like a teenage girl, stupid behavior for a grown ass woman. "I'll make sure to have a pot of fresh coffee and some lunch for you."

Oh hell, no.

"Ms. Creemore," I say firmly. "I'll come over to look at the leak. That's my job. No need for fresh coffee or lunch, it's not a social visit and I won't take long." Before she has a chance to respond I disconnect. That's when Beth starts laughing, her eyes sparkling with amusement, mouth wide showing her pretty white teeth. I reach out, grab her arm and pull her hard against me. She immediately slides her arms around my waist, head tilted back looking up at me, still with the big smile on her face.

"Trouble in paradise, baby?"

"Watch it, woman," I grunt as I lean in and kiss the smile off her face.

"So who is this?" Joe asks from the passenger seat.

I'd called Gus to let him know we were on our way to the hospital, but that I would drop Beth off and head out for a quick check on a job. He suggested Neil, who was our bodyguard for the day, would stay with Beth in the hospital. He would call Joe, who was in town anyway, checking in with the sheriff's office, and would meet me at the hospital.

"A pain in my ass is what she is. Doesn't understand the meaning of 'I'm not interested,' and has her eyes set on one or the other Mason brother. Been there, done that, and have the T-shirt."

Joe hisses between his teeth. "Sounds like a story."

"It is. It's a long and complicated one, but it's done. One day over a beer, maybe."

"Fair enough." Joe, good guy that he is, drags my thoughts back to where they should be. "Besides, you've got Beth. Nothing like the love of a good woman to put shit in perspective."

"You've got that right."

We say nothing more until we pull into Sarah's drive. She's already standing on the porch, waiting with a big smile on her painted face. Dressed to the fucking gills in a skin tight dress that leaves nothing to the imagination, since her tits are spilling out the top, and the bottom barely covers her crotch.

"Fuck me sideways," I curse, as Joe says, "Holy shit," at the same time.

"Probably should come in with me. Don't trust the bitch."

"I'm thinking not a bad idea. No worries, I've got your back," Joe mutters, getting out of the truck.

After Clint kissed me goodbye, thoroughly and not caring about Neil and Joe watching, he took off with Joe taking my place in the passenger seat. Off to see to a leak. Whatever. I turn, smile up at Neil and slip my arm through his.

"Walk me inside, handsome?"

273

He does as I ask, despite my attempt to lighten the heavy pall hanging over us and the resulting small lift of the corner of his mouth, Neil is all business. Which in turn makes me all antsy. There's something in the air.

"Hey."

"Hey. You're looking a bit better. But we seriously have to find some better places to meet. You guys get a family discount or something?" I joke, earning a smile from Jed.

"Surprised to see you without my brother attached to your side. Where is he?"

"Had to go see to a leak," I smile when I see Jed pull up an eyebrow, "at your favorite customer's home." A laugh bubbles up when I see Jed's face go from questioning to confused, finally twisting in a look of utter disgust.

"Sarah Creemore? Holy shit, I hope he brought some reinforcement because that woman's like a piranha. She's gonna chew him up."

"No worries. He's got Joe with him for muscle." I snicker at the thought of a bunch of big, brawny, grown men shivering over some woman. "I've got Neil. He got Joe."

"Things coming to a head?" Jed wants to know, his expression one of concern now.

"I don't know. There's something oppressive in the air though, but that could just be my imagination. Ready for this to be over. I miss my babies."

"Still nothing on Dylan?"

"Not even a hint. But Gus had a theory that he shared with Clint yesterday. Says if anything really bad had happened to him, we'd likely have found him by now. He thinks Dylan had help from someone to stay out of sight."

"You don't say?" Jed covers his mouth when a big yawn escapes on the last word.

"Why don't you grab a nap? I'll go see about something to eat. It's coming on lunchtime. Can I bring you something back?"

"Maybe I will, didn't sleep a lot last night. Don't need anything from the caf though. I'm still on restricted diet," he reminds me.

"Shit. Sorry, totally forgot about that. Anyway, just rest. I'll be back in a bit."

I find Neil chatting in the hallway, a little ways down, with one of Drew's deputies. Just as Gus has had someone cover Clint and me at all times, turns out Drew has made sure someone had an eye on Jed in the hospital. Neil's eyes turn to me when he sees me walking up to them.

"Jed's having a nap. I'm gonna see if I can grab something at the cafeteria. You guys want something?"

"I'm good, thanks," the deputy says, but Neil pushes away from the wall and grabs my hand to pull it through his arm.

"I'm coming with," he states, marching us down the hall.

It's busy inside the hospital cafeteria. Seems we've just caught a shift change or something, because most of the crowd is hospital staff by the looks of it. I grab yogurt and a muffin, just something to tide me over until Clint gets back, and shuffle in the line to the cash register. Once I paid—something Neil made me fight over—I walk away with the win and out the door, when his phone rings. He stops in the hallway to answer it and I keep going toward Jed's door, giving Neil some privacy. The deputy must've gone for a bathroom break or something because his chair is empty when I pass it to go into Jed's room.

"Oh, I'm sorry, I can come back later," I mumble when I find a male nurse bent over Jed's IV line. He turns to me and smiles.

"No worries, I'm just giving him the last of his intravenous antibiotics."

Jed still appears to be sleeping, since he's not reacting, but a small niggle of worry has me walk over to the bed and lean over him.

"Jed?" I barely get his name out before an arm slips tight around my neck, and I feel the pinch of a needle at my neck. Then the world turns black.

"Jesus that woman is something else."

"Jed calls her a piranha, but she's more like an octopus to me," I tell Joe, who's still shaking his head, after we finally manage to get away from the Creemore woman. She'd been completely in my space at every damn turn. Going so far as to step over me as I'm on my belly with my head in the vanity to tighten up the connections that were loose, giving me a full view of her very bare pussy under the much too tight dress she was wearing. Not adverse to exposed pussy normally, this woman's wares are not a turn on. Not when basically stuck in my face. Fuck. That shit makes me feel almost violated.

She wasn't too happy when I asked her, barely hanging on to my temper, to move her ass out of the way so I could get up. Next thing you know, she turns to Joe, rubbing her tits against his arm. By the look of revulsion on his face, he's no more welcoming to her attention as I was. Christ what a morning.

"Figure she loosened that shit herself?" Joe asks.

"Wouldn't put it past her. Glad I had you there. Figure it kept her from literally throwing herself at me. Although, judging from what almost looked like a vertical lap dance she treated you with, she's an equal opportunity man-eater." An involuntary shiver runs through me.

"Don't say it often, but that chick needs to get laid in the worst possible way, but I pity the man who steps up to the task." Joe does his own light shake of the shoulders.

We're on our way back to the hospital, to check on Jed and hook up with Beth, when Joe's phone rings. Just as I hear him swear loudly, I have to slam on my brakes when I turn the corner onto the hospital parking lot. A Healthcare Laundry van comes tearing out of the loading dock, barely missing my front fender. When I look back at the loading dock where it came from, I see Neil jumping down the platform and running for his ride.

"Go after it!" Joe yells from beside me, pointing at the van that's now turning right onto North Mildred Road, barreling toward the 160. Takes only a second for me to react, but then I have both hands on the wheel and my foot all the way down on the gas, tearing out of the parking lot.

"Putting you on speaker phone," I hear Joe say, and then Gus's voice sounds clear in the cab of the truck, freezing the blood in my veins.

"Clint, buddy. Beth's in that van. Someone got to Beth from inside Jed's room. Neil was in the hallway, saw a hospital employee come out the door with a laundry cart. He checked the room, found Beth gone and took off after the guy with the cart, only to see them load it in the van and take off. Keep a cool head and listen to Joe."

"Beth…" is the only thing I manage to get out of my mouth.

"We'll get her," Gus says firmly.

"But—" I try again, but he cuts me off.

"No buts. We'll *get* her. Now focus on driving. Neil's behind you, he may slip in front, given the chance, and you're gonna let him. Get me?" Gus's tone demands a confirmation, so I give it to him.

"I got you."

"Good, leave the line open, Joe, and give me play by play."

"Will do. Coming up behind him at the intersection with the 160, and he just got through in easterly direction. I repeat, he's on the 160 in the direction of Mancos." To me he says, "Get behind him. Now."

Disregarding all other traffic, I plow into the intersection and with the sounds of screeching tires all around me, I manage to turn left in pursuit.

"Fuck. Please tell me I didn't leave a massive accident behind," I tell Joe, who briefly looks over his shoulder.

"Doesn't look like it, although some may have shit their pants and will need their cars detailed. Quite the maneuver there, Clint," Joe says, a hint of appreciation in his tone.

"Good man," comes Gus's mumble over the phone, but I barely hear anything right now, I'm so focused on the van's back doors.

"Once out of city limits, Neil's planning to come around you and you'll try to box him in. Take his lead. Got a gun?" Gus wants to know.

"Glove compartment."

Joe fumbles around and comes up with my weapon, checking it for ammunition. Should be loaded, which is how I've had it the last while.

"Ready and loaded," he reports to Gus.

"They're gonna come up shooting, I'm sure. At least two in the van. Driver and the guy in scrubs. Be prepared."

Joe puts my gun on my leg and checks his own, pulled from a shoulder holster under his jacket.

The van is weaving in and out of traffic, and I do my best to stick close. I'm pretty positive they know they're being followed, and I'm wondering what they're leading us into.

"Keep an eye out. We're approaching Denny Park, once past there, I'm thinking Neil will make his move," Joe points out, but Gus comes with some new information.

"Actually, I've signed into the tracking software Neil's installed, and Beth's bleep is moving. I'm thinking they took her purse with them, or she had her phone in her pocket. I suggest you drop back a little, let them think they have a chance at dodging you. Then when their guard is down, we can go in and have surprise on our side. I'd much rather that than a shootout."

"Gotcha," I tell him, easing back on the gas to let them get ahead some. It goes against the grain, not racing after them to grab my woman back, but it makes me feel a hair better that Gus has a bead on her whereabouts. I'm not an idiot, I know my friends have the experience and know-how to deal with a situation like this, where I don't. I'm simply ruled by the basic need to protect her, but given the nature of the adversary we face, my instincts will not likely be a match for Jablonski's ruthless cunning. At least that's who I assume has her.

"They're turning right. There's an access road to a KOA camp on the south side of the park. They've taken that. Pull over and wait for Neil to take lead."

Biting down my frustration at taking a backseat, I nevertheless roll onto the shoulder of the road, waiting for Neil, who's three cars behind me, to pull ahead. The instant he passes, my foot is back on the gas, and I'm hugging his bumper. I'll let him go ahead, but I'm not about to let him get far.

"Camp would be closed this time of year, right?" I throw out, wondering out loud.

"Open May through end of October, so yeah—it's shut down. No one should be there. Hang on one sec, Damien is on the other line." I hear Gus's voice in the background as I turn behind Neil's truck onto a gravel path that runs into the trees. Through the open line I can hear Gus's conversation get heated.

"Like hell I'm standing down—You're playing with lives here, Damien—I don't give a flying fuck about your men needing time to set up a takedown, this gets done now. Not gonna wait around for you guys to pull your heads out of your collective asses—"

I can only hear Gus's side of the conversation when Neil pulls off to the side of the road and stops. I have no choice but to pull over behind him. Then Gus starts speaking again and the tone of his voice has turned dangerous.

"Say what? You'd better be fucking joking, because if I find out you've been playing us—not to mention used the woman they now have their hands on—to make your case for you, I'm gonna rip your fucking head off and shove it up your ass. Where it belongs." A bang and a series of colorful swearwords later, Gus's voice comes through clear.

"Feds are five minutes behind you. Ignore the fuckers, just go in silent and assess, but do it quickly. I want to use the element of surprise, and the moment those clowns get there, that'll be lost. They're planning on coming in with heavy artillery. Neil, Joe, you got me?" A firm yes from Joe and some mumbling in the background, which I assumed to be Neil on an open line as well, in response. "Clint, be ready and stay alert. You go in half-cocked and that could cost lives. You got me?"

My teeth grind when I bite off, "Got you."

"Good. Neil's got vests in his truck. Grab one, put it on. You guys are going in on foot. You drive up, they'll see you coming. For now they're thinking they ditched you. That's what we want."

Joe slips an earbud in, grabs the phone, taking it off speaker, and tucks it in his pocket before getting out. I follow suit on the other side, snagging my gun and like Joe, gently close the door instead of slamming it shut. Neil is already out, and from the toolbox in the bed of his truck, he pulls Kevlar vests, tossing one to me. Mirroring the guys, I take off my jacket, my shirt and strap the vest on against my skin before quickly dressing again. Fuck it's cold.

"Why underneath?" I want to know.

"If it's visible, the likelihood is bigger they'll shoot to avoid hitting the vest. If hidden we might get lucky. Anyone with a bit of common sense will aim for the largest part of the body, the torso. A shot in the limbs you'll survive, the head is difficult to hit, so they'll try for the upper body," Joe quietly explains, while redressing himself over his vest. "You get hit, you'll be winded and likely bruised, but alive."

Right.

Motioning me behind Neil and in front of Joe, we walk down to a slight bend in the path where Neil holds up his hand.

"Straight line from here to the gate, and visible," he whispers, "so we slip into the trees. Stick behind me."

Although I have to fight my instincts to run in like a bull in a china shop, I heed his words and slip in behind him, traipsing through underbrush and trees on the side of the road. We've walked maybe five hundred yards in silence when Neil puts up his hand again and turns back to us, whispering.

"Gus established satellite view. There's a dirt track up ahead, cutting through the woods to a maintenance shack. Two cars parked behind it, laundry van in front. One guy out front, no others visible. We get within range, you guys sit tight, I'm gonna see what we have for windows. Wanna know if they can see us coming. If I can take out the guy standing sentry I will."

CHAPTER TWENTY-THREE

"How much you give her?"

"Not much. Enough to get her quietly out of the hospital."

The first voice has a slightly nasal sound, with a thick accent, the second one sounds like a heavy smoker. I'd noticed him wheezing when he pulled me out of the laundry basket. I'd woken up, almost folded in half, and surrounded by dirty hospital linens and had to fight not to make a sound or move. Had no intention of letting on I was awake, and so far have been able to fake it, keeping my body slack and heavy and my breathing deep and slow. Was almost impossible when I was hauled out of the basket and rough hands searched me, but it seems I got away with it. My hands are tied at my back and the cold is creeping in, since I'm without my coat. It's probably still at the hospital. It's difficult to stop my body from shivering.

"You sure there was no tail?" The man with the accent asks.

"Lost them on the way out of town," the other guy says. My heart does a little jump at the knowledge someone knew I'd been taken. I know they'll be able to find me as long as I stick close to that van. I dropped my phone at the bottom of the basket that's in the back of it, afraid they'd take it off me once they got me out. I remembered the tracking app Neil had installed weeks ago and hope I did the right thing.

A sudden splash of cold water hits my face, and I can't stop my body from reacting. My hands pull at the ties, my eyes pop open, and I gasp at the impact. Okay, *now* I'm fucking cold. I'm also terrified when the man with the bucket in his hand, the same guy who was in Jed's room, steps aside revealing a man in suit and overcoat, donning a large knife in his hand. His eyes are the palest blue and without emotion. He seems younger than I'd have expected—maybe around my age. I had thought he would be a decade or maybe two older. At least if this is who I think it is: Jablonski.

"Ah yes. Ms. Franklin. Or Beth is better?" His voice is soft and syrupy, creeping me out. I'd rather he was yelling. I keep my mouth firmly shut. I'm not giving an inch, not that I have anything worth giving. I don't know where my son is, or even where Max is, so I can't even accidentally spill. For the first time I'm glad I know nothing. He can do whatever he wants to me, but he'll never use me to get to my babies. With that I lift my chin and look at him straight, my mouth firmly closed.

"I see you don't wish to cooperate. Pity. For you. For me it is bonus. I like challenge and I like playing with my knife."

I try to suppress the shudder his thick rolling words evoke, and try not to look at the white gunk collecting in the corners of his mouth. It's disgusting. Instead I tilt my head higher, which he seems to find amusing, judging by the crooked smirk on his face. Never mind wanting to curl up in a ball and cry for help, I have a feeling he'd get off on that. There is no way in hell I'll give that to him. I can't stop myself from praying silently for someone to come rescue me. I have a feeling one way or another, this is not going to end well for me.

That is only confirmed when he brings the tip of the knife to my cheek and presses lightly with the tip into the skin. I can't help the automatic flinch and hate myself for it when I see his eyes light up at my reaction. The fucking freak gets off on this.

"I'd like to know where is your son, Ms. Franklin. I'm afraid I cannot let him walk, he knows too much. He would not leave his mother without informing of his destination, *No?*" He lets the tip of the blade scrape my cheekbone. I hold my breath, only to release it in a *woosh* when, with a swift move of his hand, he slices across my skin. The sharp sting of the blade takes a few minutes to take effect, and my eyes fill with tears at the burn. I'm still not speaking. Even if I had the information he wants, I wouldn't give it to him. Looking in those ice blue, emotionless eyes, I know it wouldn't matter anyway; I'm already dead to him. Another reason why I won't speak. I figure as long as I provide him with a challenge, I buy some time. The moment he cottons on I really have nothing to contribute, I'll be dead. And I'll be damned if I give him my fear to feed off of, even if I can smell the stink of it on myself. Ignoring the tears slipping from my eyes, and the warm blood running down my cheek and into my mouth, I lift my chin again and see, with no small measure of satisfaction, a hint of surprise slip over his features.

"Not a smart woman, Ms. Franklin. Opposing me will not help," he hisses, his face so close to mine I can smell his foul breath and can't stop the involuntary shiver that runs down my spine. "There are many ways to make a woman willing, if pain will not work, but I enjoy cutting." With another flick of his wrist he has the front of my shirt open and a long red stripe bisecting my chest. Shallow, I see looking down, thank God. Blood beading along the edges of the cut. But this time I can't stop the fear. I start shaking from head to toe. I won't fucking cower to him. As long as I'm offering a challenge, he stays willing to play. He may cut me, but if I keep his attention, he won't kill me. Yet.

"I think perhaps my men would like to try their way?" He throws a look over his shoulder at the other guy, who's been leaning with his back against the wall, not interfering but simply observing. The smile that breaks through on his face at Jablonski's words is far scarier than his knife-wielding boss. My skin crawls as his eyes slide proprietarily down my exposed chest and linger on my breasts. He pushes away from the wall, walks up, and traces the cut down my chest with his filthy finger, gathering blood in its path, before licking it off with a disgusting slurping sound. His hand reaching out again, this time going for my breast and I squeeze my eyes shut. But I'm still not talking. A dull thud from outside the single door has me snap them open. Jablonski and his lackey have heard as well. With slow measured moves, Jablonski gets up from the crate he was sitting on in front of me and stalks to the side of the doorway. The other guy moves behind me, the cold barrel of a gun pressed against my head. His other hand grabs my throat and pulls me up against his front. Jablonski slides his back along the wall to the side of the door, keeping his knife along his leg, his head tilted, listening. I try to listen too, but don't hear a thing. Suspended in time, for what seemed like a very long period but was likely no more than minutes at most, I finally hear a light scraping at the door and feel the guy behind me go on alert. Jablonski visibly primes himself for attack with an intensity that I can taste across the cluttered room. The hand around my neck tightens, as I'm being pulled behind the bulk of a riding lawnmower. With a click the door unlatches and a hand pushes it inward from outside. Sensing Jablonski's move, I can't hold back.

"Knife!" I scream as loud as I can, which isn't saying much, since the hand at my throat is barely affording me the passage of air, so it comes out garbled. But whomever is on the other side hears enough to pull back at the same time Jablonski lashes out, catching only the hand with the sharp blade. Immediately a body rolls in from outside, surprising Jablonski, who jumps to the side instinctively to avoid being bowled over and mayhem ensues.

"Knife!"

The moment I hear Beth's voice, I ignore Joe's restraining hand and push up the old rolling garage door at the back of the building as the shots start flying, some pinging off the metal door so close to my hands I can feel the vibrations. But I don't stop. My Bean is in there. Joe has sidled up to me.

"Hold on to the door while I go under," he says, his hands gripping the door next to mine, but rather than do as he says, I let go, drop to roll through the gap under the door and into the fray.

First thing I see is Beth, who is clutching onto the arm of a man holding her by the throat, blood coating her face. His eyes whip from the front of the shed to the tussle I can hear there, to me. The moment his eyes hit mine, the gun he was waving around settles on Beth's head. *Fuck*. My eyes settle on her scared ones, making my gut burn. It isn't until I notice the front of her clothes, hanging awkwardly spread open, leaving her torso bare with a long cut running down the centre, that I lose my mind and charge. I hear the gun go off and register Beth dropping down, but nothing can stop my attack. Not even the volley of bullets flying my way, one of which almost knocks me on my ass but I keep going, despite the fact my lungs aren't getting any air.

"FBI!"

I feel myself pulled away from the man, whose face more resembled ground beef than the ugly mug he was toting before. I hear Joe's voice in my ear, but it takes a while for me to register what he says.

"You've got him. He's done, brother. He's done."

It's then I notice the room filled with FBI agents, all decked out in bullet proof vests and signature dark jackets, sporting the familiar letters on their back, all staring at me. Fuck that. Ignoring them, my eyes are drawn immediately to Beth, who is sitting on the ground still completely exposed. My fucking knuckles are bleeding and something else is, but I crawl my way over to her and pull her in my arms, dropping my face in her neck.

"I thought he—" my voice doesn't sound right and I try again. "I thought—"

"Shhh. I'm here, I'm good." The sound of her voice such a relief, I can't hold back the sob escaping.

"Sir, we need to—" One of the agents approaches but Joe, who's sticking close, shoves him back.

"Back away. Both of them need medical care and until cleared by a doctor at the hospital, you're getting dick-all. Now move the fuck away."

"Sir, we need to take a statement."

I look at the door, where Special Agent Damien Gomez is holding out his badge. I don't need to see it to know who he is, Gus pointed him out when he briefed me on their earlier telephone conversation, the one that left Gus swearing up a storm.

Beth and I are sharing a treatment room in the ER, neither of us wanting to be separated from the other. The cut on Beth's cheekbone is deep, but apparently very clean, and according to the plastic surgeon who was in to stitch her up, the scar it'll leave a barely distinguishable thin line. I sure as fuck hope so. Not that it matters one iota to me, but I don't want to have her reminded of the nightmare she lived through each and every morning she looks in the mirror. No fucking way. She had, quite literally, dodged a bullet when I made my move and had dropped down right away. The guy was so preoccupied with me coming for him, she slipped easily from his hands.

I was peeled out of the Kevlar vest I was very fortunately wearing, since two slugs apparently lodged in the hardy material. Still, when the vest came off, I wasn't prepared for the massive bruising that had already started on my chest. Joe chuckled and said it was a rite of passage, to get shot at. Beth got pissed at that, said loudly and for everyone to hear, that it was enough of a rite of passage to get your head bashed in, no need to hold out for the bullets. That only made Joe laugh out loud.

"Think of it this way, Bethie. He's had it all now, he's done for the rest of his life."

"I fucking hope so," she spit out, not at all amused.

The bruising will fade, although I was warned it could be sore. Whatever. The third bullet took a chunk out of my bicep and that ticked me off. I hadn't even noticed it. Not when it happened, and not when I was whaling on Jablonski's sidekick. Beth noticed that some of the blood I was covered in, was actually partially mine. So while she was being stitched up, luckily her chest wasn't deep and just needed cleaning and dressing, the attending was stitching me up as well.

That's when Gus came in and briefed us on that bastard, Damien Gomez.

So now that he's standing in the door of the room, where I'm trying to comfort a crying Beth on my lap, still trying to come to terms with the fact I nearly killed the guy who was hurting her. I don't even think. I get up and let Beth's legs slide down to the floor, never taking my eyes of that fucking son of a bitch as I urge her to sit down. When she does, it takes two steps for me to be in range to swing at his face. He obviously wasn't expecting that, since he didn't even move, and I'm shaking out my fist, that was already throbbing from the earlier beating I handed out.

"That's assault, your second for the day," the ignorant prick dares suggest, making me even angrier as I grab him by the collar.

"You self-serving bastard. You dangled my woman like a fucking carrot for fucking *weeks*! All because you were so desperate to get your hands on Jablonski. You let her believe for fucking *weeks* that her son was alone and unprotected somewhere out there, planting his phone for Jablonski to find, so he'd think Dylan took off. Knowing full fucking well that he'd use any information on that phone to try and find him. Also knowing full well that when you did that, you left his mother out to swing in the wind. You fucking did all this knowingly, when all the time you had him confined to a safe house, refusing him the call that would've put his mother's mind and heart at ease." I twist his collar, tightening it on his throat. "You refused to take action when you first saw her being beaten on in the parking lot, and the second time when she was drugged and kidnapped from the hospital. To top that off, you slacked off on the follow up, allowing them to cut my woman."

I lean in to where my nose is almost touching his. "In the fucking face!" I feel a hint of satisfaction when I see him flinch as I bellow the last right in his mug.

From behind me I feel a hand slide across my back.

"Big Guy, let me in here," she whispers, the tears still evident in her voice. I move back just a little, letting go of his neck while Beth inserts herself between us. "You can send in someone else to take a statement," she hisses in his face, "'cause you'll be too busy nursing *this.*" With that she hauls out her arm and with her full bodyweight behind it, slams her fist in his face. Something he obviously didn't expect. His hands come up to cover his nose, but only after my Bean managed to find it with great precision. Slipping my arms around her waist, I pull her back with me while she shakes out her hand.

"Jesus. You broke my nose," Damien mumbles from behind his hands.

"Lucky that's all she did," Gus announces, walking in the room and taking stock of the situation. "Better get that looked at," he suggests with the hint of a smile in his voice. "Beth's got a mean right hook."

Without a word, just a dirty look, Damien slinks out of the room and Gus turns to face us.

"Feel better?" he asks Beth, who is still nursing her hand but doesn't hesitate in answering.

"Fuck yes."

"Good, cause that's the only shot you'll get. I'll have a word to try and make it so that this doesn't blow back on you. Word to the wise though, assault on an FBI agent is generally not a good idea. Although, this one was more deserving than most." He stands with his arms folded over his chest and still his admonishment doesn't quite have the desired effect. Maybe because he can't seem to fight the smile that steals over his face.

Neil walks in, crooked grin on display, carrying a baggie of ice he hands to Beth. "Put that on there, Slugger, but keep moving your fingers so they don't stiffen up." His hand was sliced in the altercation, and had required some stitches, but he refused the bandages the nurse had tried to wrap around it, claiming it would interfere with his keyboarding. Computer techie covering up a kick-ass operative. He'd struggled Jablonski to the ground, avoiding any further damage from the knife he was wielding, and managing to dodge the shots from the other guy's gun at the same time. Definitely someone you'd want on your side. I was looking at Neil with a whole new level of respect.

"They're gonna have to talk to you at some point, might as well get it over with," Gus suggests. "Why don't I see if we can move this show to Drew's offices. May be a good idea to have him sit in at the same time. Saves everyone time."

God that felt good. What didn't feel so good was the throbbing of my hand after, a small sacrifice to make. After icing it for a bit, the ER doc came in to have a look; said it was fine but to be prepared for it to smart for a bit. With a shake of his head, he told both Clint and I we were good to go.

So after a quick check in with Jed, we go straight from the hospital to a meeting in the conference room at the sheriff's office. After the interview with two FBI agents—Damien nowhere in sight, thank God—as well as Drew, Neil, Joe, Gus and both Clint and I that lasted two hours, we finally are home.

Home being Clint's house. I carefully snuggle up to Clint, who is laying on his back in bed. Each of us nursing our battle wounds.

"I can't believe they're gonna keep Dylan in hiding," I mumble against his good shoulder. After letting me talk to Dylan finally—a tearful conversation on both sides, full of remorse on the part of my son—I was told that for his own safety, seeing as they want him to testify, Dylan would be held in protective custody indefinitely.

"Sucks. But I can see it'd be safer that way," Clint's deep rumble soothes over me. "Max'll be here tomorrow when Caleb and Katie bring him back, and you can love on him without worry. Dylan's safe where he is. He was out there somewhere, Jablonski wouldn't hesitate keeping after him, and therefore *you*. With him in custody, they have the head of the snake, but the body is still writhing. Until they can decimate the entire organization, you know he wouldn't be safe. His testimony is crucial." His hand draws lazy circles on my shoulder as he talks and my eyes are getting heavy. Been a long day and it's nearly midnight, but I can't quite stop my head from spinning, reorganizing everything I thought I knew since Max was dropped off on my doorstep. A disturbing thought enters my mind and I lift my head.

"What about Tammy? Max's mom?" I clarify when I see the blank look on Clint's face. "Where is she? Why hasn't she come forward? Her brother is still being held in jail, and I can't imagine her walking away like that, without ever checking in with her family or more importantly, her child."

Clint lifts his hand and tucks my hair behind my ear. "We'll ask Gus tomorrow if he's heard something, yeah? Let's get some rest now, babe. Tomorrow that little monster will be tearing up the house again, we're gonna need our energy."

293

With a hand on my neck, he pulls me down to his mouth, kissing me deeply before releasing his hold. I put my head down on his shoulder and with his arms firmly around me, breathing in the smell of shower gel on his skin, I let myself slide into sleep. Last thing I hear him whisper in my hair is, '*Love you*'.

CHAPTER TWENTY-FOUR

"He's loving it."

I'm watching Beth walk toward me from the back door, where she was watching Max climb the few steps it takes to get onto the finished platform and tree house we finished building yesterday. Since my injuries had slowed me down some in the progress, we had our first minor snowfall last week threatening to halt construction until spring, I didn't hesitate when all the guys showed up yesterday, armed with tool belts and offered to finish it with me. With Gus, Mal, Joe, Seb, Caleb, and Neil all helping out, it took less than six hours to put the walls and roof up, build stairs and a railing around the platform. The women all congregated in the kitchen and living room, keeping Max and Mattias occupied and cooking up a feast. When it was all done, I found our home filled with friends spread out over the house, eating, drinking, and laughing. I can't remember a time I felt this at home.

This morning is better, seeing the look on the little guy's face when I brought him outside. He's been glued to our sides ever since Caleb and Katie brought him back. I realize I've fallen in love with him as much as with his grandmother. Hearing his bright little voice calling for his 'Gammy' every morning, filling the tiny hole in my heart that always waited for children to fill one day.

I'm sitting with my back against the shed, my hat on my head keeping the chill off, watching Beth move to me. The smile on her face so big, it draws almost all the attention from the still bright red scar across her cheek. Almost, because every time I see it I remember the uncontrollable rage that came over me seeing her cut and bleeding. Hair loose, cascading down her shoulders, having given up tying it back, when I just continue to pull it free, and her soft body wrapped in a quilt from the back of the couch. When she gets close, I open my legs, pull her back against my front and wrap her in my arms, my chin resting on her shoulder.

"He's a little monkey, the way he goes up and down that ladder. Never thought a two-year-old could be so agile," I mumble in her hair.

"Should've seen his dad. I had to pull him down from the pantry shelves, more than a few times, when he was that age. Obsessed with animal crackers that kid was. No hiding place was safe, he always managed to zoom in on them. So it stands to reason he passed on some of this to his boy." Her voice sounds a bit wistful when talking about Dylan. She's talked to him a few times over the past few weeks, but always short and coming away none the wiser on when she'd be able to see him. We did start taking pictures of Max that we were able to send to an email provided to us, and in talking to Dylan, we know he gets every last one of them. At least that's something. My anger at Dylan has slowly evaporated. Yes, the kid made a stupid move, but he tried to rectify it without anyone getting dragged down. He hadn't counted on one Damien Gomez of the FBI to let the heat come down on his mother. That part was on Damien, not Dylan. So I could let that grudge go. Word is, it'll be months before Jablonski's case goes to trial, and the progress on rolling up the rest of his syndicate is slow. Hence, Dylan's return to his family won't be any time soon, either.

We're still being careful, never knowing if there will be additional blow back our way, but things have been quiet.

Beth's returned to work at the diner, only taking the dinner shifts so that I work during the day, and she works a few hours at night. One of us is always with Max that way, although it doesn't leave a whole lot of time for the two of us together. That's why Sunday and Monday are sacred, and I've adjusted my hours to fit that. With Jed still recuperating in Gus and Emma's guesthouse, which they so graciously offered him this last week since he's been home, I've put more responsibility on the shoulders of our foremen, who are stepping up to the plate.

Still, I feel like life is suspended, and I'm itching to do something about that. In a short period of time, my roots here in Cedar Tree have grown deep and solid. I can't see myself anywhere else when I have good friends, a successful business, and a woman, who's enriched my life in a way I'd never dreamed possible right here. Christmas is coming up in a little over a week, and I'm finding myself looking forward to it for the first time since leaving home.

"You're thinking so hard, I can hear the wheels turning." Beth twists her head back and smiles at me and I don't hesitate. I take her smiling mouth and pour everything I'm feeling into it.

"Clint..." she whispers when I pull up a little. Her hand comes up and strokes the scruff on my jaw. "Love you, honey," she says, her eyes bright.

"This here, right now, is everything to me," I tell her. "You cozy in my arms, telling me you love me. Our little guy happy and playing in the tree house I've always wanted to build for my children. We've been through some shit, but here we are on the other side, with all *this* in our life. Not a religious man, Bean, but I feel blessed. Only thing that would make this better would be you hauling the rest of your shit over here and making this your permanent home."

Her eyes mist over and she covers her mouth with her hand. "Big Guy…"

"Baby. We're both forty-six and have already spent too much time fucking around. I want you in my life. And more so, I want that in a way that is permanent."

Lifting up she brushes her lips against my mouth. "Okay, honey. I'll haul my shit over here and set up shop permanent-like." The little smile on her face tells me she's teasing before she gets serious. "I'm just not ready to sell my little house yet. Maybe we can rent it out?"

Before I have a chance to answer, Max lets himself be known, effectively drawing all attention. "Gammy!"

"Yes, little man?" Beth slips from my arms and walks over to the ladder, looking up at Max's big smile.

"Me hungwy."

I laugh, seeing as not much more than an hour ago, Max was wolfing down a stack of pancakes that could rival mine. The kid can eat.

"How about we go inside, clean up a bit and I'll make some grilled cheese for lunch?" Beth suggests, which apparently meets with Max's approval, his loud "Yay!" and dive off the platform into Beth's arms evidence.

"That's enough."

Clint slips his arms around my body from behind and I feel his lips on my neck. He put Max down for a nap, who seems to have tuckered himself out after lunch, and I'm just cleaning away the last of the dishes. I crave the physical closeness and loved the way it made me feel earlier. His mood, affection, and words gave me hope, but once inside he seemed distracted. We haven't done much more than kiss and cuddle the last few weeks, and I'm missing the sex. The few times I've tried to initiate taking things a little further, I've been shut down. Not harshly, but each time he tucks me to him and tells me we're not in a rush, a little of my newfound self-esteem crumbles. Initially we both were a bit bruised and battered, and so it made sense, but now all that remains is scars; his on his shoulder and mine on my face and chest. Maybe it's the scars.

I put my arms over his and lean my head back against his shoulder, hoping he'll take what his body so obviously wants judging by the hard ridge against my ass.

"Nothing better than a soft, warm woman in the kitchen, but even better when she's willingly spread out in bed," his voice rumbles and the words are like a trigger. Three weeks ago, I wouldn't have thought twice about brushing those words off as Clint being Clint—saying stuff that doesn't sound half as good hearing as he intends it to be. But already insecure and confused with the mixed messages, it works like a red flag on a bull. And the bull in this case is me.

"Seriously, Clint? You finally make a move without me initiating it and you pushing me away, and then you go and ruin it with that antiquated sexist garbage?" I push out from between him and the counter, round the island and turn to face him at a safe distance. "For weeks you've avoided touching me in any real way, and each time I tried I got shut down. I mean, I get that Max puts a bit of a damper on things, and you were injured to boot, but I could've done all the work. We've had opportunities."

The bewildered look on his face should've been a hint he doesn't have a clue what I'm talking about, which is why when he walks over and cups my face in his hands, his next words strike hard.

"Babe—it's the scar."

And there it is.

Without hesitation I pull away and make a beeline for the bathroom down the hall, ignoring him calling my name and fighting tears. With both the door to the bedroom and the one to the hallway locked, I sink down with my back against the bathtub, grabbing a towel on my way down to muffle the sobs that are breaking free. Fuck, fuck, fuck. That was way more harsh than I'd expected. Surprised, even though he just confirmed what I'd been fearing. Shocked, because the thought had not crossed my mind initially, wouldn't have, the way I felt secure with him before I was taken—but now, after a good number of brush offs, it doesn't seem so far-fetched. The fucking scar.

"Beth, open the door," I hear him from the bedroom. "Bean—talk to me."

For a few minutes, I ignore the soft knocks and pleas before I hear his footsteps disappear down the hall. My face is pressed to my knees, and the tears are relentless in coming, when I hear him coming back just moments later. Before I can clue in to what I'm listening to, the door to the bedroom is lifted clear off the hinges.

"Baby…" Clint mumbles, as he steps in the bathroom and slides down beside me, pulling me onto his lap and folding his arms tightly around me. "I'm thinking I'm missing something. Or maybe it's that my words are not making clear what's in my mind. In my heart." One of his hands comes to lift my head from where I'm still keeping it hidden against my knees. "Talk to me."

His voice is so gentle, I can't stop my eyes from searching out his and find them full of the tenderness, also evident in his words. So I tell him what's in my mind.

"The scars. They turn you off."

This time the confusion on his face registers clearly, as does the darkness replacing it a moment later.

"What?" he whispers, but it's with barely contained anger.

"My face—my chest. I know they're not pretty, but I never thought—"

His hands grab my shoulders and give me a shake, cutting me off mid-sentence. "Shut up," he growls just before his mouth slams on mine, his tongue penetrating and taking charge. My mind freezes but my body seems to have no problem responding. But when he pulls away much too soon, his hands still on my shoulders, his anger hasn't disappeared.

"You'd honestly think those would make any fucking difference in how I feel about you? Jesus, Beth, is that how little you think of me?"

I'm stunned. Foolish me, I try to explain. "But three weeks, Clint. You've pushed me away for three weeks. It's the only thing that makes any sense." I know how much of a fool I am when he slides me off his lap, and with his hands behind him on the edge of the bathtub, pushes himself to stand over me.

"What about this? Every time I see the scars that dirtbag put on you, I can barely reel in my control. I almost killed a man, Beth, and I was so out of it with rage, I didn't even know I was doing it. Each time I see what he did to you, what I almost lost, I can barely keep myself from plowing my fist through the wall. I'm all about control, you've gotta know that. The chance I'd lose it while fucking you is one I can't take." With that he's out of the bathroom and I watch his back disappear.

301

Shit. The time it takes me to let his words sink in, and get my act together, is enough for him to have snagged his coat and keys and head out. I get to the window just as I see his truck peel out of the driveway.

Cockeyed.

That shit back there is bent. My heart is pounding like a fucking jackhammer, and I'm barely hanging onto my cool. Had to get out of there; I was *this* close to picking her up off the floor and fucking some sense into her. But in my current state I could've hurt her. I roll down the window and let the cold air blow in my face as I ease my foot off the accelerator, when I realize I'm barreling full throttle down County Road G. Not smart.

With the freezing wind blowing most of the heat out of my head and reason slowly starting to seep back in, I think about leaving Beth sitting on the bathroom floor, a look of disbelief on her face. Fucked up. Again. The day started with a beautiful promise, and I'll be damned if I'm not going to let it end the same way. Jed's out of the hospital and recuperating in Gus and Emma's guesthouse, and with Emma around there's no way he isn't looked after, and well. Max is back home with us, and Beth is ready to make her stay with me permanent. Everything seems to be settling down. I'll be damned if I'm the one screwing the pooch this time.

A quick look to make sure no traffic's coming and a sharp U-turn later, I'm heading right back where I came from. Haven't been gone for more than ten minutes, when I pull in the drive and see an unfamiliar car sitting in my spot. I pull in next to it and walk to the door, keeping my eye on the older couple standing on the step, and Beth in the doorway with a worried look on her face. The moment she spots me I see guilt marring her features, guilt that has no place there. I walk up behind the couple, who both turn around at my approach.

"Clint, honey—" Beth starts, her eyes already red from the crying earlier filling with tears again, so I cut her off, not wanting to go into that in front of an audience.

"Can I help you?" I try to sound friendly but the question still comes out as a growl. The woman grabs onto the man's arm, and he immediately tucks her against him. Already I like him and I don't know who the fuck he is. Doesn't matter though; whomever they are, they're in the way of cleaning up the mess I left behind. Something I'd prefer to be doing over standing on my step, figuring out what these people are doing here.

"Tammy's our daughter. This is Janet and I'm Des Milton. We're here to see if you know where she is. And my wife wants to see Max."

Jesus. Their son is in jail and their daughter swinging in the wind after abandoning her child. No wonder they look worn. Seeing indecision on Beth's face, I decide to take hold of the situation.

"I'm Clint and to answer your question: No, we have no idea where your girl is, and as for Max, he's just gone down for a nap. We've not heard from you or seen you all the weeks he's been with us, so forgive us if we don't invite you in right now and wake him up."

I face off with a very angry Des, who's having a hard time holding on to his control, but he does.

"We just got back from a trip to New Zealand early, suspecting something was going on back home when our phone calls weren't answered by either one of our children or Dylan. Yesterday we finally land in Durango, try calling immediately with no result, drive over to Tammy's place to see it empty and headed straight for the police station after, where we find out our dumbass son is in jail in Cortez. Drove down there this morning, got in to see him and all he'd tell us was that he has no clue where that "*bitch*" is. Sheriff didn't take to kindly to me trying to smack some sense into that kid for talking about his sister that way and just being the dumbass that he is that got him where he's at." His wife puts a hand on his stomach when he throws his eyes to the sky, probably hoping for some divine intervention. I can't say I blame him. The move seems to settle him some, because he grabs her hand and pulls it against his chest where he holds on to it, turning his eyes back to me. "I got enough to know my daughter looks to have taken the easy road, again. Spoiled her too much. As a result she avoids all things that require work and expects to have everything handed to her. Our mistake. Did not anticipate having one child turn to crime and another to walk out on her child, but there it is. Max is the one thing we've had any part in that is pure. Right now, my wife needs to see him, so she can hold on to it."

Beth is affected and in a profound way. The tears that brimmed at my approach are tracking down her cheeks, and I have to admit, I fucking feel for them too.

"Right. Janet, I'm sure Beth won't mind you peeking in on Max, and I'll set something up with your husband here for a better visit tomorrow." The grateful smile Beth sends me is enough to let me know that was the right move. I watch her put her arm around Janet and lead her inside. Turning to Des, I see he's only maybe mid-fifties, but the stress of the past days makes him look older. "Des, no offense but your visit falls right

304

in the middle of something that needs to be dealt with sooner rather than later. In the meantime, let me call the motel down the road, they will take good care of you. I'll also get some friends of mine to look harder into finding Tammy. Don't know what they'll find, if anything, or how long it's gonna take, but tomorrow I'll sit down with you and fill you in on everything that's happened, so far. I need you to brace yourself. So take tonight to kick back with the knowledge your grandson is in good hands and a stone's throw away. Take in a good home cooked meal on me at Arlene's Diner, just west of here off Main Street. In the meantime, I'll make sure things are sorted here, and we'll see you back here for lunch tomorrow?"

I get a sharp nod to indicate he's on board. No words, but I don't need them. I make a quick call to reserve them a room, after which we wait in silence, our breaths fogging in the cold until Beth leads a smiling Janet back outside.

"Thank you." Her soft melodic voice such a contrast against her husband's gruff one.

"Of course," Beth says for both of us.

Des puts his arm around his wife. "Let's go. Clint here's got a room sorted. We'll go get some rest, come back tomorrow." Janet just nods, obviously trusting her husband completely as he leads her to the car and gets her settled before rounding the hood to the driver's side. "Clint?" When I look at him he continues, "Thank you, and I suggest you deal with whatever needs sorting. Sooner better than later," before sliding into his seat, starting the engine and driving off.

I turn back to find the worried look back on Beth's face, and I don't like it directed at me. So I walk up to her, put my arm around her shoulder, and pull her in from the cold. Time to get things sorted.

CHAPTER TWENTY-FIVE

"Come sit."

Still trying to get my head around what just all happened, I'm not my usual self and follow him meekly as he leads me to the couch.

I was still standing by the window after Clint drove off earlier, kicking my own ass for being so mired in my insecurities that I couldn't see beyond them. His words were like a cold shower, the chill a quickly penetrating slap of reality. Should've talked to him before going off half-cocked like that. God, I'm ashamed for being too preoccupied to see his struggle. Not once, but twice now, he has seen me bleed. Knowing what seeing him hurt did to me, I should've expected his reaction to be no less. Let alone him losing it on that man, enough so Joe'd had to pull him off. Worry. That's what held him back. I could see now; how for a man like him that kind of loss of control was frightening. Never entered my mind. I don't blame him for walking out. Fuck, I'd have walked out too if I didn't have my grandbaby sleeping in the other room. He must be so disappointed.

That's about as far as my thoughts had a chance to go before a cream colored Chrysler 3000 pulled in the drive. Not a car I recognized, although I did recognize the people getting out. Been a long time since I'd seen Tammy's parents, who tended to stay at a distance. I was at the door before they started up the steps and had it open, waiting for them. I'd just told them

I had no idea where Tammy was, and that yes, Max was with me. I didn't feel comfortable letting them inside, though. First, it's Clint's house and second, Des was obviously angry, and not knowing them very well, I had no idea what they might do. The last couple of months have taught me to be cautious. So I was relieved, for several reasons, to see Clint's truck pull in the drive. And grateful for the way he handled Des, I don't think I would've had it in me to come up with the backbone needed.

But now I'm watching him pace the living room after having deposited me on the couch. He's making me nervous. How badly did I fuck up? That's why his words shock the hell out of me.

"I fucked up," he says, stopping in front of me. "Should've talked to you, instead of keeping it to myself. I see I hurt you, when that is exactly what I was trying to avoid. Seeing you cut? That scarred *me*, Beth. And I've never—not ever in my life, come close to killing someone, but that day I would've happily gone there. I was beside myself. Literally. Can't remember a damn thing except doling out hurt. Knowing how I like to take things to the edge sometimes in the bedroom, been scared to go there. Thinking I might lose control when seeing those cuts on you." He drops down on his knees before me and slides his fingers in my hair, palms holding my jaw. "I want to fuck you so bad, Bean. Want to mark you as mine, so I'm not reminded of those assholes who had their hands on you. So that *you're* not reminded. But I don't want to scare you."

Shaking off the shock that's kept me silent, I slide forward, my legs bracing his hips, my arms sliding around his back and hooking on to his shoulders. With my face tucked into his neck, I tell him, "You're an idiot, Clint Mason. You'd never hurt me. Not. Ever. And I'm an idiot too, for not realizing what you were struggling with. I'm not normally that dense." The last words

307

have barely left my mouth, and I'm on my back on the couch, Clint's bodyweight pinning me down, his lips closing on mine.

"Love you, Bean," he mumbles.

"Back at you, Big Guy," I whisper back.

Then we're done, with lips, teeth, tongue, and hands doing all the talking. My hands sneak under his sweater and encounter the soft skin over strong muscle, fingers tracing the rolling movement. My hips come off the couch, rubbing against his crotch when his mouth suddenly leaves mine and I gasp for air. "Holy Jesus," I manage. Barely.

"No shit," he breathes equally hard before raising himself off me. "Not big on interrupting what we've got going on here, babe, but I'm thinking the bedroom?"

I'm all for being ravaged on the couch—or any other piece of furniture, as long as Clint is the one doing the ravaging— but with a toddler having a nap only steps away, the bedroom seems the more prudent choice. Straightening my shirt, which somehow ended up under my armpits, I grab hold of Clint's proffered hand and allow him to pull me up. The mood immediately changes once we step over the threshold and into the bedroom.

"Stand here and don't move," he growls in my ear before I hear the click of the door closing behind me. Super-sensitized I flinch at the sound, which seems loud in the otherwise quiet room. I don't see or hear as much as sense him walking up behind me. He doesn't touch, but I can smell and feel his proximity as he slips by. Every instinct wants to follow to the bed but when I make the slightest move he shakes his head. Seeing as he's kept me at a distance for fear of losing control, I'm not about to make it more challenging for him now. By the bed, he sinks down on the edge, his eyes scanning me from my socks to the top of my head and back down over the scar on my face. I see him flinch, biting down whatever angry emotions seeing it evokes in him. Finally they come to rest on my eyes.

"Take your clothes off." His voice soft and deep, sending a shiver from my scalp all the way down my neck and back. I haven't even started yet and already goose bumps rise on my skin. A slight lift of his eyebrow is all it takes to get my hands moving, unzipping my jeans and sliding them down, granny panties and all, taking my socks along when I step out of them. Crossing my arms I grab the hem of my shirt and lift it over my head. It's then I notice the cups still pulled down below my breasts from our tangle on the couch, but when I reach back to undo the clasp he stops me.

"Leave it on. Just like that."

A little niggle of insecurity raises it's head, standing here naked as the day I was born. Except now with a body soft and somewhat flabby with age, not to mention my boobs spilling over top of the bra, creating what seems to me layers of flesh that can hardly be attractive. All this time Clint's eyes have not strayed from mine, but now that I'm fidgeting where I stand, he lets them drift over me. I close my eyes, not wanting to see his reaction to my body. Sure, he's seen me before, but most of the time that was when we were grappling around the bed. He's never subjected me to this kind of scrutiny, and although he sits half a room away, nothing has ever felt quite this intimate or exposing. I'm so deep inside my head, I only register the sound of a zipper when I hear his voice.

"Open your eyes, Bean. Look at what you do to me." The slight hitch in his voice has me open my eyes to find him still sitting, but lazily stroking his formidable cock, obviously released from the confines of his jeans. He watches me look at his hand sliding up and down the beautifully thick-veined shaft, a bead of moisture pooling at the tip. So luscious, I can't help running my tongue over my bottom lip. "Come here, baby," the

309

sound of his voice gritty as his focus snaps down to my mouth, but no less inviting. Every step I take makes me more aware of the slick rub of my thighs as arousal slowly leaks from me. When I'm close, he releases his cock and grabs me by the hips, pulling me firmly between his legs, his mouth reaching for an exposed nipple. His hands kneading the excess flesh on my hips, while he draws me deep inside his hot mouth. A whimper escapes me when he lets my nipple plop free. The same treatment is given to the other side, before his mouth trails down and across the rolling flesh of my stomach. All done with such reverence, that any lingering thoughts of inadequacy have long disappeared, replaced with only sensations and feelings. Bending over he slides his tongue between my legs dragging at the moisture gathered there and hums. "So good. You taste as beautiful as you are." His nostrils flare, taking in the smell of my arousal before his hands force my body around. With my dimpled ass in his face, some of those thoughts find their way back inside my head, but not for long. His callused hands massaging the cheeks of my ass, I feel his breath on me moments before his lips are there, giving my butt the same attention he did my breasts and stomach. I'm not prepared for the nip of his teeth on my flesh and almost pull away, but his hands hold me back.

With one hand sliding up along my spine, pressing gently he urges me to bend over. "Hands on your knees and spread." My face flushing red, from embarrassment and arousal at the same time, I do what he asks. Terrified of losing control of my muscles, I clench my cheeks together tightly. The deep chuckle behind me tells me it's not gone unnoticed, and I flush even deeper.

"Relax, Bean."

Really?

Just like that I'm back in my head. What kind of damn nickname is Bean anyway? And who actually says *that* when I'm bent over with my ass in the air?

"Be still," he rumbles, keeping his hand firmly on my back when I try to straighten up. Before I have a chance to voice my protest, his mouth is *right there.* His tongue slicking along the folds of my pussy and up. Oh my God. The scrape of his stubble on the back and inside of my thighs, just abrasive enough to make my nerve ends sing. The moment his lips close around my clit and suck, I'm done for. No longer able to stay quiet as demanded, I cry out as I come so hard, if not for Clint's hands holding me in place, I'd have done a face-plant on the carpet.

"Beautiful," he mutters before he has me on my stomach on the mattress, his body folded over me and his mouth in my neck. "Gonna fuck you now, Beth, and I'm doing all the work." I feel the cold air hit my back as he lifts off. From the rustling of fabric, I can tell he's finally getting naked with me.

Pulling both my arms behind me, he slides the straps of my bra down each shoulder to my elbows, where he gathers both sides in one hand effectively keeping my elbows together and tied.

"Gonna have to get your knees on the edge of the mattress, babe. You're not high enough."

With a little assistance I manage to position myself to his liking, giving him my complete trust. Despite that it seems awkward with my ass in the air once again, but this time higher than my upper body, still flat on the covers.

"Ready?" Is all he says before powering into me full force while pulling on the makeshift binds at my elbows, bringing my upper body off the bed. Deeply rooted inside me, he stills and I can hear his heavy breathing over my own. Despite having just had a doozy of an orgasm, his cock inside me, the position of our bodies and the total control he has over our movements has me already building up to the next. But he doesn't move.

"Clint? Honey…"

"Don't wanna hurt you." The strangled sound of his voice cuts me.

"You're not going to hurt me. I want it. I want you to take me hard. Mark me how you need to mark me."

"Beth…"

"Please baby, I need you," I whisper.

With one hand he keeps my upper body suspended while the other wraps in my hair. The sting makes me hiss, but it feels good. He pulls out slowly, too slowly and I whimper when I lose the fullness of him inside. Then he slides back in just as slow at first, before picking up speed and power. Before you know it, my head and back are bent back by the hair and arms, and his hips are pumping furiously, driving his cock inside me. So good.

"You okay?" Beth's soft voice penetrates my postcoital fog.

I'm lying on top of her, her face still down in the covers, my heart racing from the explosion of the pent-up orgasm that tore through me. Her soft body, soft words, and total submission, finally snapping my finely honed control and I fucked her hard. Now she asks me if I'm okay? After I pounded her six ways to Sunday? Granted, the sexy noises from her lips, that I could hear over my own grunts, sounded like she was right with me, and the vice-like clamp of her pussy when she came *hard* evidence she wasn't suffering, but still. I barely had the presence of mind to release her arms from the bra straps before I collapsed on top of her.

Now she's asking me if I'm okay, I should be asking her that.

Pushing myself up in the bed with one hand, I use the other to sweep away the damp hair that is plastered to her face and kiss her cheek. "Should be asking you that question? Did I hurt you?"

I feel her body stiffen under me before she pushes back and forces me to roll over on my back. Now she's leaning over me and there is anger in her eyes.

"Hurt me? Did I give you any indication of that? You would never."

"Babe, I was brutal."

"*Babe,*" she mocks me, "you were perfect. Fucked me just the way I wanted you to." Her face softens when she leans in closer, her breath feathering over my face. "I trusted that—and you trusted me to be able to take what you needed to give. Biggest high I've ever had. Best feeling. Like barreling down from the biggest loop of a roller-coaster with your arms high up in the air. Except better."

"Bean…" I try, the depth of emotions constricting my throat. A small smile from her before her mouth descends on mine and she *takes* all of it. God, I love this woman.

"*Gammy…*"

"The lord and master of the house beckons," she whispers against my lips, "I'd better go see to him before he tears his bed apart."

I watch as Beth slips from the bed, quickly tagging her clothes and covering up, but not before giving me a eyeful of her luscious curves.

Snow.

It's been falling steadily now for at least two hours and already you can barely see the ground anymore. A system that came in from the West Coast, a little further to the south than expected, hit the cold air and the result is snow. Copious amounts of it. According to the weather station it's virtually stationary at this point, held up by the Rockies, so we're in for a treat. Good thing the fridge is full.

"Snow!" Max has his little face pressed to the window and is watching the white stuff gather in the yard. I'm thinking I should've built him a sled instead.

I drove Beth into work, under protest, but I wasn't gonna let her take the slick roads in that old rust bucket of hers with four bald tires. Seb said he'd drop her off back here, so I didn't have to pack the little guy in the truck again to pick her up.

Max and I have been hanging out, and I just fed him mac and cheese with hotdogs, apparently a favorite 'cause he gobbled that shit up. I could barely get it down. Not a big fan of Kraft Macaroni and Cheese, I caved after spending a good half hour on the phone with Gus, filling him in on the arrival of Tammy's parents and their concern about their daughter. He was going to talk to that rat-bastard, Damien, to see if he could have a word with Dylan. He might have some insight as to where she's gone off to. He was also going to get Neil on the old desktop computer that had been in their house when Mal went to clean it up. By the time I got off the phone, Max had climbed on my lap, was patting my cheek with his little hand and kept saying, "hungwy." I took his insistence seriously, given that he hadn't had anything since lunch and that's how I ended up with the box of Kraft in my hand.

"Wanna go outside with me, buddy? Dress really warm and play in the snow for a bit?" His little head nods and his smile almost splits his face in half. Guess I have my answer. I know it's time for him to go to bed, but looking at his excited face, I know there won't be much sleep yet, anyway. Better let him get some of that energy out of his system.

Dusk has set in, but there was still a little bit of light out, with the back door light on we'll still be able to see what we're doing. I dress him in the snowsuit Beth unearthed from one of the bags of clothes from his house. Not an easy feat, with little arms and legs hyped up on excitement over the first taste of snow. I pull on my own parka, which hasn't seen light since last year's snowfall, and instead of my cowboy hat, pull a beanie over my head. I'll enjoy the lack of hair come summer, but for now it is fucking cold.

The moment I open the back door, Max runs past my legs and throws himself on the snow-covered lawn, giggling loudly. I watch him, smiling, thinking 'what the hell' and throw myself down beside him. Doesn't take long to teach him to make a fine snow angel, which he proceeds to do all over the yard.

That's how Beth finds us.

Last thing I expected to find coming home is an empty house. When I walk through, dumping my bag and coat on the couch, I hear high-pitched giggles, along with much deeper chuckles, coming from the backyard. Opening the sliding door,

I spot my two guys rolling in the snow and despite the now bitter cold, a solid warmth settles deep in my chest.

"Gammy's home!" Max spots me and comes running, jumping up in my arms, making me wish I hadn't thrown off my coat before checking outside. His snow-covered body plastered against my front, I can feel the moisture seeping into my clothes. Clint follows close behind, the black beanie a worthy replacement for his ratty cowboy hat; he looks scrumptious. Even with his red nose, ice clumps in his scruff and almost blue lips.

"Hey," he murmurs, his icy lips warming themselves on mine.

"You guys are freezing! Get inside." I smile as my teeth start chattering. Reason for Clint to take charge, pluck Max from me and push me backward into the warm house.

"Run a bath, Bean. You're soaked through and shivering. You can take Max in with you." His head dips down and he lays a deep kiss on me. Almost enough to warm me up, but not quite. A bath sounds great actually, although the variety foremost in my mind includes bubbles, candles, and a good book. I'm pretty sure bathtime with Max looks a bit different. Setting out towels within reach and fixing the temperature of the water, not too hot for the little guy, I strip out of my clothes and sink in, just as Clint walks in with a shivering and buck naked little boy.

"Gotta go throw his bedding in the dryer," Clint says, as he plops Max in the tub in front of me. "Before I caught up with him, he had most of his gear off and tossed in his crib. Even soaked the mattress pad."

"Okay," I mumble, settling back against the tub, my hands on Max who is happily splashing in the warm water. Not a moment later I shoot up straight when I hear Clint yell.

"What the ever-loving FUCK?"

CHAPTER TWENTY-SIX

"You're back."

Arlene approaches our booth, eyes on Des and Janet.

We'd called them this morning, suggesting we meet at the diner since those roads would be plowed. It hadn't stopped snowing until early this morning, and the road to Clint's place was still covered. It would probably not be taken care of until later this afternoon. His truck would do fine with the four-wheel drive, but Tammy's parents might have a problem getting through in their Chrysler. So we bundled Max up, strapped him in the seat in the back, and maneuvered our way through the drifts.

Beautiful—Cedar Tree covered in snow. It's pretty any time of year, but there is something magical about the first, pristine, fluffy white layer of the season covering everything in sight. Despite the late hour last night and the unexpected discovery Clint made, I feel invigorated this morning. Ready to take on the world. Clint had taken the day off, leaving his business in the capable hands of his foremen, and we'd made plans to go see Jed later.

I'd left Clint in deep discussion with Gus and Joe last night, barely even able to keep my eyes open. Clint had scared the crap out of me when he yelled out. When unzipping the mattress pad from Max's crib, he'd found a stash of money taped to cardboard slipped between the two foam layers of the mattress. Almost ten thousand dollars worth. As I was scrambling to get Max and myself out of the tub, he'd already nabbed the phone and was obviously talking to Gus, by the time I carried my little guy into his bedroom.

"Yeah, I'll see you in a bit. Careful, the roads are treacherous," he cautioned before turning to me.

"What in the blazes?" I couldn't quite grasp the sight of a piece of cardboard that looked to be lined with money and wrapped in plastic, leaning against the crib. Clint walked up and wrapped an arm around me.

"Found that. Not a clue who'd do that, stick a wad of cash into a baby's mattress, but there it is." He waved his other hand at the money. "First thing Gus said, when I called him, was that it finally made sense why that brother of Tammy's was so eager to get in my house. Figures money like that could drive a man like that to break and enter."

"How did we miss that? I mean, we moved that damn mattress twice." I turned to Gus, wanting to know.

Clint shrugs his shoulders. "Never had cause to take the pad off before and both times it went in the back of a truck. The cardboard's not heavy, is flat and was stuck between the foam layers. Wouldn't have noticed either, unless we'd tried to fold it or—like what happened—we pulled the pad off."

It may have made sense to Gus and even Clint, but it was still muddled in my head. By the time he and Joe finally got here, Max's bed was made up with dry sheets, sans money this time, which was neatly stacked on the coffee table, and I'd just finished putting him down. The three of them sat down to brainstorm when I found myself nodding off on the couch. An emotional day, a busy one, and a good four hours running around the diner followed by a warm bath had done me in.

"Go to bed, Bean. You're practically sleeping already," Clint says softly, leaning over me, after which he kisses me softly on the lips. Company be damned. I quietly comply, pushing up from the couch, and bidding goodnight to the guys, who look on with amused smiles. Whatever.

This morning Clint woke me with coffee and Max in bed and told me the plan. This is now something else to discuss with Des and Janet and will likely not be easy to hear for parents.

"Mornin'," Des rumbles at Arlene, who is oblivious to the grumpy and slightly abrasive man across the table. Janet just smiles sweetly, a little distracted by our shared grandson, sitting at the end in a highchair and playing with her bracelet.

"Hey, Arlene," I say a bit more upbeat, which earns me a smile. From Arlene that's something. Clint's "Hi, girl," goes even further. He gets teeth with his. And of course Max is totally ignorant to all the tension flying around the table and just reaches his arms out to her, which is rewarded with a raspberry in his neck that leaves him giggling loudly. Janet smiles at this, but Des looks sour. The man's in a mood, although I can't really blame him, his son in jail and daughter on the lam. Still…

"I've already told Seb my scrumptious nugget is here, so he's pulling out the chicken fingers, but what can I get you folks? Lunch special is—"

"Just bring me a club sandwich and a coffee," Des cuts Arlene off, which has Janet admonishing him under her breath. The mumbled, "sorry" that follows, barely audible.

"I'd like to hear the special," Janet says, immediately cementing herself in my good book. Des may be under stress but he's still being an ass. That's why Arlene, never one to hide her feelings, sends him a dirty look and turns her best smile on Janet. The one *with* teeth.

"Smart move, the special is awesome, because my husband is a great cook. Hungarian stuffed peppers in spicy red pepper and tomato sauce. Not too spicy," she adds quickly, noticing the look of concern on Janet's face, "but just enough to warm you up from the inside out."

"Can vouch for those," Clint rumbles beside me, "had them before and I'm having them again. Sign me up, girl."

"Me too, please, Arlene," I add my order in.

"Okay, I'm convinced. Me three," Janet adds with a little flair, before eyeing her husband with her eyebrow raised.

"I'll just stick with my club," he says stubbornly.

"Spoilsport…" I distinctly hear Janet say, even though she's pretending to be busy, folding her napkin on her lap.

I'm not alone holding back a laugh, Arlene whips around and takes off to the kitchen without a word, but I see her shoulders moving, and Clint's hand resting on my shoulder is squeezing hard.

"You're telling me someone stuck ten thousand dollars in the mattress?" Des is incredulous and I can't really blame him. After we've eaten, Clint and I recount the entire story, beginning to end, and hearing all at once it does all seem incredible.

Janet on the other hand, puts her hand on my arm. "Are you okay? I mean, are you going to be?" she says carefully, doing her best not to look at the scar on my cheek and only partially succeeding.

"I'm fine now, and am only going to get better once I hug my son, we find your Tammy, and we figure out whose money that is."

"Right," she says, before turning her attention back to Max, who's happily chewing on some fries.

"Seriously?" I hear Clint's growl and follow his glare to the diner's entrance, at Special Agent Damien Gomez who just walked in. Afraid of further confrontations, I put my hand over Clint's, which he has fisted on the table.

Fucker's got a nerve, walking in here. Fucking Damien Gomez. If not for Beth's restraining hand, and the fact that Tammy's parents are at the table, I'd have been up and hauling his ass outside. Noticing his scan around the diner settle on our booth, I know we're in for some unpleasantness. The moment he reaches our table, he lifts his hands in defense.

"I've got news. Gus is on his way over since he apparently has some news too. Told me to meet him here, but I had no idea you were, too."

"We were just having lunch," Beth offers, seeing as I'm unable to answer, too busy grinding my teeth. "Don't think you've met Tammy's parents, the Miltons, yet? Des, Janet, this here is Special Agent Gomez." Beth's introductions done, she leans back and slightly sideways, boxing me in my seat. I know what she's doing and let her know by flipping my hand over under hers, so I can lace our fingers.

"Nice to meet you and rather perfect timing, I was going to look you up after. Saves me a trip," Gomez tells them, pulling up a chair from the table behind us and setting it on the far side of Max, who quietly stares at him, the cold fry in his hand forgotten. The bastard barely acknowledges the little guy. More reason not to like him.

"Ah, here is Gus now." His eyes are on the door where Gus, Joe, and Neil are entering, walking straight over to our table.

"We're gonna need a bigger table," Neil decrees and takes off to find Arlene. More introductions and a bit of shuffling later, we are seated at the big corner table, with plenty of room for all, including Max's highchair. Janet has taken the seat next to him and seems to be keeping him occupied, while Arlene takes orders from the latecomers.

"Who wants to go first," Gus asks and that puts an end to my patience.

"Does it matter? Just spill."

Beth's eyes turn on me and she mouths, '*easy*' as Gus gives Damien the go ahead.

"I assume everyone here is up to date so far?" He looks directly at Des, who nods curtly. He hasn't really said a whole lot, just watched the collection of big burly guys enter and move around like they own the place. He'll find out what a tight knit group we are.

"Alright then. I got a call yesterday afternoon from Gus, telling me you had concerns about your daughter." This he addresses to Tammy's parents. "I questioned Dylan, who is fine by the way," he directs at Beth, before turning back to the table. "He only knew her email address at her part time job, and she hadn't been there since taking off. I think we may have all, at some point, tried that route. He did tell me that she liked spending time on the computer in chat rooms, supposedly with old college friends who'd moved away. I got in touch with Neil, since he'd be on it faster than one of our own IT guys. He apparently had already been digging up what he could from their desktop computer. With the information he found, we know she was planning to meet up with someone in Flagstaff. Here's the tricky part," he turns back to Des and Janet before continuing, "she made these plans months ago."

That's a bit of a shocker. We'd all been under the assumption she left as a result of the fight she had with Dylan, but this would imply her disappearance was preplanned. A total shock to her parents, who both turn pale at the news.

"She had an account with Ashley Madison," Damien continues and I hear Beth gasp. We all know what that means, its membership just recently hacked and publicly listed. "She hooked up with a married real estate agent in Flagstaff and has been engaged in an online affair with him since. They planned to end up together, after dissolving their respective marriages."

"Where is she?" Des barks, his face set to thunder, his wife hanging onto his arm, obviously distraught.

"We have his name and a number and called last night, but his wife answered. She told us he'd been gone for over a month. Needless to say she wasn't very happy with our call, but was able to provide us with a number and his new address."

"I need the address," Des pipes up again.

"Mr. Milton—all due respect, but your daughter is an adult, I hardly think—" Gus joins in but Des cuts him off.

"You had a girl out there mucking up her life, would you sit back?" He blasts Gus, who takes it with a shrug.

"I imagine not. Regardless, let agent Gomez finish his part, I'll tell you our news and then you decide. Yeah?"

324

He doesn't draw a response, but the demonstrative folding of the arms and sitting back against his seat is enough of an answer. Des will sit back. For now.

"Right, so rather than calling, I called our field office in Flagstaff this morning and had them pay a visit. They found Tammy at the address, her new boyfriend apparently at his office, and took the opportunity to ask her some questions. The main question being how money ended up inside her son's mattress. She claims she had no clue. At first. Until her brother called her at work, the last day she was there."

I fucking knew it. The little prick had something to do with it. I keep my tongue, letting Damien continue.

"Claims Brian knew there was heat coming down on Dylan and called to suggest she take off. Then he took her by surprise when he asked her to remove money he had hidden inside her son's mattress before she left. She says she told him she didn't want to get involved with his shady dealings and hung up. That's all she claims to know."

"She left her son sleeping on that mattress? You're telling me, she walked out of that house, knowing that?" This from Janet, who I'd seen sitting up straighter and straighter as Gomez was talking.

"Settle down, Janet." Her husband tries to pull her back, but she slaps at his hand.

"Settle down? Are you crazy? That's our grandson she walked out on. Our precious baby, she may well have put in danger, knowing what she knew when she walked away. There's no settling down from that, Des. There just isn't." With that she slips out of her seat and runs into the washrooms. Immediately, Beth nudges me so she can get out. Now Max starts crying, because both his 'Gammys' have left him at a table with mostly angry looking men, so I pick him from his seat and try to soothe him.

"Looks good on you, old man," Neil says with a smirk on his face.

"Watch it, smartass," I fire back, to Max's great hilarity, because with big crocodile tears still wetting his cheeks, he pats his little hands on my face.

"Smaddass!"

"You teaching my little man swear words already, Clint? Come here little man, Auntie Arlene will take you to clean your ears out." With Max plucked from my arms and settled on her hip, Arlene disappears into the kitchen.

"You guys all related or something?" Des asks, looking at me, but Joe answers.

"We're better than related. We're close friends. Not gonna find family as tight as those you pick yourself, Mr. Milton."

With a 'hmpf,' Des sits back down, eyeing each of us in turn.

"To finish up, we've asked your daughter if she'd like to come back to meet up with us, but she declined. We have nothing on her that could force her hand. I can't tell you her address because of confidentiality, but what I can do is call her later, and let you talk to her."

Gomez surprises me. For a goal-obsessed, take-no-prisoners fed, he actually shows some compassion. He keeps his eyes patiently on Tammy's father, allowing him to work it out.

"That would probably please my wife," he finally says, disappointment evident on his face.

"Right, then as soon as we're done here, we'll do that in the privacy of my truck."

"I can wait for the ladies to get back," Gus says, "but given the results of this morning's talk with Tammy, what I have to add isn't much, since Brian was less than forthcoming and swore by high and low that he knew nothing of the money. This new information is reason to sit down with him again, but perhaps this time in the presence of Special Agent Gomez?" He looks pointedly at Damien who nods once. "Right, I'll let you set that up with Joe then, Damien. I'm sorry, I know he's your son, Milton, but I have little patience for the likes of him on a good day. Now that I know he's played us, I'm better off not questioning him. Joe is the better choice."

By the time Beth leads a red-eyed Janet back to the table, the boys are digging in to their lunches delivered by Seb, saying he couldn't drag Arlene away from her office, where she was getting her 'baby-fix' from Max. Damien leads Des and Janet outside, and I watch them go with a heavy heart. She's a sweetheart and he's an ass, but neither deserves this kind of disappointment and pain at the hands of their children. Makes me kind of glad I went straight to grandparenthood, the place where you can give the kid back to its parents when they get to be too much. *And* do it guilt-free.

"You okay?" I ask Beth, who's been rather quiet and withdrawn, which is not really like her. She looks at me with a sad little smile.

"I will be," she assures me, not quite convincing enough. "I feel for them." I follow her eyes out the window, where the large FBI truck is parked and Des and Janet are climbing in the front seat with Damien.

"She's nice, but too soft. He's an ass and too hard. They seem to work together, but they didn't have a lot of luck with their children," I offer.

"You can say that again," Beth agrees, before turning to me. "I'm surprised at you."

"Yeah? How come?"

"Thought for sure I'd have to bail you out of jail this time for assault on an officer of the law, but you were in total control, even when I left your side."

I shrug, still looking at the truck. "He stays a bastard and will never darken our door, if I can help it, but he was being careful with Tammy's parents. Figure there's some sense of compassion in that large frame somewhere. Just enough for me not to beat him over the head with the highchair."

She chuckles at that, "Max was in that highchair most of the time."

"Semantics," I tell her, pulling her into me as I see Damien leave the truck and stand beside the door, obviously giving the Miltons some privacy. "Besides, Max loves to do stuff with me, I figure he'd have helped."

Beth bursts out laughing and lays her head on my shoulder, just as I watch Des wrap his arms around Janet, who's clearly upset. Guess that didn't go too well. I turn to my Bean and kiss her on the top of her head, enjoying the sound of her laugh.

Blessed.

I didn't have to turn around to know that when the door to the diner opened a little later, it would be just Damien coming in.

"They gone?" Gus asks when he reaches the table.

"Yeah. Was not a good scene. They went back to the motel to pack their gear. Plan on heading back to Durango. Said they'd be in touch with you at some point," he says to Beth, who simply nods. "Fucked up situation." That earns agreement from everyone. Damien raps his knuckles on the table but has his eyes on Joe. "Right then, I'm off to see a man about a mattress. You coming?"

"I'm ready," Joe says, bending over when he slides behind Beth's chair and kissing her cheek. "Almost over, Bethie." He smiles at her before following Damien out the door.

"Finally," Arlene pipes up from behind me. "See Max? Grumpy grandpa and Federal Bureau of Idiots man are gone, isn't that great?"

She swings Max from her hip back in the highchair, where he bangs on the tray in front of him.

"Idjit?"

Everyone bursts out laughing and Arlene backs away from the table, her eyes big, her hands up, shrugging her shoulders and mouthing, 'Oops' before she turns around and practically runs into the sanctuary of the kitchen.

CHAPTER TWENTY-SEVEN

Almost over, my ass.

I've thought about those words Joe gave me almost two weeks ago at the diner.

He did come by the day after, to let us know that Brian finally caved. It'd been Dylan's money, given to Brian to pay down Dylan's debt with Sam. Except Brian, who'd been acting as go-between, decided to keep it. Figured he could get away with it, never considering that Sam would believe Dylan over him. When Dylan was approached by Sam, who demanded money, he clued in that Brian must've kept it. Joe said they suspect that's the 'meeting' the feds apparently caught after which they approached Dylan. With Dylan trying to get hold of him over the missing money, and Sam questioning his loyalty, he left town. No way he'd be able to get in the house and retrieve the stacks he had hidden in Max's mattress as a big 'fuck you' to Dylan. Less funny when he couldn't get his hands on it. That's when he tried to get his sister to retrieve it for him, telling her about the trouble Dylan was in. She wanted nothing to do with it or him. He was surprised to find both her and Dylan gone when he got back in town a week later. And shocked to find the house empty and up for rent. Apparently he remembered Tammy once mention Dylan came from Cedar Tree, which is how he ended up at Clint's house eventually.

That makes me think of lunch with the Miltons. Probably the weirdest lunch I ever had. I can't even imagine what it was like for them and cringe when I think what it will do to them, when they find out the complete extent of their son's role in this.

Janet's called me once last week, and I purposely didn't ask how the talk with Tammy went. It was obvious from what went down outside the diner, but she did volunteer some information.

"She's my daughter, but I'll be damned if I know who she is. She had no answers when I asked her how she could turn her back on her son, and it was obvious she had no real interest in having contact with us. Hard as it is, Des has convinced me we've gotta let it go. Both her and Brian. We really thought we did alright by them, never saw this coming, especially from her. I just hope when Dylan comes home, he'll not hold our children's behavior against us, but I can't blame him if he does."

"I don't think he will."

"We'll see. In any event, Des has decided to take me on another trip. A cruise to Alaska over Christmas. He says it'll keep my mind off the empty house we'd otherwise face. Maybe he's right, I don't know. Just know I'll miss Max. I put a package in the mail for him, it should arrive in time for Christmas. Hope that's okay?"

She sounded so sad, it brought tears to my eyes and I didn't hesitate. "Of course. And Janet? You are always welcome here, in my house. No matter what Dylan decides for himself, if he wants you in his life or not, I'll make sure Max always will be."

It wasn't long after she hung up.

I received her package this morning. The day before Christmas. I tuck it under the tree we'd gone out to cut last weekend. A bit late to start decorating, but we've had other things on our minds. Clint's back at work, and even Jed is back half time. Only in the office, but Clint says it makes a big difference to have him take care of tenders and sub-trades, scheduling, and payroll, as well as most anything else that requires sitting down in an office. That's apparently never been Clint's strong suit. He's not happy unless he's working with his hands. Jed's been talking about heading back to Durango when he's fully recovered, since he has nothing tying him down anywhere else anymore. I think it made Clint a little sad that he wouldn't be settling in Cedar Tree, but Jed pointed out that it would be much easier for them to build the business if they had someone running a satellite office there. More cost effective and Jed could build his own crews there. There certainly seems to be enough work. He'd continue to keep doing payroll, but Clint was already looking for someone to run his office here. I'd talked about it with Arlene, asking her if she knew of anyone, to let me know.

I've been working nights from four till nine. It seems to work out with Max, although I've got to say, I'd like it if Clint and I had more time to spend together. I've not been able to rent my house yet, and the cost of the mortgage and the care for Max is hacking away at my part-time hours *and* my tips. I was hoping I could hang on to it. Although I've not mentioned it out loud, I dream that maybe once Dylan comes back after the trial, from wherever they're keeping him, he'd be interested in moving in.

The doorbell ringing pulls me out of my thoughts, and I automatically look out the back window to the shed, where I know Clint is putting the last hand on a beautiful handcrafted sled he's been building, a few hours every night. I see his back bent over the treads, sanding them smooth. Secure in my knowledge he's close, I head for the door. I'm still a little apprehensive after all that's happened, but I'm getting better.

"Hey, woman!" Arlene almost shouts as she blows past me into the house, leaving me to shut the door.

"Boots," I remind her. She's used to running in and out of the diner without taking off shoes or boots, but I don't need crap all over the floors with Max around.

"Where's Max?" Arlene asks, as she pulls of her boots with the toe of the other foot.

"In bed, so mind the volume."

"Whatever," she says, rolling her eyes. "You've become so damn domesticated the last few months, I hardly recognize you."

For some reason that comment makes me tear up. Arlene tosses her boots toward the entrance while I turn my back, trying to fight them back. She walks up around me, takes one look at me, and tilts her head.

"What's wrong? You're crying. You don't cry. Like, not ever."

That makes me laugh through my tears, because I never did, not that anyone'd know anyway. Not even Arlene. "I've changed," I point out.

"I know, that's what I'm saying."

"I know you are. You pointed out I'm different. That you hardly recognize me."

I can tell the moment she clues in. Her mouth falls open in a silent, 'oh' and she blinks her eyes a few times before blurting out, "Happy! I didn't mean it in a bad way, just meant to say I don't recognize you so happy. Geeze Louise, I'm getting to be as bad as Clint with my mouth. Seb's on my case all the time that I should think before saying shit, but who's got the time?" Instantly she's right in front of me, her forearms resting on my shoulders and her face close. "You're even better than before, honey. I mean, you were gooder than good. Actually you were the *best* before, but now you're... well, better."

"Gooder than good?" I can't help but smile.

"No. Better than best," she corrects me, giving me the good smile. *With* teeth. So I slip my arms around her waist and give her a hug.

"Thanks."

No sooner has the word left my lips or she shoves me back. "See what I mean? Enough with the mushy shit. Got coffee? I'm thinking we'll need some."

A little puzzled, I nevertheless head for the kitchen and pop a pod in my Tassimo. I was so happy to bring it over from my house, makes life a lot easier.

"Clint not home? It's frickin' Christmas Eve."

"Back there, finishing up that sled he built for Max." I point at his flannel covered back, still visible inside the shed.

"Good, I wanted you alone anyway. For now at least. Brought some gifts for the tree, for Max tomorrow morning. For you too, but that's not what I need to talk to you about."

"Really?" I slide Arlene's cup on the counter in front of her and grab a bottle of water for myself.

Curious, I pull out a stool and sit next to her at the counter, waiting for her to spill.

"You told me Jed's leaving for Durango after the holidays and Clint's looking for someone to man the office. I was thinking that with Max here for however long, and with Clint running the show by himself again, it may be time to make some changes." She's hedging, I can tell. Not really her style, but whatever she's got on her mind, she's having a hard time just coming out with it.

"Where are you going with this?"

"I'm thinking it's time you considered a career change."

My mouth falls open in disbelief. She's fucking letting me go? After spending my entire adult life at the diner, she's sending me packing? Before I can push back from the counter, she has my wrist in a firm grip.

"Let me finish. Maybe it's because I don't have my face in it that closely, but it seems to me there's a pretty simple solution for you. You take over the office for Clint."

Well, that stops me in my tracks, if her vice-grip on my wrist wasn't already preventing flight.

"Say what?"

"Think about it. The hours you work at the diner, simply transfer those over to Mason Brothers. I don't know how much Clint can pay you, but I doubt it'll be less than what I pay, it's not like he's hurting. I figure with the money you'd save in gas, you could pay for a few hours of daycare. At least you'd get to spend a bit more time together in the evenings. You'll need it."

I'm reeling at her suggestion. It's not that it's *never* crossed my mind, it's just that I've never allowed myself to think it. I simply couldn't see myself away from the diner, where I've spent more than half my life. I also didn't want to think of leaving Arlene, but having *her* come up with the suggestion, it bears considering.

"I don't know…" I mutter undecidedly, "There's just so much to consider."

"Like what?"

"Well, I'd have to find daycare for half days," I offer.

"Emma's already on it. And she wants first dibs."

"Emma?"

"She's gonna start taking Mattias after Christmas, while Katie works in the office. Caleb's going back in the field on short stints."

"Seriously? But that's different, Katie will just be in a different space under the same roof." Emma and Gus had a guesthouse and a totally outfitted office space, complete with boardroom, added to their house a few years ago. Gus basically worked from home, unless he was on a job.

"How different? Better different, yes—things get too much for Emma or something happens, God forbid, Katie is right there."

"It might actually work," I admit, "but I don't even know if Clint would want me there, I've never really worked in an office before."

"Reckon you can run that damn diner on your own, the times you've jumped in over the years, running my shop should be a piece of cake." Clint's voice from behind startles me, I turn and only now notice him standing on the doormat by the back door. I was so engrossed, I never heard the sliding door.

"How long have you been there?" I want to know and his mouth tilts up slightly.

"Long enough to know you're too worried about everyone else and not worried enough about what you want. What do you want Beth? Cause I can tell you, it'd make my fucking life even better than it already is, with us growing the business and tending a family, together."

"Thinking my job is done here, I feel mushy coming on, and once a day is already more than enough," Arlene chuckles, getting up and pulling on her boots in the hallway. "You can let me know after the holidays, take some time to think. I'll leave the bag with presents by the door. Don't forget to grab it when you're... done."

I hear the click of the door, that's it. I'm still staring at Clint, who's staring right back at me. "You mean that?"

"What do you mean, do I mean that? Of course I mean that. I'd love to have you deal with the likes of Sarah Creemore. Saves me the aggravation." He's only half serious, clear from the sparkle of humor in his eyes, but it's true that Sarah Creemore has been a big pest. He's told me she's still trying to get him to come over to 'fix' things. Fact that he's been sending his sixty year old, bow-legged foreman over, is apparently not appreciated. Had me a good chuckle over that.

"Wow. Guess that means we have a plan now?" I watch Clint toe off his boots, unwrap the scarf around his neck, and pull off the beanie he's taken to wearing in place of his hat. He stalks to me slowly, his teeth bright white in his growing beard. When he gets to me, he first bends his mouth, and takes mine in a soul shattering kiss. One that has me glad I'm already sitting down or it would've put me on my ass. Then he pulls me off the stool, turns me in the direction of the hallway and gently steers me to the bedroom.

Oh yeah.

"Pwesents?"

Max is pointing up at the Christmas tree, sitting in the middle of a pile of wrapping paper he industriously ripped off every last one of his presents. And ours. All except one last one,

337

a little one, that was dangling off a branch out of his reach. Doesn't mean he doesn't spot it.

He really should have no concept of Christmas yet, but still he woke us up at five thirty this morning, just like any other kid at Christmas. Still dark as night outside, I decided to light candles and set them where Max can't reach, with the only lamplight coming from the kitchen. Getting coffee ready, a pot this time, for Clint and myself and a sippy cup of milk for Max, it only took a minute to pop the cinnamon rolls Arlene left by the front door last night in the oven. Along with the box of rolls, there'd been a bag with a variety of gourmet goodies: premium coffee, which was brewing, chocolate covered strawberries, a folded paper bag with marshmallows, graham crackers, and the good slabs of Lindt chocolate. A note on the bag had said, *Breakfast is on us, love Seb & Arlene.* Lastly there'd been a bottle of nice champagne. At least I think it's nice, because it says Moët & Chandon, and I know Queen, one of my favorite bands of all time, sings about it. I was ready to dig in last night, but Clint made me put it all in the fridge for today. Party-pooper.

I'd set it out early this morning, while the cinnamon rolls were heating up and the coffee was percolating, but the moment Clint walked into the kitchen with Max on his arm, he handed Max to me and started putting everything back in the fridge.

"Save it for later. First let's get this little guy at his presents, he's chomping at the bit."

He was hardly chomping, cause by the time I settled on the couch, with a coffee in front of me and Max on my lap with his milk, he was almost dozing off. Of course that didn't last long, because the moment Clint handed him a present, he slid on the floor and proceeded to decimate the pretty wrapping paper without even paying it attention.

"Bean," Clint leaned over and drew my attention. I guess I must've looked funny, because he chuckled, "ripping wrapping paper is half the fun when you're two."

Right. I keep reminding myself with every prettily wrapped gift that got ripped to bits, and all with the biggest smile. I know Clint is saving the sled for after breakfast, so they can go out and try it right away.

But there is that little present, dangling from the tree and I have no idea how it got there. I didn't do it and I know Clint didn't do it, cause both of us agreed that gift giving at Christmas should be reserved for kids. Maybe Arlene?

She's curious as hell about the gift, I can tell. The wheels are turning and she can barely keep her eyes off it. Even if she wanted to ignore it, she can't. Max won't let her since he's been pointing at it and chanting, 'pwesent,' incessantly. I want her to take it down herself, so I'm almost sitting on my hands to keep from pulling it down and handing it to her myself.

Arlene had been good. She's known since last Wednesday, when she picked me up from my office to drive the two hours into Durango. Her call, since according to her, that's where the good stores were. The decision was easy, since both of us decided the moment we saw it. It was perfect for Beth. We were back in Cedar Tree at one, where she dropped me off at the office with a pat on my cheek and a compliment. "You did good," is what she said. The rest of it, I asked her to plan and she did. Hence the goodies she left here last night. Surprised me, she could keep a secret that well.

Finally, she gets up and walks to the branch I had hung the little box on last night, after leaving her sated, and in deep sleep in our bed.

"This?" she asks Max with a smile, and is about to hand it over to him to 'unwrap.'

"Maybe you should unwrap it," I suggest, her eyes now big as saucers. She sits down on the edge of the couch and looks down at the gift, and then back up to me.

"From you?"

I don't say anything, just shrug, sitting down beside her as she starts carefully picking at the tape holding the paper together and driving me to distraction. "Maybe we should've given it to Max after all. Unwrapping this way could take us to dinnertime."

Her eyes flash at me before returning to the little box in her hands. She's usually sharp as a tack, Beth is, but for some reason it's taking her a long time to clue in. I can pinpoint the moment it happens, her spine snaps straight and one of her hands comes up to cover her mouth. She doesn't have it open yet, but the logo of the jeweler's is prominent on the lid.

My turn now.

Taking the box from her hand, I slide down on the floor in front of her feet and flip up the lid, displaying the simple square cut diamond Arlene and I both picked out.

"Oh my God…"

"Beth—" I start what I've rehearsed for two weeks, but Beth grabs my hand. The one holding the box up.

"Oh my God, Clint."

"Bean, I—"

"YES!" she screams. So loud that Max's bottom lip starts quivering.

"Babe! Can I ask you first?" But it's no use, she's up and running for the phone, and I'm still sitting on the floor with the box in my hand. Max crawls on my lap, and the two of us watch her jump up and down, squealing into the phone.

"He gave me a ring! I've never had a ring before. Like…NEVER! — What? Yes of course I said yes, you think I'd say no? I never thought at forty-six years old, I'd ever get asked. I've wanted to hear those words only my whole life. — What he said? I…uh. I've gotta go. — I'll call you back, I gotta go now!"

She puts down the phone, turns to face Max and I and that's when it happens.

"I'm so sorry…" she whispers, big tears rolling down her face. "I ruined it. I'm so sorry."

I set Max on the floor, who is easily distracted by the rustle of wrapping paper, get up, and walk over to where she's hanging on to the counter for dear life. I'd lie if I said I wasn't a little irritated that she'd turn into a lunatic when I gave her the ring. It simply hadn't occurred to me that she'd never had this before. I don't know if I'd have planned it differently, but the things she said on the phone to, I assume Arlene, evaporated any annoyance I might have felt. So I pull her against me and let her get herself together for a minute. Cause come what may, I *am* going to ask her that question. The one she's never had asked before.

"Hush," I whisper in her hair, as she continues to mumble, '*sorry,*' over and over again, until finally she settles, her arms around my middle and her hands fisted in the T-shirt on my back. "I still have a question to ask you, even though I think I might already know the answer."

341

Her head tilts back. Although her face is blotchy and wet from crying, she's the prettiest thing I've ever laid eyes on. So I tell her.

"It's those liquid brown eyes that can shoot sparks when you're angry, twinkle when you laugh, turn bright when you're happy, and intensely hot when you're turned on. But when they go soft, and I can feel the love you feel for me touch me with your gaze, that's when you are at your most beautiful. I love all those parts: the fiery, funny, happy, and passionate Beth. I waited for a long time for you to let me see all the different aspects of you, and with each one you revealed, you hooked me even deeper. I'm never gonna let you go, you know? Thought I had it once, but it doesn't even deserve to be in the shadow of what I have now, and I know it. Marry me, Bean?"

I barely hear her response this time, but it doesn't matter, she shouted it loud enough the first time. What matters is that she throws her arms around me and kisses me like she means it.

"I love you. I'm so glad I held out," she says after breaking away from the kiss, smile bright on her face.

"Not half as glad as I am. I'd have been an idiot not snap you up."

Max who has been quietly playing for a few minutes, suddenly jumps to his feet and runs over. He stops next to us, one hand on each of our legs and tilts his head back, big smile on his face.

"Idjit?"

EPILOGUE

March

"I can't believe you'll be here soon."

Beth's been waiting for this day for a long time.

February 26th was the first day Jablonski's trial was before the court. It was the first time in months Beth had been able to see and touch her son. The small room in the back of the courthouse was too small to contain all the people crammed in there. FBI agents, prosecutors, Beth and I were already in there when Special Agent Gomez showed up with his prize witness. Despite all the bodies, there was no one in the room when Beth closed Dylan in her arms.

We'd driven to Denver and planned to stay for the duration. Jed had decided to hold off on expanding to Durango until after the trial. This so he could take over while I made sure my woman would get all the closure she needed on this ugly episode in her life. For two weeks we stayed and attended each and every day, and on the fifth day of the trial, Dylan was called to the stand. I'd had to hold Beth back when Jablonski's defense attorney was cross-examining and seemed intent on ripping Dylan's testimony and credibility apart, going so far as to claim him a deadbeat father, who abandoned his child. I'd almost had to muzzle her to shut her up because the prosecutor was throwing concerned glances our way and even the judge threw some irritated looks in our direction. Jablonski's lawyer didn't get very far though, especially when Beth was called to testify to the circumstances under which Max was left at the house, which she explained in great detail, as well as her experience

343

when she was kidnapped and cut. She was a rock on the stand, just like her son, and I was proud as hell of her. The hardest was when they showed slides of the damage done to her by Jablonski's knife. The scars are barely visible now, thank goodness, but the pictures were taken in the hospital before she'd been clean up and stitched. It looked pretty gruesome and it showed in the demeanor of the jury.

At the end of the two weeks, we were relieved, although not surprised, that Stan Jablonski was sentenced to life in prison. Not solely for the attack on Beth, but for a multitude of other charges, all added consecutively. Even so, just the sentence for the charge of attempted murder on Beth, netted him the maximum allowable, twenty-four years. Given that the man is late forties, that alone would've made him an old man by the time he was up for release. But with all the other charges added together, his sentence ended up to total ninety-three years. No chance of parole. He'd never see the light of day again, and with that, my Bean had the closure she needed to sleep well at night.

It's a week after the sentencing and we've been back in Cedar Tree, waiting for Dylan to come home. Gomez had warned it would likely not be an immediate thing, since they wanted some time to sit down with him, and with the information gleaned at trial, see if there was anything that might've come up. Seemed a bit odd to me, but Beth didn't question it, so I didn't either. I just had a brief and rather enlightening conversation with Gus, who seems quite familiar with the inner workings of the FBI. The answers I got there are not ones I'm ready to share with Beth. Not yet. Not going to cause her more worry before she has a chance to enjoy her son home and safe.

"He says they're just driving through Cortez. Do I look okay?" I chuckle at her fiddling with her clothes and hair, earning me a dirty look. "I've gotta look my best, Clint. My boy's coming home today."

"Sugar, you'd look good in a potato sack."

"You're just saying that because…well, because you're *you*," she spits out, "Dylan's not *you,* and I want to make sure I look good."

"I promise you look beautiful." That nets me a little smile but then I go and put my foot in. "But did you remember to take those pills Naomi suggested you take?"

See, Beth had been having some symptoms: nightmares, night sweats, mood swings, and even hot flashes. She'd kept on insisting it would pass, it was just stress, but I wasn't buying it, so I insisted taking her to see Naomi. I didn't know, I just thought if it was really the events leading up to Christmas that were having such an impact on her, perhaps Naomi could convince her to go see a counsellor or something. When she walked out of Naomi's office, she immediately turned on me.

"It's all your fault," were her words, and Naomi, who'd come out of the office behind her started giggling. "I've hit early menopause, and I could've lived happily without having my decline in age thrown in my face. That's on you."

My face was working hard to hide the smile, but not hard enough, because she noticed and immediately her anger turned to tears. There was nothing to do but take her in my arms. Looking over her head, Naomi winked at me.

"Beth, honey? Get that prescription filled, I promise those supplements will make you feel better."

345

Those are the pills I'm referring to, and apparently reminding her of the fact she's menopausal is not improving her frantic mood, cause now she's crying. Again.

"Babe, don't cry," I try, knowing full well each time I do, and I do it a lot these days, she only cries harder.

"I did take my pills, but now my makeup is ruined," she sobs. I don't have the heart to point out that the moment Dylan walks in that door, she'll be bawling and messing it up anyway. So I pull her to me and let her cry it out, getting black guck all over my good shirt. Not that I mind, holding Beth in my arms is never a hardship.

"Gammy!"

"Oh my God, Max is already awake, and Dylan will be here soon." She pulls from my arms, grabs a box of tissues from the counter and starts wiping furiously at her face.

"Relax. I'll grab Max out of bed and you keep an eye out for Dylan." And for that I deserve a big smile. So big, it brightens the room.

Before I'm done getting Max dressed, I hear the front door open and Beth squealing, "You're here!" I turn to Max who is chewing on his stuffed animal.

"Guess who's here?" I whisper to him. "Is that your daddy?"

"Big gah?"

"No," I try again, "your daddy."

"Daddy?"

And now it's my turn to smile big as I lift him up and carry him to see his father.

June

"Hello, Mrs. Mason."

Clint's deep voice rumbles in my ear, and I slowly open my eyes to the bright sunshine.

First day of our honeymoon and we're spending it in Hawaii. Always wanted to go to Hawaii, but it was simply never in the cards. Because we had a simple wedding, something both of us wanted, with only close friends and family thus half of the population of Cedar Tree, Clint pointed out we could easily afford Hawaii. Who am I to argue?

We had gorgeous weather, not a cloud in the sky and not yet hot enough to be bothersome. The ceremony was simple and performed on Katie and Caleb's back deck. They undisputedly have the best view. Arlene was standing up for me and Jed had his brother's back. That's it, no gaggles of bridesmaids or flower girls, although we did have Max carry the pillow with the rings, which Dylan had to rescue when Max tossed it over the railing and Blue, Katie's dog, went after it thinking it was a game. The ceremony was short and sweet. Although I was wearing white, Arlene insisted, and Clint was in a suit, and can I say he looked hotter than Hades in it, we had placed no expectations on anyone else regarding dress code. There simply was none. Our wish was for everyone to feel comfortable and have fun. Despite that everyone still made an effort to look nice. Max had dark jeans and a nice dress shirt, the tie Dylan insisted he wear was lost somewhere on the way from my old house, where Dylan now lives; yes, another wish come true, and the

Barn, as everyone calls Caleb and Katie's place. I wasn't very happy when I discovered shortly after Dylan's return, that he'd been recruited by the FBI and was going to leave in July for a few months of training. For that reason, he felt it best that Max simply live with us for the time being, provided Clint and I were all right with that. I was surprised to find Clint blurting out, "of course," before I even had a chance to say anything. Dylan would take him regularly and it was good to see the bond grow between those two. Tammy, of course, was not heard from again, although every now and then Dylan would talk about her.

A full pig roast was organized for the party after, with Malachi in charge, who seemed a little quiet these days. Not that he'd ever been particularly talkative, but I'd noticed anyway. For a bit, I thought he was dating Kendra, or at least that's what I heard through the grapevine. I'd only seen them together once, but then he hadn't been around much these past months either. I just assumed he was mostly out of town on assignment.

Seb had taken care of hors d'oeuvres, and Emma insisted on making the wedding cake, which was absolutely stunning, two tiers of delicious almond cake, because we didn't have a big enough crowd to warrant three, covered in chocolate fondant and decorated with handcrafted, sugar paste white roses. Just gorgeous. Seemed like a shame to eat it, but we did, although Emma assured us she'd made a smaller one and had wrapped it tight and frozen it. For our first wedding anniversary.

We partied until late in the night, in no hurry to call it a day, because we weren't scheduled to go on our honeymoon for a few days yet.

That was then, this is now. I'm Mrs. Beth Mason. Weird. I've never been a Mrs. before. Needless to say, last night when we arrived, we barely got our bags in the room before Clint was all over me. I didn't object... much. But as a result I've not seen a damn thing of the resort we're staying at, since we arrived late at night.

"I want to see this place," I mumble into his shoulder, where I'm hiding from the bright sunlight. "I want to walk on the beach, I've never done that before, and I want to go zip lining, I hear it's fun." From the shaking under my cheek, I know Clint is laughing at me, something he does a lot of, but I don't mind. At least not anymore, not since those damn pills kicked in.

"Zip lining, babe? You couldn't think of something else? Like collecting shells or something? Learn to hula dance?"

"What? You think I'm too old for that?" I'm gearing myself up to be indignant, but I have to say, lazing in bed with no place to be and nothing to be done, not to mention being plastered against a mighty fine male specimen, I can't quite muster up the fire.

"Old? Hell no, not too old, but don't you think it's risky?"

Now it's my turn to chuckle. "Scared to? You don't have to come, you can just stay on the ground and watch me whip by."

A sharp sting on my ass, where he just smacked me. "Clint!"

"Careful, babe, you know what happens when you taunt me. I'm not afraid of anything. I'll go with you, but you'll have to convince me to let you out of this bed first," he says, rolling me to my back and settling on top of me. With his nose almost touching mine, he smiles sweetly and with teeth. Almost as rare as when Arlene does it. "I'll make sure you get to do it all.

Everything you ever wanted, I'll spend the rest of my life making sure you get it."

My hands come up to cup his jaw.

"Honey, you've already given me all." I lift my head so I can kiss him. but then he firmly takes over the kiss. Typical. When he lets me up for air I quickly add, "Except maybe control in the bedroom."

Laughing out loud, he buries his face in my neck, and proceeds to show me in a variety of ways that it's not necessarily such a bad thing, not having the upper hand.

We finally left our room two days later and I got to see the beautiful scenery around the resort. I walked on the beach, letting warm sand squeeze up between my toes.

And then we went zip lining.

——THE END——

ACKNOWLEDGEMENTS:

If it seems like I'm always thanking the same people, that's because I am. My family to whom I owe a great deal of gratitude for accepting me for who I am and supporting me always, regardless of which path I choose to walk. They may not always agree with the choices I make but that doesn't stop them from wanting it all for me and helping me get there. I am very fortunate, and I know it.

There is no way I can *not* acknowledge my beta-readers, quite a few of whom have been there from the very first book. They tell me straight up when things don't make sense, or when I make mistakes. And I do. Lots of them. The version they get to read is a raw as it can be and they work hard at cleaning my mess to get it ready for edit.

Chris Alderson Kovacich, Kerry-Ann Bell, Debbie Bishop, Deb Blake, Pam Buchanan, Leanne Hawkes, Sam Price, Catherine Scott, Nancy Huddleston—I love you guys forever!

I so appreciate the ongoing support I receive from the Indie community and its authors. There isn't a group more generous than these men and women who work so very hard to bring you the best they have to offer, and *still* manage to help each other out.

The invaluable bloggers and reviewers who take the time to read an enormous number of advanced reading copies for upcoming books, just to give you some idea of what is on offer in the book world. Not only that, they are worth their weight in gold when it comes to promoting our books and they do this without any compensation. The Indie community would be on its ass without them.

This time I want to highlight my oldest brother Hans, who without fail, manages to pick out the few spelling mistakes that inevitably fall through the cracks and for which I am solely responsible. Love you!

And of course you, the readers, who have been growing steadily in numbers, supporting and encouraging me. Those of you who have come to visit me at one of the author signings, I so appreciate that! It's wonderful to have an opportunity to interact directly with readers.

The final thank you comes from the bottom of my heart and goes to Karen Hrdlicka. If Karen wasn't already a friend long before I asked her to edit Upper Hand, she certainly would be now. It was an absolute pleasure working with you, doll. Love your face!! xox

ABOUT THE AUTHOR

Freya Barker craved reading about 'real' people, those who are perhaps less than perfect, but just as deserving of romance, hot monkey sex and some thrills and chills in their lives – So she decided to write about them.

Always creative, from an early age on she danced and sang, doodled, created, cooked, baked, quilted and crafted. Her latest creative outlets were influenced by an ever-present love for reading. First through blogging, then cover art and design, and finally writing.

Born and raised in the Netherlands, she packed her two toddlers, and eight suitcases filled with toys to move to Canada. No stranger to new beginnings, she thrives on them.

With the kids grown and out in the world, Freya is at the 'prime' of her life. The body might be a bit ramshackle, but the spirit is high and as adventurous as ever. Something you may see reflected here and there in some of her heroines.... none of who will likely be wilting flowers.

Freya

https://www.freyabarker.com

https://www.goodreads.com/FreyaBarker

https://www.facebook.com/FreyaBarkerWrites

https://tsu.co/FreyaB

https://twitter.com/freya_barker

or mailto:freyabarker.writes@gmail.com

ALSO BY THIS AUTHOR

CEDAR TREE SERIES:

Book #1

SLIM TO NONE

myBook.to/SlimToNone

Book #2

HUNDRED TO ONE

myBook.to/HundredToOne

Book #3

AGAINST ME

myBook.to/AgainstMe

Book #4

CLEAN LINES

myBook.to/CleanLines

AS WELL AS:

FROM DUST

(A dark emotional romance)

Amazon (universal):
myBook.to/FromDust

B&N:
http://bit.ly/1DuO7ZD

Kobo:
http://bit.ly/1gae320

iBooks:
http://apple.co/1ILipDC

COMING SOON

LIKE ARROWS

(Cedar Tree #6)

Coming January, 2016

Unedited excerpt

CHAPTER ONE

"I'll have a chicken salad and a glass of water, please."

Her voice is as timid as her appearance. Like a little mouse, she slipped in behind me and sat down at the furthest booth. Shocked I tried my best not to show any reaction to her showing up here. I never expected to have one of the people I've been keeping an eye on show up at Arlene's Diner. Sure, it's popular around these parts, but given that I live in the apartment above and take most my meals here, it feels like more than a coincidence. This is why I'm keeping my back turned and my ears perked.

Arlene tags her the minute she comes out of the kitchen and is taking her order. Fucking chicken salad and water, who lives on that? I've had reason to keep her in my sights since taking on this assignment and the woman rarely eats more than that from what I've seen. Seems to feel comfortable in the real estate office she works, but the moment she steps out she seems to want to disappear in the shadows. Head always low, never making eye contact and wrapping herself up in that godawful blanket thing: some kind of poncho.

357

It's her boss I'm really keeping track of. Gus got a call from the Ute reservation a few weeks ago. The council had concerns about two farms backing onto reservation lands. The chief mentioned that both had sold within a month of the other through Martin Vedica, the little mouse's boss, and they had moved out within days. A third farm, owned by an older couple was being targeted as well. The couple, Ezhno and Tiva Walker, had moved off the reservation some thirty years earlier to raise their family. They didn't go far, since their property backs right onto McElmo Creek near Finley Canyon, which is on reservation lands. In fact, it is wedged between reservation boundaries and the southern border of Canyons of the Ancients National Park.

Gus asked me to keep an eye out and I have, but with Vedica out of town since yesterday, I'd been using the time to do some online digging, but so far have come up with little or nothing.

Keeping my eye on the stainless steel backsplash behind the counter, I can see in the reflection that her face is turned my way. It isn't busy in the diner right now, being lunch time, but there are still a few booths occupied. Still I know they are her eyes burning in my back, and I wonder if she could possibly have spotted me before.

Kimeo Lowe. A rather exotic name for a plain little mouse like that. Soft voice, soft brown eyes and from what I've been able to distinguish, a soft rounded body. Hardly the description for anyone associated with some kind of nefarious real estate deal, but you never know. Looks can be deceiving.

"Your burger," Arlene says, plopping a plate loaded with sweet potato fries and Seb's juicy signature burger on the counter in front of me. Seb is married to Arlene and the cook and part owner of the diner. They're also my landlords.

"Thanks." I lift my eyes to smile at her.

I don't hesitate to dig in, starving, which pretty much is a constant state for me. Wicked fast metabolism or something, because I've always been able to eat whatever I want and none of it seems to stick. A healthy appetite. Maybe that's why seeing the woman listlessly pick at a bowl of salad just seems wrong to me. My eyes are back on her reflection where I can see her playing with her food, but not putting much of it in her mouth. She seems a little skittish, and when the door to the diner opens, her head whips around to see who's entered. I resist the urge to turn my head to see and keep focus trained on her.

"Hey stranger, how's it going?" The familiar voice has me turn my head. Kendra, the pretty physical therapist who joined Doc Waters the end of last year in the new clinic, is smiling at me. I smile back easily. She's a nice woman and since coming to town has fitted into our circle of friends easily. At some point I thought there might be something there, and we'd actually gone out a couple of times. After a movie in Cortez on our third date, I took our earlier, almost friendly kisses a step further when I dropped her off. The kiss fell flat. Where I thought there might have been sparks before, they fizzled out the moment my mouth hit hers. No heat, and fucking awkward as hell. Almost felt like kissing your sister. The kiss ended very quickly and Kendra could barely keep a straight face. We both burst out laughing, and the memory puts a smile on my face.

"Hey yourself. You in for lunch?"

"Just picking something up for Naomi and me. We've got solid appointments well into the evening. Ugh."

Naomi is Doc Waters, the new town doctor and also married to former sheriff, now colleague, Joe Morris. He and I are the latest additions to GFI, an investigations and security company owned and run by Gus Flemming.

"You guys have really hit the ground running with the clinic, haven't you?" Arlene pipes up, having heard Kendra's comment.

"Sure have. Makes you wonder where the population of Cedar Tree went before Naomi decided to open up shop here," Kendra responds.

"Most of us would go to Cortez, but it's mighty convenient having you around the corner." Arlene smiles. "What can I get you?"

While Kendra places her order, I suddenly remember the focus of my earlier attention and lift my eyes to the backsplash. Nothing, the table little mouse was sitting at is empty. I turn on my stool to look to the parking lot where the little blue Honda I've seen her drive was parked. My eyes hit two soft brown ones staring at me through the diner window, before they turn away and I see her head duck down as she slips into her car. I'm up and off my stool by the time she backs out of the parking spot and have my eyes peeled when I see her turning west.

"Be back. Add it to my tab," I tell Arlene as I pass by her followed by a, "Later, Kendra," and with a chin lift to Seb I'm through the kitchen and out the back door where my truck is parked.